Regency Buck

Regency Buck

Georgette Heyer

SOURCEBOOKS CASABLANCA™
AN IMPRINT OF SOURCEBOOKS, INC.®
NAPERVILLE, ILLINOIS

Published by Sourcebooks Casablanca, an imprint of Sourcebooks, Inc.
P.O. Box 4410, Naperville, Illinois 60567-4410
(630) 961-3900
Fax: (630) 961-2168
www.sourcebooks.com

Library of Congress Cataloging-in-Publication Data

Heyer, Georgette, 1902-1974.
  Regency buck / Georgette Heyer.
    p. cm.
  ISBN-13: 978-1-4022-1349-6
  ISBN-10: 1-4022-1349-2
  I. Title.
PR6015.E795R455 2008
823'.912—dc22

                        2008018026

        Printed and bound in the United States of America
            VP 10 9 8 7 6 5 4 3 2

One

NEWARK WAS LEFT BEHIND AND THE POST-CHAISE-AND-FOUR entered on a stretch of flat country which offered little to attract the eye, or occasion remark. Miss Taverner withdrew her gaze from the landscape and addressed her companion, a fair youth who was lounging in his corner of the chaise somewhat sleepily surveying the back of the nearest post-boy. 'How tedious it is to be sitting still for so many hours at a stretch!' she remarked. 'When do we reach Grantham, Perry?'

Her brother yawned. 'Lord, I don't know! It was you who would go to London.'

Miss Taverner made no reply to this, but picked up a *Traveller's Guide* from the seat beside her, and began to flutter the leaves over. Young Sir Peregrine yawned again, and observed that the new pair of wheelers, put in at Newark, were good-sized strengthy beasts, very different from the last pair, which had both of them been touched in the wind.

Miss Taverner was deep in the *Traveller's Guide*, and agreed to this without raising her eyes from the closely printed page.

She was a fine young woman, rather above the average height, and had been used for the past four years to hearing herself proclaimed a remarkably handsome girl. She could not, however, admire her own beauty, which was of a type she was inclined to despise. She had rather have had black hair; she thought the fairness of her gold curls insipid. Happily, her brows and lashes were dark, and her eyes which were startlingly blue (in the manner of a wax doll, she once scornfully told her brother) had a directness and a fire which gave a great deal of character to her face. At first glance one might write her down a mere Dresden china miss, but a second glance would inevitably discover the intelligence in her eyes, and the decided air of resolution in the curve of her mouth.

She was dressed neatly, but not in the first style of fashion, in a plain round gown of French cambric, frilled round the neck with scolloped lace; and a close mantle of twilled sarcenet. A poke-bonnet of basket-willow with a striped velvet ribbon rather charmingly framed her face, and a pair of York tan gloves were drawn over her hands, and buttoned tightly round her wrists.

Her brother, who had resumed his slumbrous scrutiny of the post-boy's back, resembled her closely. His hair was more inclined to brown, and his eyes less deep in colour than hers, but he must always be known for her brother. He was a year younger than Miss Taverner, and, either from habit or careless-ness, was very much in the habit of permitting her to order things as she chose.

'It is fourteen miles from Newark to Grantham,' announced Miss Taverner, raising her eyes from the *Traveller's Guide*. 'I had not thought it had been so far.' She bent over the book again. 'It says here – it is Kearsley's *Entertaining Guide*, you know, which you procured for me in Scarborough – that it is *a neat and populous town on the River Witham. It is supposed to have been a Roman station, by the remains of a castle which have been dug up.* I must say, I should like to explore there if we have the time, Perry.'

'Oh, lord, you know ruins always look the same!' objected Sir Peregrine, digging his hands into the pockets of his buckskin breeches. 'I tell you what it is, Judith: if you're set on poking about all the castles on the way we shall be a full week on the road. I'm all for pushing forward to London.'

'Very well,' submitted Miss Taverner, closing the *Traveller's Guide*, and laying it on the seat. 'We will bespeak an early breakfast at the George, then, and you must tell them at what hour you will have the horses put-to.'

'I thought we were to lie at the Angel,' remarked Sir Peregrine.

'No,' replied his sister decidedly. 'You have forgot the wretched account the Mincemans gave us of the comfort to be had there. It is the George and I wrote to engage our rooms, on account of Mrs Minceman warning me of the fuss and to-do she had once when they would have had her go up two pair of stairs to a miserable apartment at the back of the house.'

Sir Peregrine turned his head to grin amicably at her. 'Well, I don't fancy they'll succeed in fobbing you off with a back room, Ju.'

'Certainly not,' replied Miss Taverner, with a severity somewhat belied by the twinkle in her eye.

'No, that's certain,' pursued Peregrine. 'But what I'm waiting to see, my love, is the way you'll handle the old man.'

Miss Taverner looked a little anxious. 'I could handle Papa, Perry, couldn't I? If only Lord Worth is not a subject to gout! I think that was the only time when Papa became quite unmanageable.'

'All old men have gout,' said Peregrine.

Miss Taverner sighed, acknowledging the truth of this pronouncement.

'It's my belief,' added Peregrine, 'that he don't want us to come to town. Come to think of it, didn't he say so?'

Miss Taverner loosened the strings of her reticule, and groped in it for a slender packet of letters. She spread one of these open. '"Lord Worth presents his compliments to Sir Peregrine and Miss Taverner and thinks it inadvisable for them to attempt the fatigues of a journey to London at this season. His lordship will do himself the honour of calling upon them in Yorkshire when next he is in the North." And that,' concluded Miss Taverner, 'was written three months ago – you may see the date for yourself, Perry: 29th June, 1811 – and not even in his own hand. I am sure it is a secretary wrote it, or those horrid lawyers. Depend upon it, Lord Worth has forgotten our very existence, because you know all the arrangements about the money we should have were made by the lawyers, and whenever there is any question to be settled it is they who write about it. So if he does not like us to come to London it is quite his fault for not having made the least attempt to come to us, or to tell us what we must do. I think him a very poor guardian. I wish my father had named one of our friends in Yorkshire, someone we are acquainted with. It is very disagreeable to be under the governance of a stranger.'

'Well, if Lord Worth don't want to be at the trouble of ordering our lives, so much the better,' said Peregrine. 'You want to cut a dash in town, and I daresay I can find plenty of amusement if we haven't a crusty old guardian to spoil the fun.'

'Yes,' agreed Miss Taverner, a trifle doubtfully. 'But in common civility we must ask his permission to set up house in London. I do hope we shall not find him set against us, regarding it as an imposition, I mean; perhaps thinking that my uncle might rather have been appointed than himself. It must appear very singular to him. It is an awkward business, Perry.'

A grunt being the only response to this, she said no more, but leaned back in her corner and perused the unsatisfactory communications she had received from Lord Worth.

It was an awkward business. His lordship, who must, she reflected, be going on for fifty-five or fifty-six years of age, showed a marked disinclination to trouble himself with the affairs of his wards, and although this might in some circumstances be reckoned a good, in others it must be found to be a pronounced evil. Neither she nor Peregrine had ever been farther from home than to Scarborough. They knew nothing of London, and had no acquaintance there to guide them. The only persons known to them in the whole town were their uncle, and a female cousin living respectably, but in a small way, in Kensington. This lady Miss Taverner must rely upon to present her into society, for her uncle, a retired Admiral of the Blue, had lived upon terms of such mutual dislike and mistrust with her father as must preclude her from seeking either his support or his acquaintance.

Sir John Taverner had never been heard to speak with the smallest degree of kindness of his brother, and when his gout was at its worst, he had been used to refer to him as a damned scoundrelly fellow whom he would not trust the length of his own yard-arm. There were very few people whom Sir John had ever spoken of with much complaisance, but he had from time to time given his children such instances of their uncle's conduct as convinced them that he must indeed be a shabby creature, and no mere victim of Sir John's prejudice.

Lord Worth might think it singular that he who had not set eyes on his old friend once in the last ten years should have been appointed guardian to his children, but they, knowing Sir John, found it easily understandable. Sir John, always irascible, could never be brought during the last years of his life to live on terms of cordiality with his neighbours. There must always be quarrels. But from having lived secluded on his estates ever since the death of his wife and not having met Lord Worth above three times in a dozen years, he had had no quarrel with him, and had come by insensible degrees to consider him the very person to have the care of his children in the event of his own decease. Worth was a capital fellow; Sir John could trust him to administer the very considerable fortune he would leave his children; there was no fear of Worth warming his own pockets. The thing was done, the Will drawn up without the smallest reference to it being made either to Worth or to the children themselves – a circumstance, Miss Taverner could not but reflect, entirely in keeping with all Sir John's high-handed dealings.

She was aroused from these musings by the rattle and bump of the chaise-wheels striking cobblestones, and looked up to find that they had reached Grantham.

As they drew into the town the post-boys were obliged to slacken the pace considerably, so much traffic was there in the streets, and such a press of people thronging the pathways, and even the road itself.

All was bustle and animation, and when the chaise came at last within sight of the George, a huge red-brick structure on the main street, Miss Taverner was surprised to see any number of coaches, curricles, gigs, and phaetons drawn up before it.

'Well,' she said, 'I am glad I followed Mrs Minceman's advice and wrote to bespeak our rooms. I had no notion we should find Grantham so crowded.'

Sir Peregrine had roused himself, and was leaning forward to look out of the window. 'The place seems to be in the devil of a pucker,' he remarked. 'There must be something out of the way going forward.'

In another moment the chaise had turned in under the archway to the courtyard, and come to a standstill. There an even greater bustle reigned, every ostler being so fully occupied that for some minutes no one approached the chaise or gave the least sign of having observed its arrival. A post-boy already booted and spurred, with a white smock over his uniform, who was leaning against the wall with a straw between his teeth, did indeed survey the chaise in a disinterested manner, but since it was no part of his business to change the horses, or inquire after the travellers' wants, he made no movement to come forward.

With an exclamation of impatience Sir Peregrine thrust open the door in the front of the chaise, and sprang down, briefly admonishing his sister to sit still and wait. He strode off towards the lounging post-boy, who straightened himself respectfully at his approach, and removed the straw from his mouth. After a short colloquy with the boy, Sir Peregrine came hurrying back to the chaise, his boredom quite vanished, and his eyes fairly sparkling with anticipation.

'Judith! The best of good fortune! A mill! Only think of it! Out of all the days in the year to have come to Grantham, and by the veriest chance!'

'A mill?' echoed Miss Taverner, drawing her brows together.

'Yes, am I not telling you? The Champion – Tom Cribb, you know – is to fight Molyneux to-morrow at some place or another – I did not perfectly catch the name – close by here. Thank God for it you had the good sense to bespeak our rooms, for they say there is not a bed to be had for twenty miles round! Come, don't be dawdling any longer, Ju!'

The intelligence that she had come to Grantham on the eve of a prize-fight could scarcely afford Miss Taverner gratification, but from having spent the greater part of her life in the company of her father and brother, and from having been used to hear a great deal of talk about manly sports and to think them perfectly proper for gentlemen to take part in, she readily acquiesced in Peregrine's desire to be present at this fight. For herself she had rather have been otherwhere. Prize-fighting could only disgust her, and although there would naturally be no question of her being a witness of the spectacle, she must expect to hear of it all at second-hand, and to find herself, in all probability, the only female in an inn full to overflowing with sporting gentlemen. She did attempt a slight remonstrance, without, however, much hope of being attended to. 'But, Perry, consider! If the fight is for to-morrow, that is Saturday, and we must stay here until Monday, for you would not care to travel on Sunday. You know we were counting on being in London to-morrow.'

'Oh, pooh, what in the world does that signify?' he replied. 'I would not miss this mill for a hundred pounds! I tell you what: you may explore your Roman ruins as much as you choose. You know that is what you wanted. And only to think of it! Cribb and Molyneux! You must have heard me speak of the fight last year, and wish I might have been there. Thirty-three rounds, and the Black resigned! But they say he is in better fig-ure to-day. It will be a great mill: you would not wish me to miss it! Why, when they met before it lasted fifty-five minutes! They must be devilish even-matched. Do come down, Ju!'

No, Miss Taverner would not wish Peregrine to miss any-thing that could give him pleasure. She picked up the *Traveller's Guide*, and her reticule, and taking his hand stepped down from the chaise into the courtyard.

The landlord met them upon their entrance into the inn but seemed to have very little time to bestow on them. The coffee-room was already crowded and there were a dozen gentlemen of consequence demanding his attention. Rooms? There was not a corner of his house unbespoken. He would advise them to have a fresh team put to and drive on to Greetham, or Stamford. He did not know – he believed there was not an inn with accommodation to offer this side of Norman's Cross. He was sorry, but they would understand that the occasion was extraordinary, and all his bedchambers had been engaged for days back.

This, however, would not do for Judith Taverner, accustomed her whole life to command. 'There is some mistake,' she said, in her cool decided voice. 'I am Miss Taverner. You will have had my letter a full week ago. I require two bedchambers, accom-modation for my maid, and for my brother's valet, who will be here presently, and a private parlour.'

The landlord threw up his hands in a gesture of despair, but he was impressed a little by her air of authority. He had been at first inclined to underrate a couple so modestly dressed, but the mention of a maid and a valet convinced him that he had to do with persons of quality, whom he would not wish to offend. He embarked on a flood of explanation and apology. He was sure Miss Taverner would not care to stay under the circumstances.

Judith raised her brows. 'Indeed! I fancy I am the best judge of that. I will forgo the private parlour, but be good enough to make some arrangement for our bedchambers at once.'

'It is impossible, ma'am!' declared the landlord. 'The house is as full as it can hold. Every room is engaged! I should have to turn some gentleman out to oblige you.'

'Then do so,' said Judith.

The landlord looked imploringly towards Peregrine. 'You must see, sir, I can't help myself. I'm very sorry for the fault, but there's no help for it, and indeed the company is not what the lady would like.'

'Judith, it does seem that we shall have to go elsewhere,' said Peregrine reasonably. 'Perhaps Stamford — I could see the fight from there, or even farther.'

'Certainly not,' said Judith. 'You heard what this man said, that he believed there is not a room to be had this side of Norman's Cross. I do not mean to go on such a wild-goose chase. Our rooms were bespoke here, and if a mistake has been made it must be set right.'

Her voice, which was very clear, seemed to have reached the ears of a group of persons standing over against the window. One or two curious glances were directed towards her, and after a moment's hesitation a man who had been watching Miss Taverner from the start came across the room, and made her a bow.

'I beg pardon — I do not wish to intrude, but there seems to be some muddle. I should be glad to place my rooms at your disposal, ma'am, if you would do me the honour of accepting them.'

The man at her elbow looked to be between twenty-seven and thirty years of age. His manner proclaimed the gentleman; he had a decided air of fashion; and his countenance, without being handsome, was sufficiently pleasing. Judith sketched a curtsy. 'You are very good, sir, but you are not to be giving up your rooms to two strangers.'

He smiled. 'No such thing, ma'am. We cannot tell but what my rooms should properly be yours. My friend and I —' he made a slight gesture as though to indicate someone in the group behind him — 'have acquaintances in the neighbourhood, and may readily command a lodging at Hungerton Lodge. I — rather I should say *we* — are happy to be of service.'

There was nothing to do but thank him, and accept his offer. He bowed again, and withdrew to rejoin his friends. The landlord, relieved to be extricated from a difficult situation, led the way out of the coffee-room, and delivered his new guests into the care of a chamber-maid. In a very little time they found themselves in possession of two respectable apartments on the first floor, and had nothing further to do than to await the arrival of their trunks.

It was one of Miss Taverner's first concerns to discover the name of her unknown benefactor, but by the time she had seen her baggage bestowed, and arranged for a truckle-bed to be set up in the room for her maid, he had left the inn. The landlord did not know him; he had arrived only a few minutes before themselves; he was not an habitual traveller upon that road.

Judith was disappointed, but had to be satisfied. There was no finding out in the crowd flocking to Grantham who one individual might be. She owned herself pleased with him. He had a well-bred air; the delicacy with which he had managed the whole business; his withdrawing just when he ought, all impressed her in his favour. She would not be sorry to make his better acquaintance.

Peregrine agreed to his being a civil fellow, owned himself much beholden to him, would be glad to meet him again, thought it odds they must run across each other in the town, but was more immediately concerned with the means of getting to the scene of the fight next day. It was to be at Thistleton Gap, some eight or more miles to the south-west of Grantham. A conveyance must be found; he would not go in his chaise: that was unthinkable. A curricle must be hired, or a gig, and before he could sit down to his dinner he must be off to see whether he could come by one.

It was four o'clock, and Miss Taverner had not been used to fashionable hours. She would dine at once, and in her room. Sir Peregrine patted her shoulder, and said she would be more comfortable in her own room.

Judith curled her lip at him. 'Well, you like to think so, my dear.'

'You couldn't dine in the coffee-room,' he assured her. 'It may do very well for me, but for you it won't answer.'

'Go and find your curricle,' said Judith, between amusement and exasperation.

He needed no further encouragement; he was gone in a trice, nor did he return until after five o'clock. He came in then, highly elated, full of his good fortune. There was no coming by a curricle – no gentleman's carriage to be had at all, but he had heard of a gig owned by some farmer, a shabby affair, scarce an inch of paint on it, but it would serve – and been off immediately to drive the bargain. The long and short of it was he had driven the gig back, and was ready now to do all that a brother should for his sister's entertainment in taking her out to see ruins, or whatever else she chose. Dinner? Oh, he had eaten a tight little beefsteak in the coffee-room, and was entirely at her disposal.

Miss Taverner could not but feel that with the town seething with sporting company, it was hardly the moment for an expedition, but she was heartily sick of her own room, and agreed to the scheme.

The gig was found upon inspection to be not quite so bad as Peregrine described, but still, a shabby affair. Miss Taverner grimaced at it. 'My dear Perry, I had rather walk!'

'Walk? Oh, lord, I have had enough of that, I can tell you! I must have tramped a good mile already. Don't be so nice, Ju! It ain't what I'd choose, but no one knows us here.'

'You had better let me drive,' she remarked.

But that, of course, would not do. If she thought she could drive better than he, she much mistook the matter. The brute was hard-mouthed, not a sweet-goer by any means, no case for a lady.

They went down the main street at a sober pace, but once clear of the town Sir Peregrine let his hands drop, and they jolted away at a great rate, if not in the best style, bumping over every inequality in the road, and lurching round the corners.

'Perry, this is insupportable,' Judith said at last. 'Every tooth rattles in my head! You will run into something. Do, I beg of you, remember that you are to take me to see the Roman castle! I am persuaded you are on the wrong road.'

'Oh, I had forgot that curst castle!' he said ruefully. 'I was meaning to see which road I must take to-morrow – to Thistleton Gap, you know. Very well, very well, I'll turn, and go back!' He reined in the horse as he spoke, and began at once to turn, quite heedless of the narrowness of the road at this point, and the close proximity of a particularly sharp bend in it.

'Good God, what will you do next?' exclaimed Judith. 'If anything were to come round the corner! I wish you would give me the reins!'

She spoke too late. He had the gig all across the road, and seemed in danger of running into the ditch if his attention were distracted. She heard the sound of horses travelling fast and made a snatch at the reins.

Round the corner swept a curricle-and-four at breakneck speed. It was upon them; it must crash into them; there could be no stopping it. Peregrine tried to wrench the horse round, cursing under his breath; Judith felt herself powerless to move. She had a nightmarish vision of four magnificent chestnuts thundering down on her, and of a straight figure in a caped overcoat driving them. It was over in a flash. The chestnuts were swung miraculously to the off; the curricle's mudguard caught only the wheels of the gig, and the chestnuts came to a plunging standstill.

The shock of the impact, though it was hardly more than a glancing scrape, startled the farmer's horse into an attempt to bolt, and in another moment one wheel of the gig was in the shallow ditch, and Miss Taverner was nearly thrown from her seat.

She righted herself, aware that her bonnet was crooked, and her temper in shreds, and found that the gentleman in the curricle was sitting perfectly unmoved, easily holding his horses. As she turned to look at him he spoke, not to her, but over his shoulder to a diminutive tiger perched behind him. 'Take it away, Henry, take it away,' he said.

Wrath, reproach, even oaths Miss Taverner could have pardoned. The provocation was great; she herself longed to box Peregrine's ears. But this calm indifference was beyond everything. Her anger veered irrationally towards the stranger. His manner, his whole bearing, filled her with repugnance. From the first moment of setting eyes on him she knew that she disliked him. Now she had leisure to observe him more closely, and found that she disliked him no less.

He was the epitome of a man of fashion. His beaver hat was set over black locks carefully brushed into a semblance of disorder; his cravat of starched muslin supported his chin in a series of beautiful folds; his driving-coat of drab cloth bore no less than fifteen capes, and a double row of silver buttons. Miss Taverner had to own him a very handsome creature, but found no difficulty in detesting the whole cast of his countenance. He had a look of self-consequence; his eyes, ironically surveying her from under weary lids, were the hardest she had ever seen, and betrayed no emotion but boredom. His nose was too straight for her taste. His mouth was very well-formed, firm but thin-lipped. She thought it sneered.

Worse than all was his languor. He was uninterested, both in having dexterously averted an accident, and in the gig's plight. His driving had been magnificent; there must be unsuspected strength in those elegantly gloved hands holding the reins in such seeming carelessness, but in the name of God why must he put on an air of dandified affectation?

As the tiger jumped nimbly down on to the road Miss Taverner's annoyance found expression in abrupt speech: 'We don't need your assistance! Be pleased to drive on, sir!'

The cold eyes swept over her. Their expression made her aware of the shabbiness of the gig, of her own country-made dress, of the appearance she and Peregrine must present. 'I should be very pleased to drive on, my good girl,' said the gentleman in the curricle, 'but that apparently unmanageable steed of yours is – you may have noticed – making my progress impossible.'

Miss Taverner was not used to such a form of address, and it did not improve her temper. The farmer's horse, in its frightened attempts to drag the gig out of the ditch, was certainly plunging rather wildly across the narrow road, but if only Peregrine would go to its head instead of jobbing at it, all would be well. The tiger, a sharp-faced scrap of uncertain age, dressed in a smart blue and yellow livery, was preparing to take the guidance of matters into his own hands. Miss Taverner, unable to bear the indignity of it, said fiercely: 'Sir, I have already informed you that we don't need your help! Get down, Perry! Give the reins to me!'

'I have not the slightest intention of offering you my help,' said the exquisite gentleman, rather haughtily raising his brows. 'You will find that Henry is quite able to clear the road for me.'

And, indeed, by this time the tiger had grasped the horse's rein above the bit, and was engaged in soothing the poor creature. This was very soon done, and in another minute the gig was clear of the ditch, and drawn up at the very edge of the road.

'You see, it was quite easy,' said that maddening voice.

Peregrine, who had till now been too much occupied in trying to control his horse to take part in the discussion, said angrily: 'I'm aware the fault was mine, sir! Well aware of it!'

'We are all well aware of it,' replied the stranger amicably. 'Only a fool would have attempted to turn his carriage at this precise point. Do you mean to keep me waiting very much longer, Henry?'

'I've said I admit the fault,' said Peregrine, colouring hotly, 'and I'm sorry for it! But I shall take leave to tell you, sir, that you were driving at a shocking pace!'

He was interrupted somewhat unexpectedly by the tiger, who lifted a face grown suddenly fierce, and said in shrill Cockney accents: 'You shut your bone-box, imperence! He's the very best whip in the country, ah, and I ain't forgetting Sir John Lade neither! There ain't none to beat him, and them's blood-chestnuts we've got in hand, and if them wheelers ain't sprained a tendon apiece it ain't nowise your fault!'

The gentleman in the curricle laughed. 'Very true, Henry, but you will have observed that I am still waiting.'

'Well, lord love yer, guv'nor, ain't I coming?' protested the tiger, scrambling back on to his perch.

Peregrine, recovering from his astonishment at the tiger's outburst, said through his teeth: 'We shall meet again, sir, I promise you!'

'Do you think so?' said the gentleman in the curricle. 'I hope you may be found to be wrong.'

The team seemed to leap forward; in another minute the curricle was gone.

'Insufferable!' Judith said passionately. '*Insufferable!*'

O ONE USED TO THE SILENCE OF A COUNTRY NIGHT SLEEP AT the George Inn, Grantham, on the eve of a great fight was almost an impossibility. Sounds of loud revelry floated up from the coffee-room to Miss Taverner's bedchamber until an early hour of the morning; she dozed fitfully, time and again awakened by a burst of laughter below-stairs, voices in the street below her window, or a hurrying footstep outside her door. After two o'clock the noise abated gradually, and she was able at last to fall into a sleep which lasted until three long blasts on a horn rudely interrupted it at twenty-three minutes past seven.

She started up in bed. 'Good God, what now?'

Her maid, who had also been awakened by the sudden commotion, slipped out of the truckle-bed, and ran to peep between the blinds of the window. She was able to report that it was only the Edinburgh mail, and stayed to giggle over the appearance presented by the night-capped passengers descending from it to partake of breakfast in the inn. Miss Taverner, quite uninterested, sank back upon her pillows, but soon found that peace was at an end. The house was awake, and beginning to be in a bustle. In a very short time she was glad to give up all attempt to go to sleep again, and get up.

Peregrine was knocking on her door before nine o'clock. She must come down to breakfast; he was advised to start in good time for Thistleton Gap if he wanted to procure a good place, and could not be dawdling.

She went down with him to the coffee-room. There were only a few persons there, the passengers on the Edinburgh mail having been whisked off again on their journey south, and the sporting gentlemen who had made so much uproar the evening before apparently preferring to breakfast in the privacy of their own apartments.

As she had guessed, Peregrine had been of the company overnight. He had made the acquaintance of a set of very good fellows, though he could not recall their names at the moment, and had cracked a bottle with them. The talk had been all of the fight; his talk was still of it. He would back the Champion: Judith must know he had been trained by Captain Barclay of – of – he thought it was Ury, or some such queer name, but he could not be sure. At all events, he was the man who went on walking matches – she might have heard of him. It was said he had reduced Cribb to thirteen stone six pounds. Cribb was in fine fettle; he did not know about the Black, though there was no denying he could give Cribb four years. Cribb must be going on for thirty now. So it went on, while Judith ate her breakfast, and interpolated a yes or a no where it was required.

Peregrine had no qualms about leaving her to her own devices for the morning: the town would be empty, and she might walk abroad with perfect propriety; need not even take her maid.

Soon after he had finished his breakfast he was off, with a packet of sandwiches in one pocket and a bottle in the other. He had no difficulty in finding out the way: he had only to follow the stream of traffic a distance of eight miles. Everyone was bound for Thistleton Gap, in every conceivable kind of conveyance, from unwieldy coaches to farm-carts, and a great number, those who could not beg or buy a place in a wagon, afoot.

Progress was necessarily slow, but at last the scene of the fight was reached, a stubble-field, not far from Crown Point. It seemed already thick with people. In the middle men were busily engaged in erecting a twenty-five-foot stage.

Peregrine was directed to a quarter of the ground where the carriages of the gentry were to be ranged, and took up a position there, as close to the ring as he might. He had some time to wait before the fight was due to begin, but he was in a mood to be pleased, and found plenty to interest him in watching the gradually thickening crowd. The company was for the most part a rough one, but as midday approached the carriages began to outnumber the wagons. The only circumstances to mar Peregrine's enjoyment were the facts of his having not one acquaintance amongst the Corinthians surrounding him, of his gig being out of the common shabby, and of his coat boasting no more than three modest capes. These were evils, but he forgot them when someone close to him said: 'Here's Jackson arrived!'

Loneliness, coat and gig were at once nothing: here was Gentleman Jackson, one-time champion, now the most famous teacher of boxing in England.

He was walking towards the ring with another man. As soon as he jumped up on to the stage the crowd set up a cheer for him, which he acknowledged with a smile and a good-humoured wave of his hand.

His countenance was by no means prepossessing, his brow being too low, his nose and mouth rather coarse, and his ears projecting from his head; but he had a fine pair of eyes, full and piercing, and his figure, though he was over forty years of age, was still remarkable for its grace and perfect proportions. He had very small hands, and models had been made of his ankles, which were said to be most beautifully turned. He was dressed in good style, but without display, and he had a quiet, unassuming manner.

He left the ring presently, and came over to speak with a red-headed man in a tilbury near to Peregrine's gig. A couple of young Corinthians hailed him, and there was a great deal of joking and laughter, in which Peregrine very much wished that he could have joined. However, it would not be very long now, he hoped, before he, too, would be offering odds that he would pop in a hit over Jackson's guard at their next sparring. And no doubt John Jackson would refuse to bet, just as he was refusing now, with that humorous smile and pleasant jest, that it would be no better than robbery, because everyone, even Sir Peregrine Taverner, who had never been nearer to London than this in his life, knew that none of his pupils had ever managed to put in a hit on Jackson when he chose to deny them that privilege.

Jackson went back to join a group of gentlemen beside the ring in a few minutes, for he was to act as referee presently, and as usual had been put in charge of most of the arrangements. Peregrine was so busy watching him, and thinking about his famous sparring school at No. 13, Old Bond Street, and how he himself would be taking lessons there in a very short while, that he failed to notice the approach of a curricle-and-four, which edged its way in neatly to a place immediately alongside his own gig and there drew up.

A voice said: 'Starch is an excellent thing, but in moderation, Worcester, for heaven's sake in moderation! I thought George had dropped a hint in your ear?'

The voice was a perfectly soft one, but it brought Peregrine's head round with a jerk, and made him jump. It belonged to a gentleman who drove a team of blood-chestnuts, and wore a greatcoat with fifteen capes. He was addressing an exquisite in an enormously high collar and neck-cloth, who coloured and said: 'Oh, be damned to you, Julian!'

As ill-luck would have it, Peregrine's start had made him tighten the reins involuntarily, and the farmer's horse began to back. Peregrine stopped him in a moment, but not in time to prevent his right mudguard just grazing the curricle's left one. He could have sworn aloud from annoyance.

The gentleman in the curricle turned, brows lifted in pained astonishment. 'My very good sir,' he began, and then stopped. The astonishment gave place to an expression of resignation. 'I might have known,' he said. 'After all, you did promise yourself this meeting, did you not?'

It was said quite quietly, but Peregrine, hot with chagrin, felt that it must have drawn all eyes upon himself. Certainly the gentleman in the high collar was leaning forward to look at him across the intervening curricle. He blurted out: 'I hardly touched your carriage! I could not help it if I did!'

'No, that is what I complain of,' sighed his tormentor. 'I'm sure you could not.'

Very red in the face, Peregrine said: 'You needn't be afraid, sir! This place will no longer do for me, I assure you!'

'But what is the matter? What are you saying, Julian?' demanded Lord Worcester curiously. 'Who is it?'

'An acquaintance of mine,' replied the gentleman in the curricle. 'Unsought, but damnably recurrent.'

Peregrine gathered up his reins in hands that were by no means steady; he might not find another place, but stay where he was he would not. He said: 'I shall relieve you of my presence, sir!'

'Thank you,' murmured the other, faintly smiling.

The gig drew out of the line without mishap and was driven off with unusual care through the press of people. There was by this time no gap in the first row of carriages into which a gig might squeeze its way, and after driving down the length of the long line Peregrine began to regret his hastiness. But just as he was about to turn up an avenue left in the ranks to get to the rear a young gentleman in a smart-looking whisky hailed him good-naturedly, and offered to pull in a little closer to the coach on his right, and so contrive a space for the gig.

Peregrine accepted this offer thankfully, and after a little manoeuvring and some protests from a party of men seated on the roof of the coach, room was made, and Peregrine could be comfortable again.

The owner of the whisky seemed to be a friendly young man. He had a chubby, smiling countenance, with a somewhat roguish pair of eyes. He was dressed in a blue single-breasted coat with a long waist, a blue waistcoat with inch-wide yellow stripes, plush breeches, tied at the knee with strings and rosettes, short boots with very long tops, and an amazing cravat of white muslin spotted with black. Over all this he wore a driving-coat of white drab, hanging negligently open, with two tiers of pockets, a Belcher handkerchief, innumerable capes, and a large nosegay.

Having satisfied himself that Peregrine, in spite of his gig and his old-fashioned dress, was not a mere Johnny Raw, he soon plunged into conversation; and in a very little while Peregrine learned that his name was Henry Fitzjohn, that he lived in Cork Street, was not long down from Oxford, and had come to Thistleton Gap in the expectation of joining a party of friends there. However, either because they had not yet arrived, or because the crowd was too dense to allow him to discover their position, he had missed them, and been forced to take up a place without them or lose his chance of seeing the fight. His dress was the insignia of the Four Horse Club, to which, as he naïvely informed Peregrine, he had been elected a member that very year.

He had backed the Champion to win the day's fight, and as soon as he discovered that Peregrine had never laid eyes on him – or, indeed, on any other of the notables present – he took it upon himself to point out every one of interest. That was Berkeley Craven, one of the stake-holders, standing by the ring now with Colonel Hervey Aston. Aston was one of the Duke of York's closest friends, and a great patron of the ring. Did Peregrine see that stoutish man with the crooked shoulder approaching Jackson? That was Lord Sefton, a capital fellow! And there, over to the right, was Captain Barclay, talking to Sir Watkin Williams Wynne, who was always to be seen at every fight. Mr Fitzjohn fancied that none of the Royal Dukes was present; he could not see them, though he had heard that Old Tarry Breeks – Clarence, of course – was expected to be there.

Peregrine drank it all in, feeling very humble and ignorant. In Yorkshire he had been used to know everyone and be known everywhere, but it was evident that in London circles it was different. Beverley Hall and the Taverner fortune counted for nothing; he was only an unknown provincial here.

Mr Fitzjohn produced an enormous turnip watch from his pocket and consulted it. 'It's after twelve,' he announced. 'If the magistrates have got wind of this and mean to stop it it will be a damned hum!'

But just at that moment some cheering, not unmixed with cat-calls and a few derisive shouts, was set up, and Tom Molyneux, accompanied by his seconds, Bill Richmond, the Black, and Bill Gibbons, arbiter of sport, came up to the ring.

'He looks a strong fellow,' said Peregrine, anxiously scrutinising as much as he could see of the negro for the enveloping folds of his greatcoat.

'Weighs something between thirteen and fourteen stone,' said Mr Fitzjohn knowledgeably. 'They say he loses his temper. You weren't at the fight last year? No, of course you weren't: I was forgetting. Well, y'know it was bad, very bad. The crowd booed him. Don't know why, for they don't boo at Richmond and he's a Black, too. I daresay it was just from everyone's wanting Cribb to win. But it was not at all the thing, and made the Black think he had not been fairly treated, though that was all my eye and Betty Martin, of course. Cribb is the better man, best fighter I ever saw in my life.'

'Did you ever see Belcher?' asked Peregrine.

'Well, no,' admitted Mr Fitzjohn regretfully. 'Before my time, you know, though I did have the chance of being at his last fight, a couple of years ago, when he was beaten by Cribb. But I don't know that I'm sorry I missed it. They say he was past it and then, of course, there was his eye – he only had one then, you know. My father said there was never a boxer to come near him in his day. Always remember my father telling me how he was at Wimbledon when Belcher knocked Gamble out in five rounds. Fight only lasted seven minutes. There were twenty thousand people there to see it. My father told me how the ring was within sight of the gibbet, and all the while they could hear Jerry Abershaw, who was hanging there in chains, creaking every time the wind caught him. Holla, this looks like business! There's old Gibbons tying his man's colours to the ropes. Crimson and orange, you see. Cribb sports the old blue bird's eye. Ha, there's John Gully! Cribb must have arrived! Who is his bottle-holder, I wonder? They'll be throwing their castors in the ring any moment now. Cribb was lying at the Blue Bull on Witham Common last night, and I believe Molyneux was at the Ram Jam. Can't make out why they're behind time. Lord, listen to them cheering! That must be Cribb sure enough! Yes, there he goes! He has Joe Ward with him. He must be his bottle-holder. Looks to be in fine feather, don't he? I've laid a monkey on him, and another he gives the first knock-down. The only thing is that he *is* slow. No denying it. But excellent bottom, never shy at all.'

The Champion's hat had been tossed into the ring by now, and he had followed it, and was acknowledging with a broad smile, and a wave of his hand, the cheers and yells of encouragement that greeted him. He was an inch and a half taller than the

Black, a heavy-looking fighter, but neat on his feet. He did indeed look to be in fine feather, but so, too, did Molyneux, emerging from his greatcoat. The Black had an enormous reach, and huge muscular development. He looked a formidable customer, but the betting was steady at three to one on Cribb.

In another few moments the seconds and bottle-holders left the ring, and at eighteen minutes past twelve precisely (as Mr Fitzjohn verified by a glance at his watch) the fight began.

For about a minute both men sparred cautiously, then Cribb made play right and left, and Molyneux returning slightly to the head, a brisk rally followed. The Champion put in a blow to the throat, and Molyneux fell.

'Nothing to choose between 'em, so far,' said Mr Fitzjohn wisely. 'Mere flourishing. But Cribb always starts slow. Stands well up, don't he?'

At setting-to again the Champion showed first blood, at the mouth, and immediately a brisk rally commenced. Cribb put in a good hit with his right; Molyneux returned like lightning on the head with the left flush, and some quick fighting followed at half-arm. They closed, and after a fierce struggle the Black threw Cribb a cross-buttock.

Mr Fitzjohn, who had risen from his seat in his excitement, sat down again, and said there was nothing in it. Peregrine, observing the Champion's right eye to be nearly closed from the last rally, could not but feel that Molyneux was getting the best of it. He had a tremendous punch, fought with marked ferocity, and seemed quicker than Cribb.

The third round opened with some sparring for wind; then Cribb put in a doubler to the body which pushed Molyneux away. A roar went up from the crowd, but the Black kept his legs, and rushed in again. For one and a half minutes there was some quick, fierce fighting; then they closed once more, and again Molyneux threw Cribb.

'The Black will win!' Peregrine exclaimed. 'He fights like a tiger! I'll lay you two to one in ponies the Black wins!'

'Done!' said Mr Fitzjohn promptly, though he looked a trifle anxious.

In the fourth round Molyneux continued fighting at the head, and putting in some flush hits, drew blood. Mr Fitzjohn began to fidget, for it was seen that both Cribb's eyes were damaged. Molyneux, however, seemed to be in considerable distress, his great chest heaving, and the sweat pouring off him. The Champion was smiling, but the round ended in his falling again.

Peregrine was quite sure the Black must win, and could not understand how seven to four in favour of Cribb could still be offered.

'Pooh, Cribb hasn't begun yet!' said Mr Fitzjohn stoutly. 'The Black's looking as queer as Dick's hat-band already.'

'Look at Cribb's face!' retorted Peregrine.

'Lord, there's nothing in the Black having drawn his cork. He's fighting at the head all the time. But watch Cribb going for the mark, that's what I say. He'll mill his man down yet, though I don't deny the Black shows game.'

Both men rattled in well up to time in the next round, but Molyneux had decidedly the best of the rally. Cribb fell, and a roar of angry disapproval went up from the crowd. There were some shouts of 'Foul!' and for a few moments it seemed as though the ring was to be stormed.

'I think the Black hit him as he fell,' said Mr Fitzjohn. 'I think that must have been it. Jackson makes no sign, you see; it can't have been a foul blow, or he would.'

The disturbance died down as both fighters came up to the mark for the sixth round. It was now obvious that Molyneux was greatly distressed for wind. Cribb was still full of gaiety. He avoided a rather wild lunge to left and right, and threw in a blow to the body. Molyneux managed to stop it, but was doubled up immediately by a terrific blow at the neck. He got away, but was dreadfully cut up.

'What did I tell you?' cried Mr Fitzjohn. 'Good God, the Black's as sick as a horse! He's all abroad! Cribb has him on the run!'

The blow seemed indeed to have shaken the Black up badly. He was hitting short, dancing about the ring in a way that provoked the rougher part of the crowd to jeers and yells of laughter. Cribb followed him round the ring, and floored him by a hit at full arm's length.

The odds being offered rose to five to one, and Mr Fitzjohn could scarcely keep his seat for excitement. 'The next round ends it!' he said. 'The Black's lost in rage!'

He was wrong, however. Molyneux came up to time, and charged in, planting one or two blows. Cribb put in some straight hits at the throat, stepping back after each. The Black bored in, fell, but whether from a hit or from exhaustion neither Peregrine nor Mr Fitzjohn could see.

Richmond got Molyneux up to time again. He rallied gamely, but his distance was ill-judged. Cribb did much as he liked with him, got his head into chancery, and fibbed till he fell.

'Lombard Street to a China orange!' exclaimed Mr Fitzjohn. 'Ay, you can see how Richmond and Bill Gibbons are working on him, but it's my belief he's done . . . No, by God, he's coming up to the mark again! Damme, the fellow's got excellent bottom, say what you will! But he's dead-beat, Taverner. Wonder Richmond don't throw the towel in. . . . Hey, that's finished him! What a left! Enough to break his jaw!'

The Black had gone down like a log. He was dragged to his corner, apparently insensible, and it seemed impossible that he could recover in the half-minute. But Cribb, who, in spite of his disfigured countenance, seemed as full of gaiety as ever, gave away his chance, and hugely delighted the crowd by dancing a hornpipe round the stage.

Molyneux got off his second's knee, but it was obvious that he could do no more. He made a game attempt to rally, but fell almost at once.

'I believe Cribb did break his jaw,' said Mr Fitzjohn, who was watching the Black closely. 'Damn it, the man's done! Richmond ought to throw in the towel. No sport in this! Lord, he's up again, full of pluck! No, he's done for! There'll be no getting him on his feet again. Ah, you see – Richmond knows it! He's going to throw in his towel.' Here Mr Fitzjohn broke off to join in the cheering.

On the stage the Champion, and Gully, his second, were engaged in dancing a Scotch reel to announce the victory. Peregrine joined Mr Fitzjohn in waving his hat in the air, and cheering, and sat down again feeling that he had seen a great fight. The knowledge that he had lost quite a large sum of money on it did not weigh with him in the least. He exchanged cards with Mr Fitzjohn, accepted some advice from that knowledgeable young gentleman on the best hotel to put up at in London, promised to call on him in Cork Street to pay his debts at the first opportunity, and parted from him with the agreeable conviction that he now had at least one acquaintance in London.

Three

MISS TAVERNER SPENT A PLEASANT MORNING EXPLORING the town. There was scarcely anyone about, and that circumstance, coupled with the fineness of the weather, tempted her to take another stroll after her luncheon of cakes and wine. There was nothing to do at the George beyond sit at her bedroom window and wait for Peregrine's return, and this prospect did not commend itself to her. Walking about the town had not tired her, and she understood from the chambermaid that Great Ponton church, only three miles from Grantham, was generally held to be worth a visit. Miss Taverner decided to walk there, and set out a little before midday, declining the escort of her maid.

The walk was a pretty one, and a steep climb up the highroad into the tiny village of Great Ponton quite rewarded Miss Taverner for her energy. A fine burst of country met her eyes, and a few steps down a by-road brought her to the church, a very handsome example of later perpendicular work, with a battlemented tower, and a curious weathervane in the form of a fiddle upon one of its pinnacles. There was no one of whom she could inquire the history of this odd vane, so after exploring the church, and resting a little while on a bench outside, she set out to walk back to Grantham.

At the bottom of the hill leading out of the village a pebble became lodged in her right sandal and after a very little way began to make walking an uncomfortable business. Miss Taverner wriggled her toes in an effort to shift the stone, but it would not answer. Unless she wished to limp all the way to Grantham she must take off her shoe and shake the pebble out. She hesitated, for she was upon the highroad and had no wish to be discovered in her stockings by any chance wayfarer. One or two carriages had passed her already: she supposed them to be returning from Thistleton Gap: but at the moment there was nothing in sight. She sat down on the bank at the side of the road, and pulled up her frilled skirt an inch or two to come at the strings of her sandal. As ill-luck would have it these had worked themselves into a knot which took her some minutes to untie. She had just succeeded in doing this, and was shaking out the pebble, when a curricle-and-four came into sight, travelling at a brisk pace towards Grantham.

Miss Taverner thrust the sandal behind her and hurriedly let down her skirts, but not, she felt uneasily, before the owner of the curricle must have caught a glimpse of her shapely ankle. She picked up her parasol, which she had allowed to fall at the foot of the bank, and pretended to be interested in the contemplation of the opposite side of the road.

The curricle drew alongside, and checked. Miss Taverner cast a fleeting glance upwards at it, and stiffened. The curricle stopped. 'Beauty in distress again?' inquired a familiar voice.

Miss Taverner would have given all she possessed in the world to have been able to rise up and walk away in the opposite direction. It was not in her power, however. She could only tuck her foot out of sight and affect to be quite deaf.

The curricle drew right in to the side of the road, and at a sign from its driver the tiger perched up behind jumped down and ran to the wheel-horses' heads. Miss Taverner raged inwardly, and turned her head away.

The curricle's owner descended in a leisurely fashion, and came up to her. 'Why so diffident?' he asked. 'You had plenty to say when I met you yesterday.'

Miss Taverner turned to look at him. Her cheeks had reddened, but she replied without the least sign of shyness: 'Be pleased to drive on, sir. I have nothing to say to you, and my affairs are not your concern.'

'That – or something very like it – is what you said to me before,' he remarked. 'Tell me, are you even prettier when you smile? I've no complaint to make, none at all: the whole effect is charming – and found at Grantham too, of all unlikely places! – but I should like to see you without the scowl.'

Miss Taverner's eyes flashed.

'Magnificent!' said the gentleman. 'Of course, blondes are not precisely the fashion, but you are something quite out of the way, you know.'

'You are insolent, sir!' said Miss Taverner.

He laughed. 'On the contrary, I am being excessively polite.'

She looked him full in the eyes. 'If my brother had been with me you would not have accosted me in this fashion,' she said.

'Certainly not,' he agreed, quite imperturbably. 'He would have been very much in the way. What is your name?'

'Again, sir, that is no concern of yours.'

'A mystery,' he said. 'I shall have to call you Clorinda. May I put on your shoe for you?'

She gave a start; her cheeks flamed. 'No!' she said chokingly. 'You may do nothing for me except drive on!'

'Why, that is easily done!' he replied, and bent, and before she had time to realise his purpose, lifted her up in his arms, and walked off with her to his curricle.

Miss Taverner ought to have screamed, or fainted. She was too much surprised to do either; but as soon as she had recovered from her astonishment at being picked up in that easy way (as though she had been a featherweight, which she knew she was not) she dealt her captor one resounding slap, with the full force of her arm behind it.

He winced a little, but his arms did not slacken their hold; rather they tightened slightly. 'Never hit with an open palm, Clorinda,' he told her. 'I will show you how in a minute. Up with you!'

Miss Taverner was tossed up into the curricle, and collapsed on to the seat in some disorder. The gentleman in the caped greatcoat picked up her parasol and gave it to her, took the sandal from her resistless grasp, and calmly held it ready to fit on to her foot.

To struggle for possession of it would be an undignified business; to climb down from the curricle was impossible. Miss Taverner, quivering with temper, put out her stockinged foot.

He slipped the sandal on, and tied the string.

'Thank you!' said Miss Taverner with awful civility. 'Now if you will give me your hand out of your carriage I may resume my walk.'

'But I am not going to give you my hand,' he said. 'I am going to drive you back to Grantham.'

His tone provoked her to reply disdainfully: 'You may think that a great honour, sir, but –'

'It is a great honour,' he said. 'I never drive females.'

'No,' said his tiger suddenly. 'Else I wouldn't be here. Not a minute I wouldn't.'

'Henry, you see, is a misogynist,' explained the gentleman, apparently not in the least annoyed by this unceremonious interruption.

'I am not interested in you or in your servant!' snapped Miss Taverner.

'That is what I like in you,' he agreed, and sprang lightly up into the curricle, and stepped across her to the box-seat. 'Now let me show you how to hit me.'

Miss Taverner resisted, but he possessed himself of her gloved hand and doubled it into a fist. 'Keep your thumb down so, and hit like that. Not at my chin, I think. Aim for the eye, or the nose, if you prefer.'

Miss Taverner sat rigid.

'I won't retaliate,' he promised. Then, as she still made no movement, he said: 'I see I shall have to offer you provocation,' and swiftly kissed her.

Miss Taverner's hands clenched into two admirable fists, but she controlled an unladylike impulse, and kept them in her lap. She was both shaken and enraged by the kiss, and hardly knew where to look. No other man than her father or Peregrine had ever dared to kiss her. At a guess she supposed the gentleman to have written her down as some country tradesman's daughter from a Queen's Square boarding school. Her old-fashioned dress was to blame, and no doubt that abominable gig. She wished she did not blush so hotly, and said with as much scorn as she could throw into her voice: 'Even a dandy might remember the civility due to a gentlewoman. I shall not hit you.'

'I am disappointed,' he said. 'There is nothing for it but to go in search of your brother. Stand away, Henry.'

The tiger sprang back, and ran to scramble up on to his perch again. The curricle moved forward, and in another minute was bowling rapidly along the road towards Grantham.

'You may set me down at the George, sir,' said Miss Taverner coldly. 'No doubt if my brother is come back from the fight he will oblige you in the way, I, alas, am not able to do.'

He laughed. 'Hit me, do you mean? All things are possible, Clorinda, though some are – unlikely, let us say.'

She folded her lips, and for a while did not speak. Her companion maintained a flow of languid conversation until she interrupted him, impelled by curiosity to ask him the question in her mind. 'Why did you wish to drive me into Grantham?'

He glanced down at her rather mockingly. 'Just to annoy you, Clorinda. The impulse was irresistible, believe me.'

She took refuge in silence again, for she could find no adequate words with which to answer him. She had never been spoken to so in her life; she was more than a little inclined to think him mad.

Grantham came into sight; in a few minutes the curricle drew up outside the George, and the first thing Miss Taverner saw was her brother's face above the blind in one of the lower windows.

The gentleman descended from the curricle, and held up his hand for her to take. 'Do smile!' he said.

Miss Taverner allowed him to help her down, but preserved an icy front. She swept into the inn ahead of him, and nearly collided with Peregrine, hurrying out to meet her. 'Judith! What the devil?' exclaimed Peregrine. 'Has there been an accident?'

'Judith,' repeated the gentleman of the curricle pensively. 'I prefer Clorinda.'

'No,' said Judith. 'Nothing of the sort. This – gentleman – constrained me to ride in his carriage, that is all.'

'Constrained you!' Peregrine took a hasty step forward.

She was sorry to have said so much, and added at once: 'Do not let us be standing here talking about it! I think he is mad.'

The gentleman gave his low laugh, and produced a snuff-box from one pocket, and held a pinch first to one nostril and then to the other.

Peregrine advanced upon him, and said stormily: 'Sir, I shall ask you to explain yourself!'

'You forgot to tell him that I kissed you, Clorinda,' murmured the gentleman.

'What?' shouted Peregrine.

'For heaven's sake be quiet!' snapped his sister.

Peregrine ignored her. 'You will meet me for this, sir! I hoped I might come upon you again, and I have. And now to find that you have dared to insult my sister. You shall hear from me!'

A look of amusement crossed the gentleman's face. 'Are you proposing to fight a duel with me?' he inquired.

'Where and when you like!' said Peregrine.

The gentleman raised his brows. 'My good boy, that is very heroic, but do you really think that I cross swords with every country nobody who chooses to be offended with me?'

'Now, Julian, Julian, what are you about?' demanded a voice from the doorway into the coffee-room. 'Oh, I beg pardon, ma'am! I beg pardon!' Lord Worcester came into the hall with a glass in his hand, and paused, irresolute.

Peregrine, beyond throwing him a fleeting glance, paid no heed to him. He was searching in his pocket for a card, and this he presently thrust at the gentleman in the greatcoat. 'That is my card, sir!'

The gentleman took it between finger and thumb, and raised an eyeglass on the end of a gold stick attached to a ribbon round his neck. 'Taverner,' he said musingly. 'Now where have I heard that name before?'

'I do not expect to be known to you, sir,' said Peregrine, trying to keep his voice steady. 'Perhaps I am a nobody, but there is a gentleman who I think – I am sure – will be pleased to act for me: Mr Henry Fitzjohn, of Cork Street!'

'Oh, Fitz!' nodded Lord Worcester. 'So you know him, do you?'

'Taverner,' repeated the gentleman in the greatcoat, taking not the smallest notice of Peregrine's speech. 'It has something of a familiar ring, I think.'

'Admiral Taverner,' said Lord Worcester helpfully. 'Meet him for ever at Fladong's.'

'And if that is not enough, sir, to convince you that I am not unworthy of your sword, I must refer you to Lord Worth, whose ward I am!' announced Peregrine.

'Eh?' said Lord Worcester. 'Did you say you were *Worth's* ward?'

The gentleman in the greatcoat gave Peregrine back his card. 'So you are my Lord Worth's wards!' he said. 'Dear me! And – er – are you at all acquainted with your guardian?'

'That, sir, has nothing to do with you! We are on our way to visit his lordship now.'

'Well,' said the gentleman softly, 'you must present my compliments to him when you see him. Don't forget.'

'This is not to the point!' exclaimed Peregrine. 'I have challenged you to fight, sir!'

'I don't think your guardian would advise you to press your challenge,' replied the gentleman with a slight smile.

Judith laid a hand on her brother's arm, and said coldly: 'You have not told us yet by what name we may describe you to Lord Worth.'

His smile lingered. 'I think you will find that his lordship will know who I am,' he said, and took Lord Worcester's arm, and strolled with him into the coffee-room.

Four

𝒥T WAS WITH DIFFICULTY THAT MISS TAVERNER SUCCEEDED IN preventing her brother from following the stranger and Lord Worcester into the coffee-room and there attempting to force an issue. He was out of reason angry, but upon Judith's representing to him how such a scene could only end in a public brawl which must involve her, as the cause of it, he allowed himself to be drawn away, still declaring that he would at least know the stranger's name.

She pushed him up the stairs in front of her, and in the seclusion of her own room gave him an account of her adventure. It was not, after all, so very bad; there had been nothing to alarm her, though much to enrage. She made light of the circumstance of the stranger's kissing her: he would bestow just such a careless embrace on a pretty chambermaid, she dared say. It was certain that he mistook her station in life.

Peregrine could not be content. She had been insulted, and it must be for him to bring the stranger to book. As she set about the task of arguing him out of his determination, Judith realised that she had rather bring the gentleman to book herself. To have Peregrine settle the business could bring her no satisfaction; it must be for her to punish the stranger's insolence, and she fancied that she could do so without assistance.

When Peregrine went downstairs again to the coffee-room the strange gentleman had gone. The landlord, still harassed and busy with company, could not tell Peregrine his name, nor even recall having served Lord Worcester. So many gentlemen had crowded into his inn to-day that he could not be blamed for forgetting half of them. As for a team of blood-chestnuts, he could name half a dozen such teams; they might all have drawn up at the George for anything he knew. Peregrine could only be sorry that Mr Fitzjohn was already on his way back to London: he might have known the stranger's name.

By dinner-time Grantham was quiet. A few gentlemen stayed on overnight, but they were not many. Miss Taverner could go to bed in the expectation of a night's unbroken repose.

She thought herself reasonably safe from any further talk of the fight. It had been described to her in detail at least five times. There could be no more to say.

There was no more to say. Peregrine realised it, and beyond exclaiming once or twice during breakfast next morning that he never hoped to see a better mill, and asking his sister whether he had told her of this or that hit, he did not talk of it. He was out of spirits; after the excitement of the previous day, Sunday in Grantham was insipid beyond bearing. He was cursed flat, was only sorry Judith's scruples forbade them setting forward for London at once.

There was nothing to do but go to church, and stroll about the town a little with his sister on his arm. Even the gig had had to be returned to its owner.

They attended the service together, and after it walked slowly back to the George. Peregrine was all yawns and abstraction. He could not be brought to admire anything, was not interested in the history even of the Angel Inn, where it was said that Richard the Third had once lain. Judith must know he had never cared a rap for such fusty old stuff. He wished there were some way of passing the time; he could not think what he should do with himself until dinner.

He was grumbling on in this strain when the pressure of Judith's fingers on his arm compelled his attention. She said in a low voice: 'Perry, the gentleman who gave up his rooms to us! I wish you would speak to him: we owe him a little extraordinary civility.'

He brightened at once, and looked round him. He would be glad to shake hands with the fellow; might even, if Judith was agreeable, invite him to dine with them.

The gentleman was approaching them, upon the same side of the road. It was evident that he had recognised them; he looked a little conscious, but did not seem to wish to stop. As he drew nearer he raised his hat and bowed slightly, and would have passed on if Peregrine, dropping his sister's arm, had not stood in the way.

'I beg pardon,' Peregrine said, 'but I think you are the gentleman who was so obliging to us on Friday?'

The other bowed again, and murmured something about it being of no moment.

'But it was of great moment to us, sir,' Judith said. 'I am afraid we thanked you rather curtly, and you may have thought us very uncivil.'

He raised his eyes to her face, and said earnestly: 'No, indeed not, ma'am. I was happy to be of service; it was nothing to me: I might command a lodging elsewhere. I beg you won't think of it again.'

He would have passed on, and seeing him so anxious to be gone Miss Taverner made no further effort to detain him. But Peregrine was less perceptive, and still barred the way. 'Well, I'm glad to have met you again, sir. Say what you will, I am in your debt. My name is Taverner – Peregrine Taverner. This is my sister, as perhaps you know.'

The gentleman hesitated for an instant. Then he said in rather a low voice: 'I did know. That is to say, I heard your name mentioned.'

'Ay, did you so? I daresay you might. But we did not hear yours, sir,' said Peregrine, laughing.

'No. I was unwilling to – I did not wish to thrust myself upon your notice,' said the other. A smile crept into his eyes; he said a little ruefully: 'My name is also Taverner.'

'Good God!' cried Peregrine in great astonishment. 'You don't mean – you are not related to us, are you?'

'I am afraid I am,' said Mr Taverner. 'My father is Admiral Taverner.'

'Well, by all that's famous!' exclaimed Peregrine. 'I never knew he had a son!'

Judith had listened with mixed feelings. She was amazed, at once delighted to find that she had so unexpectedly amiable a relative, and sorry that he should be the son of a man her father had mistrusted so wholeheartedly. His modesty, the delicacy with which he had refrained from instantly making himself known to them, his manners, which were extremely engaging, outweighed the rest. She held her hand out to him, saying in a friendly way: 'Then we are cousins, and should know each other better.'

He bowed over her fingers. 'You are very good. I have wished to speak to you, but the disagreements – the estrangement, rather, between your father and mine made me diffident.'

'Oh well, there's no reason why that should concern us!' said Peregrine, brushing it aside with an airy gesture. 'I daresay my uncle is as hasty as my father was, eh, Judith?'

She could not assent to it; he should not be speaking of their father in that fashion to one who was quite a stranger to them.

Mr Taverner seemed to feel it also. He said: 'I believe there were grave faults, but we can hardly judge – I certainly must not. You will understand – it is difficult for me. But I have already said too much.'

He addressed himself more particularly to Judith. She fancied there was a faint bitterness in the way he spoke. She found herself more than ever disposed to like him. His manner indicated – or so she thought – that he was aware of some behaviour on his father's part which he could not approve. She respected him for his reticence; he seemed to feel just as he ought. It was with pleasure that she heard Peregrine invite him to dine with them.

He was obliged to excuse himself: he was engaged with his friends; he wished it had been in his power to accept.

He was obviously sincere; he looked disconsolate. For her part Judith was sadly disappointed, but she would neither press him, nor permit Peregrine to do so.

Mr Taverner bowed over her hand again, and held it a moment. 'I am more than sorry. I should have liked excessively – But it must not be. I am promised. May I – you will be open with me, cousin – may I give myself the pleasure of calling on you in town?'

She smiled and gave permission.

'You have a guardian who will advise you,' he said. 'I am not acquainted with Lord Worth, but I believe him to be generally very well-liked. He will put you in the way of everything. But if there is at any time anything I can do for you – if you should feel yourselves in want of a friend – I hope you will remember that the wicked cousin would be only too happy to be of service.' It was said with an arch look, and the hint of a smile. He gave Peregrine his card.

Peregrine held it between his fingers. 'Thank you. We shall hope to see more of you, cousin. We mean to put up at Grillon's for the present, but my sister has a notion of setting up house. I don't know how it will end. But Grillon's will find us.'

Mr Taverner noted it down in his pocket-book, bowed again, and took his leave of them. They watched him walk away down the street.

'I'll tell you what, Ju,' said Peregrine suddenly. 'I wish he may tell me the name of his tailor. Did you notice his coat?'

She had not; she had been aware only of a certain elegance. There was nothing of the fop about him.

They strolled on towards the George wondering about their cousin. A glance at his card informed them that his name was Bernard, and that he was to be found at an address in Harley Street, which Miss Taverner knew, from having heard her father speak of an acquaintance living there, to be a respectable neighbourhood.

The rest of the day passed quietly; they went to bed in good time to be in readiness for an early start in the morning.

Consultation of the *Traveller's Guide* convinced Miss Taverner at least that the rest of the journey could not be accomplished with comfort in one day. It was in vain that Peregrine argued that by setting forward at eight in the morning they could not fail to reach London by nine in the evening at the latest. Miss Taverner placed no dependence on his reckoning. The post-horses might, as he swore they would, cover nine miles an hour, but he made no allowance for changing them, or for the halts at the turnpikes, or for any other of the checks they would be sure to encounter. She had no wish to be travelling for as much as twelve hours at a stretch, and no wish to arrive in London after nightfall. Peregrine was forced to give way, though with an ill-grace.

However, by the time they had reached Stevenage, shortly after three o'clock on the following afternoon, he was heartily tired of sitting in the chaise, and very glad to get down at the Swan Inn, and stretch his limbs, and bespeak dinner and beds for the night.

They were off again directly they had breakfasted next morning. They had only thirty-one miles to cover now, and with London drawing nearer every moment they were both impatient to arrive, and alert to catch sight of every milestone.

Barnet was their last stage, and here they seemed to be at last within hail of London. The town was busy, for the traffic of the Holyhead road, as well as that of the Great North road, passed through it. There were any number of inns, and two great houses which were solely devoted to posting business. The smaller of these, the Red Lion, took most of the north-going vehicles, while the larger, the Green Man, which was situated in the middle of the town and kept no less than twenty-six pairs of horses and eleven post-boys, seized on the chaises travelling south.

The rivalry between the two was fierce in the extreme; it was said that on more than one occasion private chaises had been intercepted and the horses forcibly changed at one or other of the inns.

Some sign of this was evident in the way the ostlers of the Green Man came running out at the approach of the Taverners' chaise, and led it into the big stable yard. A glass of sherry was handed up to Peregrine, and sandwiches were offered to his sister, this being one of the superior attractions of the Green Man over the Red Lion that its customers had free refreshments pressed on them.

The change of horses was accomplished in two minutes; a couple of post-boys cast off the smocks they wore over their blue jackets to keep them clean, and sprang into the saddles; and almost before the travellers had time to fetch their breath they were out of the stable yard again, and trotting off towards London.

Another two miles brought them to the village of Whetstone, and the turnpike which marked the beginning of Finchley Common.

The very name of this famous tract of land was enough to conjure up terrifying thoughts, but on this fine warm October day the heath seemed kindly enough. No masked figures came galloping to hold up the chaise; nothing more alarming than a stage-coach painted all the colours of the rainbow was to be met with; and in a short space the village of East End was reached, and whatever terrors the Common might hide were left safely behind.

Highgate afforded the travellers their first glimpse of London. As the chaise topped the rise and began the descent upon the southern side, the view spread itself before Miss Taverner's wondering eyes. There were the spires, the ribbon of the Thames, and the great huddle of buildings of which she had heard so much, lying below her in a haze of sunlight. She could not take her eyes from the sight, nor believe that she was really come at last to the city she had dreamed of for so long.

The way led down until the view was lost, and the chaise entered on the Holloway road, a lonely track which ran, still descending, between high banks until Islington Spa was reached. This was a charming village, with tall elm trees growing on the green, a rustic pound for strayed cattle, and a number of coaching inns.

The last toll-gate was passed, and the ticket which opened it given up to the gate-keeper. In a very little while the chaise was bowling between lines of houses, over a cobbled surface.

Everything seemed to flash by in an instant. Miss Taverner tried to read the names of the streets down which they drove, but there was too much to look at; she began to be bewildered. It was so very large and bustling.

They seemed to have been driving through the town for an age when the chaise at last stopped. Leaning forward, Miss Taverner saw that the street in which they now stood was lined on either side with very genteel-looking houses, and had an air of being extremely well-kept, unlike some of those through which they had come.

The door of the chaise was opened, the steps let down, and in another minute Miss Taverner was standing inside Grillon's hotel.

It was soon seen that Mr Fitzjohn had not advised Peregrine ill. Grillon's hotel offered its guests everything that could be imagined in the way of comfort. The bedchambers, the saloons, the furnishings, all were in the best of taste. Miss Taverner, who had been inclined to doubt the wisdom of following a strange young gentleman's advice, was satisfied. There could be no need to inspect the sheets at Grillon's.

The first thing to be done was to see her trunks unpacked, and her clothing tidily bestowed; the next to pull the bell-rope for the chambermaid, and bespeak some hot water.

On her way through one of the saloons to the staircase she had seen some of the other visitors to the hotel. There was a gentleman in tight pantaloons, reading a newspaper; two ladies in flimsy muslin dresses, talking by the window; and a stately dowager in a turban, who stared at Miss Taverner in a haughty manner that made her feel that her bonnet was dowdy, and her dress crushed from sitting in the post-chaise for so long.

She put on her best gown for dinner, but she was afraid, looking doubtfully at her reflection in the long mirror, that it was not fashionable enough for so modish a hotel. However, her pearls at least were incomparable. She clasped the string round her neck, pulled on a pair of silk mittens over her hands, and sat down to wait for Peregrine.

They dined at six, which seemed a very late hour to Judith, but which Peregrine, who had been in conversation with some of the other guests while she was unpacking and had contrived to glean a quantity of odd information, assured her was not late at all, but on the contrary, unfashionably early.

Peregrine was agog with excitement, his blue eyes sparkling, and all his doldrums vanished. He wanted to be up and doing, and tried to coax Judith into going with him to the play after dinner. She refused it, but urged him to go without her, not to be thinking himself tied to her apron strings. For herself, she was very tired, and would go to bed at the earliest opportunity.

He went, and she did not see him again until next morning, when they met at the breakfast-table. He had been to Covent Garden, to see Kemble; he had kept the playbill for her; he was devilish sorry she had not been there, for she would have liked it of all things. Such a great theatre, with he knew not how many boxes, all hung with curtains, and supported on pillars, and the roomiest pit! He dared not say how many candles there were: everything was a blaze of light; and as for the company, why, he had never seen so many dressed-up people in his life; no, nor half so many quizzes neither!

She listened to it all, and asked him a dozen questions. He could not tell her very much about the play; he had been too much taken up with watching all the fashionables. He thought it had been *Othello*, or some such thing. He was nearly sure it was *Othello*, now he came to think of it; famous stuff, but he had enjoyed the farce more. And now what were they to do? For his part he thought they had best call on Lord Worth, and get it done with.

She agreed to it, and went up to her room after breakfast to put on her hat and gloves. She hoped Lord Worth would not be angry with them for having come to London against his advice, but now that she was so near to seeing him in person she owned to a slight feeling of nervousness. But Peregrine was right: nothing could be done until they had presented themselves to their guardian.

Since neither she nor Peregrine had the least notion where Cavendish Square was to be found, and since neither of them cared to betray their ignorance by inquiring the way, Peregrine called up one of the hackneys with which the streets seemed to abound and gave the coachman the direction.

Cavendish Square was soon reached, and the hackney, drawing up before a great stucco-fronted house with an imposing portico. Peregrine handed his sister down, paid off the coachman, and said stoutly: 'Well, he can't eat us, Ju, after all.'

'No,' said Miss Taverner. 'No, of course not. Oh Perry, wait! Do not knock! There is a straw in your shoe; you must have picked it up off the floor of that horrid carriage.'

'Lord, what a lucky chance you saw it!' said Peregrine, removing the straw, and giving a final twitch to the lapels of his coat. 'Now for it, Ju!' He raised his hand to the knocker, and beat a mild tattoo on the door.

'They will never hear that!' said his sister scornfully. 'If you are afraid I certainly am not!' She stepped forward and grasping the knocker firmly, beat an imperious summons with it.

In the middle of this operation the door opened, rather to Miss Taverner's discomfiture. A very large footman confronted them, inclining his head slightly to learn their business.

Miss Taverner, recovering her composure, inquired if Lord Worth were at home, and upon being asked civilly for her name, replied grandly: 'Be good enough to inform his lordship, if you please, that Sir Peregrine and Miss Taverner are here.'

The footman bowed, as though he were much impressed by this speech, and held the door wide for them to pass through into the house. Here a second footman took them in charge, and begging them to follow him, led the way across what seemed to be a vast hall to a mahogany door which opened into a saloon. He ushered them into this apartment and left them there.

Peregrine passed a finger inside his cravat. 'You carried that off mighty well, Ju,' he said approvingly. 'I hope you may handle the old gentleman as prettily.'

'Oh,' said Miss Taverner, 'I don't expect there will be the least need. Do you know, Perry, I have been thinking that we have made Lord Worth into an ogre, between us, and ten to one but he is perfectly amiable?'

'He may be, of course,' conceded Peregrine, without much hope. 'He has a devilish fine house, hasn't he?'

It was indeed a fine house, fitted up, apparently, in the first style of elegance. The saloon in which they stood was a noble apartment hung with a delicate blue paper, and with tall windows giving on to the square. The curtains, which were of blue and crimson silk, were draped over these in tasteful festoons, and tied back with cords, to which were attached huge silken tassels. An Axminster carpet covered the floor; there were one or two couches with gilded scroll ends and crimson upholstery; a satin-wood sofa-table; some Sheraton chairs; a secretaire with a cylinder front and the upper part enclosed in glazed doors; a couple of thimble-footed window-stools; and a handsome console-table, supported by gilded sphinxes.

There were a number of pictures on the walls, and Miss Taverner was engaged in contemplating one of these when the door opened again and someone came in.

She turned quickly, just as a stifled exclamation broke from Peregrine, and stood rooted to the ground, staring in blank astonishment at the man who had entered. It was the gentleman of the curricle.

He was no longer dressed in a caped greatcoat and top-boots, but in spite of his close-fitting coat of blue cloth, and his tight pantaloons, and his shining Hessians with their little gold tassels, she could not mistake him. It was he.

He gave no sign of having recognised her, but came across the room and bowed formally. 'Miss Taverner, I believe?' he said. Then, as she did not answer, being quite bereft of speech, he turned to Peregrine, and held out his hand. 'And you are, I suppose, Peregrine,' he said. 'How do you do?'

Peregrine put out his own hand instinctively and almost snatched it back again. 'What are *you* doing in this house?' he blurted out.

The thin black brows rose in an expression of faint hauteur. 'I can conceive of no one who has a better right to be in this house,' the other replied. 'I am Lord Worth.'

Peregrine recoiled. 'What!' An angry flush mounted to his cheeks. 'This is nothing but an ill-mannered jest! You are not Lord Worth! You cannot be!'

'Why can I not be Lord Worth?' said the gentleman.

'It is impossible! I don't believe it! Lord Worth is – must be – an older man!' cried Peregrine.

The gentleman smiled slightly, and drew an enamelled snuff-box from his pocket, and unfobbed it with a flick of his forefinger. The gesture brought the picture of him, as he had stood in the hall of the George Inn, back to Judith's mind. She found her tongue suddenly, and engaging Peregrine's silence with a movement of her hand, said in a level voice: 'It is true? Are you indeed Lord Worth?'

His glance swept her face. 'Certainly I am,' he said, and took a pinch of snuff from the box, and delicately sniffed it.

She felt her brain to be reeling. 'But it is surely – You, sir, cannot have been a friend of my father?'

He shut the box again, and slipped it back into his pocket. 'I regret, madam, I had not that honour,' he said.

'Then – oh, there is some mistake!' she said. 'There must be a mistake!'

'Quite possibly,' agreed his lordship. 'But the mistake, Miss Taverner, was not mine.'

'But you are not our guardian!' Peregrine burst out.

'I am afraid there is no loophole for escape,' replied Worth. 'I am your guardian.' He added kindly: 'I assure you, you cannot regret the circumstance more than I do.'

'How can this be?' demanded Judith. 'My father did not mean it so!'

'Unfortunately,' said Worth, 'your father's Will was drawn up nine months after the death of mine.'

'Oh!' groaned Miss Taverner, sinking down upon one of the gilt and crimson couches.

'But the name!' said Peregrine. 'My father must have written the name down!'

'Your father,' said Worth, 'left you to the sole guardianship of Julian St John Audley, Fifth Earl of Worth. The name was certainly my father's. It is also mine. The mistake – if it is a mistake – is in the title. Your father named mine the Fifth Earl in error. I am the Fifth Earl.'

An unfilial expression was wrenched from Miss Taverner. 'He would!' she said bitterly. 'Oh, I can readily believe it!'

Peregrine gulped, and said: 'This must be set right. We are not your wards. We had rather be anything in the world than your wards!'

'Possibly,' said the Earl, unmoved. 'But the distressing fact remains that you are my wards.'

'I shall go at once to my father's lawyer!' declared Peregrine.

'Certainly. Do just as you please,' said the Earl. 'But do try and rid yourself of the notion that you are the only sufferer.'

Miss Taverner, who had been sitting with one gloved hand covering her eyes, now straightened herself, and folded both hands in her lap. It was evident to her that this conversation led nowhere. She suspected that what Worth said was true, and they would find it impossible to overset the Will. If that were so this bickering was both fruitless and undignified. She quelled Peregrine with a frown, and addressed herself to the Earl. 'Very well, sir, if you are indeed our guardian perhaps you will be good enough to inform us whether we are at liberty to establish ourselves in London?'

'Subject to my permission you are,' replied Worth.

Peregrine ground his teeth, and flung over to the window, and stood staring out on to the square.

Miss Taverner's fierce blue eyes met her guardian's cool grey ones in a long look that spoke volumes. 'You may, through an error in my father's Will, be our guardian in name, sir, but that is all.'

'You cannot have read the Will, Miss Taverner,' said the Earl.

'I am aware that the control of our fortune is in your hands,' snapped Miss Taverner. 'And I am anxious to come to an agreement with you!'

'By all means,' agreed Worth. 'You will not find me at all difficult. I shall not, I hope, find myself obliged to interfere in your lives very much.' He added, with the flicker of a smile: 'I am not even going to make myself unpleasant to you on this question of your coming to London against my advice.'

'Thank you,' said Miss Taverner witheringly.

He moved towards the secretaire and opened it. 'That was, after all, a piece of advice given to suit my own convenience. I have no real objection to your having come to town, and I will do what lies in my power to see you comfortably established.' He picked up a document and held it for Miss Taverner to see. 'I have here the lease of a furnished house in Brook Street which you may move into at your earliest convenience. I trust you will find it to your liking.'

'You are extremely obliging,' said Miss Taverner, 'but I do not know that I should care to lodge in Brook Street.'

The smile gleamed again. 'Indeed, Miss Taverner? And in which street would you care to lodge?'

She bit her lip, but replied with dignity. 'I am as yet wholly unacquainted with London, sir. I should prefer to wait until I can decide for myself where I desire to live.'

'While you are making up your mind,' said Worth, 'you may lodge in Brook Street.' He put the lease back into its pigeon-hole, and closed the secretaire. 'The task of engaging your servants can be left to my secretary. I have instructed him to attend to this.'

'I prefer to engage my own servants,' said Miss Taverner, goaded.

'Certainly,' replied Worth suavely. 'I will instruct Blackader to direct those he considers the most suitable to call on you at your hotel. Where are you putting up?'

'At Grillon's,' said Miss Taverner in a hollow voice. A vision of butlers, footmen, housekeepers, serving-maids, grooms, all streaming into Grillon's hotel to be interviewed, most forcibly struck her mind's eye. She began to perceive that the Earl of Worth was a foe well worthy of her steel.

The Earl lowered his sword – or so it seemed to her. 'Unless you would prefer to see Blackader himself, and give him your commands?'

Miss Taverner, with a chilly haughtiness that concealed her inward gratitude, accepted this offer.

Peregrine looked over his shoulder, and said belligerently: 'I shall be sending to Yorkshire, for certain of my horses, but we shall be needing others, and a carriage for my sister.'

'Surely you can buy a carriage without my assistance?' said Worth in a weary voice. 'You will probably be cheated in buying your horses, but the experience won't harm you.'

Peregrine choked. 'I did not mean that! For sure, I don't need your assistance! All I meant was – what I wished to make plain –'

'I see,' said Worth. 'You want to know whether you may set up your stable. Certainly. I have not the least objection.' He came away from the secretaire, and walked slowly across the room to the fireplace. 'There remains, Miss Taverner, the problem of finding a lady to live with you.'

'I have a cousin living in Kensington, sir,' said Miss Taverner. 'I shall ask her if she will come to me.'

He glanced down at her meditatively. 'Will you tell me, Miss Taverner, what precisely is your object in having come to London?'

'What is that to the point, sir?'

'When you are better acquainted with me,' said the Earl, 'you will know that I never ask pointless questions. Is it your intention to live upon the fringe of society, or do you mean to take your place in the world of Fashion? Will the Pantheon do for you, or must it be Almack's?'

She replied instantly: 'It must be the best, sir.'

'Then we need not consider the cousin living in Kensington,' said Worth. 'Fortunately, I know a lady who (though I fear you

may find her in some ways extremely foolish) is not only willing to undertake the task of chaperoning you, but has the
undoubted entrée to the world you wish to figure in. Her name
is Scattergood. She is a widow, and some sort of a cousin of
mine. I will bring her to call on you.'

Miss Taverner got up in one swift graceful movement. 'I had
rather anyone than a cousin of yours, Lord Worth!' she declared.

He drew out his snuff-box again, and took a pinch between
finger and thumb. Over it his eyes met hers. 'Shall we agree, Miss
Taverner, to consider that remark unsaid?' he suggested gently.

She blushed to the roots of her hair. She could have cried
from vexation at having allowed her unruly tongue to betray
her into a piece of school-girlish rudeness. 'I beg your pardon!'
she said stiffly.

He bowed, and laid his snuff-box down open on the table. He
had apparently no more to say to her, for he turned to Peregrine,
and called him away from the window. 'When you have visited
a tailor,' he said, 'come to me again, and we will discuss what
clubs you want me to put your name up for.'

Peregrine came to the table, half sulky, half eager. 'Can you
have me made a member of White's?' he asked rather shyly.

'Yes, I can have you made a member of White's,' said the Earl.

'And – and – Watier's, is it not?'

'That will be for my friend Mr Brummell to decide. His
decision will not be in your favour if you let him see you in that
coat. Go to Weston, in Conduit Street, or to Schweitzer and
Davidson, and mention my name.'

'I thought of going to Stultz,' said Peregrine, making a bid
for independence.

'By all means, if you wish the whole of London to recognise
your tailor at a glance,' shrugged his lordship.

'Oh!' said Peregrine, a little abashed. 'Mr Fitzjohn recommended him to me.'

'So I should imagine,' said the Earl.

Miss Taverner said with an edge to her voice: 'Pray, sir, have you no advice to offer me in the matter of my dress?'

He turned. 'My advice to you, Miss Taverner, is to put yourself unreservedly in the hands of Mrs Scattergood. There is one other matter. While you are under my guardianship you will, if you please, refrain from being present in towns where a prize-fight is being held.'

She caught her breath. 'Yes, my lord? You think, perhaps, that my being in such towns might lay me open to some insult?'

'On the contrary,' replied the Earl, 'I think it might lay you open to an excess of civility.'

Five

$\mathcal{T}$HE EVENTS AND IMPRESSIONS OF HER FIRST WEEK IN LONDON left Miss Taverner with her brain in a whirl. On the very afternoon of the day she and Peregrine called on their guardian he not only brought Mrs Scattergood to see her, but later sent Mr Blackader to discuss the question of servants.

Mrs Scattergood took Miss Taverner's breath away. She was a very thin lady of no more than medium height, certainly on the wrong side of forty, but dressed in an amazingly youthful fashion, with her improbably chestnut-coloured hair cropped short at the back, and crimped into curls in front, and her sharp, lively countenance painted in a lavish style that quite shocked the country-bred Judith.

She was dressed in a semi-transparent gown of jaconet muslin, made up to the throat with a treble ruff of pointed lace, and fastened down the back with innumerable little buttons. Her gown ended in a broad embroidered flounce, and on her feet she had lace stockings and yellow kid Roman boots. A lavender chip hat, tied under her chin with long yellow ribands, was placed over a small white satin cap beneath, and she carried a long-handled parasol, and a silk reticule.

Her twinkling eyes absorbed Judith at a glance. She stepped back as though to see the girl in perspective, and then nodded briskly. 'I am charmed! My dear Worth, I am quite charmed!

You must, you *shall* let me have the dressing of you, child! What is your name – oh no, not that stiff Miss Taverner! Judith! Worth, what do you stay for? I am to talk of fashions, you know. You must go at once!'

Miss Taverner, who had intended politely to decline Mrs Scattergood's services, felt powerless. The Earl made his bow, and left them together, and Mrs Scattergood immediately took one of Judith's shapely hands in her own tightly-gloved ones, and said coaxingly: 'You will let me come and live with you, won't you? I am shockingly expensive, but you won't mind that, I daresay. Oh, you are looking at my gown, and thinking what a very odd appearance I present. You see, I am not pretty, not in the least, never was, and so I have to be odd. Nothing for it! It answers delightfully. And so Worth has taken a house for you in Brook Street! Just as it should be: a charming situation! You know, I have quite made up my mind to it you are to be the rage. I think I should come to you at once. Grillon's! Well, I suppose there is no more genteel hotel in town, but a young lady alone – oh, you have a brother, but what is the use of that? I had better have my boxes packed up immediately. How I do run on! You don't wish me to live with you at all, I daresay. But a cousin in Kensington! You would find she would not add to your consequence, my dear. I am sure, a dowdy old lady. She would not else be living in Kensington, take my word for it.'

So Miss Taverner yielded, and that very evening her chaperon arrived at Grillon's in a light coach weighed down by trunks and bandboxes.

Mr Blackader, who sent in his card at about four o'clock in the afternoon, was much more easily dealt with. He was a shy young man, who looked at the heiress with undisguised admiration. He seemed to be extremely conscientious, and most anxious to oblige. He frowned over the credentials of at least a dozen servants, and fluttered over the leaves of a sheaf of papers, until Miss Taverner laughingly implored him to stop.

Mr Blackader's solemnity disappeared into something remarkably like a grin. 'Well, do you know, ma'am, I think if you was to let me settle it all for you it would be quicker done?' he suggested apologetically.

So it was arranged. Mr Blackader hurried away to engage a cook, and Miss Taverner walked out to take a peep at London.

She turned into Piccadilly, and knew herself to be in the heart of the fashionable quarter. There was so much to see, so much to wonder at! She had not believed so many modish people to exist, while as for the carriages, she had never seen any so elegant. The shops, the buildings were all delightful. There was the famous Hatchard's, with its bow windows filled with all the newest publications. She could almost fancy that the gentleman coming out of the shop was the great Mr Scott himself, or perhaps, if the author of the *Lady of the Lake* was in Scotland (which was sadly probable), it might be Mr Rogers, whose *Pleasures of Memory* had beguiled so many leisure moments.

She went into the shop, and came out again after an enchanting half-hour spent in turning over any number of books, with a copy of Mr Southey's latest poem, the *Curse of Kehama*, under her arm.

When she returned to Grillon's her chaperon had arrived, and was awaiting her. Miss Taverner entered in upon her in an impetuous fashion, and cried out: 'Oh, ma'am, only to think of Hatchard's at our very door! To be able to purchase any book in the world there, as I am sure one may!'

'Lord, my dear!' said Mrs Scattergood, in some dismay. 'Never say you are bookish! Poems! Oh well, there may be no harm in that, one must be able to talk of the latest poems if they happen to become the rage. *Marmion!* I liked that excessively, I remember, though it was too long for me to finish. They say this young man who has been doing such odd things abroad is becoming the fashion, but I don't know. He was excessively rude to poor Lord Carlisle in that horrid poem of his. I cannot like him for it, besides that someone or other was telling me there is bad blood in all the Byrons. But, of course, if he is to be the fashion one must keep an eye on him. Let me warn you, my love, never be behind the times!'

It was the first of many pieces of worldly wisdom. Miss Taverner, led from warehouse to warehouse, from milliner to bootmaker, had others instilled into her head. She learned that no lady would be seen driving or walking down St James's Street; that every lady must be sure of being seen promenading in Hyde Park between the hours of five and six. She must not dare to dance the waltz until she had been approved by the Patronesses of Almack's; she must not want to be wearing warm pelisses or shawls: the lightest of wraps must suffice her in all weathers; she need extend only the barest civility towards such an one; she must be conciliating to such another. And above all, most important, most vital, she must move heaven and earth to earn Mr Brummell's approval.

'If Mr Brummell should not think you the thing you are lost!' said Mrs Scattergood impressively. 'Nothing could save you from social ruin, take my word for it. He has but to lift his eyebrow at you, and the whole world will know that he finds nothing to admire in you.'

Miss Taverner's antagonism was instantly aroused. 'I do not care *that* for Mr Brummell!' she said.

Mrs Scattergood gave a faint scream, and implored her to be careful.

Miss Taverner, however, was heartily tired of the sound of the dandy's name. Mr Brummell had invented the starched neckcloth; Mr Brummell had started the fashion of white tops to riding-boots; Mr Brummell had laid it down that no gentleman would be seen driving in a hackney carriage; Mr Brummell had his own sedan chair, lined and cushioned with white satin; Mr Brummell had abandoned a military career because his regiment had been ordered to Manchester; Mr Brummell had decreed that none of the Bow-window set at White's would acknowledge salutations from acquaintances in the street if they were seated in the club-window. And Mr Brummell, said Mrs Scattergood, would give her one of his stinging set-downs if she offended his notions of propriety.

'Will he?' said Miss Taverner, a martial light in her eye. 'Will he indeed?'

She was annoyed to find her brother inclined to be impressed by the shadow of this uncrowned king of fashion. Peregrine went to be measured for some suits of clothes at Weston's, escorted by Mr Fitzjohn, and when he debated over two rolls of cloth, unable to decide between them, the tailor coughed, and said helpfully: 'The Prince Regent, sir, prefers superfine, and Mr Brummell the Bath coating, but it is immaterial which you choose: you must be right. Suppose, sir, we say the Bath coat-ing? – I think Mr Brummell has a trifle the preference.'

Peregrine's days during that first week were quite as full as his sister's. His friend, Mr Fitzjohn, took him thoroughly in hand. When he was not being fitted for boots at Hoby's, or hats at Lock's, he was choosing fobs in Wells Street, or riding off to Long Acre to look at a tilbury, or knowingly inspecting carriage-horses at Tattersall's.

The house in Brook Street, somewhat to Miss Taverner's annoyance, proved to be admirable in every respect, the saloons handsome, and the furnishings just what she liked. She was installed there within three days of seeing Mr Blackader, and a number of her new gowns having been delivered in neat band-boxes, her hair having been fashionably cut, and her maid taught to dress it in several approved classical styles, Mrs Scattergood declared her to be ready to receive morning callers.

The first of these were her uncle, the Admiral, and his son, Mr Bernard Taverner. They came at an awkward moment, Peregrine, who had spent the great part of the morning in a brocade dressing-gown, while the barber and a breeches-maker waited on him, being at that moment engaged in trying to arrange his starched neckcloth.

His sister, who had walked unceremoniously into his room to demand his escort to Colburn's Lending Library, was an interested and rather scornful spectator. 'What nonsense it is, Perry!' she exclaimed, as with an exasperated oath he threw away his fourth crushed and mangled cravat. 'That is the fourth you have spoiled! If only you would have them made more narrow!'

Peregrine, his face and head quite obscured by his turned-up shirt collar, said testily: 'Women never understand these things. Fitz says it must be a foot high. As for four spoiled, pooh, that's nothing! Fitz says Brummell has sometimes ruined as many as a score. Now try it again, John! Fold my collar down first, you fool!'

Someone knocked on the door. Peregrine, with a neckcloth a foot wide round his neck, and his chin to the ceiling, shouted: 'Come in!' and in doing so produced a crease in the neckcloth which he felt could hardly have been bettered by the Beau himself.

The footman entered, and announced the arrival of Admiral and Mr Taverner. Peregrine was too much engaged in making further creases by the simple expedient of gradually lowering his jaw, to pay any heed, but Judith jumped up at once. 'Oh Perry, do make haste! It is our cousin! Beg the Admiral to wait, Perkins. We will come directly. Is Mrs Scattergood downstairs? Oh then, she will see to it all! Perry, will you never have done?'

The cravat had by this time been reduced to more normal proportions. Peregrine studied it anxiously in the mirror, tried with a cautious finger to perfect one of the creases, and announced gloomily that it would have to do. It was still too high to permit of his turning his head more than an inch or two either side, but this he assured Judith was nothing at all out of the way.

The next business was to get him into his new coat, an elegant blue creation made of the prescribed Bath coating, with long tails, and silver buttons. It fitted him so exactly that the services of the footman had to be engaged to assist in inserting him into it. It seemed at one time as though not even the united efforts of two able-bodied men could succeed in this, but after a grim struggle it was done, and Peregrine, panting slightly from his exertions, turned to his sister and proudly asked her how he looked.

There was a laugh in her eye, but she assured him he was quite the thing. In any other man she would have ruthlessly condemned so absurdly waisted a coat, so monstrous a cravat, such skin-tight pantaloons, but Peregrine was very much her darling, and must be allowed to dress himself up in any dandified way he pleased. She did indeed suggest that his golden locks were in considerable disorder, but upon being informed that this was intentional, and had taken him half an hour to achieve, she said no more, but took his arm and went down with him to the saloon upon the first floor.

Here they found Mrs Scattergood seated on a confidante beside a stout flushed-looking gentleman with grizzled hair, in whom Miss Taverner had no difficulty in recognising her late father's brother. Mr Bernard Taverner occupied a chair opposite to them, but upon the door opening to admit his cousins, he immediately got up, and made his bow. There was a certain warmth in his smile; his look seemed to approve, even to admire. Judith could only be glad to think that she had chosen that morning to put on the jonquil muslin dress with the lace trimming, and the new kid shoes of celestial blue.

The Admiral had got up ponderously from the confidante, and now came forward with his hand held out and a look of decided relish upon his florid countenance. 'So!' he said. 'My little niece! Well, my dear! Well!'

She had a moment's fear that he was going to kiss her, a circumstance she could not look forward to with any equanimity, since he smelled strongly of spirits. She put out her hand in a decided way, and after a moment's hesitation he took it, and held it between both of his. 'So you are poor John's daughter!' he said with a somewhat gusty sigh. 'Ah, that was a sad business! I was never more shocked in my life.'

Her brows drew together slightly; she bowed, and withdrew her hand. She could not suppose him sincere, and while determined on showing him all the observance which their relationship demanded, she could not like him. She said merely: 'My brother Peregrine, sir.'

They shook hands. The Admiral clapped his nephew on the shoulder, supposed him to be come to town to cut a dash, did not blame him, but begged him to be careful of his company, else he would find himself without a feather to fly with. This was all said with a great air of joviality, while Peregrine smiled politely, and inwardly consigned his uncle to the devil.

Mr Taverner had moved over to stand beside Judith, and now put a chair forward for her. She took it, reflecting that he did not in any way favour his father.

He drew up a back-stool, and sat down on it. 'My cousin is pleased with London?' he said smilingly.

'Yes, indeed,' she responded. 'Though I have seen very little yet. Only some of the shops, and the wild beasts at the Exeter Exchange, which Perry took me to yesterday.'

He laughed. 'Well, that is a beginning, at any rate.' He glanced at Mrs Scattergood, who was joining in the conversation between the Admiral and Peregrine, and lowered his voice. 'You have a lady of quality to live with you, I see. That is just as it should be. I had not had the pleasure before to-day of meeting her, but she is known to me a little by repute. I believe her consequence to be very just. You are fortunate.'

'We like her extremely,' Judith replied in her calm way.

'And Peregrine, I perceive, has been busy,' he said, the smile returning to lurk in his eyes. 'Will you be offended with me if I confess I looked twice before I recognised in him the young gentleman I met in Grantham?'

There was a twinkle in her own eyes. 'At us both, perhaps, sir?'

'No,' he replied seriously. 'I should always recognise you, cousin.' He became aware of the Admiral at his elbow wanting to claim Judith's attention, and rose at once. 'I beg pardon, sir. You were speaking?'

'Oh, you are pleased to be aground there, my boy, I don't doubt!' said his father, poking a finger at his ribs. 'I was saying, my dear, it's a thousand pities young Perry here wasn't put into the Navy. That's the life for you youngsters – ay, and that goes for you too, Bernard. With this war, you know, any likely fellow may make his fortune at sea. Damme, if I was but twenty years younger there's nothing would suit me better than to be commanding a snug little frigate to-day! But that's how it is with the young men nowadays! All of them as shy as be-damned of venturing a mile from town!'

'Come, come, sir, that won't do!' protested Mrs Scattergood. 'I am sure it is quite dreadful only to think of all the officers gone off to that horrid Peninsular, and here are you saying young men won't stir out of town! I could name you a dozen charming creatures gone off to be murdered by the French. I myself have a young relative' – she nodded at Judith – 'Worth's brother, you know – Charles Audley – the most delightful, audacious wretch – who is there now.'

'Oh, the Army! We do not count the Army, I can tell you, ma'am,' said the Admiral. 'Why, what do they know of the matter, playing at war as they do? They should have been with us in the Trafalgar action! Ay, that was real fighting!'

'You are not serious, sir,' interposed his son. 'They have seen some hard fighting in Spain.'

He spoke quietly, but with a decided air of reproof, fixing his expressive eyes on his father's face. The Admiral looked a little confounded, but laughed it off. He had nothing to say against the fellows in the Army; he had no doubt they were a very good set of men; all he meant was they had better have gone to sea.

It was evident from his remarks that the Admiral had less than common sense. Miss Taverner, glancing from him to his son, detected a look of contempt in the latter's face. She was sorry for it, yet could scarcely blame him. To relieve the awkwardness of the moment she turned to the Admiral, and began talking to him of the Trafalgar action.

He was pleased enough to tell it all to her, but his account, concerned as it was merely with his own doings upon that momentous day and interspersed with a great many oaths and coarse expressions, could be of little interest to her. She wanted to be hearing of Lord Nelson, who had naturally been the hero of her school-days. It was her uncle's only merit in her eyes that he must actually have spoken with the great man, but she could not induce him to describe Nelson in any other than the meanest terms. He had not liked him, did not see that he had been so very remarkable, never could understand what the women saw in him – a wispy fellow: nothing to look at, he gave her his word.

Mr Taverner had moved to one of the windows with Pere-grine, and was engaged in talking of horse-flesh with him. A servant came in with a message for Mrs Scattergood which took her away in a flutter of apologies and gauze draperies. The door had no sooner closed behind her than the Admiral's conversation took an abrupt turn. Pulling his chair a little closer to Judith's, he said in an under-voice: 'I am glad she is gone. I daresay she is very well, but a poor little dab of a woman, ain't she? You know, my dear, things are left very awkwardly. You won't like to be in a stranger's hands. And this fellow, Worth, to have the handling of your fortunes! I don't like it. He's a gamester, none too plump in the pocket, I was hearing. There's no denying that was a cork-brained Will of your poor father's. But I dare-say he was not himself, hey?'

Mr Taverner must have had remarkably acute hearing, for he turned his head sharply, looking very hard at his father, and before Judith was at the necessity of answering what she could only feel to be an impertinence, he had come across the room towards them, and said pleasantly: 'Excuse me, sir, I think such a discussion must be painful to my cousin. Judith – I may venture? – I have been trying to engage Peregrine to give me the pleasure of his company at the play. May I hope that you and Mrs Scattergood will also honour me? I think you have not visited the theatre yet.' He smiled down at her. 'May mine be the privilege of escorting you to your first play? What shall it be? There's Kemble and Mrs Siddons at Covent Garden, or Bannister at Drury Lane, if your taste should be for comedy. You have only to name it.'

Her cheeks glowed with pleasure. She thanked him, and accepted, choosing, to Peregrine's disgust, the tragedy. Her uncle was still busy congratulating his son on his good fortune in hav-ing secured such a beauty to be his guest when the door opened, and the butler announced the Earl of Worth.

Miss Taverner, taken quite by surprise, exchanged a swift glance with her brother, and began to instruct the butler to con-vey their excuses to his lordship. It was too late, however; the Earl must have followed the servant up the stairs, for he entered the room while the words of denial were on Judith's lips.

He certainly heard them, but he gave no other sign of having done so than a faint curl of his lips. His coldly appraising gaze took in the company; he bowed slightly, and said in his languid voice that he was fortunate to have found his wards at home.

Judith was obliged to present her uncle and cousin.

The Earl's visit could not have been worse-timed: she cared nothing for his opinion, but to introduce the Admiral to him must still be a mortification. She fancied she could perceive a look of disdain in his face, and it was with relief that she brought her cousin to his notice. There at least she had nothing to be ashamed of.

A few civilities were exchanged, the Earl bearing his part in these with a formality that set off Mr Taverner's easier, more open manners to advantage. A silence, which the Earl made no effort to break, soon fell, and while Judith was trying to think of something to say, and wishing that Mrs Scattergood would come back into the room, her cousin, with what she must feel to be instinctive good taste, reminded the Admiral that they had another engagement in the neighbourhood, and should be taking their leave.

The bell was pulled, the footman came up to usher the visitors out, and in a few minutes they were gone.

The Earl, who had been calmly inspecting Judith through his eye-glass, let it fall, and said: 'I see you have been taking my advice, Miss Taverner.' He glanced round the room. 'Is this house to your liking? It seems to be rather above the general run of furnished houses.'

'Have you not been inside it before?' she demanded.

'Not to my knowledge,' he said, raising his brows. 'Why should I?'

'I thought it was you who –' she broke off, cross with herself at having said so much.

'Oh no,' he replied. 'Blackader chose it.' He turned his head to look at Peregrine, and an expression of pain crossed his features. 'My good boy, are you emulating the style of Mr Fitzjohn and his associates, or is that monstrous erection round your neck due merely to the clumsiness of your valet?'

'I was in a hurry,' said Peregrine defensively, and reddening in spite of himself.

'Then do not be in a hurry again. Cravats are not to be tied in an instant. I hear you bought Scrutton's bay mare at Tattersall's.'

'Yes,' said Peregrine.

'I thought you would,' murmured his lordship.

Peregrine looked suspicious, but judged it wiser not to ask the meaning of this somewhat cryptic remark.

The Earl's gaze returned to Miss Taverner. He said softly: 'You should ask me to sit down, you know.'

Her lips quivered: she could not but appreciate his lordship's methods. 'Pray be seated, sir!'

'Thank you, Miss Taverner, but I do not stay. I came only to discuss your affairs with Peregrine,' said Worth with marked politeness.

It was too absurd; she had to laugh. 'Very well, sir. I understand there is nothing to be done with my father's unfortunate Will.'

'Nothing at all,' he said. 'You had better accept me with a good grace. You will only be made to appear ridiculous if you don't, you know.' Then, as she stiffened, he laughed, and putting out his hand tilted her face up with one careless finger under her chin. 'Poor Beauty in distress!' he said. 'But the smile was all that I hoped it might be.' He turned. 'Now, Peregrine, if you please.'

They went out of the room together, nor did she again set eyes on the Earl that day. Peregrine came running up the stairs half an hour later, and finding his sister with Mrs Scattergood, who was deep in the pages of a fashion journal, he announced impetuously that he rather thought they might do very well with Worth for their guardian.

Judith looked warningly towards Mrs Scattergood, but Peregrine was not to be checked. He had very early in their acquaintanceship insinuated himself into that lady's good graces, and treated her already with a marked lack of respect, and a good deal of affection. 'Oh, Cousin Maria don't give a fig for

Worth!' he said airily. 'But he has been talking to me, and I can tell you something, Judith, he don't mean to keep too tight a hold on the purse-strings. I fancy we shall have no trouble with him at all. Cousin Maria, do you think Worth will trouble us?'

'No, indeed, why should he? My love, I read here that strawberries crushed on the face and left all night will clear sunburn and give a delicate complexion. I wonder whether we should try it? You know, you have just the suspicion of a freckle, Judith. You will always be going out in the sun and wind, and my dear, nothing is so destructive of female charms as contact with fresh air.'

'My dear ma'am, where will you find strawberries at this season!' said Miss Taverner, amused.

'Very true, my love; I was forgetting. Then it must be the Denmark Lotion after all. I wish you will buy some, if you mean to drive with Perry.'

Judith promised and went away to put on her hat and her gloves. When she drove out presently alone with her brother, she spoke to him seriously of their guardian. 'I cannot like him, Perry. There is something in his eyes, a hardness, a – mocking look – which I don't trust. There is a lack of civility, too – oh, worse! His whole manner, his being so familiar with me – with us! It is very bad. I don't understand him. He would have us think that he wanted to be our guardian as little as we wished to be his wards, and yet is it not odd that he should busy himself so particularly with our affairs? Even Mrs Scattergood thinks it strange he should not be content to let the lawyers settle everything. She says she has never known him to exert himself so much as he does now.'

Thus Miss Taverner, in a mood of disquiet.

The Earl, however, seemed to be in no hurry to repeat his call. They saw nothing of him for some days, though their visitors were many. Lady Sefton came with one of her daughters, and Mr Skeffington, a very tall thin man with a painted face and a yellow waistcoat. He was lavishly scented, which set the Taverners instantly against him, and talked a great deal about the theatre. There did not seem to be an actor alive with whom he was not on terms of intimacy. They discovered later that he had written some plays himself, and even produced them. His manners were particularly gentle and pleasing, and it was not very long before the Taverners were quite won over to him. He was so kind one must forgive the paint and the scent.

Lady Sefton had to be liked also; and Mrs Scattergood assured her charges that neither she nor her popular husband had an enemy in the world.

Lady Jersey, another of the all-powerful patronesses of Almack's, came with Mrs Drummond-Burrell, a lady of icy good-breeding, who said little and looked to be insufferably haughty. Lady Jersey seemed to be very good-natured in her restless way. She talked incessantly throughout her short visit, and fidgeted with anything that came in the way of her fluttering hands. Getting into her carriage again when the call was over, she said: 'Well, my dear, I think – don't you? – a charming girl? Quite beautiful! And of course the fortune! They tell me eighty thousand at the very least! We shall see all the fortune-hunters at work!' She gave her fairy-laugh. 'Alvanley was telling me poor dear Wellesley Poole has left his card in Brook Street already. Well, I am sure I wish the girl a good husband. I think her quite out of the common.'

Mrs Drummond-Burrell slightly shrugged her shoulders, '*Farouche*,' she said in her cold way. 'I detest provincials.'

It was unfortunate for Miss Taverner that this judgment should soon be endorsed by another. Mr John Mills, who was called the Mosaic Dandy, went from curiosity to pay a morning call in Brook Street, and came away to spread the news through town that the new beauty might better be known as the Milk-maid. His manners had not pleased Miss Taverner. He was affected, talked with a great air of conceit, and put on so much insolent condescension that she was impelled to give him a sharp set-down.

Mrs Scattergood admitted the provocation, but was worried over it. 'I don't like the creature – I believe no one does. Brummell hates him, I know – but there's no denying, my love, he has a tongue, and can make mischief. I hope he may not try to ruin you.'

But the nickname he had bestowed on Miss Taverner was sufficiently apt to catch the fashionable fancy. Mr Mills declared that no gentleman of taste would admire such a blowsy prettiness. A great many people who had been doubtful whether to approve or condemn Judith (for her frank, decided manners were something quite new, only to be tolerated in persons of rank) were at once convinced that she was pert and presuming. Some snubs were dealt her, the throng of would-be admirers began to lessen, and more than one lady of fashion turned her shoulder.

The nickname came to Judith's ears, and made her furious. That any dandy should have it in his power to sway public opinion was not to be borne. When she discovered the extent of the harm he had worked she was not dismayed or tearful, but on the contrary eager for war. She would not change her manners to suit a dandy's taste; she would rather force Society to accept her in the teeth of them all, Brummell included.

It was in such a dangerous mood that she set out with her brother and Mrs Scattergood to make her first appearance at Almack's. Lady Jersey, adhering, even in the face of Mrs Drummond-Burrell's expressed disapproval, to her original opinion, had sent the vouchers: the most important door into Society was open to Miss Taverner. It must be for her, Mrs Scattergood said urgently, to do the rest. The door might yet close.

Privately, she thought the girl's looks should carry the day. Judith, in a ball dress of white crêpe with velvet ribbons spangled with gold, and her hair in a myriad of loose curls confined by a ribbon with a bow over her left eye, was a vision to please even the most exacting critic. If only she would be a little conciliating!

The evening began badly. Mrs Scattergood was so much taken up with her own and Judith's toilet that she had no glance to spare for Peregrine. It was not until the carriage that bore all three of them was half-way to King Street that she suddenly discovered him to be wearing long pantaloons tightly strapped under his shoes.

She gave a muffled shriek. 'Perry! Good God, was there ever anyone more provoking? Peregrine, how *dared* you put those things on? Oh, you must stop the carriage at once! No one – *no one*, do you understand? – not the Prince Regent himself! is admitted to Almack's in pantaloons! Knee-breeches, you stupid, tiresome boy! You will ruin everything. Pull the checkstring this instant! We must set you down.'

It was vain for Peregrine to argue; he did not realise how inflexible were the rules at Almack's; he must go home and change his dress – and even that would not do if he came to Almack's one minute after eleven: he would be turned away.

Judith broke into laughter, but her afflicted chaperon, bundling Peregrine out into the street, assured her it was no laughing matter.

But when the two ladies at last arrived at Almack's it did not seem to Judith that the club was worth all this to-do. There was nothing remarkable. The rooms were spacious, but not splendid; the refreshments, which consisted of tea, orgeat, and lemonade, with cakes and bread and butter, struck Miss Taverner as being on the meagre side. Dancing, and not cards, was the object of the club; no high stakes were allowed, so that the card-room contained only the dowagers, and such moderate gentlemen as were content to play whist for sixpenny points.

Lady Sefton, Princess Esterhazy, and Countess Lieven were the only patronesses present. The Austrian ambassador's wife was a little roundabout lady of great vivacity; Countess Lieven, reputed to be the best-dressed and most knowledgeable lady in London, looked to be clever, and almost as proud as Mrs Drummond-Burrell. Neither she nor the Princess were acquainted with Mrs Scattergood, and beyond staring with the peculiar rudeness of the well-bred at Miss Taverner, she at least took no further interest in her. The Princess went so far as to demand of her partner, Sir Henry Mildmay, who the Golden Rod might be, and upon hearing her name, laughed, and said rather audibly: 'Oh, Mr Mills's Milkmaid!'

It was left for Lady Sefton to come forward, which indeed she did, as soon as she perceived the new arrivals. Several persons were presented to Miss Taverner, and she presently found herself going down the dance with Lord Molyneux, her ladyship's son.

She had not heard Princess Esterhazy's comment, but she had caught the expressive look that went with it. There was an angry lump in her throat; her eyes were more than usually brilliant. She looked magnificent, but so stern that she put Lord Molyneux in a panic. The sight of Mr John Mills in conversation with a lady by one of the windows did nothing to soften Miss Taverner's mood. Lord Molyneux felt nothing but relief when the dance came to an end, and having led her to a chair against the wall escaped on the pretext of procuring a glass of lemonade for her.

It still lacked ten minutes to eleven, but although people were continuing to arrive there was no sign of Peregrine. Judith guessed him to be only too glad of an excuse not to come, for he did not care to dance, but she had never felt more lonely in her life, and hoped every moment to see him walk in.

Mrs Scattergood, having met with several of her friends, was deep in conversation, but broke off suddenly to dart up to her charge. 'Mr Brummell!' she hissed in Judith's ear. 'Do pray, my love, hold yourself up, and if he should speak to you I implore you remember what it may mean!'

The very mention of any dandy's name was quite enough at this moment to fan Miss Taverner's wrath to a flame. She looked anything but conciliating, and when she turned her eyes to the door and observed the gentleman who had just entered, an expression of undisguised contempt swept over her face.

A lady in a purple turban adorned with an aigrette bore down upon Mrs Scattergood, and drew her aside with so much condescension that Judith would hardly have been surprised to learn that it was Queen Charlotte herself. She turned away to enjoy to the full her first sight of Mr George Bryan Brummell.

She could scarcely forbear to laugh, for surely there could be no greater figure of fun. He stood poised for a moment in the doorway, a veritable puppet, tricked out in such fine clothes that he cast the two gentlemen who were entering behind him in the shade. It could not be better. From his green satin coat to his ridiculously high-heeled shoes he was just what she had expected him to be. His conceit, evidently, was unbounded. He surveyed the room through his quizzing-glass, held at least a foot away from his eye, and went mincing up to Princess Esterhazy, and made her a flourishing bow.

Judith could not take her eyes from him; he was not looking her way, so she might permit herself to smile. Indeed, the wrath had died out of her face, and given place to a twinkling merriment. So this was the King of Fashion!

She was recalled to a sense of her surroundings by a quiet voice at her elbow. 'I beg pardon, ma'am: I think you have dropped your fan?'

She turned with a start to find that a gentleman whom she recognised as one of the two who had entered behind the Beau was standing beside her, with her fan in his hand.

She took it with a word of thanks, and one of her clear, appraising looks. She liked what she saw. The gentleman was of medium height, with light brown hair brushed *à la Brutus*, and a countenance which, without being precisely handsome, was generally pleasing. There was a good deal of humour about his mouth, and his eyes, which were grey and remarkably intelligent, were set under a pair of most expressive brows. He was very well-dressed, but so unobtrusively that Judith would have been hard put to it to describe what he was wearing.

He returned her look with something of drollery in his eyes. 'It is Miss Taverner, is it not?' he asked.

She noticed that his voice was particularly good, and his manner quiet and unassuming. She said with decided friendliness: 'Yes, I am Miss Taverner, sir. I don't know how you should recognise me though, for I think we have not met, have we?'

'No, I have been out of town this week,' he replied. 'I should have called, of course. Your guardian is a friend of mine.'

This circumstance was hardly a credential in Miss Taverner's opinion, but she merely said: 'You are very good, sir. But how came you to know me?'

'You have been described to me, Miss Taverner. I could not mistake.'

A flush stole up into her cheeks; she raised her eyes and looked very steadily at him. 'By Mr Mills, perhaps, sir?'

One of his mobile brows went up. 'No, ma'am, not by Mr Mills. May I ask – or is it an impertinence? – why you should have thought so?'

'Mr Mills has made it his business to describe me in so many quarters that it was a natural conclusion,' said Judith bitterly.

'Indeed!' He looked down at her rather penetratingly. 'I am such an inquisitive creature, Miss Taverner. I hope you mean to tell me why you are looking so very angry,' he said.

She smiled. 'I should not, I know. But I must warn you, sir, it is not the fashion to be seen talking to me.'

Both brows went up at that. 'On the authority of Mr Mills?' inquired the gentleman.

'Yes, sir, as I understand. Mr Mills has been good enough to christen me the Milkmaid, and to declare that no one of fashion could tolerate my – my person.' She tried to speak lightly, but only succeeded in letting her indignation peep through.

He drew up a chair. 'Let me assure you, Miss Taverner, that there is not the least need for you to let Mr Mills's insolence distress you. May I sit down?'

She signified assent; she could only be glad that he should want to. He might not wear a green-spangled coat, and lead all London by the nose, but she had rather be talking to him than to any dandy. She said frankly: 'I know I should not – and indeed, it doesn't distress me. It only makes me angry. You see, we – my brother and I – have never been in London before, and we wanted very much to – to enter into Polite Circles. But it seems that Society agrees with Mr Mills – though a great many people have been very kind, of course.'

'Do you know, Miss Taverner, you make me feel that I have been out of town longer than I realised?' said the gentleman, with one of his comical looks. 'When I left London for Cheveley Mr Mills was not leading Society, I assure you.'

'Oh,' she said, 'you must not think I do not know who does that! I have had the name of Beau Brummell dinned into my ears until I am heartily sick of it! I am told that I must at all costs win his approval if I am to succeed, and I tell you frankly, sir, I have not the least notion of trying to do it!' She saw a slightly startled look in his eyes, and added defiantly: 'I am sorry if he should be a friend of yours, but I have made up my mind I neither wish for his good opinion nor his acquaintance.'

'You are quite safe in saying what you think of him to me,' replied the gentleman gravely. 'But what has he done to earn your contempt, ma'am?'

'Well, sir, you have only to look at him!' said Judith, allowing her eyes to travel significantly towards the gorgeous figure at the other end of the room. 'A spangled coat!' she pronounced scornfully.

His gaze followed the direction of hers. 'I am in agreement with you, Miss Taverner,' he said. 'Though I should not myself call that thing a coat.'

'Oh, and that is not all!' she said. 'I am for ever hearing of his affectations and impertinences! I am out of all patience with him.'

She had the impression that he was laughing at her, but when he spoke it was perfectly solemnly. 'Ah, ma'am, but it is Mr Brummell's folly which is the making of him. If he did not stare duchesses out of countenance, and nod over his shoulder to princes he would be forgotten in a week. And if the world is so silly as to admire his absurdities – you and I may know better – but what does that signify?'

'Nothing, I suppose,' said Judith. 'But if I cannot succeed without being obliged to court his approval I had rather fail.'

'Miss Taverner,' he replied, the smile dancing in his eyes again, 'I prophesy that you will become the rage.'

She shook her head. 'How can you think it, sir?'

He rose. 'Why, I don't think it, ma'am. I am sure of it. Every eye is even now upon you. You have held me in conversation for close on half an hour.' He made his bow. 'I may do myself the honour of calling on you?'

'We shall be glad, sir.'

'I wonder?' he said with a quizzical look, and moved away to where Lord Alvanley was standing against the wall.

Miss Taverner became aware of Mrs Scattergood at her elbow, in a twitter of excitement. 'My love, what did he say to you? Tell me at once!'

Judith turned. 'Say to me?' she repeated, bewildered. 'He asked if he might call on us, and –'

'Judith! You don't mean it? Oh, was ever anything so − Well! And you was talking for ever! Pray, what else was said?'

Judith looked at her in a good deal of surprise. 'But what can it signify, ma'am?'

Mrs Scattergood gave a suppressed shriek. 'Mercy on us! You hold Mr Brummell by your side for half an hour and then ask me what it can signify?'

Judith gave a gasp, and turned pale. 'Ma'am! Oh, good God, ma'am, that surely was not Mr Brummell?'

'Not Mr Brummell? Of course it was! But, my dearest love, I particularly warned you! What have you been about?'

'I thought you meant that odious creature in the green coat,' said Judith numbly. 'How could I imagine −' She broke off, and looked across the room at Mr Brummell.

Their eyes met; he smiled; unmistakably he smiled.

'I declare I could positively embrace him!' said Mrs Scattergood, avidly drinking in this exchange of glances. 'You are made, my dear! What a set-down for John Mills! Brummell must have heard of what he said of you, daring to try to set people against you! Such impertinence!'

'He did,' said Miss Taverner dryly. 'I told him.'

Six

WO DAYS LATER MR BRUMMELL CAME TO CALL IN BROOK Street, and stayed for three-quarters of an hour. Miss Taverner offered him a frank apology for her unwitting rudeness, but he shook his head at her. 'A great many people have heard me say rude things, ma'am, but no one has ever heard me commit the folly of apologising for them,' he told her. 'The only apology you should make me is for having mistaken Mr Frensham for me. A blow, ma'am, I confess. I thought it had not been possible.'

'You see, sir, you came in behind him – and he was so very fine,' she excused herself.

'His tailor makes him,' said Mr Brummell. 'Now I, I make my tailor.'

Miss Taverner wished that Peregrine could have been present to hear this pronouncement.

By the time Mr Brummell got up to go all the favourable impressions he had made on her at Almack's were confirmed. He was a charming companion, his deportment being particularly good, and his manners graceful and without affectation. He had a droll way of producing his sayings which amused her, and either because it entertained him to take an exactly opposite view to Mr Mills, or because he desired to oblige his friend Worth, he was good enough to take an interest in her début. He advised her not to abate the least jot of her disastrous frankness. She might be as outspoken as she chose.

Miss Taverner shot a triumphant glance at her chaperon. 'And may I drive my own phaeton in the Park, sir?'

'By all means,' said Mr Brummell. 'Nothing could be better. Do everything in your power to be out of the way.'

Miss Taverner took his advice, and straightway commissioned her brother to procure her a perch-phaeton, and a pair of carriage-horses. Nothing in his stables would do for her; she only wished that she might have gone with him to Tattersall's. She did not trust his ability to pick a horse.

Fortunately, the Earl of Worth took a hand in the affair before Peregrine had inspected more than half a dozen of the sweet-going, beautiful-stepping, forward-actioned bargains advertised in the columns of the *Morning Post*. He arrived in Brook Street one late afternoon, driving his own curricle, and found Miss Taverner on the point of setting out for the prome-nade in Hyde Park. 'I shall not detain you long,' he said, laying down his hat and gloves on the table. 'You have purchased, I believe, a perch-phaeton for your own use?'

'Certainly,' said Miss Taverner.

He looked her over. 'Are you able to drive it?'

'I should not otherwise have purchased it, Lord Worth.'

'May I suggest that a plain phaeton would be a safer con-veyance for a lady?'

'You may suggest what you please, sir. I am driving a perch-phaeton.'

'I am not so sure,' he said. 'You have not yet convinced me that you are able to drive it.'

She glanced out of the window at his tiger, standing to the heads of the restless wheelers harnessed to the curricle. The Earl was not driving his chestnuts to-day, but a team of greys. 'Let me assure you, sir, that I am not only capable of handling a pair, but I could drive your team just as easily!' she declared.

'Very well,' said the Earl unexpectedly. 'Drive it!'

She was quite taken aback. 'Do you mean – now?'

'Why not? Are you afraid?'

'Afraid? I should like nothing better, but I am not dressed for driving.'

'You may have twenty minutes,' said the Earl, moving over to a chair by the table.

Miss Taverner was by no means pleased at this cool way of dismissing her, but she was too anxious to prove her driving skill to stay to argue the point. She whisked herself out of the room, and up the stairs, set a bell pealing for her maid, and informed her astonished chaperon that there would be no walk in the Park. She was going driving with my Lord Worth.

She joined his lordship again in just a quarter of an hour, having changed her floating muslins for a severely cut habit made of some dark cloth, and a small velvet hat turned up on one side from her clustering gold ringlets, and with a curled feather hanging down on the other. 'I am ready, my lord,' she said, drawing on a pair of serviceable York tan gloves.

He held open the door for her. 'Permit me to tell you, Miss Taverner, that whatever else may be at fault, your taste in dress is unimpeachable.'

'I do not admit, sir, that there is anything at fault,' flashed Miss Taverner.

At sight of her the waiting tiger touched his hat, but bent a severely inquiring glance on his master.

Miss Taverner took the whip and reins in her hands, and mounted into the driving-seat, scorning assistance.

'Take your orders from Miss Taverner, Henry,' said the Earl, getting up beside his ward.

'Me lord, you ain't never going to let a female drive us?' said Henry almost tearfully. 'What about my pride?'

'Swallow it, Henry,' replied the Earl amicably.

The tiger's chest swelled. He gazed woodenly at a nearby

lamp-post and said in an ominous voice: 'I heard as how Major
Forrester was wanting me for his tiger. Come to my ears, it did.
Lord Barrymore too. I dunno how much he wouldn't give to
get a hold of me.'

'You had much better go to Sir Harry Peyton,' recommended
Worth. 'I will give you a note for him.'

The tiger turned a look of indignant reproach upon him.
'Yes, and where would you be if I did?' he demanded.

Miss Taverner gave her horses the office to start, and said
imperatively: 'Stand away from their heads! If you are afraid,
await us here.'

The tiger let go the wheelers and made a dash for his perch.
As he scrambled up into it he said with strong emotion: 'I've sat
behind you sober, guv'nor, and I've sat behind you foxed, and
I've sat behind you when you raced Sir John to Brighton, and
never made no complaint, but I ain't never sat behind you mad
afore!' with which he folded his arms, nodded darkly, and
relapsed into a disapproving silence.

On her mettle, Miss Taverner guided the team down the
street at a brisk trot, driving them well up to their bits. She had
fine light hands, knew how to point her leaders, and soon
showed the Earl that she was sufficiently expert in the use of the
whip. She flicked the leader, and caught the thong again with a
slight turn of her wrist that sent it soundlessly up the stick. She
drove his lordship into Hyde Park without the least mishap, and
twice round it. Forgetting for the moment to be coldly formal,
she said impulsively: 'I was used to drive all my father's horses,
but I never handled a team so light-mouthed as these, sir.'

'I am thought to be something of a judge of horse-flesh, Miss
Taverner,' said the Earl.

Strolling along the promenade with his arm in the Honourable
Frederick Byng's, Sir Harry Peyton gave a gasp, and exclaimed:
'Good God, Poodle, look! Curricle Worth!'

'So it is,' agreed Mr Byng, continuing to ogle a party of young ladies.

'But with a female driving his greys! And a devilish fine female too!'

Mr Byng was sufficiently struck by this to look after the curricle. 'Very odd of him. Perhaps it is Miss Taverner – his ward, you know. I was hearing she is an excessively delightful girl. Eighty thousand pounds, I believe.'

Sir Harry was not paying much attention. 'I would not have credited it! Worth must be mad or in love! Henry, too! I tell you what, Poodle: this means I shall get Henry at last!'

Mr Byng shook his head wisely. 'Worth won't let him go. You know how it is – Curricle Worth and his Henry: almost a byword. They tell me he was a chimney-sweep's boy before Worth found him.'

'He was. And if I know Henry he won't stay with Worth any longer.'

He was wrong. When the curricle drew up again in Brook Street, Henry looked at Miss Taverner with something akin to respect in his sharp eyes. 'It ain't what I'm used to, nor yet what I approves of,' he said, 'but you handles 'em werry well, miss, werry well you handles 'em!'

The Earl assisted his ward down from the curricle. 'You may have your perch-phaeton,' he said. 'But inform Peregrine that I will charge myself with the procuring of a suitable pair for you to drive.'

'You are very good, sir, but Peregrine is quite able to choose my horses for me.'

'I make every allowance for your natural partiality, Miss Taverner, but that is going too far,' said the Earl.

The butler had opened the door before she could think of a crushing enough retort. She could not feel that it would be seemly to quarrel with her guardian in front of a servant, so she merely asked him whether he cared to come into the house.

He declined it, made his bow, and descended the steps again to his curricle.

Miss Taverner was torn between annoyance at his high-handed interference in her plans, and satisfaction at being perfectly sure now of acquiring just the horses she wanted.

A few days later the fashionable throng in Hyde Park was startled by the appearance of the rich Miss Taverner driving a splendid match pair of bays in a very smart sporting phaeton with double perches of swan-neck pattern. She was attended by a groom in livery, and bore herself (mindful of Mr Brummell's advice) with an air of self-confidence nicely blended with a seeming indifference to the sensation she was creating. As good luck would have it Mr Brummell was walking in the Park with his friend Jack Lee. He was pleased to wave, and Miss Taverner pulled up to speak to him, saying with a twinkle: 'I am amazed, sir, that you should be seen talking to so unfashionable a person as myself.'

'My dear ma'am, pray do not mention it!' returned Brummell earnestly. 'There is no one near us.'

She laughed, allowed him to present Mr Lee, and after a little conversation drove on.

Within a week the rich Miss Taverner's phaeton was one of the sights of town, and several aspiring ladies had attempted something in the same style. But since no one, with the exception of Lady Lade, who was so vulgar and low-born (having been before her marriage to Sir John the mistress of a highwayman known as Sixteen-String Jack) that she could not be thought to count, could drive one horse, let alone a pair, with anything approaching Miss Taverner's skill, these attempts were soon abandoned. To be struggling with a refractory horse, or jogging soberly along behind a sluggish one, while Miss Taverner dashed by in her high phaeton could not add to any lady's consequence. Miss Taverner was allowed to drive her pair unrivalled.

She did not always drive, however. Sometimes she rode, generally with her brother, and occasionally with Lord Anglesey's lovely daughters, and very often with her cousin, Mr Bernard Taverner. She rode a very spirited black horse, and it was not long before Miss Taverner's black was as well known as Lord Morton's long-tailed grey. She had learned the trick of acquiring idiosyncrasies.

In a month the Taverners were so safely launched into Society that even Mrs Scattergood admitted that there did not seem any longer to be anything to fear. Peregrine had not only been made a member of White's, but had contrived to get himself elected to Watier's as well, its perpetual President, Mr Brummell, having been induced to choose a white instead of a black ball on the positive assurance of Lord Sefton that Peregrine would bring into the club not the faintest aroma either of the stables or of bad blacking – an aroma which, in Mr Brummell's experience, far too often clung to country squires.

He went as Mr Fitzjohn's guest to a meeting of the Sublime Society of Beefsteaks at the Lyceum, and had the felicity of seeing there that amazing figure, the Duke of Norfolk, who rolled in looking for all the world like a gross publican, and presided over the dinner in dirty linen and an old blue coat; ate more beefsteaks than anyone else; was very genial and good-humoured; and fell sound asleep long before the end of the meeting.

He took sparring lessons at Jackson's Saloon; shot at Manton's Galleries; fenced at Angelo's; drank Blue Ruin in Cribb's Parlour; drove to races in his own tilbury, and generally behaved very much as any other young gentleman of fortune did who fancied himself as a fashionable buck. His conversation became interlarded with cant expressions; he lost a great deal of money playing at macao, or laying bets with his cronies; drank rather too much; and began to cause his sister a good deal of alarm. When she expostulated with him he merely laughed, assured her he might be trusted to keep the line, went off to join a party of sporting gentlemen, and returned in the small hours considerably intoxicated, or – as he himself phrased it – a trifle above par.

Judith turned to her cousin for advice. With the Admiral she could never be upon intimate terms, but Bernard Taverner had very soon become a close friend.

He listened to her gravely; he agreed with her that Peregrine was living at too furious a rate, but said gently: 'You know I would do anything in my power for you. I have seen all you describe, and been sorry for it, and wondered that Lord Worth should not intervene.'

She turned her eyes upon him. 'Could not you?' she asked.

He smiled. 'I have no right, cousin. Do you think Perry would attend to me? I am sure he would not. He would write me down a dull fellow, and be done with me. It is –' he hesitated. 'May I speak plainly?'

'I wish you would.'

'Then I will say that I think it is for Lord Worth to exert his authority. He alone has the right.'

'It was Lord Worth who put Perry's name up for Watier's,' said Judith bitterly. 'I was glad at first, but I did not know that it was all gaming there. It was he who took him to that horrid tavern they call Cribb's Parlour, where he meets all the prize-fighters he is for ever talking about.'

Mr Taverner was silent for a moment. He said at length: 'I did not know. Yet he could hardly be blamed: it is his own world, and the one Perry was all eagerness to enter. Lord Worth is himself a gamester, a very notable Corinthian. He is of the Carlton House set. It may be that he is not concerning himself very closely with Perry's doings. Speak to him, Judith: he must attend to you.'

'Why do you say that?' she asked, frowning.

'Pardon me, my dear cousin, it has seemed to me sometimes that his lordship betrays a certain partiality – I will say no more.'

'Oh no!' she said, with strong revulsion. 'You are mistaken. Such a notion is unthinkable.'

He made a movement as though he would have taken her hand, but controlled it, and said with an earnest look: 'I am glad.'

'You have something against him?' she said quickly.

'Nothing. If I was afraid – if I disliked the thought that there might be some partiality, you must forgive me. I could not help myself. But I have said too much. Speak to Lord Worth of Perry. Surely he cannot want him to be growing wild!'

She was a good deal stirred by this speech, and by the look that went with it. She was not displeased: she liked him too well; but she wished him to say no more. A declaration seemed to be imminent; she was thankful that he did not make it. She did not know her own heart.

His advice was too sensible to be lightly ignored. She thought about it, realised the justice of what he had said, and went to call on Worth, driving herself in her phaeton. To request his coming to Brook Street would mean the presence of Mrs Scattergood; she supposed there could be no impropriety in a ward's visiting her guardian.

She was ushered into the saloon, but after a few minutes the footman came back, and desired her to follow him. She was conducted up one pair of stairs to his lordship's private room, and announced.

The Earl was standing at a table by the window, dipping a sort of iron skewer into what looked to be a wine-bottle. On the table were several sheets of parchment, a sieve, two glass phials, and a pestle and mortar of turned boxwood.

Miss Taverner stared in considerable surprise, being quite unable to imagine what the Earl could be doing. The room was lined with shelves that bore any number of highly glazed jars and lead canisters. They were all labelled, with such queer-sounding names as Scholten, Curaçao, Masulipatam, Bureau Demi-gros, Bolongaro, Old Paris. She turned her eyes inquiringly towards his lordship, still absorbed in his bottle and skewer.

'You must forgive me for receiving you here, Miss Taverner, but I am extremely occupied,' he said. 'It would be fatal for me to leave the mixture in its present state, or I would have come to you. Have you left Maria Scattergood downstairs, may I ask?'

'She is not with me. I came alone, sir.'

There seemed to be a fine powder in the wine-bottle. The Earl had extracted a little with the aid of the skewer and dropped it into the mortar, and had begun to mix it with what was already there, but he paused at Miss Taverner's words, and looked across at her in a way hard to read. Then his gaze returned to the mortar, and he went on with his work. 'Indeed? You honour me. Will you not sit down?'

She coloured faintly, but drew forward a chair. 'Perhaps you may think it odd in me, sir, but the truth is I have something to say to you I do not care to say before Mrs Scattergood.'

'I am entirely at your service, Miss Taverner.'

She pulled off her gloves and began smoothing them. 'It is with considerable reluctance that I have come, Lord Worth. But my cousin, Mr Taverner, advised me – and I cannot but feel that he was right. You are after all our guardian.'

'Proceed, my ward. Has Wellesley Poole made you an offer of marriage?'

'Good heavens, no!' said Judith.

'He will,' said his lordship coolly.

'I have not come about my own affairs, sir. I desire to talk to you of Peregrine.'

'Life is full of disappointments,' commented Worth. 'Which spunging house is he in?'

'He is not in any,' said Judith stiffly. 'Though I have little doubt that that is where he will end if something is not done to prevent him.'

'More than likely,' agreed Worth. 'It won't hurt him.' He picked up one of the phials from the table and delicately poured a few drops of what it contained on to his mixture.

Judith rose. 'I see, sir, that I waste my time. You are not interested.'

'Not particularly,' admitted the Earl, setting the bottle down again. 'The intelligence you have so far imparted has not been of a very interesting nature, has it?'

'It does not interest you, Lord Worth, that your ward is got into a wild set of company who cannot do him any good?'

'No, not at all; I expected it,' said Worth. He looked up with a slight smile. 'What has he been doing to alarm his careful sister?'

'I think you know very well, sir. He is for ever at gaming clubs, and, I am afraid – I am nearly sure – worse than that. He has spoken of a house off St James's Street.'

'In Pickering Place?' he inquired.

'I believe so,' she said in a troubled voice.

'Number Five,' he nodded. 'I know it: a hell. Who introduced him to it?'

'I am not perfectly sure, but I think it was Mr Farnaby.'

He was shaking his mixture over one of the sheets of parchment. 'Mr Farnaby?' he repeated.

'You know him, sir?'

His occupation seemed to demand all his attention, but after a moment he said, ignoring her question: 'I gather, Miss Taverner, that you consider it is for me to – er – guide Peregrine's footsteps on to more sober paths?'

'You are his guardian, sir.'

'I am aware. I fulfilled my part to admiration when I put his name up for the two most exclusive clubs in London. I cannot remember having done as much for anyone else in the whole course of my existence.'

'You think you did well for Perry when you introduced him to a gaming club?' demanded Judith.

'Certainly.'

'No doubt you will still be thinking so when he has gamed the whole of his fortune away!'

'On one point you may rest assured, Miss Taverner: while I hold the purse-strings Perry will not game his fortune away.'

'And after? What then, when he has learned this passion for gaming?'

'By that time I trust he will be a little wiser,' said the Earl.

'I should have known better than to have come to you,' Judith said bitterly.

He turned his head. 'Not at all. You were quite right to come to me. The mistake you made was in thinking that I did not know of Perry's doings. He is behaving very much as I supposed he would. But you will no doubt have noticed that it is not causing me any particular degree of anxiety.'

'Yes,' said Miss Taverner, with emphasis. 'I have noticed it. Your anxiety is kept for whatever it is that you are so busy with.'

'Very true,' he agreed. 'I am mixing snuff – an anxious business, Miss Taverner.'

She was momentarily diverted. 'Snuff! Do all those jars contain snuff?'

'All of them.'

She cast an amazed, rather scornful glance round the shelves. 'You have made it a life-study, I conjecture.'

'Very nearly. But these are not all for my own use. Come here.'

She came reluctantly. He led her round the room, pointing out jars and bottles to her notice. 'That is Spanish Bran: it is generally the most popular. That is Macouba, a very strongly scented snuff, for flavouring only. This is Brazil, a large-grained snuff of a fine, though perhaps too powerful flavour. I use it merely to give tone to my mixture. In that bottle is the Regent's own mixture. It is scented with Otto of Roses. Beside it is a snuff I keep for your sex. It is called Violet Strasbourg – a vile mixture, but generally much liked by females. The Queen uses it.' He took down the jar, and shook a little of the snuff into the palm of his hand, and held it out to her. 'Try it.'

An idea had occurred to her. She raised her eyes to his face. 'Do many ladies use snuff, Lord Worth?'

'No, not many. Some of the more elderly ones.'

She took a pinch from his hand and sniffed it cautiously. 'I don't like it very much. My father used King's Martinique.'

'I keep a little of it for certain of my guests. Quite a pleasant snuff, but rather light in character.'

She dusted her fingers with her handkerchief. 'If a lady wished to take snuff for the purpose of being a little out of the way, which would she choose, sir?'

He smiled. 'She would request either Lord Petersham or Lord Worth to put her up a special recipe to be known as Miss Taverner's Sort.'

Her eyes gleamed. 'Will you do that for me?'

'I will do it for you, Miss Taverner, if you can be trusted to treat it carefully.'

'What must I do?'

'You must not drench it with scent, or let it become too dry, or leave your box where it will grow cold. Good snuff is taken with the chill off. Sleep with it under your pillow, and if it needs freshening send it to me. Don't attempt anything in that way yourself. It is not easily done.'

'And a snuff-box to match every gown,' said Miss Taverner thoughtfully.

'By all means. But learn first how to handle your box. You cannot do better than to observe the methods of Mr Brummell. You will notice that he uses one hand only, the left one, and with peculiar grace.'

She began to draw on her gloves again. 'I shall be very much obliged to you, sir, if you will have the kindness to make me that recipe,' she said. She realised how far she had drifted from the real object of her visit, and led the conversation ruthlessly back to it. 'And you will stop Perry going to gaming hells, and being for ever with this bad set of company?'

'I am quite unable to stop Peregrine doing either of these things, even if I wished to,' replied the Earl calmly. 'A little experience will not hurt him.'

'I am to understand, then, that you don't choose to interest yourself in his affairs, sir?'

'There is not the least likelihood of his attending to me if I did, Miss Taverner.'

'He could be made to attend to you.'

'Do not be alarmed, Miss Taverner. When I see the need of making him attend to me I shall do so, beyond all possibility of being ignored.'

She was not satisfied, but it was obviously of no use to urge him further. She took her leave of him. He escorted her to her phaeton, and was about to go back into the house when he heard himself hailed by a couple of horsemen, who chanced at that moment to be trotting by. One was Lord Alvanley, whose round, smiling face was as usual slightly powdered with the snuff that lingered on his rather fat cheeks; the other was Colonel Hanger, a much older man of very rakish mien.

It was he who had hailed Worth. 'Holà, Worth, so that's the heiress, hey? Devilish fine girl!' he cried out as Miss Taverner's phaeton disappeared down Holles Street. 'Eighty thousand, ain't it? Lucky dog, hey? Making a match of it, hey?'

'You're so crude, Colonel,' complained Alvanley.

'Ay, plain Georgy Hanger, that's me. Take care some brave boy don't snatch the filly up from under your nose, Julian!'

'I will,' promised the Earl, quite unmoved by this raillery.

The Colonel dug the butt end of his riding-whip at Lord Alvanley. 'There's William here, for instance. Now, what d'ye say,

William? They do tell me there's more to it than the eighty thousand if that young brother were to die. Ain't that so, Julian?'

'But the chances of death at nineteen are admittedly small,' said the Earl.

'Oh, y'never know!' said the Colonel cheerfully. 'Better tie her up quick, before another gets her. There's Browne, now. He could do with a rich wife, I daresay.'

'If you mean Delabey Browne, I was under the impression that he came into a legacy not so long ago,' replied the Earl.

'Yes,' agreed Lord Alvanley mournfully, 'but the stupid fellow muddled the whole fortune away paying tradesmen's bills.' He nodded to his companion. 'Come, Colonel, are you ready?'

They rode off together, and Worth went back into the house. It seemed that the Colonel had reason on his side, for within the space of one fortnight his lordship received no less than three applications for permission to solicit Miss Taverner's hand in marriage.

The day after he had politely refused his consent to the third aspirant Miss Taverner received a letter by the twopenny post. It was quite short.

'The Earl of Worth presents his compliments to Miss Taverner and begs to inform her that he would be obliged if she would assure any gentleman aspiring to her hand that there is no possibility of his lordship consenting to her marriage within the period of his guardianship.'

Justly incensed, Miss Taverner sat herself down at her elegant little tambour-top writing-table and dashed off an impetuous note, requesting the favour of a visit from his lordship in the immediate future. This she had sent off by hand. A reply in Mr Blackader's neat fist informed her that his lordship being upon the point of setting out to spend the week-end at Woburn he was commissioned to tell her that his lordship would do himself the honour of calling in Brook Street some time during the following week.

Miss Taverner tore this civil letter up in a rage. To be obliged to bottle up her wrath at Worth's daring to refuse all her suitors (none of whom she had the smallest desire to marry) without consulting her wishes, for as much as three days, and very likely more, was so insupportable that she could not face the week-end with any degree of composure.

However, it was not so very bad. A card-party on Saturday helped to pass the time, and Sunday brought her a new and rather awe-inspiring acquaintance.

She and Mrs Scattergood attended the Chapel Royal for the morning service. Mrs Scattergood frankly occupied herself with looking about her at the newest fashions, and was not above whispering to her charge when she saw a particularly striking hat, but Miss Taverner, more strictly brought up, tried to keep her mind on what was going forward. This, when all her thoughts were taken up with the impertinence of her guardian having announced that he should not give his consent to her marriage, was not very easy. Her mind wandered during the reading of the first lesson, but was recalled with a jerk.

'And Zacchæus said: "Behold, Lord, the half of my goods I give to the poor,"' read the clergyman.

A voice which came from someone seated quite near to Miss Taverner suddenly interrupted, saying in a loud hurried way: 'Too much, too much! Don't mind tithes, but can't stand that!'

There were one or two stifled giggles, and many heads were turned. Mrs Scattergood, who had craned her neck to see who it was who had lifted up his voice in such an unseemly fashion, nipped Judith's arm, and whispered urgently: 'It's the Duke of Cambridge. He talks to himself, you know. And I think it is his brother Clarence who is with him, but I cannot quite see. And if it is, my love, I believe it to be a fact that he is parted from Mrs Jordan, and is looking about him for a rich wife! Only fancy if he should think of you!'

Miss Taverner did not choose to fancy anything so absurd, and quelled her chaperon with a frown.

Mrs Scattergood was right in her conjecture; it was the Duke of Clarence. He came out of church after the service with Lord and Lady Sefton, a burly, red-faced gentleman with very staring blue eyes and a pear-shaped head. Mrs Scattergood, who had lingered strategically on the pretext of exchanging greetings with an acquaintance, contrived to be in the way. Lady Sefton bowed and smiled, but the Duke, with his rather protuberant eyes fixed on Miss Taverner, very palpably twitched her sleeve.

The party stopped, Lady Sefton begged leave to present Mrs Scattergood and Miss Taverner, and Judith found herself making her first curtsy to Royalty.

The Duke, who had the same thick utterance that belonged to all the King's sons, said in his blunt, disconnected way: 'What's that? What's that? Is it Miss Taverner? Well, this is famous indeed! I have been wishing to meet Miss Taverner these three weeks. How do you do? So you drive a phaeton and pair, as I hear, ma'am? Well, that is the right tack for Worth's ward!'

Miss Taverner said simply: 'Yes, sir, I do drive a phaeton and pair.'

'Ay, ay, they tell me you shake the wind out of all their sails. I shall keep a weather eye lifted for you in the Park, ma'am. I am acquainted with Worth, you know: he is a particular friend of my brother York. You need not fear to haul to and take me aboard your phaeton.'

'I shall be honoured, sir,' replied Miss Taverner, wondering at his bluff geniality. She could not imagine why he should want to be taken aboard her phaeton, as he phrased it, but if he did she had not the least objection. He seemed a good-humoured easy-going Prince, not at all awe-inspiring; and (though rather elderly and stout) quite likeable in his odd way.

The Duke of Cambridge, who, unlike his brother, was extremely tall, with a fair handsome countenance, came towards the group at this moment, and the Duke of Clarence said with his boisterous laugh: 'Ah, you see, I am overhauled; I must be off. Did you ever know such a fellow as my brother, to be talking out loud in church? But he don't mean it, you know; you must not be shocked, my lady. I shall look for you in the Park, Miss Taverner; don't forget I shall be looking out for you!'

Judith curtsied and moved away with Mrs Scattergood, and beyond describing her encounter with a good deal of humour to Peregrine that evening, thought no more about it. But sure enough the Royal Tar did look out for her. She did not visit Hyde Park the next day, but on Tuesday she was there with her groom beside her, and had not gone very far when she saw the Duke waving to her from the promenade. He was walking with another gentleman, but when Miss Taverner drew up in obedience to his signal, he left his companion abruptly and came to the phaeton, and wanted to know whether she would take him up.

'I shall be honoured, sir,' she said formally, and signed to the groom to get down.

The Duke climbed up beside her, saying: 'Oh, that's nonsense – never stand on ceremony. Look, there goes my cousin Gloucester. I daresay he envies me perched up here beside you. What do you say?'

Miss Taverner laughed. 'Nothing, sir, how can I? If I agree, I must be odiously conceited, which I hope I am not; and if I demur you will think me to be asking for reassurance.'

He seemed to be much struck by the frankness of this reply, laughed very heartily, and declared they should get along famously together.

He was not at all difficult to talk to, and they had not driven more than half-way round the Park before Miss Taverner discovered him to have been a firm friend of Admiral Nelson. She was in a glow at once; he was very ready to talk to her of the admiral, and in this way they drove twice round the Park, extremely well pleased with each other. When Miss Taverner set him down, he parted from her with a vigorous handshake and a promise that he should bring to in Brook Street at no very distant date.

Seven

THE TAVERNERS WERE BOTH AT VAUXHALL THAT EVENING
with a party, to partake of ham-shavings and burnt wine
in a box, and after to see Mr Blackmore performing feats on a
slack-rope, followed by the usual display of fireworks. It was not
until the small hours that they were set down at their own door
again, and they were both extremely sleepy, Peregrine rather
more so than his sister, since he had drunk, in addition to burnt
wine, any quantity of rack-punch. He went straight off to bed,
yawning prodigiously, but Miss Taverner was not too tired to
look over a little pile of notes awaiting her on the marble-top
table in the hall. They had most of them the appearance of invitations, and since she had not been in town long enough to
think invitations dull, she gathered them all up to take with her
to her bedchamber.

While her maid was brushing her hair she ran through them.
Midway through the pile she came upon Mr Blackader's fist,
and at once pushed the rest aside and broke the seal. It was a
brief note informing her that the Earl of Worth would call at
Brook Street the following morning.

Miss Taverner, who considered that the commonest civility
should have prompted his lordship to inquire when it would
suit her to receive him, immediately made a plan to spend the
whole morning at the Botanic Gardens in Hans Town.

This plan was ruthlessly carried out, in spite of the protests of Mrs Scattergood, who had no extraordinary interest in gardens. A message for Lord Worth was left with the butler, intimating that Miss Taverner was sorry that she had not received his obliging note earlier, since she was engaged elsewhere that morning.

The message was never delivered. Miss Taverner returned from the Botanic Gardens to find that the Earl had not called at all, but had sent round a footman with a note instead.

Miss Taverner, thinking indignantly of a whole morning wasted amongst plants, broke the seal and spread open the letter. It was the ubiquitous Mr Blackader again, regretting that his lordship was unfortunately prevented from fulfilling his promise, but trusted to be able to visit Miss Taverner within the course of the next few days.

Miss Taverner tore the letter into shreds, and swept upstairs in a mood of considerable exasperation.

She dined at home with only Mrs Scattergood for company, but in the expectation of receiving her cousin later in the evening. He had promised to bring her a volume from his library which he believed she would like to read, and would call at Brook Street on his way home from Limmer's hotel, where he was engaged to dine with a party of friends.

At ten o'clock, as the butler was bringing in the tea-table, a knock was heard. Mrs Scattergood was just wondering who could be calling on them so late, and Miss Taverner had gladly put away her embroidery frame, when not her cousin, but the Earl of Worth was announced.

'Oh, is it you, Julian?' said Mrs Scattergood. 'Well, to be sure, this is very pleasant. You are just come in time to drink tea with us, for we are alone this evening, as you see, which has become a very strange thing with us, I can tell you.'

Miss Taverner, having bowed slightly to her guardian, picked up her embroidery again, and became busy with it.

Mrs Scattergood began to make tea. 'I thought you was out of town, my dear Worth. This is quite a surprise.'

'I have been at Woburn,' he replied, taking the cup and saucer she held out to him, and carrying it to Miss Taverner. 'I am fortunate to find you at home.'

Miss Taverner accepted the cup and saucer with a brief word of thanks, and setting it down on the sofa-table at her elbow, continued to ply her needle.

'Yes, indeed you are,' agreed Mrs Scattergood. 'We have been about for ever this last week. You can have no notion! Balls, assemblies, card-parties, and actually, Worth, an invitation to Lady Cork's! I tell Judith nothing could be better, for all she may think it tedious! No cards, my love – nothing of that sort, but the company of the most select, and the conversation all wit and elegance. I am sure we have to thank that dear, delightful Emily Cowper for it!'

'On the contrary, you have to thank me for it,' said the Earl, sipping his tea.

'My dear Worth, is it really so? Well, and why should I not have guessed it? To think I should forget the terms your poor Mama was upon with Lady Cork! Of course I might have known it was all your doing. It is very prettily done of you; I am excessively pleased with you for thinking of it. Is that why you are here? Did you come to tell us?'

'Not at all,' said the Earl. 'I came at the request of Miss Taverner.'

Mrs Scattergood turned a surprised, inquiring look upon Judith. 'You never told me you had invited Worth, my dear?'

'I did request Lord Worth to call here,' said Miss Taverner, carefully choosing another length of embroidery silk. 'I did not, however, mention any particular day or hour.'

'True,' said the Earl. 'I had had the intention of calling on you this morning, Miss Taverner, but – er – circumstances intervened.'

'It was fortunate, sir. I was not at home this morning.' She raised her eyes momentarily from her work to find that he was regarding her with a look of so much sarcastic amusement that the unwelcome suspicion crossed her mind that he must have seen her drive out, and changed his own plans immediately.

'This morning!' ejaculated Mrs Scattergood, with a strong shudder.'Pray do not be talking of it! Three hours – I am persuaded it was no less – at the Botanic Gardens, and I not having the least notion that you cared a rap for all those odiously rare plants!'

'The Botanic Gardens,' murmured the Earl.'Poor Miss Taverner!'

She was now sure that he must somewhere have seen her. She got up. 'If you have finished your tea, sir, perhaps you would do me the kindness of coming into the other drawing-room. You will excuse us, ma'am, I know. I have something of a private nature to say to Lord Worth.'

'By all means, my love, though I can't conceive what it should be,' said Mrs Scattergood.

Miss Taverner did not enlighten her. She went out through the door his lordship was holding open for her into the back drawing-room, and took up a stand by the table in the middle of the room. The Earl shut the door, and surveyed her with his air of rather bored amusement. 'Well, Miss Taverner?' he said.

'I desired you to visit me, sir, to explain, if you please, this letter which you wrote me,' said Judith, pulling the offending document out of her reticule.

He took it from her. 'Do you know, I never thought that you would cherish my poor notes so carefully?' he said.

Miss Taverner ground her teeth, but made no reply. The Earl, having looked her over with what she could not but feel to be a challenge in his mocking eyes, picked up his eyeglass, and through it perused his own letter. When he had done this he lowered his glass and looked inquiringly at Miss Taverner. 'What puzzles you, Clorinda? It seems to me quite lucid.'

'My name is not Clorinda!' snapped Miss Taverner. 'I wonder that you should care to call up the recollections it must evoke! If they are not odious to *you* –'

'How could they be?' said Worth. 'You must have forgotten one at least of them if you think that.'

She was obliged to turn away to hide her confusion. 'How can you?' she demanded, in a suffocating voice.

'Don't be alarmed,' said Worth. 'I am not going to do it again yet, Clorinda. I told you, you remember, that you were not the only sufferer under your father's Will.'

Her cousin's warning flashed into Miss Taverner's mind. She said coldly: 'This way of talking no doubt amuses you, sir, but to me it is excessively repugnant. I did not wish to see you in order to discuss the past. That can only be forgotten. In that letter which you are holding you write that there is no possibility of your consenting to my marriage within the year of your guardianship.'

'Well, what could be plainer than that?' inquired the Earl.

'I am at a loss to understand you, sir. Certain applications have been made to you for – for permission to address me.'

'Three,' nodded his lordship. 'The first was Wellesley Poole, but him I expected. The second was Claud Delabey Browne, whom I also expected. The third – now who was the third? Ah yes, it was young Matthews, was it not?'

'It does not signify, sir. What I wish you to explain is, how you came to refuse these gentlemen without even the formality of consulting my wishes.'

'Do you want to marry one of them?' inquired the Earl solicitously. 'I hope it is not Browne. I understand that his affairs are too pressing to allow him to wait until you are come of age.'

Miss Taverner controlled her tongue with a visible effort. 'As it happens, sir, I do not contemplate marriage with any of these gentlemen,' she said. 'But you had no means of knowing that when you refused them.'

'To tell you the truth, Miss Taverner, your wishes in the matter do not appear to me to be of much importance. I am glad, of course, that your heart is not broken,' he added kindly.

'My heart would scarcely be broken by your refusal to consent to my marriage, sir. When I wish to be married I shall marry, with or without your consent.'

'And who,' asked the Earl, 'is the fortunate man?'

'There is no one,' said Miss Taverner curtly. 'But –'

The Earl took out his snuff-box, and opened it. 'But my dear Miss Taverner, are you not being a trifle indelicate? You are not proposing, I trust, to command some gentleman to marry you? The impropriety of such an action must strike even so masterful a mind as yours.'

Miss Taverner's eyes were smouldering dangerously. 'What I wish to make plain to you, Lord Worth, is that if any gentleman whom I – if anyone should ask me to marry him whom I – you know very well what I mean!'

He smiled. 'Yes, Miss Taverner, I know what you mean. But keep my letter by you, for it tells you just as plainly what I mean.'

'Why?' she shot at him. 'What object can you have?'

He took a pinch of snuff, and lightly dusted his fingers before he answered her. Then he said in his cool way: 'You are a very wealthy young woman, Miss Taverner.'

'Ah!' said Judith, 'I begin to understand.'

'I should be happy if I thought you did,' he replied, 'but I feel it to be extremely doubtful. You have a considerable fortune in your own right. More important than this is the fact that under your father's Will you are heiress to as much of your brother's property as is unentailed.'

'Well?' said Judith.

'That being so,' said Worth, shutting his snuff-box with a snap and restoring it to his pocket, 'there is little likelihood of gaining my consent to your marriage with anyone whom I can at the moment call to mind.'

'Except,' said Miss Taverner through her teeth, 'yourself!'

'Except, of course, myself,' he agreed suavely.

'And do you suppose, Lord Worth, that there is any great likelihood of my marrying you?' inquired Judith in a sleek, deceptive voice.

He raised his brows. 'Until I ask you to marry me, Miss Taverner, not the least likelihood,' he replied gently.

For fully a minute she could not trust herself to speak. She would have liked to have swept from the room, but the Earl was between her and the door, and she could place no dependence on him moving out of the way. 'Have the goodness to leave me, sir. I have no more to say to you.'

He strolled forward till he stood immediately before her. She suspected him of meaning to take her hands, whipped them both behind her, and took a swift step backward. A large cabinet prevented her from retreating further, and the Earl very coolly following, she found herself cornered. He took her chin in his hand, and made her hold up her head, and stood looking down at her with a faintly sardonic smile. 'You are handsome, Miss Taverner; you are not unintelligent – except in your dealings with me; you are a termagant. Here is some advice for you: keep your sword sheathed.' She stood rigid and silent, staring doggedly up into his face. 'Oh yes, you hate me excessively, I know. But you are my ward, Miss Taverner, and if you are wise you will accept that with a good grace.' He let go her chin, gave her cheek a careless pat. 'There, that is better advice than you think. I am a more experienced duellist than you. I have brought you your snuff, and the recipe.'

It was on the tip of her tongue to refuse both, but she bit back the words, aware that they would sound merely childish. 'I am obliged to you,' she said in an expressionless voice.

He moved to the door, and held it open. She walked past him into the hall. He nodded to the waiting footman, who at once brought him his hat and gloves. As he took them he said: 'I beg you will make my excuses to Mrs Scattergood. Good night, Miss Taverner.'

'Good night!' said Judith, and turning on her heel, went back into the front drawing-room.

She entered with a somewhat hasty stride and shut the door behind her if not with a slam, at least with a decided snap. Her eyes were stormy; her cheeks looked hot. She flashed a look round the room, and the wrath died out of her face. Mrs Scattergood was not present; there was only Mr Taverner, seated by the window, and glancing through a newspaper.

He got up at once, and laid the paper aside. 'I am so late. Forgive me, cousin! I was detained longer than I had thought possible − hardly liked to call upon you at this hour, and indeed should have done no more than leave the book with your butler, only that he assured me that you had not retired.'

'Oh, I am glad you came in!' Judith said, holding out her hand to him. 'It was kind in you to remember the book. Is this it? Thank you, cousin.'

She picked it up from the table, and began to turn the leaves. Her cousin's hand laid compellingly over hers made her look up. He was regarding her intently. 'What is it, Judith?' he asked in his quiet way.

She gave a little, angry laugh. 'Oh, it is nothing − it should be nothing. I am stupid, that is all.'

'No, you are not stupid. Something has occurred to put you out.'

She tried to draw her hand away, but he did not slacken his hold. 'Tell me,' he said.

She looked significantly down at his hand. 'If you please, cousin.'

'I beg your pardon.' He stepped back with a slight bow.

She put the book aside, and moved towards a three-backed settee of lacquered wood and cane, and sat down. 'You need not. I know you only wish to be kind.' She smiled up at him. 'I am not offended with you, for all I may look to be in one of my sad passions.'

He followed her to the settee, and at a sign from her seated himself beside her. 'It is Worth?' he asked directly.

'Oh, yes, it is, as usual, my noble guardian,' she replied, with a shrug of her shoulders.

'Mrs Scattergood informed me that he was with you. What has he been doing or must I not ask?'

'I brought it upon myself,' said Judith, incurably honest. 'But he behaves in such a way – oh, cousin, if my father had but known! We are in Lord Worth's hands. Nothing could be worse! I thought at first that he was amusing himself at my expense. Now I am afraid – I suspect him of a set purpose, and though it cannot succeed it can make this year uncomfortable for me.'

'A set purpose,' he repeated. 'I may guess it, I suppose.'

'I think so. It was you who put me a little on my guard.'

He nodded; he was slightly frowning. 'You are very wealthy,' he said. 'And he is expensive. I do not know what his fortune is; I imagined it had been considerable, but he is a gamester, and a friend of the Regent. He is in the front of fashion; his clothes are made by the first tailors; his stables are second to none; he belongs to I dare not say how many clubs – White's, Watier's, the Alfred (or, as I have heard it called, the Half-Read), the Je ne sais quoi, the Jockey Club, the Four Horse, the Bensington – perhaps more.'

'In a word, cousin, he is a dandy,' Judith said.

'More than that. He is of the Bow-window set, I grant, but not of the Unique Four. That is composed, as you know, of only your complete Dandies – Brummell, Alvanley, Mildmay, and Pierrepoint. Worth has other interests, even more expensive.'

'So has Lord Alvanley,' she interposed.

'Very true. Lord Alvanley hunts, for instance, but he does not,
I believe, aspire to be first in so many fields as Worth. You may
hardly go to a race-meeting but you are sure to find Worth has
a horse running, while his curricle-races, the teams he drives,
are notorious.'

'It is the only thing I know of to his advantage,' Judith said. 'I
will admit him to be an excellent whip. But for the rest I find
him a mere fop, a creature of affectations, tricked out in modish
clothes, thinking snuff to be of more moment than events of real
importance. He is proud, he can be insolent. There is a reserve,
a lack of openness – I must not say any more: I shall put myself
in a rage, and that will not do.'

He smiled. 'You've no love for the dandies, Judith?'

'Oh, as to that – Mr Brummell is of all people the most
charming companion. Lord Alvanley too must always please.
But in general, no, I do not like them. I like a man to be a man,
and not a mask of fashion.'

He agreed to it, but said seriously: 'I collect there is more than
you have said. These faults, though you may despise them, are
not enough to anger you as I think you were angered this
evening, cousin.'

She was silent for a moment, her eyes smouldering again at
the recollection of her interview with the Earl. Mr Taverner laid
his hand over hers, and clasped it. 'Do not tell me unless you
choose,' he said gently, 'but believe that I only wish to serve you,
to be, if I may be no more, merely your friend.'

'You are all consideration,' she said. 'All kindness.' She smiled,
but with a quivering lip. 'Indeed, I count you very much my
friend. There is no one I can open my mind to, saving Perry, and
he is young, taken up with his new acquaintances, and amusements. Mrs Scattergood is very amiable, but she is related to
Worth – a circumstance I cannot forget. I have been thinking
how very much alone I am. There is only Perry – but I am

falling into a mood of pitying myself, which is nonsensical. While I have Perry I cannot want for protection.' She gave her head a little shake. 'You see how stupid Lord Worth makes me! We cannot meet but I find myself picking a quarrel with him, and then I become as odious as he is himself. To-night in particular – he informs me, if you please, that he shall not consent to my marriage with anyone but himself while he is my guardian! It has put me in such a rage that I declare I could almost elope to Gretna Green just to spite him.'

He started. 'My dear cousin!'

'Oh, I shall not, of course! Do not look so shocked!'

'Not that – certainly not that, but – I have no right to ask you – you have met someone? There is some man with whom you could contemplate –'

'No one, upon my honour!' she said, laughing. Her eyes met his for an instant, and then fell. She coloured, became aware of her hand under his and gently drew it away. 'Where can Mrs Scattergood be gone to, I wonder?'

He rose. 'I must go. It is growing late.' He paused, looking earnestly down at her. 'You have Peregrine to turn to, I know. Let me say just this, that you have also a cousin who would do all in his power to serve you.'

'Thank you,' she said, almost inaudibly. She got up. 'It – it is late. It was good of you to call, to bring me the book.'

He took her hand, held out to him in farewell, and kissed it. 'Dear Judith!' he said.

Mrs Scattergood, coming back into the room at that moment, looked very sharply at him, and made not the smallest attempt to persuade him into staying any longer. He took his leave of both ladies, and bowed himself out.

'You are getting to be excessively intimate with that young gentleman, my love,' observed Mrs Scattergood.

'He is my cousin, ma'am,' replied Judith tranquilly.

'H'm, yes! I daresay he might be. I have very little notion of cousins, I can tell you. Not that I have anything against Mr Taverner, my dear. He seems an agreeable creature. But that is how it is always! The less eligible a man is the more delightful he is bound to be! You may depend upon it.'

Judith began to put away her embroidery. 'My dear ma'am, what can that signify? There is no thought of marriage between us.'

'No Bath-miss airs with me, child, I implore you!' said Mrs Scattergood, throwing up her hands. 'That is very pretty talking, to be sure, but you have something more of quickness than most girls, and you know very well, my love, that there is always a thought of marriage between a single female and a personable gentleman, if not in his mind, quite certainly in hers. Now this cousin may do very well for a young lady of no particular consequence, but you are an heiress and should be looking a great deal higher for a husband. I don't say you must not show him the observance that is due to a relative, but you know, my dear, you do not owe him any extraordinary civility, and to let him kiss your hand and be calling you dear Judith, is the outside of enough!'

Judith turned. 'Let me understand you, ma'am. How much higher must I look for a husband?'

'Oh, my dear, when a female is as wealthy as you, as high as you choose! I did think of Clarence, but there's that horrid Marriage Act to be got over, and I daresay the Regent would never give his consent.'

'There is Mrs Jordan to be got over too,' said Judith dryly.

'Nonsense, my love, I have it for a fact he has quite broken with her. I daresay she will keep all the children of the connection – I believe there are ten, but I might be mistaken.'

'You informed me yourself, ma'am, that the Duke was a devoted father,' said Judith.

Mrs Scattergood sighed. 'Well, and have I not said that I believe he won't do? Though I must say, my dear, if you had the chance of becoming his wife it would be a very odd thing in you to be objecting to it merely because of a few Fitz-Clarences. But I have been thinking of it, and I am persuaded it won't answer. We must look elsewhere.'

'Where shall we look, ma'am?' inquired Judith, with a hint of steel in her voice. 'A mere commoner is too low for me, and a Royal Duke too high. I understand his Grace of Devonshire is unmarried. Shall I set my cap at him, ma'am, or should I look about me for a husband amongst – for instance – the Earls?'

Mrs Scattergood glanced up sharply. 'What do you mean, my love?'

'Would not Lord Worth make me a suitable husband?' said Miss Taverner evenly.

'Oh, my dearest child, the best!' cried Mrs Scattergood. 'It has been in my mind ever since I clapped eyes on you!'

'I thought so,' said Judith. 'Perhaps that was why his lordship was so determined you should live with me?'

'Worth has not said a word to me, not one, I promise you!' replied Mrs Scattergood, an expression of ludicrous dismay in her face.

Miss Taverner raised her brows in polite incredulity. 'No, ma'am?'

'Indeed he has not! Lord, I wish I had not spoken! I had not the least notion of uttering a word, but then you spoke of earls, and it popped out before I could recollect. Now I have put you in a rage!'

Judith laughed. 'No, you have not, dear ma'am. I am sure you would not try to force me into a marriage, the very thought of which is repugnant to me.'

'No,' agreed Mrs Scattergood. 'I would not, of course, but I must confess, my love, I am sorry to hear you talk of Worth like that.'

'Do not let us talk of him at all,' said Judith lightly. 'I for one am going to bed.'

She went to bed, and presently to sleep, but was awakened some time after midnight by a tapping on her door. She sat up, and called out: 'Who is there?'

'Are you awake? Can I come in?' demanded Peregrine's voice.

She gave permission, wondering what disaster had befallen him. He came in carrying a branch of candles, which he set down on the table beside her bed to the imminent danger of the rose-silk curtains. He was dressed for an evening party, in satin knee-breeches, and a velvet coat, and he seemed to be suffering from suppressed excitement. Judith looked anxiously up at him. 'Is anything wrong, Perry?' she asked.

'Wrong? No, how should it be? You weren't asleep, were you? I didn't think you had been asleep yet. It is quite early, you know.'

'Well, I am not asleep now,' she said, smiling. 'Do move the candles a little, my dear! You will have me burned in my bed.'

He complied with this request, and sat himself down on the edge of the bed, hugging one knee. Judith waited patiently for him to tell her why he had come, but he seemed to have fallen into a pleasant sort of dream, and sat staring at the candle flames as though he saw a picture in them.

'Perry, have you or have you not something you wish to tell me?' demanded his sister between amusement and exasperation.

He brought his gaze round to dwell on her face. 'Eh? Oh no, nothing in particular. Do you know Lady Fairford, Ju?'

She shook her head. 'I don't think I do. Ought I to?'

'No – that is – I believe – I am nearly sure she is going to call on you.'

'I am very much obliged to her. Shall I like her?'

'Oh yes, excessively! She is a most agreeable woman. I was presented to her at Covent Garden tonight. I was dining with Fitz, you know, and we thought we might as well go to the play, and they were there, in a box. Fitz is a little acquainted with the family, and he took me up, and the long and the short of it was we joined them afterwards at the ball, and Lady Fairford asked very particularly after my sister, and said she had had it in mind to call on you, but from the circumstance of her having been out of London just lately – they have a place in Hertfordshire, I believe – it had not so far been in her power. But she said she should certainly come.' He gave her a fleeting glance, and began to study his finger-nails. 'She may – I do not know – but she may bring her daughter,' he added, rather too off-handedly.

'Oh!' said Judith. 'I hope she will. Has she only the one daughter?'

'Oh no, I believe she has a numerous family, but Miss Fairford is the only one out. Her name,' said Peregrine rapturously, 'is Harriet.'

Miss Taverner knew her duty, and immediately replied: 'What a pretty name, to be sure.'

'Yes, it is, isn't it?' said Peregrine. 'She – I think she is very pretty too. I do not know how she may strike you, but I certainly consider her uncommonly handsome.'

'Is she dark or fair?' inquired his sister.

But to this question he could not give any very certain answer. He rather thought Miss Fairford's eyes were blue, but they might be grey: he could not be sure. She was not tall, quite the reverse, yet Judith must not be imagining a dab of a girl. It was no such thing: but she would see for herself.

After a good deal in this strain he took himself off to bed, leaving his sister to her reflections.

She had not been used to see him in the toils of a young woman, and could hardly be blamed for feeling a certain jealousy. She did her best to banish it, and succeeded very fairly. When Lady Fairford, who turned out to be a kindly sensible woman in the early forties, came to pay her promised call, she did bring her eldest daughter with her, and Judith had leisure to observe Peregrine's charmer.

Miss Fairford was not long out of the schoolroom, and had all the natural shyness of her seventeen years. She regarded Judith out of a pair of large dove-like eyes with a great deal of awe, coloured a little when directly addressed, and allowed her soft mouth to tremble into a fugitive, appealing smile. She had pretty brown curls, and a neat figure, but to Judith, who was built on Juno-esque lines, she could not seem other than short.

When Peregrine came in, which he presently did, Lady Fairford greeted him with marked complaisance, and took the opportunity to beg the company both of him and his sister to dinner on the following Tuesday. The invitation was accepted: Peregrine had in fact accepted it before Judith could recollect her own engagements. On the pretext of showing Miss Fairford a book of views which Judith had previously been looking at, he contrived to draw her a little apart, a manœuvre which was observed by the lady's mama without provoking her to any other sign than a faint smile. Miss Taverner concluded that her visitor would be inclined to look favourably upon a possible match. She was not surprised. Peregrine was well-born, handsome, and possessed of a large fortune. No mother with five daughters to see suitably established could be blamed for giving so eligible a suitor just a little encouragement.

Upon inquiry, the Fairfords were found to be a very respectable family living in good style in Albemarle Street. They moved in the best circles, without aspiring to belong to the Carlton House set; had one son in the army, one at present at Oxford, and a third at Eton.

When Tuesday came the company invited to dinner was found to be not numerous, but extremely select, and the party went off without any other hitch than that occasioned by Lord Dudley and Ward, who, from the circumstance of his being excessively absent-minded and fancying himself in his own house, apologised very audibly to Miss Taverner for the badness of one of the entrées. He said that the cook was ill.

The gentlemen soon joined the ladies after dinner; a whist-table was formed, and the rest of the party sat down, some to play a few rubbers of Casino, and the rest to a game of lottery tickets. Miss Fairford having placed herself at the lottery-table, Judith was amused but not surprised to see Peregrine taking a chair beside her. She reflected with an inward smile that this was just such an evening as a week ago he would have voted very poor sport.

Eight

*C*ONTRARY TO HIS SISTER'S EXPECTATIONS, PEREGRINE'S INFATU-
ation for Miss Fairford showed no sign of abating. He
continued to go about town a great deal, but whenever opportunity offered he was to be found, if not on the Fairford doorstep,
certainly at any party where they were likely to be present. Miss
Taverner informed her cousin that she did not know whether to
be cross or glad. A love-lorn Peregrine was tiresome, but if Miss
Fairford's attractions could keep him out of gaming clubs and tav-
erns she must certainly be glad. When she found his thoughts to
be dwelling on marriage she was a little dubious. He seemed to
her to be too young to be thinking of such a thing.

However that might be, within one month of having met
Miss Fairford he had come to such a good understanding with
her that he took his courage in both hands, and sought an interview with her parents.

Lady Fairford, who besides wishing to see her daughter so
triumphantly bestowed, was in a fair way to loving Peregrine
quite for his own sake, showed a marked inclination to accept
him into her family without any more ado, but Sir Geoffrey, with
greater common sense, thought the young couple would do well
to wait. He was by no means anxious to lose his daughter, and
might conceivably feel some doubt of her suitor's stability, but
even he must feel that the match would be a better one than he

had ever hoped to see his Harriet make. He would not forbid the engagement, but his notions of propriety, which were very nice, made him refuse to listen to any offer that was made without Lord Worth's knowledge or approval.

This pronouncement had the effect of sending Peregrine off hot-foot to his guardian.

Worth, however, proved to be somewhat elusive. Three consecutive calls at his house failed to discover him, and after an abortive attempt to compose a letter which should explain everything to his lordship, Peregrine hit upon the notion of looking for him at his clubs.

This plan was more successful. After being told at White's that the Earl had gone out of town, and at the Alfred that he had not been inside the club for six months, he finally ran him to earth at Watier's, where he was playing macao.

'Oh!' said Peregrine. 'So you are here! I have been searching for you all over town!'

The Earl cast him a look of faint surprise, and gathered up his cards. 'Well, now that you have found me, do you think you could sit down – keeping me under observation, if you like – until after the game?' he said.

'I'm sorry, I didn't mean to interrupt you!' said Peregrine. 'Only they told me at White's you were out of town, and when I called at the Alfred they said you had not been there for months.'

'Come and take a hand,' said Lord Alvanley kindly. 'You should not have wasted your time at the Half-Read, my boy. They have seventeen bishops there, so I hear. Worth and I gave it up after the eighth. As for White's, it is my belief Worth taught them always to say he was out of town. Do you care to join us?'

Peregrine, much flattered, thanked him, and took a place between Sir Henry Mildmay and a gentleman with very red hair and very blue eyes, whom he discovered later to be Lord Yarmouth. The stakes at the table were extremely high, and he soon found that his luck was quite out. This did not trouble him much, for he did not think Worth could very well refuse to pay any debts he might incur over and above what little remained of the quarter's allowance. He took his losses in good part, and cheerfully wrote a number of I O Us, which Worth, who held the bank, accepted with an unmoved countenance.

Mr Brummell, who had come over to observe the game, lifted an eyebrow, but said nothing. The hour was considerably advanced, and the table broke up before the bank changed hands. Mr Brummell took the Earl away with him in search of iced champagne, and murmured: 'Must he play at your table, Julian? Really, you know, it does not look well.'

'Young fool,' said the Earl, unemotionally.

'Just a little out of place,' said Brummell, taking a glass from the tray a waiter was presenting to him.

The Duke of Bedford came up at that moment with Lord Frederick Bentinck and Mr Skeffington, forming the nucleus of the circle that very soon gathered round Mr Brummell, and nothing more was said of Peregrine and his losses. The Duke, who was a great personal friend of the Beau, wanted his opinion on a matter of some importance. 'Now George, tell me!' he said earnestly. 'I have changed my tailor, you know, and this is the coat my new man has made for me. What do you say? Will it answer? Do you like the cut of it?'

Mr Brummell continued to sip his champagne, but over the rim of his glass he gazed thoughtfully at his grace, while the circle about him waited in interested silence for his verdict. The Duke stood anxiously showing himself off. Mr Brummell's eyes dwelled for an appreciable time upon the coat's very bright gilt buttons; he gave a faint sigh and the Duke blenched.

'It sets well; I like the long tails,' said Lord Frederick. 'Who made it, Duke? Nugee?'

'Turn round,' said Mr Brummell.

The Duke pivoted obediently, and stood craning his head over his shoulder to see what effect this aspect of the garment produced on the Beau. Mr Brummell examined him from head to foot, and walked slowly round him. He studied the length of the tails, and pursed his lips; he observed the cut across the shoulders, and raised his brows. Lastly, he took one of the lapels between his finger and thumb, and carefully felt it. 'Bedford,' he said earnestly, '*do* you call this thing a coat?'

The Duke, with a ludicrous expression, half of dismay, half of amusement, on his face, interrupted the laughter of the circle. 'No, really, George, that's too bad of you! Upon my word, I have a good mind to call you out for it!'

'You may call me, Bedford, but there it will end, I warn you,' replied Brummell. 'I haven't the least intention of putting a period to my existence in such a hideous way as that.'

'Did you ever fight a duel, Brummell?' inquired Mr Montagu, astride a cabriole chair.

'Thank God, no!' said the Beau, with a shudder. 'But I once had an affair at Chalk Farm, and a dreadful state I was in: never in my life shall I forget the horrors of the previous night!'

'Any sleep, George?' asked Worth, smiling.

'None, not a wink. It was out of the question. Dawn was to me the harbinger of Death, and yet I almost hailed it with pleasure. But my second's step on the stair soon spoiled *that* feeling, for what must he do but carefully explain all the horrid details to me, thus annihilating the little – the very little – courage that had survived the anxieties of the night! We left the house, and no accident, no fortunate upset occurred on our way to the rendezvous, where we arrived, according to my idea, much too soon, a quarter of an hour before the time named.' He paused, closing his eyes as though overcome by the recollection.

'Go on, George: what happened?' demanded the Duke, highly entertained.

Mr Brummell opened his eyes again, and fortified himself with champagne. 'Well, Bedford, there was no one on the ground, and each minute seemed an age as in terror and semi-suffocation I awaited my opponent's approach. At length the clock of the neighbouring church announced that the hour had come. We now looked in the direction of town, but there was no appearance of my antagonist. My military friend kindly hinted that clocks and watches varied, a fact I was well aware of, and which I thought he might have spared me the pleasure of hearing him remark upon: but a second is always such a "damned good-natured friend"! The next quarter of an hour passed in awful silence. Still no one appeared, not even on the horizon. My friend whistled, and, confound him! looked much disappointed. The half-hour struck – still no one; the third quarter; at last the hour. My Centurion of the Coldstream now came up, this time in *truth* my friend and said to me, and I can tell you they were the sweetest accents that ever fell on my ear: "Well, George, I think we may go." You may imagine my relief! – "My dear fellow," I replied, "you have taken a load off my mind: let us go *immediately*!"'

The shout of laughter that greeted this climax brought several other people over to the group, Peregrine amongst them, who arrived in time to hear his guardian say: 'Had your blood-thirsty opponent met with the accident that did *not* befall you, George, or was his second less determined than yours?'

'I am inclined to believe,' replied the Beau gravely, 'that he realised in time the social solecism he had committed in calling me out at all.'

Peregrine worked his way through the knot of persons to Worth's side, and touched his sleeve. The Earl turned his head, frowning a little. 'Well, Peregrine, what is it?'

'I thought you had gone,' said Peregrine in a low voice. 'I must have a word with you; you know that is what I came for.'

'My good boy, you cannot be private with me at Watier's, if that is what you want. You may come and see me at my house to-morrow morning.'

'Yes, but will you be there?' objected Peregrine. 'I have been to your house three times already, and you are never at home. Could I not walk back with you now?'

'You may call at my house to-morrow,' repeated the Earl wearily. 'In the meantime you are interrupting Mr Brummell.'

Peregrine blushed, begged pardon, and withdrew in some haste just as Lord Alvanley came up. Lord Alvanley's chubby face wore a look of concern. He laid his hand on Worth's shoulder. 'Julian, I am such a stupid fellow! do pray forgive me! But, do you know, you were so curt with the boy, and he looked so uncomfortable, that I had to ask him to join us.'

'If only you would not be kind-hearted!' said the Earl. 'I had snubbed him quite successfully when you intervened.'

'Oh well, of course, he should not have broken in on the table as he did,' admitted Alvanley. 'But he's very young, after all, and quite a nice boy, from what I have seen.'

'Quite,' said Worth. 'He will be still nicer when he has been snubbed a few more times. George, you might attend to it.'

Mr Brummell shook his head. 'My dear Worth, you really cannot expect me to do any more for your ward. Why, I once gave him my arm all the way here from White's!'

'Ah, perhaps that may account for his presumption,' said Worth. 'You had better have given him one of your cuts.'

'But I thought you wanted me to do what I could to bring him into fashion,' said the Beau plaintively.

Whether from a natural impatience, or from a fear of once more missing his guardian, Peregrine was in Cavendish Square by half-past ten next morning, only to be informed that his lordship was dressing. He had nothing to do, there-fore, but to kick his heels in the saloon for half an hour, skim through the newspaper, and silently rehearse all he meant presently to say.

At eleven o'clock the footman came back, and informed him that his lordship would receive him. He followed the man up the broad stairway, and was ushered into the Earl's bedroom. This was a large apartment with a canopy bed occupying the whole of one wall. It was an extremely fine piece, supported by two bronze gryphons, and with crimson silk hangings caught up by a pair of smaller gryphons on pedestals. A fifth gryphon surmounted the canopy with its wings spread ready for flight, and all the hangings depending apparently from its claws. Peregrine was so much struck by the splendour of this edifice that for some moments he could only stand and gaze at it.

The Earl, who was seated before a mahogany dressing-table with the drawer pulled out and the top pushed back to disclose a central mirror, cast him a fleeting glance, and went on attending to his toilet.

Peregrine, having taken in the bed in all its details, looked round for his guardian, and, perceiving him, blinked a little at the elegance of the brocade dressing-gown he was wearing, and wished that he could achieve the exquisite disorder of his lordship's black locks. These were brushed into a style which Peregrine at once recognised as being *au coup de vent*. He himself had wasted half an hour in trying to arrange his own yellow curls in the same manner, and had had to be content in the end with a cherubim style.

'Good morning, Peregrine. You choose a very early hour for your calls,' said the Earl. 'You need not wait, Foster. Stay, hand me the packet you will find on that table. Thank you; you may go.'

The valet put a chair forward for Peregrine, and went away. Peregrine sat down, looking rather uneasily at the papers the man had fetched for the Earl. He had not the least difficulty in recognising them, and blurted out: 'Those are my I O Us, are they not?'

'Yes,' said the Earl. 'Those are your I O Us. Shall we settle before we go any further?'

Peregrine fixed his eyes anxiously on that calm profile, and moistened his lips. 'Why – why, the fact of the matter is – I don't think I can,' he confessed. 'I'm not perfectly certain how much I lost last night, but –'

'Oh, not much above four thousand, I fancy,' said the Earl.

'Not much above – Oh! Well – well, that is not such a vast sum after all, is it?' said Peregrine valiantly.

'That,' said the Earl, taking a slender knife from the open drawer, and beginning to pare his nails with it, 'depends very largely on the size of your fortune.'

'Yes,' agreed Peregrine. 'Very true. I – I have a considerable fortune, haven't I?'

'At the moment,' replied Worth, 'you have what I should rather call an independence.'

'You mean I have what you allow me,' said Peregrine in a dissatisfied voice.

'I am glad to find that you realise that,' said Worth. 'I was beginning to be afraid that you did not.'

'Of course I do. But the money's there, ain't it? It's only a matter of advancing me some of it.'

The Earl laid the knife down, and dipped his hands in a bowl of water, placed at his elbow. Having rinsed them he began to dry them carefully on a fine napkin. 'But I have not the least intention of advancing you any of it,' he said.

Peregrine stiffened. 'What do you mean?' he asked.

The Earl raised his eyes for a moment, and coldly looked his ward over. 'Between you, you and your sister credit me with an obscurity of meaning which I am unaware of having done anything to deserve. It really doesn't amuse me. I mean precisely what I say.'

'But you can't refuse to let me have money to pay my debts of honour!' said Peregrine indignantly.

'Can't I?' said the Earl. 'I was under the impression that I could.'

'Damme, I never heard of such a thing! I must pay my debts!'

'Naturally,' agreed the Earl.

'Well, how the devil can I if you won't loosen the purse-strings?' demanded Peregrine. 'You must know my pockets are pretty well to let till next quarter!'

'I didn't know it, but I don't find it very hard to believe. You have all my sympathy.'

'Sympathy! What's the use of that to me?' cried Peregrine, a good deal injured.

'I'm afraid it isn't of any use to you at all,' said Worth. 'We are wandering a little from the point, are we not? You owe me something over four thousand pounds – if you look over those I O Us you may find out the exact sum for yourself – and I am anxious to know when you propose to pay me.'

'You are my guardian!' said Peregrine hotly. 'You have control of all my fortune!'

The Earl lifted one well-manicured hand. 'Oh no, Peregrine! You must leave me as your guardian quite out of this discussion, if you please. As your guardian I have already intimated that I have no intention of assisting you to game your fortune away. As your creditor I am merely desirous of knowing when it will suit your convenience to redeem these notes.'

By this time Peregrine was feeling very limp, but he kept his chin up, and said in as even a voice as he could manage: 'In that case, sir, I shall have to ask you to have the goodness to wait until next quarter-day, when I shall be able to pay you – not all, but a large part of the sum I owe you.'

The Earl once more looked him over in such a way that made the unfortunate Peregrine feel very small, and hot, and uncomfortable. 'Perhaps I should have told you – in the character of your guardian – that it is customary to settle your debts of honour at once,' he said gently.

Peregrine flushed, gripped his hands together on his knee, and muttered: 'I know.'

'Otherwise,' said the Earl, delicately adjusting one of the folds of his cravat, 'you may find yourself obliged to resign from your clubs.'

Peregrine got up suddenly. 'You shall have the money by to-morrow morning, Lord Worth,' he said, his voice trembling. 'Had I known – had I guessed the attitude you would choose to assume I should have arranged the payment before ever I called on you.'

'Let me make one thing quite plain to you – I am speaking once more as your guardian, Peregrine. – If I find at any time during the next two years that you have visited my friends Howard and Gibbs, or, in fact, any other moneylender, you will return to Yorkshire until you come of age.'

Very white about the mouth, Peregrine stared down at the Earl, and said rather numbly: 'What am I to do? What can I do?'

The Earl pointed to the chair. 'Sit down.'

Peregrine obeyed, and sat with his eyes fixed anxiously on his guardian's face.

'Do you quite understand that I mean what I have said? I will neither advance you money for your gaming debts, nor permit you to go to the Jews.'

'Yes, I understand,' said poor Peregrine, wondering what was to become of him.

'Very well then,' said Worth, and picked up the little sheaf of papers, tore them once across, and dropped them into a waste-paper-basket under the dressing-table.

Peregrine's first emotion at this unexpected action was one of staggering relief. He gave a gasp, and his colour came flooding back. Then he got up quickly, and thrust his hand into the basket. 'No!' he said jerkily. 'I don't play and not pay, sir! If you will neither advance me the money nor permit me to obtain it in my own way, keep my notes till I come of age, if you please!'

The Earl's hand closed over his wrist, and the grip of his slender fingers made Peregrine wince. 'Let them fall,' he said quietly.

Peregrine, who had caught up the torn notes, continued to clutch them in his prisoned hand. 'I won't! I lost the money in fair play, and I don't choose to put myself under such an obligation to you! You are very good – extremely kind, I am sure – but I had rather lose my whole fortune than accept such generosity!'

'Let them fall,' repeated the Earl. 'And do not flatter yourself that in destroying the notes I am trying to be kind to you. I do not choose to figure as the man who won over four thousand pounds from his own ward.'

Peregrine said sulkily: 'I do not see what that signifies.'

'Then you must be very dull-witted,' returned the Earl. 'I should warn you that my patience is by no means inexhaustible. Put those notes down!' He tightened his grip as he spoke. Peregrine drew in his breath sharply, and allowed the crumpled papers to fall back into the basket. Worth let him go. 'What was it you wanted to say to me?' he asked calmly.

Peregrine swung over to the window, and stood staring blindly out, one hand fidgeting with the curtain-tassel. His whole pose suggested that he was labouring under a strong sensation of chagrin. The Earl sat and watched him, a slight smile in his eyes. After a moment, as Peregrine seemed still to be struggling with himself, he got up and slipped off his dressing-gown, tossing it on to the bed. He strolled over to get his coat, and put it on. Having adjusted it carefully, flicked a speck of dust from his shining Hessians, and scrutinised his appearance critically in the long mirror, he picked up a Sèvres snuff-box from his dressing-table, and said: 'Come! We will finish this conversation downstairs.'

Peregrine turned reluctantly. 'Lord Worth!' he began on a long breath.

'Yes, when we get downstairs,' said the Earl, opening the door.

Peregrine made a stiff little bow, and stood back for him to go first.

The Earl went in his leisurely fashion down the stairs, and led the way into a pleasant library behind the saloon. The butler was just setting a tray bearing glasses and a decanter on the table. He arranged these to his satisfaction, and withdrew, closing the door behind him.

The Earl picked up the decanter, and poured out two glasses of wine. One of them he held out to Peregrine. 'Madeira, but if you prefer it I can offer you sherry,' he said.

'Thank you, nothing for me,' said Peregrine, with what he hoped was a fair imitation of his lordship's own cold dignity.

Apparently it was not. 'Don't be stupid, Peregrine,' said Worth.

Peregrine looked at him for a moment, and then, lowering his gaze, took the glass with a murmured word of thanks, and sat down.

The Earl moved towards a deep chair with earpieces. 'And now what is it?' he asked. 'I apprehend it to be a matter of some importance, since it sends you looking all over town for me.'

His guardian's voice being for once free from its usual blighting iciness, Peregrine, who had quite determined to go away without mentioning the business which had brought him, changed his mind, shot a swift, shy look at the Earl, and blurted out: 'I want to talk to you on a – on a very delicate subject. In fact, marriage!' He gulped down half the wine in his glass, and took another look at the Earl, this time tinged with defiance.

Worth, however, merely raised his brows. 'Whose marriage?' he asked.

'Mine!' said Peregrine.

'Indeed!' Worth twisted the stem of his wineglass between his finger and thumb, idly watching the light on the tawny wine. 'It seems a trifle sudden. Who is the lady?'

Peregrine, who had been quite prepared to be met at the out-set with a flat refusal to listen to him, took heart at this calm way of receiving the news, and sat forward in his chair. 'I daresay you will not know her, sir, though I think you must know her parents, at least by repute.'

The Earl was in the act of raising his glass to his lips, but he lowered it again. 'She has parents, then?' he asked, an inflexion of surprise in his voice.

Peregrine stared. 'Of course she has parents! What can you be thinking of?'

'Evidently of something quite different,' murmured his lordship. 'But continue: who are these parents who are known to me by repute?'

'Sir Geoffrey and Lady Fairford,' said Peregrine, watching very anxiously to see how this disclosure would be met. 'Sir Geoffrey is a member of Brooks's, I believe. They live in Albemarle Street, and have a place near St Albans. He is a Member of Parliament.'

'They sound most respectable,' said Worth. 'Pour yourself out another glass of wine, and tell me how long you have known this family.'

'Oh, a full month!' Peregrine assured him, getting up and going over to the table.

'That is certainly a period,' said the Earl gravely.

'Oh yes,' said Peregrine, 'you need not be afraid that I have just fallen in love yesterday. I am quite sure of my mind in this. A month is fully long enough for that.'

'Or a day, or an hour,' said the Earl musingly.

'Well, to tell you the truth,' confided Peregrine, reddening, 'I was sure the instant I set eyes on Miss Fairford, but I waited, because I knew you would only say something cut –' He broke off in some confusion. 'I mean –'

'Something cutting,' supplied the Earl. 'You were probably right.'

'Well, I daresay you would not have listened to me,' said Peregrine defensively. 'But now you must realise that it is perfectly serious. Only, from the circumstances of my being under age, Sir Geoffrey would have it that nothing could be in a way to be settled until your consent was gained.'

'Very proper,' commented the Earl.

'Sir Geoffrey will have no scruple in agreeing to it if you are not against it,' urged Peregrine. 'Lady Fairford, too, is all complaisance. There is no objection *there*.'

The Earl threw him a somewhat scornful but not unkindly glance. 'It would surprise me very much if there were,' he said.

'Well, have I your permission to address Miss Fairford?' demanded Peregrine. 'It cannot signify to you in the least, after all!'

The Earl did not immediately reply to this. He sat looking rather enigmatically at his ward for some moments, and then opened his snuff-box, and meditatively took a pinch.

Peregrine fidgeted about the room, and at last burst out with: 'Hang it, why should you object?'

'I was not aware that I had objected,' said Worth. 'In fact, I have little doubt that if you are of the same mind in six months' time I shall quite willingly give my consent.'

'Six months!' ejaculated Peregrine, dismayed.

'Were you thinking of marrying Miss Fairford at once?' inquired Worth.

'No, but we – I had hoped at least to be betrothed at once.'

'Certainly. Why not?' said the Earl.

Peregrine brightened. 'Well, that is something, but I don't see that we need wait all that time to be married. Surely if we were betrothed for three months, say –'

'At the end of six months,' said Worth, 'we will talk about marriage. I am not in the mood today.'

Peregrine could not be satisfied, but having expected worse, he accepted it with a good grace, and merely asked whether the betrothal might be formally announced.

'It can make very little difference,' said the Earl, who seemed to be fast losing interest in the affair. 'Do as you please about it: your prospective mother-in-law will no doubt inform all her acquaintance of it, so it may as well be as formal as you like.'

'Lady Fairford,' said Peregrine severely, 'is a very superior woman, sir, quite above that sort of thing.'

'If she is above trying to secure a husband with an estate of twelve thousand pounds a year for her daughter she is unique,' said the Earl with a certain tartness.

Nine

HE BETROTHAL WAS ANNOUNCED IN THE COLUMNS OF THE *Morning Post*, and its most immediate effect was to bring Admiral Taverner to Brook Street with a copy of the paper under his arm, and an expression of strong indignation on his face. He wasted no time in civilities, and not even the presence of Mrs Scattergood had the power to prevent him making known his mind. He demanded to know what they were all about to let Peregrine make such wretched work of his future. 'Miss Harriet Fairford!' he said. 'Who is Miss Harriet Fairford? I thought it had not been possible when I read it. "Depend upon it," I said (for Bernard was with me), "Depend upon it, it is all a damned hum! The lad will not be throwing himself away on the first pretty face he sees." But you don't speak; you say nothing! Is it true then?'

Miss Taverner begged him to be seated. 'Yes, sir, it is quite true.'

The Admiral muttered something under his breath that sounded like an oath, and crumpling up the paper threw it into a corner of the room. 'It does not signify talking!' he said. 'Was there ever such an ill-managed business? Damn me, the boy's no more than nineteen! He is not to be getting married at his age. Upon my soul, I wonder at Worth! But I daresay this is done without his knowledge?'

Miss Taverner was obliged to banish the gleam of hope in her uncle's eyes by replying quietly that the betrothal had been announced with the Earl's full consent.

The Admiral seemed to find this difficult to believe. He exclaimed at it, blessed himself, and ended by saying that he could not understand it. 'Worth has some devilish deep game on hand!' he said. 'I wish I knew what it may be! Married before he is twenty! Ay, that will mean the devil to pay and no pitch hot!'

Mrs Scattergood, at no time disposed in the Admiral's favour, shut up her netting-box at this, and said in a tone of decided reproof: 'I am sure I do not know what you can mean, sir. Pray, what game should my cousin be playing? It is no bad thing, I can tell you, for a young man inclined to wildness to be betrothed to a respectable female such as Miss Fairford. It will steady him, and for my part I have not the least doubt she will make him a charming wife.'

The Admiral recollected himself. 'Mean! Oh, damn it, I don't mean anything! I had forgot you were related to the fellow. But Perry with his fortune to be throwing himself away on a paltry baronet's daughter! It is a pitiful piece of work indeed!'

He was evidently much put out, and Miss Taverner, guessing as she must the real reason behind his annoyance, could only be sorry to see him expose himself so plainly. She had no means of knowing what else he might have said, for the footman opening the door to announce another caller the conversation had to be abandoned.

This second visitor was none other than the Duke of Clarence, who came in with a smile on his good-humoured face, and a bluff greeting for both ladies.

Miss Taverner was distressed that he should have come when her uncle was sitting with her, but the Admiral's manners when confronted by Royalty underwent a distinct change. If he did not, with his red face and rather bloodshot eyes, present a very creditable appearance, at least he said nothing during the Duke's visit to mortify his niece. His civilities were too obsequious to please the nice tone of her mind, but the Duke seemed to find nothing amiss, so that she supposed him to be too much in the way of encountering such flattery to think it extraordinary. He stayed only half an hour, but his partiality for Miss Taverner, which he made no attempt to conceal, did not escape the Admiral's notice. No sooner had the Duke made his bow, and gone off, than the Admiral said: 'You did not tell me you was on such easy terms with Clarence, my dear niece. This is flying high indeed! But you will be very ill-advised to encourage *his* attentions, you know. Ay, you may colour up, but you won't deny he is in a way to make you the object of his gallantry. But there is nothing to be hoped for in that quarter. These morganatic marriages are not for you. Nothing could be worse! Think of Mrs Fitzherbert, gone off to live at Golders Green! Think of that poor creature Sussex married in Rome – and *she* was of better birth than you, my dear, but it was all annulled, and there she is, I don't know where, with two children, and a beggarly allowance, quite cast-off.'

'Your warning, sir, is quite unnecessary,' said Miss Taverner coldly. 'I have no intention of marrying the Duke of Clarence even if he should ask me – an event which I do not at all anticipate.'

The Admiral evidently felt that he had said enough. He begged pardon, and presently took himself off.

'Well, my love,' remarked Mrs Scattergood, 'I should not wish to be severe on a relative of yours, but I must say that I do not think the Admiral quite the thing.'

'I know it,' replied Miss Taverner.

'It is quite plain to me that he does not like to think of Perry with a nursery-full of stout children standing between him and the title. You must forgive me, my dear, but I do not perfectly know how things are left.'

'My uncle would inherit the title if Perry died without a son to succeed him, and also a part – only what is entailed, and it is very little – of the estate,' Judith answered. 'It is I who would inherit the bulk of the fortune.'

'I see,' said Mrs Scattergood thoughtfully. She seemed to be on the point of making some further remark, but changing her mind merely proposed their ordering the carriage and driving to a shop in Bond Street, where she fancied she would be able to match a particularly fine netting cotton.

Miss Taverner, having a book to change at Hookham's Library, was quite agreeable, and in a short time both ladies set forth in an open barouche, the day (though it was November) being so extremely mild that even Mrs Scattergood could not fear an inflammation of the lungs, or an injury to the complexion.

They arrived in Bond Street soon after two o'clock and found it as usual at that hour very full of carriages and smart company. Several tilburies and saddle-horses were waiting outside Stephen's Hotel, and as Miss Taverner's barouche passed the door of Jackson's Boxing Saloon she saw her brother going in on Mr Fitzjohn's arm. She waved to him, but did not stop, and the carriage drawing up presently outside a haberdasher's shop she set Mrs Scattergood down and drove on to the library.

She had just handed in *Tales of Fashionable Life*, and was glancing through the volumes of one of the new publications when she felt a touch on her sleeve and turned to find her cousin at her elbow.

She gave him her hand, gloved in lemon kid. 'How do you do? I believe one is sure of meeting everyone at Hookham's, soon or late. Tell me, have you read this novel? I have just picked it at random from the shelf. I don't know who wrote it, but do, my dear cousin, read where I have quite by accident opened the volume!'

He looked over her shoulder. Her finger pointed to a line.

While he read she watched him, smiling, to see what effect the words must produce on him.

> 'I am glad of it. He seems a most gentleman-like man; and I think, Elinor, I may congratulate you on the prospect of a very respectable establishment in life.'
> 'Me, brother! What do you mean?'
> 'He likes you. I observed him narrowly, and am convinced of it. What is the amount of his fortune?'
> 'I believe about two thousand a year.'
> 'Two thousand a year?' and then working himself up to a pitch of enthusiastic generosity, he added: 'Elinor, I wish with all my heart it were twice as much for your sake.'

A laugh assured Miss Taverner that this passage had struck her cousin just as she believed it must. She said, closing the volume: 'Surely the writer of that must possess a most lively mind? I am determined to take this book. It seems all to be written about ordinary people, and, do you know, I am quite tired of Sicilians and Italian Counts who behave in such a very odd way. *Sense and Sensibility!* Well, after *Midnight Bells* and *Horrid Mysteries* that has a pleasant ring, don't you agree?'

'Undoubtedly. I think it has not yet come in my way, but if you report well of it I shall certainly bespeak it. Are you walking? May I be your escort?'

'My carriage is waiting outside. I have to call at Jones's for Mrs Scattergood. I wish you may accompany me.'

He was all compliance, and having handed her into the carriage, took his seat beside her, and said with a grave look: 'I believe my father has been to call on you this morning.'

She inclined her head. 'Yes, my uncle was with us for about an hour.'

'I can guess his errand. I am sorry for it.'

'There is no need. He considers that Perry is too young to be thinking of marriage, and in part I agree with him.'

'Perry's friends must all feel the truth of that. It is a pity. He has seen very little of the world, and at nineteen, you know, one's taste is not fixed. My father has never been a believer in early marriages. But it may yet come to nothing, I daresay.'

'I do not think it,' Judith said decidedly. 'Perry is young, but he knows his own mind, and once that is made up there is generally no changing it. I believe the attachment to be deep; it is certainly mutual. And, you know, however much I may regret an engagement entered into so soon I could not wish to see it broken.'

He assented. 'It would be very bad. We can only wish him happy. I am not acquainted with Miss Fairford. You like her?'

'She is a very amiable, good sort of girl,' responded Judith.

'I am glad. The wedding, I conclude, will not be long put off?'

'I am not perfectly sure. Lord Worth spoke of six months, but Perry hopes to be able to induce him to consent to its taking place sooner. I don't know how he will succeed.'

'I imagine Lord Worth will be more likely to find the means of postponing it.'

She turned an inquiring look upon him. He shook his head. 'We shall see, but I own myself a little worried. I don't understand Worth's consenting to this marriage. But it is possible that I misjudge him.'

The barouche drew up outside the haberdasher's, and Mrs Scattergood coming out of the shop directly Judith could not pursue the subject further. Her cousin stepped down to help Mrs Scattergood into the carriage. He declined getting in again; he had business to transact in the neighbourhood; they left him on the pavement, and drove slowly on down the street. Coming opposite to Jackson's again some little press of traffic obliged the coachman to pull his horses in to a standstill, and before they could move on two gentlemen came out of the Saloon, and stood for a moment on the pavement immediately beside the barouche. One was the Earl of Worth; the other Colonel Armstrong, a close friend of the Duke of York, with whom Miss Taverner was only slightly acquainted. Both gentlemen bowed to her; Colonel Armstrong walked away up the street, and Worth stepped forward to the barouche. 'Well, my ward?' he said. 'How do you do, cousin?'

'Do you go our way?' inquired Mrs Scattergood. 'May we take you up?'

'To the bottom of the street, if you will,' he answered, getting into the carriage.

Miss Taverner was gazing at a milliner's window on the opposite side of the road, apparently rapt in admiration of a yellow satin bonnet embossed with orange leopard-spots, and bound with a green figured ribbon, but at Mrs Scattergood's next words she turned her head and unwillingly paid attention to what was being said.

'I am excessively glad to have fallen in with you, Julian,' Mrs Scattergood declared. 'I have been wanting to ask you these three days what you were about to let Perry tie himself up in this fashion. Not that I have a word to say against Miss Fairford: I am sure she is perfectly amiable, a delightful girl! But you know he might do much better for himself. How came you to be giving your consent so readily?'

He said lazily: 'I must have been in an uncommonly good temper, I suppose. Don't you like the match?'

'It is respectable, but not brilliant, and I must say, Worth, I think Perry much too young.'

He made no reply. Miss Taverner raised her eyes to his face. 'Do you think it wise to let him be married?' she asked.

'I think he is not married yet, Miss Taverner,' replied Worth.

The carriage began to move forward. Judith said: 'Now that it has been so publicly announced it must be a settled thing.'

'Oh, by no means,' said Worth. 'A dozen things might happen to prevent it.'

'He cannot in honour turn back from an engagement.'

'True, but I might turn him back from it if I thought it proper to do so,' said the Earl.

'If you do not like the engagement why did you permit him to enter into it?' asked Miss Taverner rather sternly.

'Because I had not the smallest desire to see him persuade Miss Fairford into a runaway match,' replied Worth.

She frowned. 'I am to understand that you don't wish to see him married?'

'Not at all. Why should I?' He turned to address the coachman, desiring to be set down at the corner. The carriage turned into Piccadilly, and stopped. He got out, and stood for a moment with his hand on the door. His face softened as he looked at Miss Taverner, but he only said: 'Believe me, I have your affairs well in hand. Where do you go from here? Shall I direct your coachman?'

'Oh, we are going to look at the new bridge across the river,' said Mrs Scattergood. 'But he knows. Well, I am glad we met you, and I have no doubt there is a great deal in what you say. You are off to White's, I suppose? I am sure I do not know what you gentlemen would do if there were no clubs to spend the day in!'

He returned no answer to this observation, but merely bowed and stepped back.

'Well, my love,' said Mrs Scattergood as the carriage moved on, 'you may say what you will, but excepting only Mr Brummell, there is no one in town who dresses so well as Worth! Such an air of fashion! I believe you may see your face in his boots as well as in your mirror.'

'I have never denied Lord Worth's ability to be in the mode,' replied Miss Taverner indifferently. 'The only thing that surprises me is to see him come out of a boxing saloon.'

'Oh, my dear, I daresay he went only to accompany Colonel Armstrong,' said Mrs Scattergood excusingly.

'More than likely,' agreed Judith, with a contemptuous smile.

Peregrine, who had entered the saloon as Worth was on the point of leaving, had also been surprised. That his lordship had been indulging in sparring exercise was evident, for he was just coming out of the changing-room, and had paused in the doorway to exchange a few words with Mr Jackson. He caught sight of Peregrine at the other end of the Saloon, nodded to him, and said: 'How does that ward of mine shape, Jackson?'

Jackson glanced over his shoulder. 'Sir Peregrine Taverner, my lord? Well, he shows game; always ready to take the lead, you know, but sometimes rather glaringly abroad. Good bottom, but not enough science. Do you care to see him in a round or two?'

'God forbid!' said Worth. 'I can well imagine it. Tell me, Jackson, could you lay your hand on a promising young heavyweight who would be glad to earn a little money out of the way – not in the Ring?'

Jackson looked at him rather curiously. 'Cribb knows most of the young 'uns, my lord. Lads thankful to be fighting for a purse of five guineas – is that it?' Worth nodded. 'Any number of them to be found,' Jackson said. 'You know that, my lord. But do *you* stand in need of one?'

'It has just occurred to me that I might,' said the Earl, negligently playing with his gloves. 'I'll see Cribb.' He turned as Colonel Armstrong came out of the changing-room. 'Are you ready, Armstrong?'

'I suppose I am,' replied the Colonel, who was looking very hot. 'I'll swear you've sweated pounds off me, Jackson. I don't know how you both contrive to look so cool.'

The ex-champion smiled. 'His lordship was taking it very easily today.'

'What, fighting shy?' said the Colonel, with a twinkle.

'No, not shy; just trifling,' said Jackson. 'But you should be coming to me more regularly, Colonel. It was bellows to mend with you after three minutes of it, and I don't like those plunges of yours.'

'Trying to land you a facer, Jackson,' grinned the Colonel.

'You won't do it like that, sir,' said Jackson, shaking his head. 'If you'll excuse me, gentlemen, I'll go over and set Mr Fitzjohn to a little singlestick with one of my young men.'

'Oh ay, we're just off,' said Armstrong. 'Are you coming, Worth?'

'Yes, I'm coming,' answered the Earl. He looked at Jackson. 'Do what you can with my ward. And, Jackson, by the way – on that other matter, I feel sure I can rely on your discretion.'

'You can always be sure of that, my lord.'

The Earl nodded, and went out with his friend. Mr Jackson turned his attention to the new-comers, matched Mr Fitzjohn at singlestick with one of his instructors, and stood critically by while Peregrine, stripped to the waist, hit out at a punchball. He presently took the eager young man on in a sparring match, gave Mr Fitzjohn a turn, and dismissed them both to cool off.

'Oh, damn it, why can't I pop in a good one over your guard?' panted Mr Fitzjohn. 'I try hard enough!'

'You don't try quick enough, Mr Fitzjohn. You want to look to your footwork more. I shan't let you hit me till you deserve to.'

'What about me?' asked Peregrine, wiping the sweat out of his eyes.

'You're shaping, sir, but you must keep your head more. You rattle in too hard. Go along to the Fives Court next Tuesday for the sparring exhibition, and you'll see some very pretty boxing there.'

'I can't,' said Peregrine, draping a towel round his shoulders. 'I'm going to the Cock-Pit. The Gentlemen of Yorkshire against the Gentlemen of Kent, for a thousand guineas a side, and forty guineas each battle. You should come, Jackson. I'm fighting a Wednesbury grey – never been beaten!'

'Give me a red pyle!' said Mr Fitzjohn. 'I don't fancy any of your greys, or blues, or blacks. Red's the only colour for your true game-cock.'

'Why, good God, Fitz, that's the greatest piece of nonsense ever I heard! There's nothing to touch a Wednesbury grey!'

'Except a red pyle,' said Mr Fitzjohn obstinately.

'There are good cocks of all colours,' interposed Jackson. 'I hope yours wins his fight, Mr Peregrine. I'd come, but I've promised to help Mr Jones with the arrangements at the Fives Court.'

The two young men went off to the changing-room together, and forgot their difference of opinion in splashing water over themselves, and being rubbed down by the attendant. But as Peregrine put on his shirt again he recollected the argument sufficiently to invite Mr Fitzjohn to come to the Cock-Pit Royal on Tuesday and see the match. Mr Fitzjohn agreed to it very readily, and was only sorry that from the circumstances of his being Sussex-born he could not enter his own red pyle for a battle with Peregrine's grey. 'What's his weight?' he asked. 'Mine turns the scale of four pounds exactly.'

'Mine's just over,' replied Peregrine. 'Three years old, and the sharpest heel you ever saw. My cocker has had him preparing these six weeks. He's resting him now.' He bethought him of something. 'By the by, Fitz, if you should chance to meet my sister you need not mention it to her. She don't above half like cocking, and I haven't told her I've had my bird brought down from Yorkshire.'

'Lord, I don't talk about cocking to females, Perry!' said Mr Fitzjohn scornfully. 'I'll be there on Tuesday. What's the main?'

'Sixteen.'

'Bad number. Don't like an even set,' said Mr Fitzjohn, shaking his head. 'Half-past five, I suppose? I'll meet you there.'

He was not a young gentleman who made a habit of punctuality, but his watch being, unknown to himself, twenty minutes ahead of the correct time, he arrived at the Cock-Pit Royal, in

Birdcage Walk, on Tuesday evening just as the cocks were being weighed and matched. He joined Peregrine, and saw the grey taken out of his bag, and looked him over very knowingly. He admitted that he was of strong shape; closely inspected his girth; approved the beam of his leg; and wanted to know whose cock he was matched with.

'Farnaby's brass-back. It was Farnaby who suggested I might enter my bird, but he'll make that brass-back look like a dung-hill cock, eh, Flood?'

The cocker put the grey back into his bag, and looked dubious. 'I don't know as I'd say just that, sir,' he answered. 'He's in good trim, never better, but we'll see.'

'Don't think much of your bag,' remarked Mr Fitzjohn, who liked bright colours.

The cocker gave a slow smile. '"There'll come a good cock out of a ragged bag," sir,' he quoted. 'But we'll see.'

The two young men nodded wisely at the saw, and moved away to take up their places on the first tier of benches. Here they were joined by Mr Farnaby, who squeezed his way to them, and after a slight altercation prevailed on a middle-aged gentleman in a drab coat to make room for him to sit down beside Peregrine. Behind them the benches were being rapidly filled, and higher still the outer ring of standing room was tightly packed with the rougher members of the crowd. In the centre of the pit was the stage, on which no one but the setters-on was allowed. This was built up a few feet from the ground, covered with a carpet with a mark in the middle, and lit by a huge chandelier hanging immediately above it.

The first fight, which was between two red cocks, only lasted for nine minutes; the second was between a black-grey and a red pyle, and there was some hard hitting in the pit, and a great deal of noisy betting amongst the spectators. During this and the next fight, which was between a duck-winged grey and a red pyle, Peregrine and Mr Fitzjohn grew much excited, Mr Fitzjohn betting heavily on the red's chances, extolling his tactics, and condemning the grey for ogling his opponent too long. Peregrine in honour bound backed the grey to win, and informed Mr Fitzjohn that crowing was not fighting, and nor was breaking away.

'Breaking away! You've never seen a red pyle break away!' said Mr Fitzjohn indignantly. 'There! Look at him! He's fast in the grey; they'll have to draw his spurs out.'

The fight lasted for fifteen minutes, both birds being badly mauled; but in the end the red sent the grey to grass, dead, and Mr Fitzjohn shook a complete stranger warmly by the hand, and said that there was nothing to beat a red pyle.

'Good birds, I don't deny, but I'll back my brass-back against any that was ever hatched,' said Mr Farnaby, overhearing. 'You'll see him floor Mr Taverner's grey, or my name's not Ned Farnaby.'

'Well, you'd better be thinking of a new one then, for our fight's coming on now,' retorted Peregrine.

'Pooh, your bird don't stand a chance!' scoffed Farnaby.

The setters-on had the cocks in the arena by this time, and Mr Fitzjohn, critically looking them over, declared there to be very little to choose between them. They were well matched; their heads a full scarlet; tails, manes, and wings nicely clipped; and spurs very long and sharp, hooking well inwards. 'If anything I like Taverner's bird the better of the two,' pronounced Mr Fitzjohn. 'He looks devilish upright, and I fancy he's the largest in girth. But there ain't much in it.'

The birds did not ogle each other for long; they closed almost at once, and there was some slashing work which made the feathers fly. The brass-back was floored, but came up again, and toed the scratch. Both birds knew how to hold, and their tactics were cunning enough to rouse the enthusiasm of the crowd. The betting was slightly in favour of the grey, which very much delighted Peregrine, and made Mr Fitzjohn shake his head, and say that saving his own red pyle he did not know when he had seen a cock he liked better. Mr Farnaby did not say anything, but looked at Peregrine sideways once or twice and thrust out his under-lip.

The cocks had been fighting for about ten minutes when the brass-back, who had till now adopted more defensive tactics than the grey, suddenly rushed in, striking and slashing in famous style. The grey responded gallantly, and Mr Fitzjohn cried out: 'The best matched pair I ever saw! There they go, slap for slap! I'll lay you any odds the grey wins! No, by God, he's down! Ha, spurs fast again!'

The setters-on having secured their birds, and the brass-back's spurs being released, both were again freed. The grey seemed to be a little dazed, the brass-back hardly less so. Both were bleeding from wounds, and neither seemed anxious to close again with his opponent. They stayed warily apart, ogling each other while the timekeeper kept the count, and fifty being reached before either showed any disposition to continue fighting, setting was allowed. The setters-on each took up his bird and brought him to the centre of the arena, and placed him beak to beak with the other. The grey was the first to strike, a swift, punishing blow that knocked the brass-back clean away.

A sudden commotion arose amongst the spectators. Mr Farnaby sprang up, shouting: 'A foul! A foul! The grey was squeezed!'

Someone called out: 'Nonsense! No such thing! Sit down!'

Peregrine swung round to stare at Farnaby. 'He was not squeezed! I was watching the whole time, and I'm ready to swear my man did no more than set him!'

The setters-on, pending the referee's decision, had each caught his bird, a lucky circumstance for the brass-back, who seemed to have been badly cut up by the last blow. The referee gave it in favour of the grey, and Mr Fitzjohn said testily: 'Of course the grey was not squeezed! Sit down, man, sit down! Hey, no wonder your cock's shy! I believe the grey got his eye in that last brush. Perry, that's a rare bird of yours! We'll match him with mine one day, down at my place. Ha, that finishes it! The brass-back's a blinker now – or dead. Dead, I think. Well done, Perry! Well done!'

Mr Farnaby turned with an ugly look on his face. 'Ay, well done indeed! Your cock was craven, and was squeezed to make him fight.'

'Here, I say, Farnaby, learn to take your losses!' said Mr Fitzjohn with strong disapproval.

Peregrine, a gathering frown on his boyish countenance, lifted a hand to hush his friend, and fixed his eyes on Farnaby's. 'You can't know what you're saying. If there was a fault the referee must have seen it.'

'Oh,' said Farnaby, with a sneer, 'when rich men fight their cocks referees can sometimes make mistakes.'

It was not said loud enough to carry very far, but it brought Peregrine to his feet in a bound. 'What!' he cried furiously. 'Say that again if you dare!'

Though no one but those immediately beside Farnaby could have heard his words, it was quite apparent to everyone by this time than an altercation was going on, and the rougher part of the gathering at once began to take sides, some (who had lost their money on the brass-back) loudly asserting that the grey had been squeezed, and others declaring with equal fervour that it had been a fair fight. Above the hubbub a shrill Cockney voice besought Peregrine to darken Mr Farnaby's daylights – advice of which he did not seem to stand in much need, for he was clenching his fists very menacingly already.

Mr Fitzjohn, who had also heard Farnaby's last speech, tried to get between him and Peregrine, saying in a brisk voice:

'That's enough of this foolery. You're foxed, Farnaby. Ought to be ashamed of yourself.'

'Oh, I'm foxed, am I?' said Farnaby, keeping his eyes on Peregrine's. 'I'm not so foxed but what I can see when a bird's pressed to make him fight, and I repeat, Sir Peregrine Taverner, that money can do queer things if you have enough of it.'

'Oh, damn!' said Mr Fitzjohn, exasperated. 'Pay no heed to him, Perry.'

Peregrine, however, had not waited for this advice. As Mr Fitzjohn spoke he drove his left in a smashing blow to Farnaby's face, and sent that gentleman sprawling over the bench. There were a great many cheers, a shout of 'A mill, a mill!' some protests from the quieter members of the audience; and the man in the drab coat, across whose knees Mr Farnaby had fallen, demanded that the Watch should be summoned.

Mr Farnaby picked himself up, and showed the house a bleeding nose. The same voice which had counselled Peregrine to strike shouted gleefully: 'Drawn his cork! Fib him, guv'nor! Let him have a bit of home-brewed!'

Mr Farnaby held his handkerchief to his nose and said: 'My friend will call on yours in the morning, sir! Be good enough to name your man!'

'Fitz?' said Peregrine curtly, over his shoulder.

'At your service,' replied Mr Fitzjohn.

'Mr Fitzjohn will act for me, sir,' said Peregrine, pale but perfectly determined.

'You will hear from me, sir,' promised Farnaby thickly, and strode out, still holding his reddened handkerchief to his nose.

Ten

$\mathscr{M}$R FITZJOHN, BREAKFASTING IN HIS LODGINGS IN CORK Street next morning, wore an unusually sober expression on his face, and when his man came in to inform him that a gentleman had called he got up from the table with a sigh and a shake of his head.

The gentleman's card, which Mr Fitzjohn held between his finger and thumb, told him very little. The name was unknown to him, and the address, which was a street in the labyrinth lying between Northumberland House and St James's Square, did not impress him favourably.

Captain Crake was ushered into the room, and Mr Fitzjohn, with a shrewdness belied by his cherubic countenance, instantly decided that his military rank was self-bestowed. He was displeased. He had been brought up by a careful father with a nice regard for etiquette, and one glance at Captain Crake was sufficient to convince him that he was not one whom any gentleman would desire to have for a second in an affair of honour. The first duty of a second was to seek a reconciliation; it was evident that Captain Crake had no such thought in mind. He came only to arrange a place and a time of meeting, and to choose on behalf of his principal pistols for weapons.

To this Mr Fitzjohn agreed, but when the Captain, assuming Mr Farnaby to have been the injured party, stipulated for a range of twenty-five yards he unhesitatingly refused to consent to it. Such a range must be all in favour of the more experienced duellist, and however many wafers Peregrine might be able to culp at Manton's Gallery, Mr Fitzjohn felt reasonably certain that he had not before been engaged in an actual duel.

He would not consent, and upon the Captain's attempting to take a high hand with him, said bluntly that he could by no means agree that Mr Farnaby was the injured party. Sir Peregrine had indeed struck the blow, but the provocation had been strong.

After some argument the Captain gave way on this point, and a range of twelve yards was agreed to. There could be no further hope of reconciliation. Mr Fitzjohn, well versed in the Code of Honour, was aware that no apology could be extended or received after a blow, and Captain Crake's attitude now convinced him that, however much Mr Farnaby might know himself to have been in the wrong, no dependence could be placed on his tacitly acknowledging it on the ground by *deloping*, or firing into the air.

When Captain Crake had been shown out of the room Mr Fitzjohn did not immediately resume his interrupted meal, but stood instead staring gloomily into the fire. Though not particularly acquainted with Mr Farnaby, he knew him a little by repute. The man was a hanger-on to the fringes of society, and was generally to be seen in the company of raw young men of fortune. His reputation was not good. Nothing was precisely known against him, but he had been mixed up in more than one discreditable affair, and was known to be a crack shot. Mr Fitzjohn did not anticipate a fatal outcome to the following day's meeting: the consequences would be too serious, he thought; but he was not perfectly at his ease. Farnaby had not been drunk, nor had there been the least sign of foul play in the Cock-Pit. It looked suspiciously as though this quarrel had been thrust on Peregrine. Yet he could find no object in it, and was forced to conclude that he was indulging a mere flight of fancy. As soon as he had finished his breakfast he picked up his hat and gloves and set out to walk the short distance to Brook Street. Arriving at the Taverners' house he sent in his name and was taken immediately upstairs to Peregrine's bedroom.

Peregrine was still engaged in the arduous task of dressing, and was anxiously arranging his cravat when Mr Fitzjohn came in. He said cheerfully: 'Sit down, Fitz, and don't move, don't speak till I've done with this neck-cloth!'

Mr Fitzjohn obeyed, choosing a chair from which he could observe his friend's struggles. Having guessed that the next morning's meeting would be Peregrine's first, he was very well satisfied with his careless unconcern. It was evident that he would have nothing to blush for in his principal; the lad was game as a pebble. He was not to know with what desperate courage Peregrine had forced himself to utter his cheerful greeting, nor how many sleepless hours he had spent during the night.

The cravat being at last adjusted Peregrine dismissed his valet, and turned. 'Well, have you arranged it all, Fitz?' he asked.

'To-morrow at eight, Westbourn Green,' said Mr Fitzjohn briefly. 'I'll call for you.'

Peregrine had the oddest sensation that none of this was really happening. He heard his own voice, surprisingly steady, say: 'Westbourn Green? Is that near Paddington?'

Mr Fitzjohn nodded. 'Are you a good shot, Perry? The fellow's chosen pistols.'

'You have seen me at Manton's — or have you not?'

'I haven't seen you at Manton's, but I've seen Farnaby,' said Mr Fitzjohn rather grimly. 'You'll keep a cool head, won't you, Perry, and remember it's everything to be quick off the mark?'

There was an unpleasant dryness in Peregrine's mouth, but he said with a good attempt at nonchalance: 'Of course. I shan't aim to kill him, however.'

'No, don't,' agreed Mr Fitzjohn. 'Not that I think he means to make it a killing matter either. I can't see why he should. He'd have to make a bolt for it if he did, and I fancy that wouldn't suit him. What are you doing to-day?'

Peregrine achieved a shrug of the shoulders. 'Oh, the usual round, my dear fellow! I am engaged to dine at the Star, I believe. I daresay we shall look in at the play, and sup at the Piazza afterwards.'

'You'll do,' said Mr Fitzjohn approvingly. 'But see it ain't a boozy party, and don't sit up too late. I'm off to engage a surgeon now. I daresay we shan't need him, but he'll have to be there. I like that waistcoat you have on.'

'Yes, I flatter myself it's uncommonly handsome,' replied Peregrine. He moistened his lips. 'Fitz, I have suddenly remembered – do you know, I believe I have no duelling pistols by me?'

'Leave that to me, I'll see to it,' said Mr Fitzjohn, getting up. 'I'm going now. I'll call for you at a quarter-past seven to-morrow.'

Peregrine smiled jauntily. 'I shall be ready. Don't oversleep!'

'Never fear!' said Mr Fitzjohn.

He let himself out of Peregrine's bedroom and descended the stairs to the hall. Here he rather unfortunately met Miss Taverner, who was dressed for the street, and had just come out of the breakfast-parlour.

She looked a little surprised to see him so early in the morning, and glanced laughingly at the clock. 'How do you do? Forgive me, but I did not think you were ever abroad until midday! As for Perry, he is a sad case: did you find him in his bed?'

'No, no, he is up,' Mr Fitzjohn assured her. 'I had a little business with him; nothing of importance, you know, but I thought I might call.'

Miss Taverner, who was holding a very pretty buhl snuff-box in her left hand, flicked it open, and took a pinch with an elegant turn of her wrist. 'I think it must have been important to bring you out before noon,' she said.

Mr Fitzjohn, watching her manoeuvres with the snuff-box in a good deal of astonishment, said: 'Oh no, just a trifling question of a horse he had a mind to purchase. But Miss Taverner – don't be offended – in the general way I don't like to see a lady take snuff, but upon my word, you do it with such an air! It passes everything!'

Miss Taverner, who had spent a week in practising the art, was more than satisfied with the effect it had produced on her first audience.

Mrs Scattergood appearing at that moment at the head of the stairs, Mr Fitzjohn took his leave, and went out of the house into the street. He paused for a moment on the steps, considering which surgeon he should engage, shook his head at a couple of chairmen who were signalling their readiness to carry him anywhere he pleased, and after staring abstractedly at a shabbily dressed lad who was lounging against the railings of an adjacent house, set off in the direction of Great Ormond Street.

Arrived there, he ran up the steps of Dr Lane's establishment, knocked loudly on the door, and was soon admitted. He came out again presently with all the satisfied air of one who has successfully accomplished his task, called up a hackney, and drove back to Cork Street.

Half an hour later a tilbury drove up Great Ormond Street, and stopped outside Dr Lane's house. A second gentleman knocked on the doctor's door, and was admitted. His visit lasted a little longer than Mr Fitzjohn's, but when he at length emerged he, too, wore the look of one perfectly satisfied with the success of his mission.

Meanwhile Peregrine, when Mr Fitzjohn had left him, finished his toilet with less than his usual care, and tried not to think too much about the morrow. His thoughts, however, showed a disposition to creep back to it, and he found himself recalling all the fatal duels of which he had heard. Happily none of these was very recent. The only recent duels he could call to mind were the Duke of York's meeting with Colonel Lennox (which had taken place three years before his own birth), and Lord Castlereagh's late affair with Mr Canning. Neither of these meetings had proved fatal, but Peregrine could not but acknowledge that there might have been a score of others between lesser persons of which he had never heard. An exchange of shots between himself and Farnaby would, in all probability, end the quarrel, but the possibility of a more serious outcome had to be faced. With a sigh and a heavy heart Peregrine went down to the saloon to compose a letter to his sister.

He was engaged on this difficult task when Mr Bernard Taverner was shown into the room.

Peregrine looked up with a start, and quickly concealed his letter under a blank sheet of paper. 'Oh, it's you, is it? Good morning; did you come to see me or Judith? She's out, shopping with Maria, you know.'

Mr Taverner scrutinised him rather closely for a moment. He said, coming further into the room: 'Then I am unfortunate. She mentioned the other day that she had an ambition to see Madame Tussaud's Waxworks, and I came to propose escorting her. But another morning will do as well. I am not interrupting you, I trust? You were busy, I think, when I came in.'

'Oh, not in the least; it is of no particular moment,' said Peregrine, stretching out his hand to pull the bell. 'You'll take a glass of wine, won't you?'

'Thank you, a little sherry, if I may.'

The servant came, the order was given, and Peregrine begged his cousin to be seated. Mr Taverner began to talk on a number of idle topics. Peregrine's replies were delivered in a mechanical way; it was plain that his thoughts were elsewhere. When the wine had been brought, and the servant had gone away again, Mr Taverner said in his quiet voice: 'Forgive me, Perry, but has anything happened to put you out?'

Peregrine disclaimed at once, and tried to start some other topic for conversation. His cousin's eyes were upon him, however, and he presently gave up the attempt to appear at his ease, and said with a jerky little laugh: 'I see you have guessed it; my mind is occupied with another matter. I have certain dispositions to make. Well, you are a good fellow, Bernard: I can trust you. The fact is I am engaged to meet Farnaby to-morrow morning at – well, it's no matter where.'

Mr Taverner put down his wine-glass. 'Am I to understand an affair of honour? You cannot mean that!'

Peregrine shrugged. 'There was no avoiding it. The fellow insulted me, I landed him a facer, and received his challenge.'

'I am sorry for it,' Mr Taverner said, with a grave look.

'Oh, as to that I do not anticipate any very serious consequences,' said Peregrine. 'But it is well to be prepared, you know. I was writing a letter to Judith, and another to – to Miss Fairford when you came in, in case I should be fatally injured.'

'I take it it is impossible for you to draw back?'

'Quite impossible,' said Peregrine decidedly. 'I need not engage your silence, I am sure. You will understand that I don't want the affair to come to my sister's or to Miss Fairford's ears.'

Mr Taverner bowed. 'Certainly. You may trust me in that. Who acts for you?'

'Fitzjohn.' Peregrine fidgeted with his fob. 'Bernard, if anything should happen to me – if I should not return, in short – you will keep your eye upon Judith, won't you? She is in Worth's hands, of course, but she don't like him, and you are our cousin, and will see she don't come to harm.'

'Yes,' said Mr Taverner rather curtly. He got up. 'I'll leave you now; you have your affairs to settle. Believe me, I am sorry for this.'

Peregrine spent the rest of the day very sensibly. He went to Jackson's Saloon, and forgot his troubles in sparring; and from there drove to Albemarle Street to solicit permission to take Miss Fairford in the Park in his tilbury. Dinner at Richardson's Hotel, a visit to Drury Lane, and supper at the Piazza Coffee House ended the day, and he returned soon after midnight to Brook Street too weary to be kept long awake by his thoughts.

His valet, who had of necessity been taken into his confidence, drew back the bed-curtains at six o'clock next morning and began to get the shaving tackle ready, while Peregrine, with his night-cap over one eye, sat up and sipped a cup of hot chocolate. One of the chambermaids brought in a faggot, and kindled a fire in the empty grate. It was a raw morning, and the fact of being obliged to dress by candle-light was curiously depressing. When the chambermaid had gone Peregrine got out of bed, put on his dressing-gown, and sat down before the mirror to be shaved. His valet, whom he had brought with him from Yorkshire, was looking very gloomy, and when Peregrine made a careful choice amongst his many suits of clothes he heaved a gusty sigh, and seemed to think such particularity frivolous. But Peregrine, wondering in his heart whether this might be the last choice he would make, was determined not to let it appear that he had not cared to bestow all his usual attention on his appearance. He put on a pair of buff pantaloons and a light waistcoat, arranged his cravat with great nicety, struggled into a blue coat with silver buttons, and pulled on a pair of Hessians with swinging tassels. 'My new hat, John, and I will wear the large driving-coat with the Belcher handkerchief.'

'Oh, sir!' groaned the valet, 'I never thought to live to see this day!'

Peregrine's underlip trembled slightly, but a gleam entered his eyes, and he said with the quiver of a laugh: 'You! Why, it is I who might rather be wondering whether I shall live to see very much of this day!'

'If only we had never come to London!' said the valet.

'Tush!' said Peregrine, who found no comfort in this conversation. 'What's o'clock? Past seven, is it? Very well, help me into this coat, and I'll be off. You can snuff the candles now; it is growing quite light. You have those letters I gave you?'

'I have them in my pocket now, sir, but please God I won't be called on to do more than burn them!'

'Why, certainly,' said Peregrine, picking up his hat and gloves. He stretched out his right hand, and watched it closely. It was steady enough. That cheered him a little. He went softly out of the room and down the stairs, followed by the valet, who carried a branch of candles to light the darkened stairway, and drew back the bolts of the front door.

A neat town-coach was drawn up outside the house, and Mr Fitzjohn was standing on the pavement, muffled in a greatcoat and consulting his watch.

'Good-bye, John,' said Peregrine. 'And if I don't see you again – well, good-bye, and don't forget the letters. I'm not late, Fitz, am I?'

'Bang up to the mark,' Mr Fitzjohn assured him. He ran an eye over Peregrine's person, and seemed satisfied. 'Get in, Perry. Did you sleep well?'

'Sleep! Lord, yes! Never stirred till my man roused me this morning!' replied Peregrine, taking his place in the coach.

'Damme, you might be an old hand!' remarked Mr Fitzjohn approvingly. 'Is this your first meeting, or have you been out before?'

'Well, no, as a matter of fact, it is my first,' confessed Peregrine. 'But not, I hope, my last.'

'No fear of that,' said Mr Fitzjohn, rather too heartily. He began to prod the opposite seat with the tip of his walking-cane. 'You don't want to kill him, and I can't for the life of me see why he should want to kill you. At the same time, Perry, it don't do to take chances, and you'll fire the moment the word's given, do you see? You've shot at Manton's, haven't you? Well, you know how to come up quick on to the mark, and all you have to do is to fancy yourself at the Gallery, firing at a wafer. There's no difference.'

Peregrine withdrew his gaze from the passing houses and gave his friend a long clear look. 'Is there no difference?' he asked.

Mr Fitzjohn met his eyes for a moment, and then studied the head of his cane. 'Yes, there is a difference,' he said. 'But my father once told me that the secret of a good duellist is to imagine that there is none.'

Peregrine nodded and picked up the flat case that lay on the seat opposite and opened it. A pair of plain duelling pistols lay in it.

'You can handle 'em; they're not loaded,' said Mr Fitzjohn.

Peregrine lifted one from its bed, weighed it in his hand, and tested the pull. Then he laid it down again and shut the case. 'Nicely balanced,' he remarked.

'Yes, they're a first-rate pair,' agreed Mr Fitzjohn. 'Hair trigger, of course. It'll go off at a touch.'

The coach stopped in Great Ormond Street to pick up the doctor, who came out of his house almost as soon as the horses pulled up, and jumped nimbly into the coach. He had a black case under his arm, which Peregrine knew must contain the instruments of his profession. Oddly enough, the sight of it affected him more unpleasantly than the case of pistols had done.

'You are in good time, gentlemen,' said the doctor, rubbing his hands together. 'It is a cold morning, is it not?'

'Cold enough,' said Mr Fitzjohn. 'But it won't be long before we are all of us drinking hot coffee in a place I know of hard by the Green.'

'Myself, I never touch coffee,' said the doctor. 'I hold it to be injurious to the stomach. Cocoa, now – there is no harm in a cup of cocoa; I have even known it to prove in some cases extremely beneficial.'

Interested in his subject, and possibly with some notion of diverting Peregrine's mind from the coming duel, he went on to discuss the effects of wine and tea on the human system, and was still talking when the coach arrived at the hamlet of Westbourn Green.

The meeting-place was at no great distance from the road; the coach was able to drive within sight of it over a field.

'First on the ground,' said Mr Fitzjohn, jumping down. 'But we shan't have long to wait, for it's close on eight now. Unless, of course, our man has thought better of it. Perry, if there's any offer of apology I shall accept it.'

'Very well,' said Peregrine, who was finding it increasingly difficult to talk.

He got down from the coach and walked beside his friend to the ground. The day, though dull, was by this time quite light. A sharp wind was blowing, and some scudding clouds overhead gave warning of rain to come. Peregrine thrust his hands into his pockets to keep them warm, and glanced up at the sky. He had rather an uncomfortable sensation in the pit of his stomach, but apart from that he felt curiously detached.

Hardly five minutes after their arrival another conveyance, this time a travelling chaise, drove into the field, and Mr Farnaby and Captain Crake got out.

Mr Fitzjohn, observing the chaise, was conscious once more of that faint feeling of unease. Unless he was much mistaken there was a box strapped to the back of the chaise, and although the vehicle was only drawn by a pair of horses with one postilion, it had all the appearance of being about to make a journey of some distance. His lips tightened; he began to suspect Mr Farnaby of having a sterner purpose than he had supposed possible, and determined, in the event of Peregrine's receiving a mortal wound, to put every obstacle in the way of his opponent's flight.

Both the new-comers were stamping their feet on the ground and slapping their hands on their arms, but Captain Crake soon came across the field to where Mr Fitzjohn awaited him, and after the briefest of greetings the pair set about the task of inspecting and loading the pistols. No second shot was to be allowed, so that only Mr Fitzjohn's pistols (a very fine pair of Manton's, ten inches in length in the barrels, and with steel sights) were loaded.

This done, Mr Fitzjohn rejoined Peregrine, and said in a low voice: 'Twelve paces. You can't miss, Perry. Let him have it!'

'Yes, if I can I will,' answered Peregrine, beginning to unbutton his greatcoat. 'Do you advise fighting in this coat or without it?'

'Without it,' said Mr Fitzjohn, grimly surveying the very large mother-of-pearl buttons with which the coat was adorned. 'I should have warned you to wear a black coat. Close it up to the throat, and remember not to stand square to the fellow, but give your side only, and keep your arm well in to it. And don't lower it until Farnaby's shot, Perry! Here comes the fellow now. You must salute him, of course, but I need not tell you that.' He waited until this formality had been gone through, and then said: 'Listen to me, Perry! Make up your mind where you mean to hit him, and don't trouble your head with wondering where he means to hit you! Take your aim when I say "All's ready," keep your eye on the handkerchief, and when I let it drop, shoot! If you kill him I'll get you away somehow.'

'It sounds mighty desperate,' said Peregrine, forcing his pale lips into a smile. 'You're a curst good friend, Fitz. Thank you, and – oh, well, just thank you!'

Mr Fitzjohn gripped his shoulder. 'Breakfast in my lodgings afterwards,' he said, and walked off to measure the paces with Captain Crake.

Peregrine buttoned up his coat to the throat, observing as he did so that Mr Farnaby, who was wearing black, had done the same. Mr Farnaby, after his salute, had not looked at him again. He seemed to be impatient, and kept calling to his second to make haste, and not keep them all standing in the cold. When called upon to leech he came at once to the spot, took the pistol Mr Fitzjohn handed him at half-cock, and stood with the muzzle pointed to the ground.

Peregrine was given the second pistol, and realised that the palms of his hands were sweating slightly. He wiped them on his pantaloons, took the pistol carefully (for the slightest touch would make a duelling pistol go off when set at half-cock, as he very well knew), and put himself into position.

The doctor turned his back, and the seconds retreated to a distance of eight paces. Peregrine was conscious of a sharp wind, ruffling his yellow locks; he fixed his eyes on Farnaby, trying to decide on some object on his dress to choose as his mark.

Mr Fitzjohn was holding up a handkerchief; it fluttered in the wind, a splash of white against a background of grey.

Then, before the word could be given, an interruption took place. A third coach, this time a heavy, lumbering affair, had driven up, and several men now jumped down from it, and came running towards the duellists, shouting: 'In the name of the Law! Hold!'

Peregrine jerked his head round, heard a stifled oath from Farnaby, and the next minute was in the grip of a burly officer. 'I arrest you the name of the Law!' puffed this individual. 'Attempt to break the peace! I shall have to take you before a magistrate.'

Mr Fitzjohn, who admitted afterwards that he had never been so glad to see a constable before, heaved one long sigh of relief, and said: 'Oh, very well! Nothing for it, Perry; you had better put your coat on again.'

Mr Farnaby, in the grip of a second constable, showed a disposition to resist. 'Who set you on?' he demanded.

'Acting on information received,' was the curt reply. 'Now give me that pistol, sir! It ain't no use resisting.'

An unwelcome suspicion crossed Peregrine's mind. He said quickly: 'Do you know who lodged the information?'

'No, nor it ain't my business,' answered the constable. 'You put on your coat, sir, and come with us.'

Mr Fitzjohn went to lend Peregrine a hand. 'Do you suspect someone?' he asked in an under-voice.

'By God I do, and I mean to know the truth!'

'Who knew of it?'

'My cousin,' said Peregrine. 'But I did not tell him the place of rendezvous – of that I am perfectly certain! How he found that out, if it was he –'

'But, Perry, surely he wouldn't inform the magistrates if you told him in confidence, which I suppose you must have?'

'I don't know, but I shall find out!' said Peregrine, buttoning up his greatcoat.

Mr Fitzjohn turned with sudden suspicion to the doctor, who was standing beside them. 'I take it you know nothing of this, Lane?'

The doctor replied in a dry tone: 'I did not lay information against your principal, sir, but I am forced to admit that it may be through me that this duel has been interrupted. If it was so I cannot regret it, though I certainly did not intend it.'

'What the devil do you mean?' said Mr Fitzjohn.

The doctor tucked his case of instruments under his arm. 'Yesterday, sir,' he said, 'not long after you called on me, I received a visit from another gentleman requiring my services in an affair of honour to-day. I told him that it was quite out of my power, since I was already engaged. He gave me to understand that he was acting as second to your opponent – a fact I could readily believe, as it would be an odd, almost an unprecedented occurrence, for two duels to be fought in London upon the same day. I informed this gentleman that I could not disclose the name of my principal, though I should have no objection to attending his man as well if he should prove to be the unknown adversary. He realised the propriety of my scruples, and at once made it plain to me that he was conversant with your affair by giving me the names of yourself and Sir Peregrine Taverner. I said that I should be happy to do what I could for his principal, and, as I recollect, we fell into some slight conversation, during the course of which I might easily mention the place of rendezvous. When your opponent came on to the ground, sir, and I perceived his friend to be totally unlike my visitor, I own I felt surprise. But upon reflection I could not recollect that my visitor actually stated that he was acting as a second in the affair, and I concluded that I had misunderstood him, and that he had come to me in place of the second.'

'What was he like?' demanded Peregrine, who had listened to this speech with considerable impatience. 'Was he tall, rather dark, and elegantly dressed?'

'Yes,' said the doctor. 'Certainly he was tall. I should describe him as very dark. He was a gentleman-like man, quiet in his manner, and with a pronounced air of fashion.'

'I knew it!' said Peregrine. 'My cousin to the life!'

At this point one of the constables came up to request their following him to the coach. They could only obey, and in a few minutes the whole party was being driven off to the nearest magistrate.

It was fully an hour before the principals were at liberty to go their several ways. Both were bound over to keep the peace, a great many formalities were gone through, sureties were paid, the magistrate read them a lecture, and Mr Fitzjohn longed for his breakfast. At last they were set free. Mr Farnaby and his second, both wearing the blackest of scowls, drove away in their chaise, and Peregrine and Mr Fitzjohn went off to Cork Street, the doctor having gone away in a hackney some time previously.

Eleven

*T*HE SECRET OF THE DUEL WAS SOON OUT. PEREGRINE ARRIVED in Brook Street shortly after eleven o'clock to find his valet, who had given him up for lost an hour before, standing over Miss Taverner while she read her brother's farewell letter.

'O God!' burst from Miss Taverner's lips just as Peregrine walked into the room. The sheets of the letter fluttered to the ground. Miss Taverner sprang up crying: 'I must go at once! What have they done to him? Where is Fitzjohn?' Then she caught sight of Peregrine in the doorway, and the next instant was in his arms. 'Perry! Oh, Perry, my darling, you are safe!'

'Yes, yes, of course I am safe,' said Peregrine, clumsily patting her shoulder. 'What the devil do you mean by making all this stir, John? You fool, did I not charge you to wait until you heard from Mr Fitzjohn?'

His sister grasped the lapels of his coat. 'Tell me at once, Peregrine, what has happened?'

'Nothing has happened. I can tell you, I am in a pretty rage, Ju! A rare fool I am made to look! We are informed against, and I have a strong notion who laid the information!'

'Whoever he is he has earned my undying gratitude!' declared Judith, still shaken from the fright she had had. 'How could you go out to fight without a word to me? Oh, how I hate the practice of duelling! How I despise all you men for thinking it a way to settle a quarrel.'

'Stuff!' said Peregrine, disengaging himself from her clasp. 'As for you, John, be off to your work! You've meddled enough for one day! If I had dreamed the fellow was not to be trusted – but I might have known! I had no business to be taken in by him. My father warned us against his, and you may depend upon it the son is no better.'

'Do you speak of my cousin? Is it possible that it was he who saved you from this terrible affair?'

'Lord, Ju, don't talk in that silly way! You don't understand these things. Ay, it was our cousin; I am persuaded it was he. I am off to settle with him on the instant.'

She detained him. 'You need not; I expect him here at any minute. He is to take Mrs Scattergood and me to Madame Tussaud's Exhibition. Indeed, I do not know what should be keeping him, for he said he would be here quite by eleven, and you see it is past eleven now.'

'That's cool, upon my word!' exclaimed Peregrine. 'He has the impudence to get me had up before a beak, and takes my sister out on the top of it! A very pretty fellow is this Bernard Taverner!'

'Do I hear my name?' The voice, a quiet one, came from the doorway behind Peregrine. 'Ah, Peregrine! Thank God!'

Peregrine swung round to confront his cousin. 'Ay, you are surprised to see me, are you not?'

'I am glad,' Mr Taverner replied steadily. 'You imposed silence upon me; it has been hard for me to stand by. But I guessed I must hear certain tidings of you by this time. You have taken no hurt?'

'Silence!' ejaculated Peregrine. 'Will you tell me you have kept silence over this?'

His cousin looked at him intently, and from him to Judith. She had sunk down on the sofa, and could only smile at him rather tremulously. 'Will you tell me what you mean me to understand by that?' he asked in an even tone.

'Who was the man who laid the information against us, and had us arrested on the ground?' Peregrine flung at him.

Mr Taverner continued to look at him, his brows a little knit. Peregrine said angrily: 'Who was the man who induced the surgeon to disclose the place of rendezvous? Who else knew of the meeting but you?'

'I cannot answer that question, Perry. I have no means of telling who else knew of it,' responded Mr Taverner.

'Give me a plain yes or no!' snapped Peregrine. 'Did you lay that information?'

Mr Taverner said slowly: 'I can understand and pardon your indignation, but consider a moment, if you please! You engaged my silence: do you accuse me of breaking faith with you?'

The niceties of the male code of honour being beyond Miss Taverner's sympathy she cried impatiently: 'What could that signify in face of such danger to Perry? What other course could be open to any friend of his than at all costs to stop the meeting?'

Mr Taverner smiled, but shook his head. Peregrine, a little confounded, stammered: 'I don't wish to be doing you an injustice, but you do not answer me! Only one other person knew of the meeting – my valet, and he does not fit the description Dr Lane gave.'

'And what, may I ask, was that description?'

'It was of a tall, gentleman-like man, dark, and with an air of fashion!'

Mr Taverner looked rather amused. 'My dear Perry, am I the only man in town answering to that description? Is that all that you base your suspicions on? Have you not considered that your opponent may very likely have spoken of the meeting as well as you?'

'Farnaby?' Peregrine was disconcerted. 'No, it had not occurred – that is to say, I do not think it probable –'

'Why, what is this? Is it more probable, then, that I laid the information?'

'Of course if you assure me you did not I am bound to accept your word,' said Peregrine stiffly.

'I am glad of that,' said his cousin. 'I will confess, at the risk of offending you afresh, that however little I may have had to do with it I am more than pleased to find that information *was* laid.'

'You are very good,' said Peregrine, eyeing him a trifle askance.

Mr Taverner laughed. 'Well, were you so anxious to be shot at? Come, you are not to be picking a quarrel with me, you know! Judith, do you go to the Exhibition? Is Mrs Scattergood ready?'

Judith got up. 'She went into the breakfast-parlour to write a note before you came. Shall we fetch her?'

'By all means. We are behind time, I believe. I was detained, and should beg pardon.' He nodded pleasantly to Peregrine and held open the door for Judith to pass out.

In the hall she waited for him to close the door, and then said in a low voice: 'You did not deny it.'

He raised his brows, looking down at her quizzically. 'Are you also to pick a quarrel with me, Judith?'

'No, indeed,' she said earnestly. 'Perry is only a boy; he has these nonsensical notions. You are wiser. Oh, do not tell me! Indeed, you need not! You saved him, and I am – you do not know how grateful!'

He took her hand in both of his. 'To earn your good opinion there is nothing I would not do!' he said.

Her eyes fell before the look in his. 'You have earned it. From the bottom of my heart I thank you.'

'I want more than gratitude,' he said, holding her fast. 'Tell me, may I hope? I dare not press you; you have seemed to show me that you do not wish me to speak, and yet I must! Only assure me that I may hope – I ask no more!'

She was most strangely moved, and knew not how to answer him. Her hand trembled; he bent and kissed it. She murmured: 'I do not know. I – I have not thought of marriage. I wish you would not ask me yet. What can I answer?'

'At least tell me that there is no one else?'

'There is no one, cousin,' she said.

He continued to hold her hand a minute, and when she made a movement to disengage herself pressed it slightly, and released it. 'I am content. We will go and look for Mrs Scattergood.'

In another part of the town, Mr Farnaby was still talking the affair over with his second, who was by this time heartily sick of the subject. His principal seemed to him so much put out over it that he presently said: 'What's your game, Ned? There's more to it than you've told me, eh? Who wants that young sprig put away? You're being paid, and paid handsomely for the task, ain't you?'

'I don't know what you're talking about,' said Farnaby. 'Taverner hit me in the face.'

'I can see he did,' said his friend, interestedly surveying the contusion that marred Mr Farnaby's countenance.

Farnaby flushed. 'You should know I am not the man to stomach an insult!' he declared.

'Not unless you were paid to,' agreed Captain Crake.

Mr Farnaby said with dignity that the Captain forgot himself.

'I don't forget myself, but it seems to me that you have,' said the Captain frankly. 'If there was money in this, where was my share? Tell me that!'

'There is no money,' said Mr Farnaby, and closed the interview.

He spent the rest of the day in a mood of bitter discontent, and betook himself in the evening to the King's Arms, at the corner of Duke Street and King Street, to solace himself with gin and the company of such of his cronies as he might find there.

The King's Arms was owned by Thomas Cribb, champion heavyweight of England. All sorts and conditions of men, from titled gentlemen to coal-heavers, frequented it, but it was not every visitor's fortune to be admitted into the famous parlour. Mr Farnaby for one did not rank amongst the privileged. Since gin and not boxing-talk was what he came for, this did not trouble him, and he was quite content to ensconce himself in a cosy corner of the tap-room and watch the prize-fighters and the Corinthians drift past him to the inner sanctum. The tavern was always crowded; every young buck came to it, every prize-fighter of note, and it was not unusual for some ambitious person to walk in and pick a quarrel with the genial host for the privilege of being able to boast afterwards that he had exchanged blows with the Champion. This practice had of late become less popular, as Cribb had formed a disappointing habit of hailing his would-be assailants straight before a magistrate, on the score that if he obliged every man who wanted to be knocked down by him he would have no peace at all.

Mr Farnaby found a nook in the tap-room on this particular evening, and settled down to his glass of daffy, keeping a look-out for any acquaintance who might come in.

Plenty of people did come in, but although he might nod to some of them, or exchange a brief greeting, his particular friends were not amongst them. Tom Belcher, the great Jem's brother, strolled in arm in arm with old Bill Gibbons; Warr stood chatting awhile with Cribb before he went through into the parlour; Gentleman Jackson arrived with a party of Corinthians whom he was amusing with one of his stories. Mr Farnaby watched them all without envy, and called for another glass of daffy.

The tap-room was full almost to overflowing when the door was pushed open and the Earl of Worth walked in. He stood on the threshold for a moment, looking round through the smoke of a score of pipes, and Tom Cribb, who had just come out of the parlour, saw him, and crossed the room to his side. 'Good evening, my lord,' he said. 'Glad to see your lordship. You'll find a snug little gathering in the parlour to-night. Lord Yarmouth's there, Colonel Aston, Sir Henry Smyth, Mr Jackson, and I don't know who besides. Will you go through, my lord?'

'Presently,' said the Earl. 'I see someone here I want a word with first.'

'Here, my lord?' said Cribb, looking round at the company with a wrinkled brow.

'Yes, here,' said the Earl, and went past him with a swing of his caped driving-coat straight up to the table at which Mr Farnaby was sitting.

Mr Farnaby, who was idly watching a couple of men throwing dice at a neighbouring table, did not see the Earl until he stood right over him. He looked up then, and came to his feet in a hurry.

'Good evening,' said the Earl politely.

Farnaby made him a bow. 'Good evening, sir,' he returned, looking sideways at the Earl.

Worth laid his cane on the table and began to draw off his gloves. 'You were expecting me, no doubt,' he said.

'Oh no, hardly!' replied Farnaby, with a sneer. 'I know your lordship is in the habit of frequenting Cribb's Parlour, but I had no expectation of being recognised by you.'

The Earl drew out a chair on the opposite side of the table and sat down. From under the shade of his curly-brimmed hat, which he wore tilted rather over his face, his eyes mocked unpleasantly. 'You think I might be chary of being seen in your company? Very true, but I believe my credit with the world to be fairly good. My reputation may yet survive. You may sit down.'

'I have every intention of so doing,' retorted Farnaby, suiting the action to the word and tossing off what remained of his second glass of daffy. 'I am sure I am highly honoured to have your lordship's company.'

'Make the most of it then,' advised the Earl, 'for it is not an honour that is likely to befall you again.'

Farnaby's hand fidgeted with his empty glass; he was watching the Earl covertly. 'Indeed! And what may your lordship mean?'

'Merely that I shall have no further need of your company after to-night, Farnaby. Circumstance has caused our paths to cross, but they diverge again now, quite widely, I assure you.'

'If I had the pleasure of understanding your lordship – !'

'I should not have thought that you would derive much pleasure from that,' said the Earl. 'But if you do, enjoy it to the full, for I think you understand me tolerably well.'

'I assure you I do not, sir. I am at a loss to discover why you should take this tone with me, and I may add, my lord, that I resent it!'

The Earl took out his snuff-box and opened it. He inhaled a pinch with deliberation. 'You are not in a position to resent any tone I may choose to take, Farnaby,' he said. He laid his box down open on the table and leaned back in his chair, his driving coat falling open to show a glimpse of a light waistcoat and a blue coat, and the irreproachable folds of his cravat. 'Let us be frank,' he said. 'You have made a stupid bungle of a very simple affair, Farnaby.'

Farnaby shot a quick look round. 'Sir!'

'Don't be alarmed,' said Worth. 'No one is listening. You were hired to put Sir Peregrine Taverner out of the way, and you have failed to earn your hire.'

Farnaby's hands clenched; he leaned forward. 'Damn you, shut your mouth!' he whispered. 'You daren't say I was hired!'

Worth raised his brows. 'What makes you think that?' he inquired.

'You can't say it!'

'On the contrary, I can say it with the greatest of ease, my good Farnaby, and if you give me any trouble I shall say it.

And – my credit being good with the world, as I have already pointed out to you, I think my word will be believed before yours. We will put it to the test, if you like.'

Farnaby was rather white; he looked at the Earl with a good deal of fear in his eyes, and said breathlessly: 'Everyone knows what happened! Taverner's cock was squeezed, and I said so, and I'll have you know, my lord, there are dozens who will bear me out that it was so! Taverner struck me, I sent him a cartel, and that is the whole story!'

'Not quite the whole story,' said Worth. 'You forgot to add that through your bungling folly the duel was stopped.'

'If we were informed against that was not my fault,' said Farnaby sulkily.

'There I take leave to differ from you,' said Worth coolly. 'To force a duel on Sir Peregrine Taverner was one thing, but to do it in such a public spot as the Cock-Pit Royal was quite another. Those were not your instructions, I think. I find it hard to believe that even you could do such a stupid thing, Farnaby. Did it not occur to you that at the Cock-Pit there must be any number of persons who might consider it their duty to carry the tidings to the proper quarter? Yet that is precisely what happened. You have blundered, Farnaby, and that ends your part in the affair.'

Farnaby was staring at the Earl as though fascinated. 'You're a devil!' he said chokingly. 'You can't say I was hired! I've not touched a penny for it!'

'Not only have you not touched a penny of it, but you are not going to touch a penny,' said Worth, taking another pinch of snuff, and dusting his fingers with a fine handkerchief. 'You were not hired to put Sir Peregrine on his guard. Had you succeeded – but you did not succeed, Farnaby, so why should we waste time in idle conjecture? What I am endeavouring to point out to you is that though the reward has still to be earned, you are not the man to earn it.'

Farnaby swallowed something in his throat. 'What do you mean?' he asked weakly.

'I mean, Farnaby, that the task of disposing of Sir Peregrine must be left to some less clumsy hireling,' said the Earl pleasantly. 'I am persuaded you will perceive that any further attempt made by you on his life would bear an extremely suspicious appearance.'

'Do you suggest – do you dare to suggest that I would – I'm not a common cut-throat, my lord!'

'You will have to forgive me for misjudging you,' said Worth scathingly. 'The scruples of persons of your kidney are, alas, hidden from me. Do not touch my snuff-box, if you please, or I shall be obliged to throw the rest of its contents into the fire!'

Farnaby, who had stretched his hand out absently towards the box, drew back with a start and flushed to the roots of his hair at the note of cold contempt in the Earl's voice. 'You are insulting, my lord! You come here to threaten me, but you won't put this on me, let me tell you!'

'No?' said the Earl, raising his eyes. 'No?'

Farnaby tried to give back that long, cool look, but his own eyes shifted under the Earl's and fell. 'No,' he said uncertainly. 'No, by God, you won't! If you dare to accuse me – if you try to put it on to me, do you think I shall have nothing to say? I shan't suffer alone, I –' He broke off and moistened his lips.

Worth was sitting very still in his chair; his glance never wavered from Farnaby's face. 'Go on, Mr Farnaby,' he said. 'I am waiting to hear what it is you will say.'

'Nothing!' Farnaby said quickly.

'Not even the name of the man who hired you?' said the Earl softly.

'Nothing, I tell you! No one hired me!'

The Earl shut his snuff-box. 'No doubt you are wise,' he said. 'He might – who knows? – take steps to put *you* out of the way, might he not? And I am afraid that even if you had the courage to divulge his name it would not be of very much use. It would be your word against his, Farnaby, and to be honest with you I hardly think yours would be heeded. You see, I have considered all that.'

'No need!' Farnaby said, glaring at him. 'I've told you I shall divulge nothing!'

'I am glad to find that you have such a wholesome regard for your skin,' murmured Worth. 'I hope that it may prompt you to keep away from Sir Peregrine in the future. I should go into the country for a while, if I were you. I have an odd notion that if anything were to happen to him while you were in town you might suffer for it.'

Farnaby forced out a laugh. 'Very interesting, my lord, but I'm no believer in premonitions!'

'Ah!' said the Earl. 'But that was more in the nature of a promise, Farnaby. One blunder may be forgiven; a second would prove fatal.' He rose and picked up his gloves and cane. 'That is all I wanted to say to you.'

Farnaby jumped up. 'Wait, my lord!' he said, gripping the edge of the table and seeming to search for words.

'Well?' said the Earl.

Farnaby licked his lips. 'I could be of use to you!' he said desperately.

'You are mistaken,' said the Earl in a tone that struck a chill into Farnaby's veins. 'No man who has bungled once is of the least use to me.'

Farnaby sank down into his chair again, looking after the Earl's tall figure with an expression of mingled venom and despair in his eyes. Worth strolled away towards the parlour door.

He had not reached it when his gaze alighted on the figure of a gentleman who had entered the tavern a few minutes earlier, and was standing at the other end of the tap-room, fixedly regarding him.

The Earl checked, gently put aside a slightly inebriated sailor who was standing in his way, and walked across the room to the newcomer. 'Your servant, Mr Taverner.'

Mr Taverner bowed formally. 'Good evening, Lord Worth.'

The fingers of the Earl's right hand began to play with the riband of his quizzing-glass. 'Well, Mr Taverner, what is it?' he asked.

Bernard Taverner raised his brows. 'What is it?' he repeated. 'What is what, my lord?'

'You seemed to me to be much interested in my movements,' said Worth. 'Or am I at fault?'

'Interested . . .' said Mr Taverner. 'I was not so much interested, sir, as surprised, since you ask me.'

'To find me here? I am often to be seen in Cribb's Parlour,' replied the Earl.

'I am aware of it. What I was not aware of, and which, I must confess, occasioned some surprise in me, was that you are also to be seen in such company as Farnaby's.'

This was said plainly enough, and with a straight look that met Worth's cynical gaze squarely. It did not, however, appear to embarrass the Earl. 'Ah, but I frequently find myself in strange company at Cribb's, Mr Taverner,' he said.

Taverner's lips tightened. After a moment's silence he said in a measured way: 'You will admit, Lord Worth, that to see you in conversation with a person who only this morning set out to fight a duel with your ward must present a very odd appearance. Or are you perhaps in ignorance of to-day's *releager?*'

The Earl's fingers slid down the riband to the shaft of his quizzing-glass. He raised it. 'No, Mr Taverner, I was not in ignorance of it.'

There was another silence, during which Bernard Taverner seemed to be trying to read what thoughts might lie behind the Earl's suave manner. 'You were not in ignorance, and yet –'

'Curiously enough,' said Worth, 'it was on that very subject that I have been talking to Mr Farnaby.'

'Indeed!'

'Yes,' said the Earl. 'But why should we fence, Mr Taverner? You suspect me, I think, of taking a large interest in the *affaire* Farnaby, and you are quite right. I have informed him – and I believe he understood me tolerably well – that his part is played. So you must not worry about him, my dear sir.'

Taverner frowned. 'I don't entirely understand you, sir. I did not come here to insult you with accusations which must be absurd, but I think it will not be inopportune to assure you that I have the interests of my cousins very much at heart, and should not hesitate to serve either of them to the utmost of my power.'

'I am profoundly moved by your assurance, Mr Taverner,' said the Earl, with an unpleasant smile, 'but I cannot help feeling that you would be wiser to refrain from meddling in your cousins' affairs.'

Taverner stiffened. 'If I read you correctly, my lord, you mean rather that I should be wiser to refrain from meddling in your affairs.'

'Well, that is to put the matter very crudely,' said the Earl, still smiling. 'Nevertheless, you do read me quite correctly. Those who meddle in my affairs do not prosper.'

'Please do not address threats to me, Lord Worth!' said Taverner quietly. 'I am not to be frightened out of a proper regard for my cousins' well-being.'

The Earl spoke so softly that no one but Taverner could catch his words. 'Let me remind you, Mr Taverner, that the well-being of your cousins does not lie in your hands, but in mine. You have been very assiduous in your attentions, but if you are cherishing dreams of a bridal, banish them. You will never marry Judith Taverner.'

Mr Taverner's hands clenched involuntarily. 'I am grateful to you for showing me your hand so plainly, sir,' he said. 'In my turn I would remind you that your jurisdiction over Miss Taverner expires within the year. It did not need this conversation to convince me that you are nursing designs which are as unscrupulous as they are shameless. Understand, if you please, that I am not to be cowed into standing out of your way.'

'As to that, Mr Taverner, you will do as seems best to you,' said the Earl. 'But you will bear in mind, I trust, that when I find an obstacle in my way I am apt to remove it.' This was said without heat, even blandly, and the Earl, not waiting to see how it was received, bowed slightly and walked away towards the parlour door.

Twelve

NOT VERY LONG AFTER THE EPISODE OF HIS FRUSTRATED duel Peregrine went off to stay in Hertfordshire with the Fairfords, who removed from London early in December with the intention of spending some weeks in the country. The invitation was cordially extended to Miss Taverner as well, but she was obliged to decline it, having received just previously a very gratifying invitation to spend a week at Belvoir Castle with the Duke and Duchess of Rutland.

The Duchess, who had lately been on a visit to town, had made the acquaintance of Miss Taverner at Almack's, Miss Taverner having been presented to her by Mr Brummell, a close friend of the Rutlands. The Duchess remembered Miss Taverner's father, seemed to be pleased with the daughter, kept her talking for some time, and ended by sending her, a few weeks later, an invitation to join a house-party at Belvoir.

Miss Taverner journeyed north in a private chaise, and arrived to find herself one of a distinguished company. Chief amongst the guests was the Duke of York, who had arrived a day previously. His visit being quite unexpected, some slight disturbance had been caused, for the Duke of Dorset had been allotted the rooms that were invariably kept for York, and had had to be dispossessed in a hurry. However, as it was quite an understood thing that York and Brummell should both have their particular apartments both at Belvoir and at Cheveley, his grace of Dorset acquiesced in the alteration, and was only glad that so notable a whist-player should have joined the party.

Frederick, Duke of York, was the second son of the King, and had been living for the last few years in a sort of retirement consequent upon the Clarke scandal. He had lately been reinstated as Commander-in-Chief, and at this present date, when Miss Taverner had the honour to be presented to him, he seemed to be in excellent spirits, and not at all the sort of man who could be suspected of selling Army promotions through the machinations of his mistress. He was nearing fifty, a tall, stout man, with a florid complexion and a prominent nose. He had a ready laugh, a kindly, inquisitive blue eye, and was easily amused. He was married to a Prussian princess from whom he lived apart on very excellent terms. The Duchess resided at Oatlands, where she led an eccentric but blameless existence, surrounded by as many as forty pet dogs of every imaginable breed. The Duke was used to bring down parties of his friends to spend the weekends at Oatlands. The Duchess had not the least objection, and without making any change in her own manner of life, entertained her guests in a charming and unceremonious way that endeared her to everyone who knew her. No one was ever known to refuse an invitation to Oatlands, though the first visit there must always astonish, and even dismay. The park was kept for the accommodation of a collection of macaws, monkeys, ostriches, kangaroos; the stables were full of horses which were none of them obtainable for the use of the guests; the house swarmed with servants, whose business never seemed to be to wait on anyone; the hostess breakfasted at three in the morning, spent the night in wandering about the grounds, and was in the habit of retiring unexpectedly to a four-roomed grotto she had had made for herself in the park. Dinner was always at eight; the Duke never rose from the table till eleven, and when he did rise it was to play whist for five-pound points and twenty-five pounds on the rubber, until four in the morning.

The Duke, who never saw his wife except at Oatlands, had naturally not brought her with him to Belvoir. He was accompanied only by Colonel Wyndham, a smart man-about-town, for whom the Duchess had an inordinate dislike.

The other guests, besides the Duke and Duchess of Dorset, consisted of what seemed at first sight to Miss Taverner an enormous number of ladies and gentlemen, most of whom were unknown to her. Lord and Lady Jersey, Mr Brummell, and Lord Alvanley were her only acquaintances amongst them. She felt a little shy, and was not as displeased as she might otherwise have been when hardly an hour after her own arrival a chaise drove up and deposited Lord Worth on the doorstep.

She was bearing her part in a conversation with a very haughty young lady, who seemed to eye her with great superciliousness, when Worth entered the saloon with his hostess. She looked up, and seeing him was betrayed into a smile. He came at once towards her, his rather hard face softened, and having exchanged a word of greeting with her companion, sat down beside her sofa, and asked her how she did.

The haughty young lady, who was all flattering complaisance towards him, did what lay in her power to claim and keep his attention. Miss Taverner could not but be amused: the lady was so very anxious to please, the gentleman so politely unresponsive. But Mr Pierrepoint came up presently, and took the lady away with him to inspect Mr Brummell's water-colour sketch of their hostess, and the Earl was left alone with his ward.

Miss Taverner had had time to reflect while Worth was engaged with Miss Crewe that he had not shown any surprise on meeting her. When Miss Crewe had walked off she asked him in her abrupt way whether he had expected to find her at Belvoir.

'Why, yes,' he replied. 'I believe I was informed of it.'

The gleam in his eye made her suspect him strongly of having had some say in her being invited. She said: 'Oh! I, on the other hand, had not the least notion of finding you here.'

'If you had you would not have come, I daresay.'

She raised her brows. 'I hope I am not so prejudiced that I cannot be staying in the same house with you.'

'That is very encouraging,' said the Earl. 'Do you know, I was presumptuous enough to think that you were quite glad to see me when I came in?'

She hesitated, and then said with a rueful smile: 'Well, perhaps I was a little glad. I have been feeling rather strange amongst a set of company I don't know. That lady – Miss Crewe, I think you called her – has been trying for the past twenty minutes to show me what a countrified nobody I am, and that, you know, when one knows it to be the melancholy truth, makes one feel sadly out of place.'

'You will have your revenge upon her if you mean to hunt to-morrow,' remarked the Earl. 'She has the worst hands imaginable, and is generally off at the first fence.'

She laughed. 'Yes, I do mean to hunt, but I hope I am not ill-natured enough to wish Miss Crewe a tumble. Shall you hunt also?'

'Certainly; to keep an eye on my ward.'

She put up her chin, a quizzical gleam in her eye. 'I will give you a lead,' she promised.

He was amused. 'Come, we begin to understand one another tolerably well,' he said. 'How do you like your snuff?'

'To tell you the truth I don't often take it,' confided Judith. 'I only pretend.'

'You are in excellent company then, for you follow the Prince Regent. Let me see you take a pinch.'

She obeyed him, extracting from her reticule a gold box with enamelled plaques on the lid and sides.

He took it from her to inspect it more closely. 'Very pretty. Where did you get it?'

'At Rundell and Bridge. I bought several there.'

He gave it back to her. 'You have good taste.'

'Thank you,' said Judith. 'To have earned the approval of so notable a connoisseur as yourself must afford me gratification.'

He smiled. 'Do not be impertinent, Miss Taverner.'

She flicked open the box, and offered it to him. 'You mistake me, Lord Worth: I was being civil – in your own manner.'

'You have not mastered the precise way of it,' he answered. 'No, don't offer your box to me; it is not a mixture that I like.'

'Indeed! How odd!' said Miss Taverner, raising a pinch to one nostril with a graceful turn of her wrist. 'I do not like it either.'

'That is probably because you have drenched it with Vinagrillo,' said the Earl calmly. 'I warned you to be sparing in the use of it.'

'I have not drenched it with Vinagrillo!' said Miss Taverner, indignantly shutting her box. 'I used two drops, just to moisten the whole!'

A gentleman who was standing beside Colonel Wyndham in the middle of the saloon had been looking at Miss Taverner in a dreamy, unconcerned way, but when he saw her take out her snuff-box a look of interest came into his eyes, and he wandered away from the Colonel, and came towards the sofa. He said very earnestly to Worth: 'Please present me! Such a pretty box! What I should call a nice visiting-box, but not suitable for morning wear. I was tempted when they showed it to me, but it did not happen to be just what I was looking for.'

Judith stared at him in a good deal of astonishment, but Lord Worth, betraying no hint of surprise, merely said: 'Lord Petersham, Miss Taverner,' and got up.

Lord Petersham begged permission to sit beside Miss Taverner. 'Tell me,' he said anxiously, 'are you interested in tea, I wonder?'

She was not interested in tea, but she knew that his lordship had a room lined with canisters of every imaginable kind, from Gunpowder to Lapsang Souchong. She confessed her ignorance, and felt that she had disappointed him.

'It is a pity, a great pity,' he said. 'You would find it almost as interesting as snuff. And you are interested in that, are you not? You have your own mixture; I saw the jar at Fribourg and Treyer's.'

Miss Taverner produced her box. 'I wish you will do me the honour of trying my sort,' she said.

'Mine will be the honour,' said his lordship, bowing. He dipped his finger and thumb in her box, and held a pinch to his nostrils, half-closing his eyes. 'Spanish bran — a hint of Brazil — something else besides, possibly a dash of masulipatam.' He turned. 'It reminds me of a mixture I think I have had in your house, Julian.'

'Impossible!' said Worth.

'Well, perhaps it is not precisely the same,' conceded Lord Petersham, turning back to Miss Taverner. 'A very delicate mixture, ma'am. It is easy to detect the hand and unerring taste of an expert.'

Miss Taverner, with her guardian's ironic eye upon her, had the grace to blush.

It was soon time to go upstairs and change her gown for dinner. She was placed at table between Lord Robert Manners and Mr Pierrepoint, nowhere near the Earl, and as he joined the Duke of York after dinner, with his host and another inveterate whist-player, whom everyone called Chig, she did not speak to him again that evening.

She was not the only lady to join the Hunt next day, but no more than three others had enough energy or enthusiasm to appear, and by no means all the gentlemen. She was somewhat surprised to find Mr Brummell attired for riding when she came down to an early breakfast, and opened her eyes at him.

He drew out a chair for her beside his own. 'I know,' he said understandingly, 'but it has a good appearance, and one need not go beyond the second field.'

'Not go beyond the second field!' she echoed. 'Why, won't you go farther, Mr Brummell?'

'No, I don't think so,' he replied very gravely. 'There is sure to be a farmhouse where I can get some bread and cheese, and you must know there is nothing I like better than that.'

'Bread and cheese instead of hunting!' she said. 'I cannot allow it to be a choice!'

'Yes, but you see, if I went very far I should get my tops and leathers splashed by all the greasy, galloping farmers,' he replied softly.

But even her partiality for him could not induce Miss Taverner to smile at such a speech as that. She looked reproachful, and would only say: 'I am persuaded you do not mean it.'

She was to discover later that he had for once spoken in all sincerity. He abandoned the Hunt after the first few fields, and was no more seen. She commented on it with strong disapproval to her guardian, who had drawn up beside her at a check, but he merely looked faintly surprised, and said that the notion of Brummell muddied and dishevelled from a long day in the saddle was too absurd to be contemplated. Upon reflection she had to admit him to be right.

Mr Brummell, encountered again at dinner, was unabashed. He had discovered a very excellent cheese in a farmhouse he had not previously known to exist, had regaled himself on it, and having satisfied himself that no speck of mud sullied his snowy tops, had ridden gently back to Belvoir to discuss with his hostess a plan for landscape gardening which had occurred to him in the night watches.

Lord Worth did not join the whist-party after dinner, but repaired to the drawing-room with several others, and was at once claimed by Lady Jersey. A rubber of Casino was being played at one end of the room, but not very seriously, and the card-players, when asked, had not the least objection to a little music. The Duchess begged that Miss Crewe's harp might be fetched, and Miss Crewe, after a proper display of bashfulness, and some prompting from her mama, consented. The Honourable Mrs Crewe, turbaned and majestic, bore down upon Lady Jersey, and informed her that she thought her ladyship would be pleased with Charlotte's performance.

'Your ladyship's mama, dear Lady Westmorland, recommended Charlotte's present master to me,' she announced. 'The result, I venture to think, has been most happy. She has learned to apply, and has in general acquired a proficiency upon the instrument – but I shall await your judgment, and yours too, Lord Worth. *Your* taste may certainly be relied on.'

The Earl had risen at her approach. He bowed, and said in his most expressionless voice: 'You flatter me, ma'am.'

'Oh no, that I am sure I do not! Anything of that sort is repugnant to my nature; you will not find me administering to anyone's vanity, I can tell you. I say exactly what I think. Charlotte is more conciliatory, I believe. I do not know where you may find a more good-natured, amiable girl: it is quite absurd!' The Earl bowed again, but said nothing. Mrs Crewe tapped his sleeve with her fan. 'You shall tell me what you think of her performance, but I do beg of you not to watch the child too closely, for I have had a great piece of work inducing her to play at all with you present. The nonsensical girl sets so much store by your opinion it is quite ridiculous! "Oh, Mama!" she said to me, as we came downstairs, "if there should be music, don't, I beg of you, press me to play! I am sure I cannot with Lord Worth's critical eyes upon me!"'

'I will engage, ma'am, to turn my eyes elsewhere,' replied the Earl.

'Oh, nonsense, I have no notion of indulging girls in such folly,' said Mrs Crewe. '"Depend upon it, my love," I told her, "Lord Worth will be very well pleased with your performance."'

The harp had been brought into the room by this time, and Mrs Crewe sailed back to fuss over her daughter, to direct Mr Pierrepoint to move a branch of candles nearer, and Lord Alvanley to bring up a more suitable chair.

Worth resumed his seat beside Lady Jersey, and gave her one expressive glance. Her eyes were dancing. 'Oh, my dear Julian, do you see? You must sit and gaze at Charlotte throughout! Now, that isn't ill-natured of me, is it? Such a detestable, matchmaking woman! I beg you won't offer for Charlotte. I shall never ask you to Osterley again if you do, and you know that would be too bad when you are one of my oldest friends.'

'I can safely promise you I won't,' replied the Earl.

His eyes had wandered by chance to where Miss Taverner was seated, at no great distance, and rested there for a moment. Miss Taverner was not looking at him; she was conversing in a quiet voice with a lively brunette.

Lady Jersey followed the direction of the Earl's glance, and shot him one quick, shrewd look. 'My dear Worth, I have always agreed with you,' she said saucily. 'She is lovely – quite beautiful!'

The Earl turned his eyes upon her. 'Don't talk, Sally: you interrupt Miss Crewe.'

And indeed by this time Miss Crewe had run one hand across the strings of the harp, and was about to begin.

Mrs Crewe, anxiously watching his lordship, had the doubtful felicity of seeing that he kept his word to her. Beyond bestowing one cursory glance upon the fair performer, he did not look at her again, but inspected instead his companion's famous pink pearls. He did indeed join in the applause that greeted the song, but with all his habitual languor. Miss Crewe was begged to sing again, though not by him, and after a little show of reluctance, complied. My Lord Worth sank his chin in his cravat, and gazed abstractedly before him.

The second piece being at an end, and Miss Crewe properly complimented and thanked, Lady Jersey leaned forward impulsively and addressed Miss Taverner. 'Miss Taverner, surely I am not mistaken in thinking that you play, and sing too?'

Judith looked up. 'Very indifferently, ma'am. I have no skill on the harp.'

'But the pianoforte! I am persuaded you could give us all great pleasure if you would!'

The Duchess at once added her entreaties to Lady Jersey's, and Lord Alvanley, deserting Miss Crewe, went across to her, and said in his cheerful way: 'Now, do pray sing for us, Miss Taverner! We can never be brought to believe that you don't sing, you know! Do you not give us all the lead in everything?'

Judith coloured, and shook her head. 'No, indeed; you put me quite out of countenance. My performance on the pianoforte is nothing at all out of the common, I assure you.'

The Duchess said kindly: 'Do not be doing anything you would rather not, Miss Taverner, but I believe I can engage for it we shall all listen to you with considerable pleasure.'

'Worth!' said Alvanley. 'Use your influence, my dear fellow! *You* can command where *we* may only supplicate!'

'Well, here is a piece of work!' exclaimed Mrs Crewe, by no means pleased at the turn events had taken. 'It is an odd thing to hear you begging the indulgence of music, Lord Alvanley. I am sure you had rather be at the card-table.'

'Oh, come, ma'am,' said Alvanley easily, 'you are giving me a sad character, you know.'

'Well, I have never known you to stay away from the whist-table before,' she persisted.

'You will make me feel you are anxious to be rid of me,' he said. 'If you can tell me if there is any chance of the Ten Tribes of Israel being discovered, I promise you I will go and play whist when I have heard Miss Taverner sing.'

'What in the world can you mean? You are the oddest creature, I protest!'

'Why, ma'am, only that I have exhausted the other two tribes, and called out the conscription of next year. Worth! you say nothing! Compel Miss Taverner!'

Judith, who had recovered her countenance, got up. 'Indeed, it is not necessary! You make me seem very ungracious, sir, and I am afraid you will be disappointed in my performance after Miss Crewe's excellence.'

Lord Worth rose, and walking over to the pianoforte opened it for her. As Alvanley led her up to it, he said in a low voice: 'Have you music? May I fetch it for you?'

She shook her head. 'I brought none. I must play from memory, and beg you all to pardon my deficiencies.'

'That is a very prettily-behaved, unaffected girl,' whispered the Duchess of Dorset to her hostess. 'Did you say eighty or ninety thousand pounds, my dear?'

Miss Taverner settled herself on the music-stool, and spread her fingers over the keys. The Earl placed himself in a chair near the pianoforte, and fixed his eyes on her face.

She sang a simple ballad; her voice, though not powerful, was sweet, and well-trained. She accompanied herself creditably, and looked so beautiful that it was not to be wondered at that her performance should be greeted with extravagant acclaim. She was begged to sing again, and accused of hiding her light under a bushel. She blushed, shook her head, sang one more ballad, and resolutely got up from the pianoforte.

'If she had had the benefit of good masters she would sing quite tolerably,' said Mrs Crewe in an undervoice to Lady Jersey. 'It is a pity she puts on such an air of consequence. But so it is always with these lanky, overgrown females!'

Miss Taverner had moved away from the instrument towards the window embrasure. The Earl followed her, and sat down beside her there. 'There is no end to your accomplishments,' he remarked.

'Please don't be absurd!' said Miss Taverner. 'You at least do not want for sense, and to talk as though my singing were in any way superior is a great piece of folly!'

'It gave me pleasure,' he answered mildly. 'Would you prefer me to tell you that you have very little voice, and no particular skill?'

She smiled. 'It would be the truth, and more what I am growing used to hear from you. But I did not mean to be rude.'

'You are absolved,' he said gravely. 'Tell me, do you like to be here? Are you enjoying your visit?'

'Yes, very much. Everyone has been so kind! I might have been acquainted with them all my life. I wish Perry could have been here. He is staying with the Fairfords, you know.' She gave a little laugh. 'His regard for Miss Fairford shows no sign of abating. I did not more than half like it when he offered for her, but I begin to think that she may do very well for him. She is the oddest little creature! so young and shy, and yet with a great deal of common sense. She makes Perry mind her already, which I could never succeed in doing.'

'How long does Peregrine mean to stay in Hertfordshire?' inquired the Earl.

'I am not perfectly sure. Certainly for a week, and I should suppose for longer.'

He nodded. 'Well, unless he contrives to break his neck on the hunting-field, he should not come to much harm there.'

'He won't do that; he rides very well, better than he drives.' She looked at him undecidedly, and opened and shut her fan once or twice. 'I spoke to you once about Perry, Lord Worth.'

'You did.'

'I am no less anxious now. He needs to be steadied. If you cannot do that will you not give another the right?'

'Whom, for instance?' asked his lordship.

'Miss Fairford,' she replied seriously.

'I was under the impression that I had given it to her.'

'If you would give your consent to an earlier marriage!' she coaxed. 'I do believe Perry's affection to be deep-rooted. He will not change.'

He shook his head. 'No, Miss Taverner. That I will not do. I cannot imagine what possessed me to countenance the betrothal at all.'

She was a little startled, and turned in her chair to look at him more fully. 'Why should you not? What is this change of face?'

He returned her gaze in a considering way, but after a slight pause, he merely said: 'He is too young.'

She felt that he had not told her the real reason; she was annoyed, but tried not to show it. 'Perhaps he is too young; I do not deny that I thought so at first. But now I feel that marriage would be the very thing for him. Miss Fairford does not like London, and I believe she would wish to reside the most of the year in Yorkshire. And it would be best for Perry, after all. He gets into dangerous scrapes in town. Only the other day –' She stopped, looked a little confused, and said after a moment: 'Well, that is nothing. It is over now, and I should not have spoken. But I have been in some alarm about him.'

'You refer, I collect, to the duel which did not take place,' said the Earl.

She raised her eyes quickly. 'You knew of that?'

'My dear Miss Taverner, when challenges are offered at the Cock-Pit it is not wonderful that there should be no secrecy attached to the subsequent meeting.'

'The Cock-Pit! That I had *not* heard! If you knew how much I detest cocking, and all that it leads to! I have had to see as many as a hundred cocks walking on my father's estate, and to know that both he and Perry – but this is beside the point. I begin to understand now how it all came about. If it had not been for the intervention of one who has proved himself very much our friend, Perry might not be alive to-day.'

The Earl turned a singularly penetrating gaze upon her. 'Pray go on, Miss Taverner. Who was this well-disposed person?'

'My cousin, Mr Bernard Taverner,' she replied.

He lifted his quizzing-glass. 'Your cousin. Are you sure that it was he who intervened?'

'Why, yes,' she said, rather surprised. 'He was to some extent in Perry's confidence. Perry taxed him with it afterwards, and he could not deny it. It is only one more instance of his consideration, his regard for us.'

The Earl kept his glass up. 'This gentleman is a good deal in your confidence, I gather.'

'I know of no reason why he should not be,' said Judith, a little stiffly. 'I believe him to be very worthy of our confidence. He is not only our cousin, but most truly our friend.'

He lowered his glass. 'He is fortunate to have so easily secured your good opinion,' he said. 'Does he advise an early marriage for Peregrine, I wonder?'

'He has not told me so,' said Judith.

'No doubt he will,' said his lordship. 'You may tell him, when he does, that I have not the least intention of permitting Peregrine to marry yet awhile.'

He got up, but she detained him. 'I don't know why you should take this tone, Lord Worth, nor why, having promised your consent to Perry's marriage next year, you should suddenly change your mind.'

'Oh,' said the Earl with a sardonic smile, 'you may take it that I have too nice a sense of my duty to allow my ward to entangle himself in matrimony so young.'

'That is not the true answer,' she said. 'For some reason it does not suit you to see Perry married. I should wish to know what that reason is.'

'At the moment,' said the Earl, 'I fear I cannot call it to mind.'

He left her considerably put out. She had been in a fair way to acknowledge herself to have been mistaken in him, and now, just as she had warmed towards him, he made her angry again. She looked after him resentfully, until her consciousness was recalled by Mr Pierrepoint, who came up to ask her if she would join a lottery-table in the next room.

She went at once, and did not set eyes on the Earl again until she went with the rest of the ladies to bed. He was in the hall with several of the other men of the party then, and he gave her her candle. As she took it from him, with downcast eyes and a very sober countenance, he clasped her wrist in a light hold, and said quietly: 'Do you dislike me as much as ever? It is a pity. Try not to let your prejudice lead you into mistrusting me. You have no need.' He paused. 'Look at me!'

She raised her eyes. He smiled faintly. 'Obedient girl! If you had as much confidence in my integrity as you have in your cousin's it would be no bad thing.'

'I do not mistrust you,' she answered in a low voice. 'We shall be remarked. Please let me go, Lord Worth!'

He released her. 'One of a guardian's privileges is to be seen talking to his ward without occasioning remark,' he said. 'I can assure you he has not many.'

She set her hand on the stair-rail, preparing to follow Lady Jersey. She looked a little arch. 'Is your position as my guardian so painful, sir?'

'It is a damnable position,' he said deliberately, and turned away, leaving her staring.

Thirteen

*N*OT ALTOGETHER TO MISS TAVERNER'S SURPRISE, PEREGRINE'S stay in Hertfordshire was prolonged beyond the original week to a fortnight, and again to three weeks. She was warned four times through the medium of the post to expect him, only to receive a hasty scrawl next day postponing his return a little longer; and remarked humorously to her cousin that the sight of the postman's scarlet coat and cockaded hat in Brook Street was beginning to mean nothing but another put-off. 'But it cannot go on for ever,' she said with a twinkle. 'Sir Geoffrey must grow tired at last of franking Perry's letters to me, and then we may expect to see him in town again.'

Meanwhile, Miss Taverner's days continued to be so fully occupied that she had little leisure for missing her brother. She received two more offers of marriage, both of which she civilly declined; sat to have her portrait taken by Hoppner at the earnest solicitation of her cousin, and twice went to the play in the company of her guardian. He said nothing to annoy her on either of these occasions, but on the contrary talked so much like a sensible man, and saw to her comfort in such a practised manner, that she was quite in charity with him, and could thank him for two pleasant evenings with perfect sincerity.

'You have nothing to thank me for,' he returned. 'Do you think I have not had a great deal of pleasure in your company?'

She smiled. 'I have not been used to hear you say things so prettily, Lord Worth.'

'No, nor have I been used to find my ward so amiable,' he replied.

She held up her finger. 'Do not let us be recalling past differences, if you please! I am determined not to quarrel with you; it is useless to provoke me.'

He looked amused. 'Ever, Miss Taverner?'

'Oh, as to that, there is no saying, to be sure! To-night I am your guest, and must accord you a little extraordinary civility, to-morrow I may abuse you with a clear conscience.'

'Indeed! do you mean to do so? Have you received another offer of marriage for me to refuse without consulting you?'

She shook her head. 'I hold it to be a bad thing for any female to talk of the offers she may have received,' she said briefly.

'Your opinion does you honour; but you may confide in me with perfect propriety. I conjecture that you have received several. Why do you look so grave?'

She raised her eyes to his face, and found that he was watching her with a softened expression, which she might almost have believed to be sympathy, had she not been persuaded that he knew nothing of so gentle an emotion. She said in a despondent tone: 'It is quite true. I have received numerous offers, but there is nothing to boast of in that, for I think not one of them would have been made had I not been possessed of a large fortune.'

He replied coolly: 'None, I imagine.'

There was no vestige of sympathy in his voice. If her spirits stood in need of support this matter-of-fact tone was no bad thing. She was obliged to smile, though she said with a faint sigh: 'It is a melancholy thought.'

'I cannot agree with you. Being born to a handsome independence you have all the consequence of being the most sought-after young woman in London.'

'Yes,' she said rather sadly, 'but to be sought after for one's fortune is no great compliment. You laugh at me, but in this respect I must think myself most uncomfortably circumstanced.'

'Depend upon it, your fortune will not frighten away an honest man,' he replied.

'Why, no, that is left for you to do,' she said playfully.

He smiled. 'I will not allow it to have been so. I have frightened away fortune-hunters, and you should be grateful to me.'

'Perhaps I am. But I am quite at a loss to know why, having said that you will not consent to my marriage while I am your ward, you raise no objection to Perry's engaging himself.'

'Miss Fairford seems to be an unexceptional girl. I am indulging in the hope that if I ever let Peregrine marry her she will relieve me of some at least of my responsibilities.'

'You should reflect that my husband would relieve you of them all,' she said.

The carriage had stopped in Brook Street by this time; as the door was opened the Earl said: 'You are mistaken: I have no wish to be relieved of them all.'

It was fortunate that in the business of being handed out of the carriage the necessity of answering should be lost. Judith had no answer ready. Her guardian's words argued an attempt at gallantry, yet his manner was so far removed from the lover-like, that she was quite at a loss to understand him. She stepped down from the carriage, remarking as she did so that it now seemed to be a certain thing that Peregrine would be in London again the following day.

He had apparently no objection to this change of subject. 'Indeed! You do not fear another put-off?'

'No, I believe we may be sure of seeing him this time. One of the children, Lady Fairford's youngest, has the sore throat, and they fear it may be found to be infectious. Perry is to come home.'

'At what hour do you expect him?'

'I do not know, but I cannot suppose that he will be late.'

The footman was holding open the front door. The Earl said: 'Very well, I must be glad for your sake. Good night, my ward.'

'Good night, my guardian,' said Miss Taverner, giving him her hand.

Peregrine arrived in London midway through the afternoon, in a glow of health and spirits. He had had a capital time, was sorry to have left; there was no place like the country, after all. He and Tom Fairford had made the journey in famous time, though not without adventure. Judith must remember that he had travelled into Hertfordshire in his own curricle, instead of going post. Well, as she might suppose, he had returned in the same way, and had engaged to reach town ahead of Tom Fairford, also driving a curricle-and-four.

'I was driving my bays, you know. Tom had a team of greys – showy, but a trifle on the large side: heavy brutes, very well for hilly work, I daresay, but no match for my bays. I drew ahead pretty soon, taking the Hatfield road, the Fairfords' place being situated, as I believe I told you, considerably to the east of St Albans. In going there I took the road through Edgware and Elstree, but found it to be in no good case.'

'No,' agreed his sister patiently. 'You wrote as much to me: you were determined to come back by the Great North road. I remember my cousin being surprised at it, thinking the other way more direct.'

'Oh yes, I believe it may be, but a bad road: no chance of springing your horses on it. Worth told me as much, advised the North Road at the outset, but I thought I would try the other. However, that's neither here nor there. We ran a ding-dong race to Hatfield, and drew level at Bell Bar, the turnpike man being deaf, as I suppose, and keeping me waiting a good three minutes before he would open the gate. But it may have been that new man of mine I had with me. He carried the yard of tin, you know, but he has no notion how to sound it – put me out of all patience. I daresay the pike-keeper might not hear it at first. So Tom drew level with me there, and we had a famous race of it to Barnet. His nags were blowing by that time, and he changed them at the Green Man. Mine had got their second wind some way back; I pushed on to Whetstone, had a fresh team harnessed up there – small quick-steppers, capital for a flat stage – and was away before Tom came in sight. Well, as you remember, Ju, you come on to Finchley Common past Whetstone. You know how we saw Turnpike's Oak, and wondered whether we should be held up by highwaymen. No sign of highwaymen *that* day, but would you believe it, I was held up to-day!'

'Good God!' Judith exclaimed. 'You were actually robbed?'

'No such thing. But I will tell you. I had not driven a great distance over the Common – had not reached Tally Ho Corner, in fact – when I caught sight of a horseman, half-hidden from me by some trees. I was travelling at a smart pace, as you may guess – nothing on the road beyond a post-chaise met with half a mile back – and I made nothing of this rider, hardly noticed him. Imagine my amazement when a shot came whistling by my head! I believe it must have killed me, only that that man of mine, chancing to catch sight of the rogue as he was about to fire, fairly knocked me out of my seat. So the bullet went wide, and there we were, Hinkson snatching at the reins, and one of the leaders with his leg over the trace. I thought we had been overset any moment. I need not tell you it did not take me long to snatch my pistol from the holster, but I'd no luck; could not well see our man for the trees. I took my shot at a venture, and missed. Hinkson thrust the reins into my hands, and just as our man comes out of the thicket, what does Hinkson do but whip out a pistol from his picket, and fire it! Did you ever hear of a groom carrying pistols before? But so it was. He fired, and our man lets a squawk, claps his hand to his right arm, and drops his barker. By that time I'd pulled out our second pistol, but there was no need to use it. The rascal was making off as fast as his horse would carry him, and when Tom came up, as he soon did, we had the leaders disentangled, and were ready to be off again.'

'Merciful heavens!' cried Mrs Scattergood. 'You might have been killed!'

'Oh well, I daresay I should not have been. I daresay the rogue only fired to frighten us, though the shot seemed to pass devilish close. If he had robbed me he would have found himself out of luck, for I'd no more than a couple of guineas in my purse. Ju, you are looking quite pale! Nonsensical girl, it was nothing! The merest brush!'

'Yes,' she said faintly. 'The merest brush. Yet to have you fired upon, the shot coming so close, and the man riding up afterwards, as though to finish his work – it terrifies me, I confess! You are safe, and unhurt, and that must satisfy me – *should* satisfy me, yet does not.'

He put his arm round her. 'Why, this is nothing but an irritation of nerves, Ju! It's not like you to quake for such a small cause. You refine too much upon it. Ten to one but the fellow had no thought of injuring me.'

'I daresay he might not. Perhaps I do refine too much upon it; it has taken strong possession of my mind, I own. The danger you so lately passed through, and now this! But I am fanciful; you need not tell me so.'

'Oh, if you are to recall that meeting, I have done!' he said, impatiently. 'There can be no connection.'

She agreed to it, and said no more. Having told his tale he did not wish to be still talking of it, and what vague fears she might still cherish she kept to herself. He began to speak of the hunting he had enjoyed, of the company to be met with in Hertfordshire, the Assembly they had attended, and a dozen other circumstances of his visit. She had time to recover her composure, and was ready, upon Peregrine's having no more to say, to recount her own diversions since their last meeting. Belvoir must be described, Worth's unusually gentle manners touched upon, and finally the Duke of Clarence's attentions laughed over.

These had become most marked. From the day of their first meeting the Duke had lost no opportunity of fixing his interest with her. She could no longer be in any doubt of his intentions. If she drove in the Park she might place a reasonable dependence on meeting him, and being obliged to take him up beside her; if she went to the play the chances were he would be there too, and would find his way to her box; if a posy of flowers, a box of sugar-plums, or some pretty trifle to ornament her drawing-room were delivered at the house, his card would almost certainly accompany it. He was for ever calling in Brook Street, and put forward so many schemes for her entertainment, including even an invitation to make one of a party at his house at Bushey for Christmas, that she was hard put to it to know how to discourage him without the appearance of incivility.

Peregrine thought it a very good joke, and the notion of a prince paying addresses to his sister provoked him to laughter whenever he happened to think of it.

'Odious boy!' Judith said, trying to frown. 'Pray, why should he not? I hope I am as respectable as Miss Tylney Long, and I believe it to be a fact that the Duke has proposed to her several times.'

'What, the Pocket Venus?' exclaimed Peregrine. 'I did not know that! I thought Wellesley Poole was casting his eyes in her direction.'

'Very possibly,' said Judith, looking scornful. 'I ought to be flattered at his casting his eyes first in my direction, I suppose. Sometimes, Perry, I could wish that I had been born merely to a respectable competence instead of to a fortune.'

'Stuff!' replied Peregrine. 'You would not like that at all, let me tell you. And as for this notion of Tarry Breeks proposing to you – pho, I'll lay you ten to one he don't do it!'

'He will not if I can prevent him,' said Judith decidedly.

This proved, however, to be a feat beyond her powers. Neither coldness of manner nor direct rebuff made the least impression on the Duke, and having made up his mind that he had found an eligible partner in Miss Taverner, he lost very little time in declaring himself.

The moment he chose was a fortunate one for him, Judith being engaged in writing letters in the drawing-room when he called, and Mrs Scattergood having driven out to buy some satin for a new cap. He was ushered into the room, carrying a tight bunch of flowers, and having warmly shaken Miss Taverner by the hand, pressed his posy upon her, remarking with a satisfied air: 'I see you are alone. Now, that is just what I had hoped! How d'ye do? But I need not ask. Such a bloom of health! You are always in looks!'

Judith, accepting the posy with a word of thanks, hardly knew how to reply to this, and could only beg him to be seated. He made her a very gallant bow, indicating the sofa with a wave of his hand, and, feeling a little helpless, she sat down in one corner of it.

He took his place beside her, and fixing his bright blue eyes on her face said jovially: 'This is a luxurious state indeed, to be finding myself tête-à-tête with you! But you know that we have not settled it that you are to spend Christmas at Bushey. Come now, you will not be so unkind as to refuse me! We will have a snug party. I will engage for your liking Bushey excessively. Everyone does! It is a neat little box, I can tell you. I was used to have a house at Richmond, but from one cause or another I gave it up, and when they made me Ranger of Bushey Park I went to live there. It suits me very well. I don't care so much for the river, do you?'

'Perhaps it may be damp to live beside,' said Judith, glad to be getting away from the subject of Christmas. 'I must own I have a decided partiality for it, however.'

'Well, for my part, I don't see what there is to make so much of in the Thames,' said the Duke. 'You are all in raptures over it, but I am quite tired of it. There it goes, flow, flow, flow, always the same!'

She was obliged to hide a smile. Before she could think of any suitable rejoinder he was off again. 'But I did not come to talk of the river, after all. Christmas! Now what do you say to it?'

'I am very grateful to you, sir – honoured as well, I am sure beyond my deserts – but it must not be.'

'Grateful – honoured! Pho, pho, don't use high-sounding phrases to me, I beg of you! You should know I am a plain sort of man, never stand upon ceremony, think it all stuff and non-sense! Why should you not come? If you are thinking it would not be just the party you would like I will engage for it it will be. You may have the ordering of it, may look over the list of guests, and have it all as you choose.'

'Thank you, thank you, but you misunderstand me, sir! Con-sider, if you please, how particular an appearance my joining your party must present! It is not what either of us could wish.'

'Well, there you are quite in the wrong,' said the Duke bluntly. 'It is of all things what I should like most. It cannot seem too particular for my taste.' He leaned towards her, and seized her hands. 'My dear, dear Miss Taverner, you cannot be unaware of my feelings! You won't expect pretty speeches from me; you know how it is with me: I am just a sailor, and say what I think: but I have the deepest regard for you – damme, I am head over ears in love with you, my dear Miss Taverner, and don't care who hears me say it!'

He had her hands clasped so tightly that she was unable to move. She could only turn her head away, saying in a good deal of confusion: 'Please say no more! You do me too much honour! Indeed, I am sorry to give you pain, but it is impossible!'

'Impossible! How so? I see no impossibility. Ah, I daresay you are thinking I am too old a fellow to be addressing you, but I have the best health of all my family, you know. You will see how I shall outlive them. Have you thought of *that?*'

She made another attempt to disengage herself. 'No, indeed, how should I? I am sure I wish you may, but it cannot concern me. It is not on the score of your more advanced age that I find myself obliged to decline your offer, but our different situations, my own feelings – I beg of you, let us speak of this no more!'

An idea dawned on him; his rather protuberant blue eyes gleamed with intelligence. 'I see how it is!' he said in his hurried way. 'I am a clumsy fellow, I do not make myself plain! But it is marriage, you know, that I am offering you – everything in proper sailing trim, upon my word of honour!'

'I did not mistake you,' she said in a suffocating voice. 'But you must perceive how impossible such an alliance would be! Were I to consent to it can you suppose that there would be no opposition from *your* family?'

'Oh, you mean my brother, the Regent! I do not know why he should oppose it. He is not at all a bad fellow, I assure you, whatever you may have heard to the contrary. There's Charlotte to succeed him, and my brother York before me. You may depend upon it he thinks the Succession safe enough without taking me into account. But you do not say anything! You are silent! Ah, I see what it is, you are thinking of Mrs Jordan! I should not have mentioned her, but there! you are a sensible girl; you don't care for a little blunt speaking. *That* is quite at an end: you need have no qualms. If there has been unsteadiness in the past that is over and done with. You must know that when the King was in his senses we poor devils were in a hard case – not that I mean anything disrespectful to my father, you understand – but so it was. We have all suffered – Prinny, and Kent, and Suss, and poor Amelia! There's no saying but that we might all of us have turned out as steady as you please if we might have married where we chose. But you will see that it will all be changed now. Here am I, for one, anxious to be settled, and comfortable. You need not consider Mrs Jordan.'

Miss Taverner succeeded at last in drawing her hands away. 'Sir, if I could return your regard perhaps the thought of that lady might not weigh with me, but surely she must be considered, cannot be put quite out of mind?'

'Oh,' said the Duke earnestly, 'I was never married to her, you know. No, no, you have that quite wrong! There are no ties binding us, none at all!'

She could not forbear giving him a look of shocked reproach. 'No ties, sir?'

'You mean the children, do you?' said the Duke eagerly. 'But you will like them excessively! I do not believe there can be better children in the world.'

'Yes, sir, indeed I have always heard – but you do not understand me! It is not on that count that I – pray believe, sir, that what you propose can never be! You must marry some lady of rank, some princess; you know it must be so!'

'Not at all, not at all!' declared the Duke, puffing out his cheeks. 'There can be no objection, no hitch of any sort. You are not to be thinking this is cream-pot love, as they say, because, when I am married, you know, Parliament will make me a grant, and I shall pay off my debts, and be all right and tight. We shall do delightfully!'

Miss Taverner got up, and moved away from him to the window. 'We should not suit, sir. I thank you for the honour you have done me, but do most earnestly beg you not to distress me by persisting in it. I cannot return your regard.'

The Duke looked very much crestfallen at this, and asked in a desponding voice whether her affections were bestowed elsewhere. 'I thought it might be so; I was afraid someone might have been before me, for all I've crowded all sail to be first with you.'

'No, sir, my affections are not engaged, but —'

'Oh well, in that case there is no need to be down in the mouth,' said the Duke, brightening. 'I have taken you too much by surprise, but when you have thought it over you will see how you will come round to it.'

'I assure you, sir, my resolution is formed. For your friendship, which you have been so kind as to bestow on me, I have the highest value; but anything of a warmer nature — you understand me: I need say no more.'

'No, no, where's the use in talking?' agreed the Duke. 'I have been too quick; you are not well enough acquainted with me yet to give me an answer.'

Miss Taverner began to despair of making any impression on him. She turned. 'It is useless, sir. Apart from my own sentiments, you must know that my guardian, Lord Worth, is resolved not to consent to my marriage while I remain his ward. He will not countenance so much as a betrothal. He has said it, and, I believe, means it.'

The Duke looked much struck by this, blinked rapidly once or twice, and began to walk about the room with his hands under his coat-tails. 'Well, well! Bless my soul!' he ejaculated. 'What should he do that for? This is very odd hearing, upon my word!'

'Yes, sir, but so it is. His mind is made up.'

'The strangest fellow! However, though I am not one to make a great parade of my rank, I hope, I am not quite anybody, and you may depend upon it Worth will sing a different tune when I see him. That is what I shall do; that will be best. I do not set a great deal of store by such things, you know, but I like to have everything ship-shape, and I will get Worth's permission to pay my addresses. I should like to have it all done with propriety. Ay, that's the best tack: I must see Worth, and then, you know, you can have no objection. And I'll tell you what! I have a famous notion in my head now! I will have Worth come to spend Christmas at Bushey with us!'

He beamed upon her with such goodwill, and seemed to have so simple a pride in his famous notion that Miss Taverner had not the heart to protest further. She could only trust in her guardian's ability to rescue her from her difficulties, and wish the Duke good-day with as much reserve of manner as was compatible with the civility she must feel to be his due. He impressed upon her once more that he should approach her guardian; she assented; and so they parted.

She was not without hope that a period of calm reflection might damp her royal suitor's ardour; she had no notion of his hurrying off post-haste to call upon Worth, and had every intention of warning the Earl at the first opportunity of what was in store for him.

With this resolve in mind she was glad when, at Almack's that evening, she perceived her guardian to be present. He was standing beside Lady Jersey when she came in, his handsome head bent to hear what her ladyship was saying, but he soon caught sight of Miss Taverner, and bowed. A very friendly smile brought him across the room to her side to beg the honour of a dance.

Judith, who was looking quite her best in Indian mull muslin draped with gold Brussels lace, expressed her willingness, but before going with him to take her place in the set which was forming, she put out her hand to draw forward Miss Fairford, who had come to the Assembly in Mrs Scattergood's charge. 'I think, sir, you are not acquainted with Miss Fairford. Harriet, you must permit me to present Lord Worth.'

Miss Fairford, who, from hearing Peregrine's unflattering description of his guardian, already stood in considerable awe of him, was quite overpowered by his commanding height and air of consequence. She hardly dared raise her eyes to his face. He bowed, and said something civil enough to embolden her to peep up at him for a moment. Her soft eyes encountered his hard ones, which seemed to be looking her over with a sort of indifferent criticism. She blushed, and retreated again to Peregrine's side.

Lord Worth led Judith into the set. 'Do you like timid brown mice?' he inquired.

'Sometimes, when they are as good as Miss Fairford,' she replied. 'Do not you?'

'I?' he said, lifting his brows. 'What a singularly stupid question! No, I do not.'

'I don't understand why you should call it a stupid question,' said Judith with spirit. 'How should I know what you like?'

'You might guess, I imagine, but I shall not gratify your vanity by telling you.'

She gave a start, and shot a quick, indignant look up at him. 'Gratify me! *That* would not gratify me, I assure you!'

'You take too much for granted, Miss Taverner. What would not gratify you?'

She bit her lip. 'You lose no opportunity to put me in the wrong, Lord Worth,' she said in a mortified voice.

He smiled, and as their hands joined in the dance pressed hers slightly. 'Don't look so downcast. I did mean just what you thought. Are you satisfied?'

'No, not at all,' said Judith crossly. 'This is a foolish conversation; I do not like it. I was glad to see you here to-night, for I wanted particularly to speak to you, but you are in one of your disagreeable moods, I see.'

'On the contrary, my temper is more than usually complaisant. But you are behindhand. I have heard the news, and must wish you joy.'

'Wish me joy?' repeated Judith, looking at him in a startled way. 'What can you mean?'

'I understand you are to become a Duchess in the near future. You must allow me to offer you my sincere felicitations.'

They were separated at this moment by the movement of the dance. Judith's brain, as she went down the set, was whirling; she could scarcely perform her part in the dance, nor contain her impatience till she and Worth came together again. No sooner were they confronting each other once more than she demanded: 'How can you talk so? What do you mean?'

'I beg pardon. Is it to be kept a secret?'

'A secret!'

'You must forgive me. I had thought that only my consent was wanting before the engagement was to be made public.'

She turned quite pale. 'Good God! You have seen him, then!'

'Certainly. Did you not send him to me?'

'Yes – no! Do not trifle with me! This is dreadful!'

'Dreadful?' said his lordship, maddeningly calm. 'You could hardly make a more brilliant match, surely! You will have all the comfort and consequence of a most superior establishment, a position of the first consideration, and a husband who must be past the age of youthful folly. You are to be congratulated; I could not have wished to see you more creditably provided for. In addition you will be assured of suitable female companionship in the person of your eldest daughter-in-law, Miss Fitzclarence, whom I believe to be near your own age.'

'You are laughing at me!' Judith said uncertainly. 'I am sure you are laughing at me! Do pray tell me you did not give your consent!'

He smiled, but would not answer. They were again separated, and when they met once more he began to talk in his languid way of something quite different. She answered very much at random, trying to read his face, and when the dance came to an end, suffered him to lead her into the tea-room, away from her own party.

He procured a glass of lemonade for her, and took up a position beside her chair. 'Well, my ward,' he said, 'did you, or did you not, send Clarence to me?'

'Yes, I did – that is to say, he said he should go to you, and I agreed, because I could not make him realise that I don't wish to marry him. I thought I might depend on you!'

'Oh!' said Worth. 'That is not precisely as I understood the matter. The Duke seemed to be in no doubt of the issue once my consent was obtained.'

'If you thought that I would ever marry a man old enough to be my father you did me a shocking injustice!' said Miss Taverner hotly. 'And if you had the amazing impertinence to suppose that his rank must make him acceptable to me you insult me beyond all bearing!'

'Softly, my child: I thought neither of these things,' said his lordship, slightly amused. 'My experience of you led me instead to suppose that you had sent your suitor to me in a spirit of pure mischief. Was that an injustice too?'

Miss Taverner was a little mollified, but said stiffly: 'Yes, it was, sir. The Duke of Clarence would not believe I meant what I said, and the best I could think of was for you to help me. I made sure you would refuse your consent!'

'I did,' said the Earl, taking snuff.

'Then why,' demanded Miss Taverner, relieved, 'did you say you wished me joy?'

'Merely to alarm you, Clorinda, and to teach you not to play tricks on me.'

'It was no trick, and you are abominable!'

'I humbly beg your forgiveness.'

She flashed an indignant look at him, and set her empty glass down on the table with a snap. The Earl offered her his

snuff-box. 'Will you try this mixture? I find it tolerably soothing to the nerves.'

Miss Taverner relented. 'I am very sensible of what an honour *that* is,' she said, helping herself to an infinitesimal pinch. 'I
suppose you could do no more.'

'Not while I continue to occupy the post of guardian,' he agreed.

She lowered her gaze, and said in a hurry: 'Did the Duke mention his plan of inviting me (and you too) to Bushey for Christmas?'

'He did,' said the Earl. 'But I informed him that you would
be spending Christmas at Worth.'

Miss Taverner drew in her breath sharply, inhaled far more of
his lordship's snuff than she had meant to, and sneezed. 'But I am
not!' she said.

'I am sorry if it should be repugnant to you, but you are certainly spending Christmas at Worth,' he replied.

'It is not repugnant, precisely, but –'

'You relieve my mind of a weight,' said his lordship satirically.
'I was afraid it might be.'

'It is very obliging of you, but since you have refused your
consent to the Duke's paying his addresses to me he cannot now
expect me to make one of his party. I should prefer to spend
Christmas with Perry.'

'Naturally,' said the Earl. 'I was not proposing that you should
come to Worth without him.'

'But Perry has no notion of going to Worth!' protested Miss
Taverner. 'I daresay he has quite different plans in mind!'

'Then he will put them out of his mind,' replied the Earl. 'I
prefer to keep Perry under my eye.'

He offered his arm, and after a slight hesitation she rose, and
laid her hand on it, and allowed him to lead her back into the
ballroom. It had occurred to her that she was by no means
averse from going on a visit to Worth.

Fourteen

*I*T WAS FORTUNATE FOR MISS TAVERNER THAT, BY REASON OF Christmas being at hand, she must soon be removed from the Duke of Clarence's neighbourhood. He by no means despaired of winning her, and though momentarily cast-down, and inclined to be indignant at Worth's refusing his consent, he was very soon consoling himself with the reflection that Miss Taverner would be free in less than a year from the Earl's guardianship. He was sanguine, and, calling in Brook Street again, assured Judith that when she came to know him better she would perceive all the advantages of the match as clearly as he did himself.

Peregrine's feelings upon being informed that he was to go to Worth were not at all complacent. He asserted that he should not go, thought it a great imposition, suspected the Earl of trying to fix his interest with Judith, and had a very good mind to write a curt refusal. However, the intelligence that Miss Fairford had received a most distinguishing invitation from Lady Albinia Forrest, the Earl's maternal aunt, to make one of the party, quite put an end to his ill-humour. The Earl became immediately a very good sort of a fellow, and from having been disconsolately expecting a party insipid beyond everything, he was brought to look forward to it with no common degree of pleasure.

Judith also looked forward to it in the expectation of considerable enjoyment. She had an ambition to see Worth, which Mrs

Scattergood had described to her in the most eulogistic terms; the party was to be select, comprised for the most part of her most particular friends; and her only regret was that the greatest of her friends, Mr Bernard Taverner, was not to be present. When she told him of the invitation and saw him look sadly out of countenance, she said impulsively that she wished he might be going with them. He smiled, but shook his head. 'The Earl of Worth would never invite me to join any party of which you were a member,' he said. 'There is no love lost between us.'

'No love lost!' she exclaimed. 'I had thought you barely acquainted with him. How is this?'

'The Earl of Worth,' he said deliberately, 'has been good enough to warn me against making your well-being my concern. He does me the honour of thinking me to stand in his way. What will be the issue I do not know. If he is to be believed, I stand in some danger of being put out of his way.' He gave a little laugh. 'The Earl of Worth does not like to have his path crossed.'

She was staring at him in great astonishment. 'This is beyond everything, upon my word! You cannot, I am persuaded, have properly understood him! Why should he threaten you? When have you met? Where did this conversation take place?'

'It took place,' said Mr Taverner, 'in a certain tavern known as Cribb's Parlour, upon the day that Perry went out to fight Farnaby. I found his lordship there in close conversation with Farnaby himself.'

'With Farnaby! Good God! what can you mean?'

He took a short turn about the room. 'I do not know. I wish that I did. It was not my intention to speak of this to you, but lately I have thought that his lordship has been making headway with you. However little I may relish the office of informer, it is only right that you should be put upon your guard. What Worth's business with Farnaby may have been I have no means of knowing. It must be all conjecture. To see them with their heads together was to me something of a shock, I own. I impute nothing; I merely tell you what I saw. The Earl, perceiving me, came across the room to my side; what passed between us I shall not repeat. It was enough to assure me that Worth regards me as a menace to whatever scheme he may have in mind. I was warned not to meddle in your concerns. Whether I am very likely to be intimidated by such a threat I leave it to yourself to decide.'

She was silent for a moment, frowning over it. She could not but perceive that there might be some jealousy at work here, on both sides perhaps. She said presently in a tone of calm good-sense: 'It is very odd, indeed, but I must believe you to be mistaken, in part at least. Lord Worth, being Perry's guardian, may easily have conceived it to be his duty to inquire more fully into the cause of that projected meeting.'

He looked at her intently. 'It may have been so, yet I shall not conceal from you, Judith, that I neither like nor trust that man.' She made a gesture as though to silence him. 'You do not wish me to speak. Perhaps I should not; perhaps I am wrong. I will only beg of you to take care how you put yourself in his power.'

She returned his look a little sternly, but as though puzzling over what he had said. 'Lord Worth told me to trust him,' she said slowly.

'That is easily said. I do not tell you to trust me. Mistrust me, if you please: I shall continue to do what I can to serve you.'

His frank, manly way of speaking induced her to stretch out her hand to him. 'Why, of course I trust you, cousin,' she said, 'even though I think you are mistaken.'

He kissed her hand, and said no more, but left her very soon to ponder over it, to recall incidents, words, that might guide her understanding. Lately, it had seemed to her as though Worth too might become a suitor to her hand, yet no man had it in his power to compel her into marriage, and she could see no reason for fearing him. Her cousin she believed to be strongly attached to her, and allowance must be made for the very natural jealousy of a man deeply in love. Neither man could like the other: it had been apparent from the first. She supposed each must find it easy to mistrust the other. She put the matter out of mind, yet was still worried by it.

A few days would now bring Christmas upon them; the Taverners, accompanied by Mrs Scattergood and Miss Fairford, were to travel into Hampshire, to Worth, upon the twenty-third of December, and every moment before their departure seemed to Miss Taverner to be occupied in writing graceful notes of acknowledgment for the shower of gifts that descended upon her. The most elegant trifles were sent for her acceptance: she was in despair, half-inclined to return them all, but dissuaded from it by her chaperon, who inspected each offering with the strictest regard for propriety, and pronounced all to be in the best of taste, quite unexceptionable, impossible to decline!

Amongst the collection of snuff-boxes, étuis, china figures, and fans that arrived for his sister, the tokens Peregrine had received made, he complained, a meagre show. Some handkerchiefs, hemmed for him by Lady Fairford, a brace of partridges from Sussex, where Mr Fitzjohn had retired for the month, a locket with his Harriet's eye painted on ivory, a small jar of snuff from which the sender's card was missing, and a fob from his cousin made up the sum of his presents. However, he was in raptures over the locket, and very well satisfied with the rest. The handkerchiefs must always be useful; the birds could be roasted for dinner; the fob was added to his already large collection; and the snuff was no doubt a capital mixture. Like a great many other young gentlemen, Peregrine never stirred out without his box, and inhaled a vast quantity of snuff without having very much taste for it, or discrimination in the sorts he chose. Brown rappee was the same to him as Spanish bran; he could detect very little difference. As for this elegant, glazed jar which had been sent to him he liked it excessively, and only wished he might know the donor. A prolonged search amongst the litter of cards, notes, and silver-paper wrappings which surrounded his sister failed to discover the missing card; he had to resign himself to its being lost.

Judith took a pinch of his snuff, and wrinkled her nose at it. 'My dear Perry, it reeks of Otto of Roses! It is detestable!'

'Pho, nonsense, you are a great deal too nice! Since you took to using snuff you think you know everything about it.'

'I know this mixture would never be tolerated by Lord Petersham, or Worth,' she retorted. 'It is not at all unlike the sort Worth has made up for the Regent, only more scented. Do not be offering it to him, I beg of you! Who can have sent it to you? How awkward it is that you have lost the card!'

'I believe there never was a card. I believe it must have been forgotten. If you do not like the mixture I am glad, for you won't be wanting to fill your box from my jar.'

'No, indeed! I imagine no one would suspect *me* of taking scented snuff,' retorted Judith.

The day of setting forward on the journey arrived at last. The trunks and the bandboxes were safely strapped to the chaise; Mrs Scattergood predicted a fall of snow; Peregrine mounted his horse; Miss Fairford was picked up in Arlington Street; and the whole party started on the journey not more than an hour later than had originally been intended.

No fall of snow occurred to render the roads impassable; the weather, though wintry, was not cold enough to make travelling insupportable; and with only one halt of any length upon the way they arrived at Worth by four in the afternoon, to be welcomed with all the comfort of large fires, hot soup, and cheerful company.

It was dusk when they turned in at the iron gates of Worth,

and no impression of the park, or the exterior of the house could be had; but the interior struck Miss Taverner at once with a sense of its elegance, noble apartments, and handsome furnishings. It was just what a gentleman's residence should be; everything spoke its owner's taste. Judith could not but be pleased with all that she saw, and wish to explore further, at a more convenient time, into the older part of the house, which she understood to date back as much as two centuries.

Lady Albinia was there to receive the travellers. She was a short-sighted, vague woman of no particular beauty, and a total disregard for the prevailing fashion. A Paisley shawl, which she wore to protect her from the draughts, was continually slipping from her shoulders and becoming entangled in the furniture. When this happened she immediately summoned up any gentleman who chanced to be near, and commanded him to disengage her tiresome fringe. She seemed incapable of helping herself, and when she dropped her fan or her handkerchief, as she frequently did, merely waited for someone to pick it up for her, breaking off in the middle of whatever she was saying, and resuming again the instant her property was restored to her. She had a habit of uttering her thoughts aloud, which was disconcerting to those not much acquainted with her, but which no one who knew her paid the least attention to. She greeted the Taverners kindly, and having led the ladies to the fire, and begged them to sit down by it and warm their chilled hands, looked Judith over with an expression of mild approval, and said in her inconsequent way: 'Such bad weather for travelling, though to be sure it does not snow, and the roads nowadays are so good that one is hardly ever in danger of being held up. Eighty thousand pounds, and quite a beauty besides! Worth is fortunate indeed if only he may have the sense to realise it.'

Miss Taverner, who had been warned by Mrs Scattergood

what to expect, tried to look unconscious, but could not prevent a blush creeping into her cheeks. Mrs Scattergood said severely: 'Albinia, where is Julian?'

It appeared that the gentlemen had gone out for a day's shooting, and were not yet returned. The travellers were escorted upstairs to their bedchambers, and left to recover from the fatigues of the journey before dressing for dinner.

By dinner-time the rest of the party had arrived, and the sporting gentlemen returned from their expedition. The remaining guests comprised Lords Petersham and Alvanley, Mr Brummell, and Mr Forrest, Lady Albinia's taciturn spouse, and Mrs and Miss Marley, particular friends of Miss Taverner. Everyone was acquainted; nothing, Mrs Scattergood declared, could have been more charming. Lord Alvanley, except for his habit of putting out his bedroom candle by stuffing it under his pillow, must always be an acceptable guest; Lord Petersham, the most finished gentleman alive, was courteous and amiable; the Earl was a calm but attentive host; Mr Brummell was in a conversable mood, and a pleasant evening was spent in one of the saloons, playing cards, drinking tea, and chatting over a noble fire. The only discomfort Judith had to endure was the sight of her brother begging Lord Petersham to give an opinion on his new snuff, the whole history of which he had been recounting a moment previous. Lord Petersham was obliging enough to help himself to a pinch, and to say courteously that he had no doubt of its being a superior mixture. Lord Worth, less polite, put up his glass when the box was offered to him, and upon hearing that it was highly scented waved it away. 'No, thank you, Peregrine. I will believe it to be all you say. I hope you are not using it, Miss Taverner?'

'No, no, I keep my own sort,' Judith assured him. 'When I want scent I do not go to my snuff-box for it, but to Mr Brummell, who is going to make me a stick of perfume.'

'A stick of Mr Brummell's perfume, my love!' exclaimed Mrs

Marley. 'Do you want to make us all envious? Do you not know that every lady among us wants one of those sticks?'

The Beau shook his head. 'Very true, but you know I cannot be giving them to everyone, ma'am. That would be to have them held very cheap. The Regent, now, is dying to get hold of one, but one has to draw the line somewhere.'

'George is feeling peevish because he has caught a cold,' remarked Alvanley. 'How did you come by it in this mild weather, George?'

'Why, do you know, I left my carriage this afternoon on my way from town, and the infidel of a landlord put me into a room with a damp stranger!' replied Brummell instantly.

It seemed the next day as though Peregrine had caught the Beau's cold. He complained of the sore throat, and coughed a little, but trusted that a day's sport (which he had been promised) would soon set matters to rights. Judith could place no such dependence on the effect of a raw, December day, but it was useless to expect Peregrine to remain indoors for no more serious reason than a slight chill. He went off with Petersham, Alvanley, and Mr Forrest to shoot over some preserves a few miles distant from Worth.

Mr Brummell put in no appearance until midday. The exigencies of his toilet occupied several hours; he had been known to spend as many as two on the nice arrangement of his clothes, to which, however, he gave not another thought once he had left his dressing-room. Unlike most of the dandies he was never seen to cast an anxious glance at a mirror, to adjust his cravat, nor to smooth wrinkles from his coat. When he left his room he was, and knew himself to be, a finished work of art, perfect in every detail from his beautifully laundered linen to his highly polished boots.

Mrs Marley also kept her room until a late hour, but the three young ladies were up in good time, and spent the morning in exploring the house under the guidance of the housekeeper, and in strolling about the gardens and shrubbery until they were called in to partake of scalloped oysters, cold meats, and fruit in one of the dining-parlours.

The sportsmen were expected to be back by three o'clock, so that it was not surprising that Miss Fairford should blushingly decline the offer of being driven out for an airing after luncheon. The Earl made the suggestion; it was met by a dismayed look and a stammered excuse, Miss Fairford hardly knowing what to say, from the fear, on the one hand, of offending her host, and, on the other, of not being present when Peregrine returned to the house. The Earl looked amused at her confusion, but forbore to tease, as Judith was half afraid he would, and said with only the faintest suggestion of a laugh in his well-bred voice: 'You had rather be writing a letter to your mama, I daresay.'

'Oh yes!' said Miss Fairford thankfully. 'I think I ought certainly to do that!'

He turned away to address Judith. 'Does Miss Taverner care to drive out with me?'

She assented to it gladly; as they left the room together the Earl looked back, and said with the hint of a smile: 'Let me have your letter when it is finished, Miss Fairford, and I will frank it for you.'

An hour spent in being driven about the country brought Miss Taverner back with glowing cheeks and in happy spirits. The Earl had been in his most pleasant mood, a sensible companion, entertaining her with easy talk, and teaching her how to loop a rein and let it run free again in his own deft fashion.

They returned quite in charity with each other to find Lady Albinia, Mrs Marley, and Mr Brummell seated in one of the drawing-rooms with a lady and two gentlemen who had driven over from a neighbouring estate to pay a call at Worth.

Upon the entrance of the Earl and his ward a greater animation seemed to enter into these visitors. Compliments were exchanged, and the lady lost no time in presenting her son to Miss Taverner. The elder of the two gentlemen, who had been talking to Mr Brummell, had less interest in the heiress, and very soon returned to Brummell. The Beau was sitting with a look of pained resignation on his face, which was accounted for by Lady Albinia, who in making the necessary introductions turned to the Earl and said: 'You see the Fox-Matthews are come to call on us, my dear Worth. So obliging of them! They have been sitting with us more than half an hour. I do not believe they will ever go.'

Mr Fox-Matthews was talking in a consequential way of the beauties of the Hampshire scenery. He would scarcely allow it to have its equal, unless perhaps one took the Lake District into account. It was soon seen that having been travelling there in the summer he now desired nothing better than to be allowed to describe the Lakes to everyone, and to tell those who had not had the good fortune to journey so far that they had missed something very fine. He did not know whether Mr Brummell had visited the Lakes; if he had not he should certainly make the effort.

Mr Brummell looked him over with that lift of the eyebrow which could always depress pretension. 'Yes, sir, I *have* visited the Lakes,' he said.

'Ah then, in that case – And which of them do you most admire, sir?'

Mr Brummell drew in his breath. 'I will tell you, sir, if you will accord me a few moments.' Then, turning to address a footman who had come in to make up the fire, he quietly desired the man to send his valet to him. Mr Fox-Matthews stared, but the Beau remained quite imperturbable, and maintained a thoughtful silence until the entrance of a neat man in a black coat, who came anxiously up to him, and bowed.

'Robinson,' said Mr Brummell, 'which of the Lakes do I admire?'

'Windermere, sir,' replied the valet respectfully.

'Ah, Windermere, is it? Thank you, Robinson. Yes, I like Windermere best,' he said, turning politely back to Mr Fox-Matthews.

Mrs Fox-Matthews, swelling with indignation, rose, and declared it to be time they were taking their leave.

Peregrine's cough, when his sister next saw him, did not appear to have benefited much from a morning spent in the fresh air. It still troubled him, and during the days that followed grew perceptibly worse. His throat was slightly inflamed, and although he would not hear of consulting a doctor, or admit that he felt in the least sickly, it was evident that he was far from being in perfect health. There was a languor, a heavy look about the eyes which worried his sister, but he ascribed it all to having caught a chill, and believed that the air at Worth might not quite suit him.

'The air at Worth,' Judith repeated. 'The air –' She broke off. 'What am I thinking? I deserve to be beaten for indulging such a wild fancy! Impossible! Oh, impossible!'

'Well, what are you thinking?' inquired Peregrine, with a yawn. 'What is impossible? Why do you look so oddly?'

She knelt down beside his chair and clasped his hands. 'Perry, how do you feel?' she asked earnestly. 'Are you sure that it is no more than a chill?'

'Why, what else should it be? What's in your mind?'

'I hardly know, hardly dare to wonder. Perry, when that man picked a quarrel with you – I am speaking of Farnaby – were you not surprised? Did it seem to you reasonable?'

'What has that to do with it?' he asked, opening his eyes at her. 'Ay, I daresay I was a trifle surprised, but if Farnaby was foxed, you know –'

'But was he? You did not say so.'

'Lord, how should I know? I did not think so, but he may have been.'

She continued to clasp his hands, looking anxiously up into his face. 'You were fired on the day you came over Finchley Common, a shot you believed might have killed you, had it not been for Hinkson. Twice you have been in danger of your life! And now you are ill, mysteriously so, for you have no chill, Perry, and you know it, but only this dry cough, which is growing worse, and the sore throat!'

He stared, sat up with a jerk, and then burst into a laugh that brought on a fit of coughing. 'Lord, Ju, you'll be the death of me! Do you think I am being poisoned? Why, who in the world should want to put me away? Of all the nonsensical notions!'

'Yes, yes, it *is* nonsensical, it must be!' she said. 'I tell myself so, and yet am unconvinced. Perry, have you not considered that if anything should happen to you the greater part of your fortune would be mine?'

This set him off into another fit of laughing. 'What! are you trying to make away with me?' he asked.

'Be serious, Perry, I beg of you!'

'Lord, how can I be? I never heard such a pack of nonsense in my life. This is what comes of reading Mrs Radclyffe's novels! It is a famous joke, I declare!'

'What is a famous joke? May I share it?'

Judith looked quickly round. The Earl had come into the room, and was standing by the table, inscrutably regarding them. How much he had heard of their conversation she could not guess, but she coloured deeply, and sprang up, turning her head away.

'Oh, it is the best thing I have heard these ten years!' said Peregrine. 'Judith thinks I am being poisoned!'

'Indeed!' said the Earl, glancing in Judith's direction. 'May I know who it is Miss Taverner suspects of poisoning you?'

She threw her brother an angry, reproachful look, and went past the Earl to the door. 'Peregrine is jesting. I believe him to have taken something that has not agreed with him, that is all.'

She went out, and the Earl, looking after her in silence for a moment, presently turned back to Peregrine, and, laying a silver snuff-box on the table, said: 'This is yours, I fancy. It was found in the Blue Saloon.'

'Oh, thank you! Yes, it is mine,' said Peregrine, picking it up and idly flicking it open. 'I did not know I had so much snuff in it, however; I thought it had been no more than half full. You know, Petersham found it to be a very good mixture. You heard him say so. I wish you would try it!'

'Very well,' said the Earl, dipping his finger and thumb in the box.

Peregrine, much gratified, also took a pinch, and inhaled it carelessly. 'I like it as well as most,' he said. 'I do not see what there is to object to in it.'

The Earl's eyes, which had been fixed watchfully on his face, fell. 'Petersham's praise should be enough to satisfy you,' he said. 'I know of no better judge.'

'Judith says it is a sort no gentleman of taste could use,' complained Peregrine. 'If *you* think that I suppose I had better throw it all away, for I daresay Petersham was only wishing to be civil.'

'Miss Taverner is prejudiced against scented snuffs,' replied the Earl. 'You need not be afraid of using this sort.'

'Well, I am glad of that,' said Peregrine. 'You know, I have a whole jar of it at home, and it would be a pity to waste it.'

'Certainly. But I hope you keep your jar in a warm room?'

'Oh, it is in my dressing-room! I do not keep a great deal of snuff, you know. I do not have a room for it, as you do. In general, I buy it as I need it, and keep it where it may be handy.'

The Earl returned some indifferent answer, and soon left the room in search of Judith. He found her presently in the library, choosing a volume from the shelves. She looked over her shoulder when he came in, coloured faintly, but said in a calm voice: 'You have such an excellent library: I daresay many thousands of volumes. At Beverley we are sadly lacking in that respect. It is a great luxury to find oneself in a library as well stocked as this.'

'My library is honoured, Miss Taverner,' he answered briefly.

She could not but be aware of the gravity in both face and voice. He was looking stern; there was something of reserve in his tone, quite different from the easy, open manner she was growing used to in him. She hesitated, and then turned more completely towards him, and said with an air of frank resolution: 'I am afraid there may be some misconstruction. I have been indulging an absurd flight of fancy, as I believe you may have heard when you came into the saloon just now.'

He did not answer immediately, and when he did at last speak it was with considerable dryness. 'I think, Miss Taverner, you will be well advised not to repeat to anyone that you believe Peregrine's indisposition to be due to the effect of poison.'

Her colour mounted; she hung down her head. 'I have been very foolish. Indeed, I do not know what possessed me to blurt out so stupid a suggestion! I have been worried about him. That duel, which, thank God! was stopped, took such strong possession of my mind that I have not been easy ever since. It seemed so wanton, so senseless! Then you must know that he was attacked upon his way home from St Albans, and escaped by the veriest miracle. I cannot rid myself of the fear that some danger threatens him. This indisposition seemed, in the agitation of the moment, to bear out my suspicion, and without pausing to consider I spoke the thought that darted through my head. I was wrong, extremely foolish, and I acknowledge it.'

He came towards her. 'Are you worried about Peregrine? You need not be.'

'I cannot help myself. If I thought that my suspicions had in them the least vestige of truth I think I should be quite out of my mind with terror.'

'In that case,' said his lordship deliberately, 'it is as well that there can be no truth in them. I have no doubt of Peregrine's being speedily restored to health. As for his rather absurd duel, and his encounter on Finchley Common, such things may befall anyone. I counsel you to put them out of your mind.'

'My cousin did not take so light a view,' she said in a low voice.

She saw his face harden. 'Have you discussed this matter with Mr Bernard Taverner?' he asked sharply.

'Yes, certainly I have. Why should I not?'

'I could tell you several good reasons. I shall be obliged to you, Miss Taverner, if you will remember that whatever your relationship with that gentleman may be, it is I who am your guardian, and not he.'

'I do not forget it.'

'Excuse me, Miss Taverner, you forget it every time you bestow on him confidences which he has done nothing to deserve.'

She faced him with a dawning anger in her eyes. 'Is not this a little petty, Lord Worth?'

A sardonic smile curled his lips. 'I see. I am jealous, I suppose? My good girl, your conquests have mounted to your head. You are not the only pretty female I have kissed!'

Her breasts rose and fell quickly. 'You are insufferable!' she said. 'I have done nothing to deserve such an insult from you!'

'If we are to talk of insults,' said the Earl grimly, 'you will come off very much the worst from that encounter. The insult of informing you that I am not a suitor to your hand is hardly comparable to the insult of ascribing to me jealousy of such a person as Mr Bernard Taverner.'

'I am very happy to think that you are not my suitor!' flashed Judith. 'I can conceive of nothing more odious!'

'There are times,' said the Earl, 'when, if I were in the habit of uttering exaggerated statements, I could almost echo that sentiment. Do not look daggers at me: I am wholly impervious to displays of that kind. Your tantrums may do very well at home, but they arouse in me nothing more than a desire to beat you soundly. And that, Miss Taverner, if ever I do marry you, is precisely what I shall do.'

Miss Taverner fought for breath. 'If ever you – Oh, if I were but a man!'

'A more stupid remark I have yet to hear you make,' commented his lordship. 'If you were a man this conversation would not be taking place.'

Miss Taverner, failing to find words with which to answer him, swung round on her heel, and began to pace about the room in a hasty manner that spoke more clearly than any words the agitation of her spirits.

The Earl leaned his shoulders against the bookshelves, and stood with folded arms, observing her perambulations. As he watched her the anger died out of his eyes; his mouth which had been set in a straight line relaxed; and he began to look merely amused. After a few minutes he spoke, saying in his usual calm way: 'Do not be striding about the room any longer, Miss Taverner. You look magnificent, but it is a waste of energy. I will apologise for the whole.'

She came to a halt beside a chair, and grasped the back of it with both hands. 'Your behaviour, your manner –'

'Both abominable,' he said. 'I beg pardon, *insufferable* was the word. I offer you my apologies.'

'Your way of speaking of a gentleman who is my cousin –'

'Whom, if you please, we will leave out of this discussion.'

She gripped the chair-back more tightly still. 'Your indelicacy, the total want of proper feeling that could prompt you to taunt me with an episode in the past which covered me, and still covers me, with shame –'

He held out his hand to her. 'That was ill-done of me indeed,' he said gently. 'Forgive me!'

She was silenced, and stood looking across at him in a frowning way for several minutes. At last she said in a more mollified voice: 'I daresay I may seem to be conceited. If you say so no doubt it is so: *you* should be a judge. But I can assure you, Lord Worth, that my conquests, as you are good enough to call them, have not led me to suppose that every gentleman of my acquaintance, including yourself, is desirous of marrying me.'

'Of course not,' he agreed.

She said uncertainly: 'I am sorry to have lost my temper in what you may have thought to have been an unlady-like manner, but you will allow the provocation to have been great.'

'I will allow it to have been impossible to withstand,' said his lordship. 'Come, shall we shake hands on it?'

Miss Taverner walked slowly across the room and put her hand reluctantly into his. He bent, and somewhat to her surprise lightly kissed it. Releasing it again he said: 'I have one more thing to say to you before we forget this conversation. It is my wish that you will not mention, either to Mr Taverner or to anyone else, this suspicion you have had of Perry's having been poisoned.' She looked questioningly at him, half-frowning. 'You can do no good by giving voice to such a suspicion; you may do harm.'

'Harm! Do you think – is it possible that I may have been right?' she asked in quick alarm.

'Extremely unlikely,' he replied. 'But since this indisposition of his has overtaken him under my roof I prefer not to be suspected of making away with him.'

'I shall not speak of it,' she said in a troubled way. 'I should not spread such a rumour without positive proof of its truth.'

He bowed, and moved away from her towards the door. Before he had reached it he looked back, and said casually: 'By the by, Miss Taverner, can you lay your hand on the lease of your house? I believe I gave it into your charge.'

'It is in my desk at home,' she said. 'Do you wish for it?'

'Blackader writes of some point to be argued. It will be necessary for me to glance at the lease. If a servant were sent to London, could your housekeeper, or some such person, find it, and give it to him to bring to me?'

'Certainly,' she said. 'Hinkson, Perry's new groom, can be sent for it.'

'Thank you, that will be best, no doubt,' he said.

A hasty step sounded at this moment outside the room, and a gay voice called: 'In the library, is he? I will find him: do not give yourself the trouble of coming with me, my dear ma'am! I have not forgot my way about.'

The Earl raised his brows in quick surprise. 'This is something quite unexpected,' he remarked, and opened the door, and held out both his hands. 'Charles! What the devil?'

A tall young man in Hussar uniform, with a handsome, laughing countenance, and his right arm in a sling, gripped one of the Earl's hands in his own left one. 'My dear fellow! How do you do? By Gad, it's famous to see you again! You observe I have got my furlough, thanks to this!' He indicated his useless arm.

'How is it?' Worth asked. 'Do you feel it as much as ever? When did you come out of hospital? There does not look to be a great deal amiss with you from what I can see!'

'Lord, no! nothing in the world! I'm come home to try my luck with the heiress. Where is she? Does she squint like a bag of nails? Is she hideous? They always are!'

The Earl stood back. 'You may judge for yourself,' he said dryly. 'Miss Taverner, little though he may have recommended himself to you, I must beg leave to present my brother, Captain Audley.'

Captain the Honourable Charles Audley started, and gazed at Miss Taverner with an expression of mingled dismay, admiration, and incredulity in his bright eyes. He said: 'Good God! is it possible?' and strode forward. 'Madam, your most obedient! What can I say?'

'You have said too much already,' remarked the Earl in a tone of amusement.

'True, very true! There is no getting away from it, indeed; Miss Taverner, you did not hear me; you were not attending!'

'On the contrary, I heard you very plainly,' said Judith, unable to withstand his smile. She held out her hand. 'How do you do? I am sorry to see your arm in a sling. I hope no lasting injury?'

'Not to my arm, ma'am; none incurred in the *Peninsula*,' he said promptly, taking her hand and kissing it.

She could not help laughing. His eyes began to dance; he said outrageously: 'You must let me tell you that in all my experience of heiresses I have never till to-day encountered one who did not give me a nightmare. You have restored my faith in miracles, Miss Taverner!'

'If you expose yourself any further, Miss Taverner will ask to have her carriage spoken for immediately,' observed the Earl.

'Not at all,' she replied. 'I am happy to think I do not give Captain Audley nightmares.' She moved towards the door. 'You will have so much to say to each other! I will leave you.'

She was gone on the words. Captain Audley closed the door behind her and turned to look at the Earl. 'Julian, you dog! you've kept her mighty dark! Are you engaged to her?'

'No,' said Worth. 'I am not.'

'You must be mad!' declared the Captain. 'Don't tell me you mean to let all that wealth and beauty slip through your fingers! I have a very good mind to try for her myself.'

'Do so, by all means. You won't succeed, but it may keep you out of mischief.'

'Ah, don't be too sure!' grinned the Captain. 'You know nothing about it, my boy.'

'I know a great deal about it,' retorted Worth. 'I am her guardian.'

'Well, upon my word!' exclaimed Captain Audley. 'Am I to understand you would forbid the banns?'

'You are,' said Worth.

The Captain perched himself on the edge of the table. 'Very well, Gretna Green let it be! My dear fellow, you're in love with her yourself! Shall I go away again?'

Worth smiled. 'Your vulgarity is only equalled by your conceit, Charles. Tell me now, how have things been with you?'

'All in good time,' said the Captain. 'First you shall tell me whether I am to hold off from the heiress.'

'Not at all; why should you? I think you may be quite useful to me. The heiress has a brother.'

'I am not the least interested in her brother,' objected the Captain.

'Possibly not, but I have a considerable interest in him,' said Worth. He looked the Captain over meditatively. 'I think, Charles – I am nearly sure – that you are going to become very friendly with young Peregrine, if he will let you. Unfortunately, he does not like me, and his prejudice may extend to you as well.'

'Alas, alas! Why do you want him to like me?'

'Because,' said the Earl slowly, 'I need someone to be in his confidence whom I can trust.'

'Good God! why?' demanded the Captain in lively astonishment.

'Peregrine Taverner,' said Worth, with a certain deliberation, 'is an extremely wealthy young man, and if anything were to happen to him his sister would inherit the greater part of his fortune.'

'Very well, let us by all means drown him in the lake,' said the Captain gaily. 'Plainly, he must be disposed of.'

'He is being disposed of,' said the Earl, without the least trace of emotion in his level voice. 'For the past five days he has been inhaling poisoned snuff.'

Fifteen

$\mathcal{T}$HE ARRIVAL OF CAPTAIN CHARLES AUDLEY WAS A HAPPY
circumstance, for the departure to London on that day of
Mr Brummell, Lord Petersham, and both the Marleys had produced all the inevitable languor attendant on the breaking-up
of a party. The Taverners, with Miss Fairford and Lord Alvanley, were engaged to remain at Worth over the week-end, but
although an Assembly at a neighbouring town, where some
militia were quartered, a day's hunting, and a card-party were
promised, there was an insipidity, a flatness, that was hard to
shake off. The appearance, however, of Captain Audley ban-
ished every feeling of regret for the absence of four of the original members of the party. His gaiety was infectious, and his
manners, for all their oddity, were so generally charming as to
render him always acceptable. His having but just come from
the Peninsula made him first in consequence; the ladies hung
on his lips, and the gentlemen, in a quieter fashion, were very
ready to hear all the information he could give them of the
state of affairs in Spain. The only respect in which he fell short
of the female expectations at least was his refusal to describe
the act of dashing gallantry to which it was felt that his wound
must have been due. He would not talk of it, insisted that the
wound was not the result of any noble action at all, and beyond
learning that it had been incurred at the affair of Arroyo del

Molinos upon the twenty-eighth day of October, and that he had been lying in hospital ever since (which Lady Albinia and Mrs Scattergood were aware of already), they could discover nothing about it. But on any other subject he was ready to converse, and his arrival was soon felt to be an advantage. He paid unblushing court to Miss Taverner, was kind to Miss Fairford, quizzed his aunt and cousin, took Peregrine secretly over to a dingy tavern in the nearest town to witness a cock-fight, and was voted in less than no time to be a most amiable young man. He was not above being pleased; he could derive as much enjoyment from making up a pool of quadrille to oblige his aunt as from playing whist for pound points; and found as much to amuse him at the local Assembly as he would have found at Almack's.

'You are blessed with the happiest nature, Captain Audley,' Miss Taverner said smilingly. 'Whatever you do, you are pleased to be doing, and *your* spirits infect everyone else with the same liveliness.'

'If I could not be pleased in such company I must be an insufferable fellow!' he replied warmly.

'You are certainly a flatterer.'

'Only so modest a creature as yourself could think so.'

'I am silenced. Do you find this mode of address generally acceptable amongst the heiresses of your acquaintance?'

'Miss Taverner, I appeal to your sense of what is fair! Is this kind? Is this right?'

'It was irresistible,' she replied mischievously.

'What is to be done? How shall I convince you?'

'You cannot; you are completely exposed.'

'I shall come about again, I warn you. My dependence is all on my brother. If he has the slightest regard for me he must assist me to convince you of my disinterestedness.'

'Dear me, how is he to do that, I wonder?'

'Why, very simply! He has only to sell you out of the three-per-cents and gamble away your whole fortune on 'Change. I may then offer you my hand and heart with a clear conscience.'

'It sounds very disagreeable. I had rather keep my fortune, I thank you.'

'Miss Taverner, you are guilty of the most shocking cruelty to one wounded in the service of his country!'

'That is very bad, certainly. What shall I do to atone?'

'You shall drive me out in Worth's curricle,' he said promptly.

'I am quite willing, but Lord Worth might view the matter in a different light.'

'Nonsense! His cattle must be honoured in being driven by you.'

'I wish he may think so, but I believe we shall do well to obtain his permission.'

'You shall be held blameless,' he promised. 'You can have no objection to my ordering the curricle to be sent round.'

She wavered. 'To be sure, I have once driven it. I suppose if you order it there can be nothing against it. You cannot do wrong in your own home after all.'

He grinned. 'We will hear my brother's comments on that. His greys are in the stable: can you handle them?'

'I can, but I have a notion I ought not. Are − are his chestnuts in the stable, too?'

'Miss Taverner,' said Captain Audley solemnly, 'Julian is the best of good fellows, and the kindest of brothers, but he has the most punishing left imaginable! Frankly, I dare not!'

'I do not know what you mean by a punishing left, but you are very right. We must not take his chestnuts. I daresay he will not mind his greys being exercised.'

'He will know nothing of the matter, in any case. He has rid over to Longhampton. The word is, *en avant*!'

The greys, which were soon brought round to the house by a reluctant groom, had not been out for several days, and were consequently very fresh. Captain Audley looked them over, and said: 'We had better take Johnson along with us. Miss Taverner, do you feel yourself equal to the task of driving them, or shall we send them away, and have out the gig?'

'A gig! By no means! I have driven this team before, and know them to be beautifully mouthed. I will engage to drive you without mishap. We will take no groom.'

'So be it!' said the Captain recklessly. 'I have one sound arm, after all.'

It was not needed, however. Miss Taverner's skill soon showed itself, and the Captain, who, never having driven with her before, had been at first holding himself in readiness to seize the reins, presently relaxed, and paid Miss Taverner the compliment of saying that she was as good a whip as Letty Lade. He directed the way, and since he gave the road to Longhampton a wide berth, it was a piece of the most perverse ill-luck that upon the way back to Worth they should come plump upon the Earl.

His lordship had stopped by the roadside to exchange a few words with one of his tenant-farmers, and was bestriding a raking bay mare. Judith was the first to catch sight of him, at a distance of a hundred yards, or more, and she gave a dismayed gasp, and exclaimed: 'What is to be done? There is your brother!'

Captain Audley regarded her quizzically. 'Oh, oh! I believe you would like to turn round and make off in the other direction!'

'Nonsense!' said Miss Taverner, sitting very erect. 'Yours is the blame, after all.'

'But I have only one arm. I depend on your protection.'

'How can you be so absurd? Ten to one he will think nothing of it.'

'You are too sanguine. We had better turn our heads away and trust to his not recognising us.'

'A man not recognise his own horses!' said Miss Taverner scornfully. 'Oh, you are laughing at me! You are quite abominable!'

At the first sound of the curricle's approach the Earl had raised his head and glanced casually up the lane. He was in the middle of making a civil inquiry into the health of his tenant's family, but he broke off abruptly. The farmer followed the direction of his eyes, and said in no little surprise: 'Why, here come your lordship's greys, or I'm much mistaken!'

'You are not mistaken,' said the Earl grimly, and wheeled his mare across the lane.

Miss Taverner, observing this manoeuvre, said: 'There! You see! We shall have to stop.'

'I see no necessity. Drop your hands and drive over him.'

Miss Taverner threw him a look of withering contempt and checked her horses. In another minute the curricle had pulled up alongside the Earl, and Miss Taverner was meeting his gaze with an expression half of defiance, half of apology, in her blue eyes. 'I am taking your brother for a drive, Lord Worth,' she said.

'So I see,' replied the Earl. 'It was very civil of you to pull up to greet me, but you must not let me be detaining you.'

Miss Taverner eyed him doubtfully. 'You must wonder at it, but –'

'Not at all,' said the Earl. 'The only thing I wonder at is that you are not driving my chestnuts.'

'I should have liked to,' said Miss Taverner wistfully, 'but Captain Audley said he dared not, and of course I knew I must not without your leave. If you are displeased I beg your pardon. Captain Audley, how odious it is of you to sit laughing, and not to say a word in my defence!'

'My brother would never listen to my excuses with half so much complaisance, I assure you,' said the Captain, with a twinkle.

Miss Taverner turned her attention to the Earl again. 'I hope you are not very angry, sir?'

'My dear Miss Taverner, I am not in the least angry, except on one account. My horses are at your service, but what are you about to have no one with you but that one-armed rattle by your side? If any accident occurred, as it might well, he would be of no assistance to you.'

'Oh, if that is all,' returned Judith, 'you must know that I have been used to drive alone. My father saw no objection.'

'Your father,' said the Earl, 'never saw you with one of my teams in hand.'

'Very true,' said Judith. 'But what is to be done? Will you lead the horses, or shall Captain Audley alight and lead yours?'

'Captain Audley begs leave to inform Miss Taverner that he will die rather!'

'Drive on – Clorinda!' said the Earl, a little smile twisting his lips.

She bowed; the team moved forward, and in another minute was trotting away down the lane. The Earl watched it out of sight, and turned back to his tenant. His business did not occupy him long; he rode home presently across country, and arrived at Worth just as Miss Taverner was ascending the stairs to change her habit for a muslin frock. She looked over her shoulder and said archly: 'Am I forgiven, Lord Worth? Do I stand in your black books?'

He came up the stairs and began to walk slowly along the gallery by her side. 'You would be disappointed if I said you had not succeeded in vexing me, Miss Taverner.'

'No, indeed. You have a very odd notion of me, to be sure! You think me shockingly unamiable.'

'I think you –' He stopped, and after a moment continued with a little constraint: 'I think you take a great delight in crossing swords with me.'

'Mine is a sad character, according to you. But I shall protest against this attack. Our quarrels have been all of your making.'

'I cannot admit it to be true; I am not at all quarrelsome.'

She smiled, but allowed it to pass. They walked on until her bedchamber door was reached. Before she could open it the

Earl spoke again. 'Are you determined, Miss Taverner, to return to Brook Street on Monday?'

She looked at him in surprise. 'Determined? I have the intention, certainly. Why do you ask me?'

'I have no knowledge of the engagements you may have made, but if it is not distasteful to you I should like you and Peregrine to extend your visit.' He saw a look of refusal in her face, and added with his sardonic smile: 'You need not be afraid: I shall not be here. I have business which will take me into the Midlands for several weeks.'

'But why do you wish us to stay here?' asked Judith.

'I believe it may be of benefit to Peregrine's health.'

'He seems to me to be better,' she said. 'He does not cough so much, I think.'

'Undoubtedly, but I do not consider an immediate return to town advisable. The air of Worth will do him more good than the air of Watier's.'

She agreed to it, but still hesitated. He said abruptly: 'Oblige me in this, Miss Taverner!'

She raised her brows. 'Is it a command?'

'I have carefully avoided giving it the least appearance of one.'

'What is your real reason, Lord Worth?'

'When I am unable to be in London to prevent you, Miss Taverner, from announcing your engagement to a Royal Duke, and Peregrine from committing some act of folly to the risk of his life or his fortune, I prefer to leave you safely provided for under my own roof.'

She said quickly: 'You do think that something threatens Perry, then!'

He shrugged. 'I think he is a rash young man who will get into trouble if he can.'

She was silent for a moment, and then said: 'Very well. If you wish it we will remain here a little longer.'

'Thank you; I do wish it. My brother will do what lies in his power to make your stay agreeable, I trust. If you can keep him from overtaxing his strength I shall be your debtor.'

She could not prevent a suspicion from crossing her mind; she said with a certain reserve: 'I cannot charge myself with such an office. I have neither interest nor influence with Captain Audley.'

There was a good deal of comprehension in his eyes, which were regarding her with something of the cynical gleam she so much disliked. 'You are mistaken, Miss Taverner.'

'I do not understand you.'

'I shall not permit you to marry my brother. You would not suit.'

Miss Taverner whisked herself into her bedroom and shut the door with unnecessary force.

When she met the Earl again at the dinner-table he seemed to be unaware of having said anything to vex her. Her manner was cold; he gave no sign of noticing it; and after a while she came to the conclusion that her most dignified course would be to assume a similar unconcern.

Lady Fairford, applied to in a letter sent express, readily gave her consent to her daughter's remaining at Worth under Mrs Scattergood's chaperonage; Miss Fairford's presence easily reconciled Peregrine to the change of plan; and the Earl left his house on Monday, confident that his guests would be all very happily engaged with each other until his return.

His confidence was not misplaced. With riding-horses at their disposal, Assemblies at Longhampton, and their own company, the younger people were well satisfied. Captain Audley made a charming host, and it was not long before Peregrine liked him as well as his sister did, and thought him the very model of what he would secretly like to be himself. Three weeks slipped by without anyone's noticing them, and by the time the party did at last break up every member of it was on excellent terms with the rest. Miss Taverner, while allowing the

Captain to come as near to flirting with her as her sense of propriety would sanction, did not fall in love with him; and upon being asked by Peregrine whether she could fancy being married to him returned a decided answer.

'Dear me, no, Perry! What should put such a notion into your head?'

'I thought you seemed to like him very well.'

'Why, so I do! I am sure everyone must.'

'Well, I will tell you what, Ju: I should not mind it if you did marry him. He is a capital fellow.'

She smiled. 'Certainly; but he is not at all the sort of man I could fancy myself in love with. There is a volatility, a habit of being too generally pleasing which must preclude my taking him in any very serious spirit.'

'I am sure he is in love with you.'

'And I am sure he is as much in love with any other passable-looking female,' replied Miss Taverner.

The matter was allowed to drop. Towards the end of January the Taverners were in London again, only to set forth a week later for Osterley Park. Even Peregrine, who had plunged once more into the pleasures of the town, thought an invitation from Lady Jersey too flattering to be declined. He raised no objection, and, indeed, after settling-day at Tattersall's was inclined to think that a further stay in the country would be a very good thing.

'Yes,' agreed his cousin dryly. 'A very good thing if at the end of one week in town you can tell me you are floored.'

'Oh, well!' replied Peregrine. 'It is not as bad as that, I daresay. I have had shocking bad luck, to be sure. Fitz gave me the office to back Kiss-in-a-Corner. I turned the brute up in Baily's Calendar – a capital steeplechaser! Yet what should win that particular race but Turn-About-Tommy, whom I'll swear no one had ever heard of! Never was there such ill-luck! I am not so well up in the stirrups as I should like, but I daresay my luck will have turned by the time I am back from Osterley.'

'I hope it may. You do not look very well. Are you in health?'

'Oh, never better! If I look a trifle baked to-day that is because Fitz, and Audley, and I had a pretty batch of it last night.' He pulled out his snuff-box and offered it. 'Do try some of my mixture! It is famous snuff, quite the thing!'

'Is this the snuff you were given at Christmas? No, I thank you! With Judith's eyes upon me I dare not be seen taking scented snuff.'

'Well, you very much mistake the matter,' said Peregrine, helping himself and shutting the box. 'Even Petersham pronounced it to be unexceptionable!'

'But I care more for Judith's opinion than for Petersham's.'

'Oh, lord! That's nonsensical!' said Peregrine, with brotherly scorn.

He soon took himself off to join Mr Fitzjohn, and Mr Taverner, turning to Judith, who sat quietly sewing by the fire, said: 'Is he in health? He looks a trifle sickly, I think. Or do I imagine it?'

'He has not been in good health,' Judith replied. 'He had a troublesome cough – a chill caught on our journey to Worth, but I believe him to be quite on the mend now.'

'You do right to take him out of London. Another run of bad luck, and he will be quite in the basket, as they say.'

She sighed. 'I cannot stop him gaming, cousin. I can only trust in Lord Worth. He is keeping Perry on an allowance, and I believe has an eye to him.'

'An eye to him! If you had said an eye to his fortune I could more readily believe you! I have it on the authority of one who was present that Lord Worth rose from the macao-table at Watier's a couple of months ago with vowels of Perry's in his pocket to the tune of four thousand pounds!'

She looked up with an expression of startled alarm in her face, but was prevented from answering him by the entrance of Captain Audley. The Captain had been walking down Brook Street, and would not pass the house without coming in to pay a morning call. Miss Taverner made the two men known to each other, and was glad to see that no such formal civility as had been the result of presenting her cousin to Worth was the outcome of this introduction. Captain Audley's manners were too easy to permit of it. A cordial hand-shake was exchanged; Mr Taverner made some polite reference to the Captain's wound; and the talk was directed at once to events in the Peninsula. The news of the storming of Ciudad Rodrigo had not long been made known; there was plenty to say; and half an hour passed apparently to both men's satisfaction. Upon the Captain's departure Mr Taverner acknowledged him to be a very pleasant fellow, and one whom he was glad to make the acquaintance of; and in discussing him the original subject of conversation was forgotten. It was recalled to Judith's mind later, and when she saw Peregrine again she repeated what their cousin had said, and desired to know the truth of it.

Peregrine was vexed. He coloured and said in a displeased voice: 'My cousin is a great deal too busy! What concern of his are my affairs?'

'But Perry, is it true, then? Do you owe money to Lord Worth? I had not thought it to have been possible?'

'No such thing. I wish you will not bother your head about me!'

'Bernard said he had it from one who was present.'

'Lord! cannot you let it be? I did play macao at Worth's table, but I don't owe him anything.'

'Bernard said Lord Worth has vowels of yours amounting to four thousand pounds.'

'Bernard said! Bernard said!' exclaimed Peregrine angrily. 'I can tell you, I don't care to recall that affair! Worth behaved in a damned unpleasant fashion – as though it were anything extraordinary that a man with my fortune should drop a few thousands at a sitting!'

'That he – your guardian – should win such a sum from you!'

'Oh, do not be talking of it for ever, Judith! Worth tore up my vowels, and that is all there is to it.'

She was conscious of a feeling of relief out of proportion to the event. The loss of four thousand pounds would not be likely to cause Peregrine embarrassment, but that Worth should win considerable sums of money from him shocked her. She had not believed him capable of such impropriety: she was happy to think he had not been capable of it.

The visit to Osterley Park passed very pleasantly, and the Taverners returned to London again midway through February with the intention of remaining there until the Brighton season commenced. Nothing was much changed in town; no new diversions were offered; no startling scandal had cropped up to provide a topic for conversation. It was the same round of balls, assemblies, card-parties, theatres; with concerts of Ancient Music in Hanover Square, or a visit to Bullock's Museum, just opened in Piccadilly, for those of a more serious turn of mind. The only novelty was supplied by Mr Brummell, who created a slight stir by the announcement that he was reforming his way of life. Various were the conjectures as to what drastic changes this might mean, but when he was asked frankly what his reforms were he replied in his most ingenuous manner: 'My reforms – ah, yes! For instance, I sup early; I take a – a little lobster, an apricot puff, or so, and some burnt champagne about twelve, and my man gets me to bed by three.'

The Duke of Clarence, after one more attempt to win Miss Taverner, returned to the siege of Miss Tylney Long, but in the clubs his chances of success were held to be slim, the lady having begun to show signs of favouring Mr Wellesley Poole's suit.

At the beginning of March all other subjects of interest faded before a new and scintillating one. One name was on everybody's lips, and no drawing-room could be found without a copy of *Childe Harold's Pilgrimage* lying upon the table. Only two cantos of this work had been published, but over these two everyone was in raptures. Lord Byron, sprung suddenly into fame, was held to have eclipsed all other poets, and happy was the hostess who could secure him to add distinction to her evening party. He had been taken up by the Melbourne House set; Lady Caroline Lamb was known to be madly in love with him, as well she might, for surely never had such beauty, such romantic mystery clung to a poet before.

'Confound this fellow Byron!' said Captain Audley humorously. 'Since *Childe Harold* came out none of you ladies will so much as spare a glance for the rest of us less gifted mortals!'

'Do not level that accusation at my head, if you please,' replied Miss Taverner, smiling.

'I am sure if I have heard you murmur raptly: "*Adieu, adieu! my native shore fades o'er the waters blue*" once, I must have heard you murmur it a dozen times! Do you know that we are all of us growing white-haired in the endeavour to be poets too?'

'Ah, his poetry! I could listen to that for ever, but pray do not confuse my admiration for that with a partiality for his lordship. I have met him at Almack's. I will allow him to be as handsome as you please, but he has such an air of pride and puts on so much melancholy grandeur that it gave me quite a disgust of him. He fixes his brilliant gaze upon one, bows, speaks two words in a cold voice, and that is all! It put me out of patience to see everyone flock about him, flattering, admiring, hanging on his lips. Only fancy! he was asked to dine in St James's Place with Mr Rogers himself, came late, refused every course that was offered, and ended by dining on potatoes mashed up with vinegar, to the astonishment, as you may imagine, of all. I heard it from one who was present, and who seemed to be much struck. For my part I think it a piece of studied affectation, and cannot smile at it.'

'Excellent! I am delighted,' said the Captain. 'I need not try to emulate his lordship, I see.'

She laughed. 'Emulate such genius! No one could do that, I am sure. You must know that my abuse of Lord Byron has its root in pique. He barely noticed me! You will not expect me to do him justice after *that*!'

Lord Byron continued to obsess the thoughts of Society. His connection with Lady Caroline was everywhere talked over, and exclaimed at; his verses and his person extravagantly extolled: even Mrs Scattergood, who was not bookish, was able to repeat two or three consecutive lines of *Childe Harold*.

Peregrine, as might be supposed, was not much interested in his lordship. He had thrown off his cough, seemed to be in good health, and had only two things to vex him: the first, that Worth could not be prevailed upon to consent to his wedding-date being fixed; the second, that not even Mr Fitzjohn would put his name up for membership to the Four-Horse Club. This select gathering of all the best whips met the first and third Thursdays in May and June in Cavendish Square, and drove in yellow-bodied barouches to Salt Hill at a strict trot. There the members dined, either at the Castle, or the Windmill, having previously lunched at Turnham Green, and refreshed at the Magpies on Hounslow Heath. The return journey was made the next day, without change of horses. Judith could not see that there was anything very remarkable in the club's performance, but for fully two months the sum of Peregrine's ambition was to have the right to join that distinguished procession to Salt Hill, driving the bay horses, which (though the colour was not absolutely enforced) were very much *de rigueur*. He could never see Mr Fitzjohn in the club's uniform without a pang, and would have given all his expensive waistcoats in exchange for a blue one with inch-wide yellow stripes.

'No, really, my dear Perry, I can't do it!' said Mr Fitzjohn, distressed. 'Besides, if I did, who should we get to second you? Peyton wouldn't, and Sefton wouldn't, and you wouldn't have asked me to put you up if you could have got Worth to do it.'

'I am pretty well acquainted with Mr Annesley,' said Peregrine. 'Don't you think he might second me?'

'Not if he has seen you with a four-in-hand,' said Mr Fitzjohn brutally. 'Anyway, you'd be blackballed, dear old fellow. Try the Bensington: I believe they are not near so strict, and there's no knowing but they may have a vacancy.'

But this would by no means satisfy Peregrine; it must be the F.H.C. or nothing for him.

'The fact of the matter is,' said Mr Fitzjohn frankly, 'you can't drive, Perry. I will allow you to be a bruising rider, but I wouldn't sit behind you driving a team for a hundred pounds! Cowhanded, dear boy! cow-handed!'

Peregrine bristled with wrath, but his sister broke into low laughter, and later reproduced the expression, which had taken her fancy, to her guardian. She came up with his curricle when she was driving her phaeton in the Park, and drawing up alongside, said prettily: 'I have been wishing to meet you, Lord Worth. I have a favour to ask of you.'

His brows rose in surprise. 'Indeed! What is it, Miss Taverner?'

She smiled. 'You are not very gallant, sir. You must say: "Anything in my power I shall be happy to do for you"; or, more simply: "The favour is yours for the asking."'

He replied in some amusement: 'I mistrust you most when you are cajoling, Miss Taverner. What is this favour?'

'Why, only that you will contrive to get Perry elected to the Whip Club,' said Judith in her most dulcet voice.

'My instinct for danger seldom fails me,' remarked his lordship. 'Certainly not, Miss Taverner.'

She sighed. 'I wish you might. He can think of nothing else.'

'Recommend him to approach his friend Fitzjohn. *He* might put him up, even though *I* shall blackball him.'

'You are very disagreeable. Mr Fitzjohn is as bad. He says Perry is cow-handed.'

'I imagine he might, but I can see no need for you to use the expression.'

'Is it very vulgar?' inquired Judith. 'I thought it excessively apt.'

'It is extremely vulgar,' said the Earl crushingly.

'Well,' said Judith, preparing to drive on, 'I am very glad I am not your daughter, Lord Worth, for you are a great deal too strict in your notions, I think.'

'My daughter!' exclaimed the Earl, looking thunderstruck.

'Yes; are you surprised? You must know I should not like to have you for my father at all.'

'I am relieved to hear you say so, Miss Taverner,' said the Earl grimly.

Miss Taverner bit back a smile at having put him out of countenance, bowed, and drove on.

It was some time before Peregrine could recover from his disappointment, but by the middle of April his thoughts took a turn in another direction, and he began to urge Judith to approach Worth on the subject of their spending two or three months at Brighton. She was very willing; London, from the circumstance of the Regent having celebrated his birthday, on April 12th, at Brighton, was growing already rather thin of company; and from all she had heard they would be in danger of missing their chance of acquiring a suitable lodging at Brighton if they delayed much longer. It was arranged between them that if Worth gave his consent Peregrine would drive down with their cousin to arrange accommodation for a date early in May.

The Earl gave his consent with the utmost readiness, but contrived to provoke Miss Taverner. 'Certainly. It will be very desirable for you to go out of town for the summer. I had fixed the 12th May as a convenient date, but if you like to go sooner I daresay it can be arranged.'

'*You* had fixed – !' repeated Miss Taverner. 'Do you tell me you have already made arrangements for our going to Brighton?'

'Naturally. Who else should do so?'

'No one!' said Miss Taverner angrily. 'It is for Peregrine and me to arrange! You did not so much as mention the matter to either of us, and we will not have our future arranged in this high-handed fashion!'

'I thought you wished to go to Brighton?' said the Earl.

'I *am* going to Brighton!'

'Then what is all this bustle about?' inquired Worth calmly. 'In sending Blackader to look over suitable houses there I have done nothing more than you wanted.'

'You have done a great deal more. Perry is going to drive down with my cousin to select a house!'

'He may as well spare himself the trouble,' replied Worth, 'there are only two to be had, and I hold an option on both. You must know that houses in Brighton for the season are excessively hard to come by. Unless you wish to lodge in a back street, you will be satisfied with one of the two Blackader has found for you. One is on the Steyne, the other on the Marine Parade.' He looked at her for a moment, and then lowered his gaze. 'I strongly advise you to choose the house on the Steyne. You will not like Marine Parade; the Steyne is a most eligible situation, in the centre of town, within sight of the Pavilion – the hub of Brighton, in effect. I will tell Blackader to close with the owner. Thirty guineas a week is asked for the house, but taking into account the position it cannot be thought excessive.'

'I think it ridiculous,' said Miss Taverner instantly. 'From what my cousin has told me I should infinitely prefer to lodge on the Marine Parade. To be situated in the centre of the town, in the midst of all the bustle, can be no recommendation. I will consult with my cousin.'

'I do not wish you to take the house on Marine Parade,' said the Earl.

'I am sorry to disoblige you,' said Miss Taverner, a martial light in her eye, 'but you will have the goodness to instruct Mr Blackader to hire that and no other house for us.'

The Earl bowed. 'Very well, Miss Taverner,' he said.

Judith, who had anticipated a struggle, was left triumphant and bewildered. But the Earl's unexpected compliance was soon explained. Captain Audley, meeting Miss Taverner in the Park, got up beside her in the phaeton, and said: 'So you are to go to Brighton, Miss Taverner! My doctor recommends sea air for me: you will certainly see me there as well.'

'We go next month,' replied Judith. 'We shall lodge on the Marine Parade.'

'Yes, I was present when Blackader came back from Brighton. The place will be full this summer. There were only two genteel houses to be had, and one was on the Steyne – no very eligible situation for you, Worth thought.'

Miss Taverner's lips parted; she turned her eyes towards the Captain, and regarded him with painful intensity. 'He wanted me to choose the other?' she demanded.

'Why, yes; I am sure he had no notion of your lodging on the Steyne. It is very smart, no doubt, but you would have your front windows for ever stared into, and all your comings and goings ogled by young bucks.'

'Captain Audley,' said Miss Taverner, controlling herself with a strong effort, 'you must get down immediately, for I am going home.'

'Good God!' exclaimed the Captain, in lively dismay. 'What have I said to offend you?'

'Nothing, nothing! It is only that I have remembered I have a letter to write which must be sent off without any loss of time.'

Within a quarter of an hour Miss Taverner was seated at her desk, furiously mending her pen, her gloves and scarf flung down on the floor beside her. The pen mended to her satisfaction, she dipped it in the standish, and drew a sheet of elegant, hot-pressed paper towards her. After that she sat nibbling the end of her pen while the ink slowly dried. At last she nodded briskly to herself, dipped the pen in the standish a second time, and began to write a careful letter to her guardian.

Brook Street, April 19th.

Dear Lord Worth [she began], *I am afraid that I behaved badly this morning in going against your wishes in the matter of the house in Brighton. Upon reflection I am bound to acknowledge that I did wrong. I write now to assure you that I have no real wish to stay on the Marine Parade, and shall obey you in lodging on the Steyne.*

Yours sincerely,
Judith Taverner.

She read this through with a pleased smile, sealed it in an envelope, wrote the direction, and rang the bell for a servant.

The note was taken round by hand, but the Earl being out when it was delivered, no answer was brought back to Miss Taverner.

By noon on the following day, however, the answer had arrived. Miss Taverner broke the seal, spread out the single sheet, and read:

Cavendish Square, April 20th.

Dear Miss Taverner, – I accept your apologies, but although your promise of obedience must gratify me, it is now too late to change. I regret to inform you that the house on the Steyne is no longer on the market, but has been snapped up by another. I have this morning signed the lease of the one on Marine Parade.

Yours, etc.,
Worth.

'My love!' cried Mrs Scattergood, coming suddenly into the room, in her street dress and hat, 'you must instantly drive with me to Bond Street! I have seen the most ravishing sea-coast promenade gown! I am determined you must purchase it. Nothing could be more desirable, more exactly suited to the seaside! It is of yellow craped muslin, confined at the bosom and down the entire front with knots of green ribbon, and bound round the neck with, I think, three rows of the same. You may imagine how neat! There is a high lace tucker, and ruffles on the sleeves, and a Zephyr cloak to wear with it, made of lace, falling in long points to the feet, with green tassels to finish each point, and a sash round the waist. You could wear your yellow morocco sandals with it, and the pebble ear-rings and necklace, and the beehive bonnet with the long veil. Oh, and what do you think, my dear? I met Charles Audley on my way, and he told me Worth is to go to Brighton too, and has taken a house on the Steyne for the whole summer. But what is the matter? Why do you look at me like that? Have you received bad news?'

Judith sprang up, and screwing the Earl's letter into a ball, hurled it into the empty grate. 'I think,' she said stormily, 'that Lord Worth is the most odious, provoking, detestable creature alive!'

Sixteen

ORTH'S DUPLICITY, WORTH'S DESPICABLE STRATEGY, WORTH'S infamous triumph, possessed Miss Taverner's mind for many days. In all the business of choosing muslins, gauzes, French cambrics, and crapes for the making up for gowns to wear at Brighton, plans for revenge on him were revolving in her head, and her thoughts wandered even when she was engaged in choosing between sandals made of white kid, and Roman boots of Denmark satin. Mrs Scattergood was in despair, and when Miss Taverner cast an indifferent glance at two hats displayed by a milliner (the one an enchanting Lavinia chip tied down with sarcenet ribbons, and the other a celestial-blue bonnet with a jockey-front edged with honey-comb trimming) and said that she liked neither, her chaperon, seriously alarmed, spoke of sending for Dr Baillie to prescribe a tonic.

Miss Taverner declined seeing a doctor, but continued to brood darkly over Worth's enormities.

Somewhat to Peregrine's disappointment, the Fairfords were not going to Brighton, but to Worthing instead, a resort much patronised by persons to whom the racket of Brighton was distasteful. Nothing but the discovery that Worthing was situated only thirteen miles from Brighton reconciled him to his sister's choice of watering-place, and with the smallest encouragement he would have forgone all the gaiety of Brighton and secured lodgings at Worthing instead. But Judith was adamant, and he was forced to be content with the prospect of riding over to see his Harriet three or four times a week.

The time for their departure from London drew near; everything was in train; all that remained to be done was to pack their trunks, and to decide upon the route to be followed. There could be little question: all the advantages of the New Road, which was shorter and in better condition than any other, were felt. At the most four carriages only could be thought necessary, and with her own horses posted on the road, Judith might expect to accomplish the journey in five hours or less. Twenty-eight stage-coaches a day ran between London and Brighton during the season, but Peregrine could not discover that any of them made the journey in less than six hours. He was of the opinion that a light travelling chaise-and-four might very well accomplish it in five, though he, driving his curricle, had every expectation of rivalling the Regent's performance in 1784, when, as Prince of Wales, he had driven a phaeton drawn by three horses, harnessed tandem-fashion, from Carlton House to the Marine Pavilion in four hours and a half.

'Though I shan't drive unicorn, of course,' he added. 'I shall have four horses.'

'My dear, you could not drive unicorn if you wanted to,' said Judith. 'Those randoms are the most difficult of all to handle. I wish I might go with you. I hate travelling boxed up in a chaise.'

'Well, why don't you?' said Peregrine.

She had spoken idly, but the notion having entered her head it took root, and she began seriously to consider whether it might not be possible. She very soon convinced herself that there could be no harm in it; it might be thought eccentric, but she who took snuff and drove a perch-phaeton for the purpose of being remarkable, could scarcely regard that as an evil. Within half an hour of having first mentioned the scheme she had decided to put it into execution.

In spite of having assured herself that no objection could be made to it, she was not surprised at encountering opposition from Mrs Scattergood. That lady threw up her hands, and pronounced the plan to be impossible. She represented to Judith all the impropriety of rattling down to Brighton in an open carriage, and begged her to consider in what a hoydenish light she must appear if she adhered to the scheme. 'It will not do!' she said. 'It is one thing to drive an elegant phaeton in the Park, and in the country you may do as you please without occasioning remark; but to drive in a curricle down the most crowded turnpike-road in the country, to be quizzed by every vulgar Corinthian who sees you, is not to be thought of. It would look so particular! Upon no account in the world must you do it! That sort of thing can be allowable only in such women as Lady Lade, and I am sure no one could wonder at whatever *she* took it into her head to do.'

'Do not make yourself uneasy, ma'am,' said Judith, putting up her chin. 'I have no apprehension of being thought to rival Lady Lade. You can entertain no scruple in seeing me drive away with my own brother.'

'Pray do not think of it, my love! Every feeling must be offended! But you only wish to tease me, I know. I am persuaded you have too much delicacy of principle to engage on such an adventure. I shudder to think what Worth would say if he were to hear of it!'

'Indeed!' said Judith, taking fire. 'I shall not allow him to be a judge of my actions, ma'am. I believe my credit may survive a journey to Brighton in my brother's curricle. You must know that my determination is fixed. I go with Perry.'

No arguments could move her; entreaties were useless. Mrs Scattergood abandoned the struggle, and hurried away to send off a note to Worth.

Upon the following day Peregrine came to his sister and said, with a rueful grimace: 'Maria must have split on you, Ju. I've been at White's that morning, and met Worth there. The long and short of it is that you are to go in a chaise to Brighton.'

An interval of calm reflection had done much to soften Miss Taverner's resolve; she could not but admit the justice of her chaperon's words, and was more than a little inclined to submit gracefully to her wishes. But every tractable impulse, every regard for propriety, was shattered by Peregrine's speech. She cried out: 'What? Is this Lord Worth's verdict? Do I understand that he takes it upon himself to arrange my mode of travel?'

'Well, yes,' said Peregrine. 'That is to say, he has positively forbidden me to take you up in my curricle.'

'And you? What answer did you make?'

'I said I saw no harm in it. But you know Worth: I might as well have spared my breath.'

'You submitted? You let him dictate to you in that insufferable fashion?'

'Well, to tell you the truth, Ju, I did not see that it was such a great matter after all. And, you know, I don't wish to quarrel with him just now, because I am in hopes that he will consent to my marriage this summer.'

'Consent to your marriage! He has no notion of doing so! He told me as much months ago. He does not mean you to be married if he can prevent it.'

Peregrine stared at her. 'Nonsense! What difference can it make to him?'

She did not answer, but sat tapping her foot for a moment, glowering at him. After a pause she said curtly: 'You agreed to it, then? You told him you would not drive me to Brighton?'

'Yes, in effect I did, I suppose. I daresay he may be right; he says you are not to be making yourself the talk of the town.'

'I am obliged to him. I have no more to say.'

He grinned at her. 'That's not like you. What have you got in your head now?'

'If I told you, you would run to Worth with the news,' she said.

'Be damned to you, Ju, I would not! If you want to put Worth in his place I wish you luck.'

She looked at him, a glint in her eye. 'I will lay you a level hundred, Perry, that I reach Brighton before you on May 12th, driving a curricle-and-four.'

His jaw dropped; then he burst out laughing, and said: 'Done! You madcap, do you mean it?'

'Certainly I mean it.'

'Worth goes to Brighton himself on the 12th,' he warned her.

'It would give me infinite pleasure to meet him on the road.'

'Lord, I would give a monkey to see his face! But do you think you should? Will it not be remarked on?'

'Oh,' she said, curling her lip. 'The rich Miss Taverner is expected to astonish the world.'

'Ay, very true; so it is! Well, I am game. It's time Worth tasted our mettle. We have been too easy with him, and he begins to interfere beyond what is reasonable.'

'No word of it to Maria!' she said.

'Not a murmur!' he promised gaily.

Mrs Scattergood, in ignorance of what was in store, and believing herself to have checkmated her charge, set about the business of departure in a mood of considerable complacence. Had she guessed that Miss Taverner's meek acquiescence in all her plans sprang from nothing but a desire to allay any suspicions she might nourish, her peace would have been quite cut up. But she had never come up against Miss Taverner's will, and had no idea of its strength. In happy unconcern she went about her affairs, instructed the housekeeper what chairs and sofas must be put into holland-covers, arranged for the servants they were to take with them to leave Brook Street not later than seven o'clock in the morning, and gave orders for the chaise that was to convey herself and Miss Taverner to be brought round at noon.

The momentous day dawned. At ten o'clock Miss Taverner, dressed in her habit, and with a handful of spare whip-points thrust through one of her buttonholes, walked into her bedroom where she was fluttering about in the midst of bandboxes and valises, and said coolly: 'Well, ma'am, I shall see you presently, I trust. I wish you a pleasant journey.'

Mrs Scattergood cast one aghast glance at her, and cried:

'Good God! what does this mean? Why have you put on your habit? What are you going to do?'

'Why, ma'am, I have engaged to race Perry to Brighton, driving the other curricle,' said Miss Taverner, preparing to depart.

'Judith!' shrieked Mrs Scattergood, sitting down plump upon her best bonnet.

Miss Taverner put her head round the door again. 'Don't be uneasy, Maria; I can out-drive Perry. I beg you won't forget to send word of it to Lord Worth, if he should still be in town.'

'*Judith!*' moaned the afflicted lady. But Miss Taverner had gone.

In the street Peregrine was tossing his driving-cloak up on to the box of his curricle. Hinkson was to accompany him, while the second curricle was in charge of Judith's own groom, a very respectable, smart-looking man, with an intimate acquaintance with every turnpike-road in England.

'Well, Ju, is it understood?' asked Peregrine, as his sister came out of the house. 'We take the New Road, and change three times only, at Croydon, Horley, and Cuckfield. The race to begin the other side of Westminster Bridge, and to end at the Marine Parade. Are you ready?'

She nodded, and taking the reins in her right hand got up on to the box of her curricle, and deftly changed the reins over. Peregrine followed suit, the grooms got to their places, and both vehicles moved forward down the street.

Until Westminster Bridge was crossed the pace was necessarily slow, but once over the bridge, Judith, who had been leading, drew up to let Peregrine come abreast, and the race began.

Very much as she had expected he would Peregrine fanned his horses to a rattling speed immediately, and went ahead. Judith kept her team at a brisk trot, and said merely: 'His horses will be blown by the time they reach the top of the first hill. No need to press mine yet.'

A mile and a half brought them to the Kennington turnpike. Peregrine was not in sight, and as the gate was shut it was to be presumed that he must have passed through some minutes previously. The groom had the yard of tin ready, and blew up for the pike in good time; as the curricle drove through he remarked with satisfaction: 'The master must be springing 'em. Brixton Hill will take the heart out of his cattle, miss. You may overtake him anywhere you please between Streatham and Croydon.'

Another two and a half miles brought Brixton Church into sight. There was no sign of Peregrine, but instead an Accommodation coach, loaded high with baggage, presented a ludicrous appearance with a wheel off, and all its disgruntled passengers sitting or standing by the roadside. No one seemed to be hurt, and Judith, checking only for a minute, drove past, and into Brixton village. She had been nursing her horses carefully, and they brought her up the hill beyond at a good pace. She steadied them over the crown, swept past a stage-coach painted bright green and gold, with its destination printed in staring white capitals on the panels, and let her horses have their heads. Peregrine's curricle came into sight a mile farther on, crossing Streatham Common. His horses were labouring, and it was evident that he had pressed them too hard up Brixton Hill. Judith gained on him steadily; he sent the lash of his whip out to touch up one sluggish leader, and the wheeler behind shied badly. Judith seized her chance, demonstrated how to hit a leader without alarming the wheel-horse by throwing her thong out well to the right, and bringing it back with a sharp jerk, and shot by at a gallop just as the Royal Mail Coach came into sight round a bend. The curricle swung over to the side of the road, and the two vehicles met and passed without mishap.

Peregrine had now no hope of overtaking his sister on the first stage, and was content to hang on as close behind as he could for the four miles that lay between them and Croydon.

A gallows-sign straddling Croydon High Street showed the position of the Greyhound, one of the two chief posting houses in the town; the groom blew a long blast for the change, and by the time the curricle had turned into the courtyard the ostlers and post-boys were bestirring themselves to be in readiness for whatever vehicle should appear.

Miss Taverner kept her seat while the horses were taken out and the new team swiftly put-to, but Judson, her groom, jumped down and ran back under the archway to watch for Peregrine's arrival. He came back in a few moments with the news that the master had passed, and was making for the King's Head, in Market Street.

A little time had to be wasted in giving the necessary directions for the return of Miss Taverner's own team, but in a very short space the curricle was away again, and bowling through the town towards the turnpike three-quarters of a mile on.

Just short of the pike the Sussex Iron Railway ran for a little way beside the road. A number of trucks loaded with coal were being hauled along iron rails by teams of horses, and the sight was so new to Miss Taverner that she slackened her speed to watch this queer form of transport.

The new team was not an ideal one to drive, one of the wheelers being a bad holder. His continual attempts to break into a canter, coupled with the sluggish disposition of his fellow, made the task of driving the whole team up to their bits a difficult one. Miss Taverner had some trouble with them, and further experienced the misfortune of coming up behind a stage-coach which obstinately held the crown of the road for a good half-mile. Its progress was erratic; it lurched and swayed along at an unusual speed for such a top-heavy vehicle, and the roof-passengers, who were all of them holding tightly to their seats, looked as though they were not enjoying their journey at all. When Miss Taverner at last succeeded in passing it, the reason for its odd progress was explained, for she saw that it was being driven by a rakish young Corinthian, who had bribed the coachman to give up his place for a stage, and was tooling the coach along at a great rate, with all the reins clubbed in his hand. It seemed probable that at the first corner the Corinthian would overset the equippage – a not uncommon ending to this particular pastime. Miss Taverner felt sorry for the other passengers, and especially for a thin, unhappy-looking man immediately behind the box-seat, who sat in imminent danger of having his hat whisked off by the Corinthian's unruly whiplash.

Once past the stage no further check was experienced, but Miss Taverner knew that she had lost valuable time, and could only hope that Peregrine would be similarly unfortunate. But a few hundred yards short of Foxley Hatch he came into sight, and caught his sister up at the toll-gate, where she was being detained by an attempt on the gate-keeper's part to fob her off with a ticket which would carry her only as far as the next pike. Judson immediately took control of the matter, and while he pithily informed the gate-keeper that he was no Johnny Raw to be cheated of the correct ticket (which opened all the gates and pikes as far as Gatton), Peregrine and Judith had time to exchange a few words.

'What sort of team, Perry?' Judith asked. 'You have got a roarer, I see.'

'Lord, yes!' replied Peregrine cheerfully. 'And a couple of regular bone-setters as well. Did you see the spill down the road? Some fellow's put the stage in the ditch. What's the trouble here? Is the gate-keeper trying to gammon you? Hi, Judson, tell him if he thinks we're flats he mistakes the matter!'

By this time, however, the dispute had been settled, and Miss Taverner's curricle was free to pass. She drove through the gateway, and once past Godstone Corner set her horses at a brisk trot up the long, straight road ascending the pass to Smitham Bottom. Bearing in mind the maxim that an unsound team was best driven fast, she took them down into Merstham, four miles on, at an easy gallop, only slackening the speed when the village was reached. A toll-gate lay just beyond Merstham, but the ticket issued at Foxley Hatch opened it, and with scarcely a check Miss Taverner swept through, and opened out her leaders on the mile stretch that led to Gatton toll-gate, which was placed by the nineteenth milestone, where the old road branched off to Reigate. Here a new ticket had to be bought, and with Peregrine hard on her heels, only waiting his opportunity to challenge her, Judith began to resign herself to the prospect of losing her lead on the second stage.

She maintained it, however, for the two miles, aided by circumstance, for twice when Peregrine would have passed her, a vehicle coming in the opposite direction made it impossible, and she was able to draw away again. Red Hill gave an advantage, for Peregrine, who was in the habit of letting his leaders do too much work on the flat, was forced to let his team drop into a walk there.

Past Red Hill the road ran in a series of switchbacks over Earlswood Common, and such magnificent bursts of country presented themselves to her gaze, that Miss Taverner almost lost sight of the fact that she was endeavouring to reach Horley before her brother in admiring the grandeur of the scene.

They were nearing the end of the long stage, and her team, which had never gone well together, were labouring. She was a little surprised that Peregrine should not challenge again, but concluded that the ups and downs of the road were not to his taste.

'The master's nursing his horses, miss,' remarked Judson. 'Hinkson will have told him where to take his chance. He'll challenge short of the Salfords pike, I'll be bound.'

'How far to Horley?' Miss Taverner asked.

'No more than a couple of miles now, miss, downhill all the way.'

She smiled. 'He may yet miss his chance.'

Over the lonely common a long, gradual fall of ground led down to the Weald, past Petridge Wood and Salfords. The team picked up their pace, and for a quarter of a mile Peregrine could not slip by. But just when Miss Taverner was entertaining reasonable hopes of maintaining her lead, her off-side leader went lame, and Peregrine dashed by in an eddy of dust.

There was nothing for it but to follow at a sober pace, and by the time the curricle stopped at the Chequers in Horley, Peregrine had accomplished his change, and was away again. His old team were being led off when Miss Taverner drew up; she caught a glimpse of his tail-board vanishing down the street; and realised, from the sight of a waiter going back into the inn with an empty tankard on a tray, that he had allowed himself time for refreshment.

The Chequers, which was the half-way house, was busy, and swarmed with ostlers. A London-bound coach, heralding its arrival with three long blasts of the horn, drove up as Miss Taverner's horses were being taken out; a bell clanged somewhere in the stables; the first turn-out was shouted for; and almost before the coach had pulled up the new team, with post-boys already mounted, was being led out.

In addition to the stage, several private vehicles, including a post-chaise carrying a smart-looking lady and gentleman, who stared curiously at Miss Taverner, were drawn up in the big yard. There was a young man with a gig, who seemed to have driven in from somewhere in the neighbourhood. Having quizzed Miss Taverner for several minutes, he started to come towards her curricle, but encountered such a frosty look from her that he changed his mind, and began to curse one of the ostlers instead. Judith had sent to procure a glass of lemonade, but finding herself the object of so much interest, she was sorry to have done so, and would have preferred to drive on with a parched throat than to have been obliged to stay in the yard to be impertinently scrutinised. She began to be uncomfortable, to wish that she had not embarked on such an adventure, and for the first time to realise the impropriety of being upon the box of a gentleman's curricle, unattended except for her groom, and upon the busiest turnpike-road in the whole south country. A very small tiger, who seemed to belong to an elegant tilbury drawn by match-greys, and with its owner's scarlet-lined driving-coat hanging negligently over one of the panels, looked her over with an expression of strong derision, openly nudged one of the ostlers, said something behind his hand, and sniggered. But just at that moment a lean, saturnine gentleman with a club-foot came out of the inn, and the grin was promptly wiped from the tiger's face, and he sprang to attention. The gentleman limped up to the tilbury, pulling on his gloves. He saw Miss Taverner, and looked her up and down till she blushed; then he shrugged his shoulders, got into his carriage, and drove off.

'That's the Earl of Barrymore, miss,' volunteered Judson. 'Him they call Cripplegate.'

The fresh team had been put-to by this time, and the lemonade drunk. Miss Taverner gave her horses the office to start, and swung out of the yard.

The tilbury was already out of sight, for which she was profoundly thankful, and if Judson was to be believed, there would be little fear of catching up with it.

Miss Taverner now had a fast team of brown horses in hand, and all the difference of strengthy, quick-actioned beasts from the badly-matched four she had been obliged to drive over the second stage was soon felt. The milestones seemed to flash by, and from the circumstances of the road being in excellent repair, and Judson knowing every inch of it, she was able to make up her lost time, and to reach Crawley not very far behind her brother, who had got himself into difficulties with a farm wagon just at the narrow part of the road by the George inn.

Past Crawley the road rose steadily to Pease Pottage. There was not much traffic to be encountered, and except for one of the leaders shying at a hen which scuttled squawking across the road, the next two miles were covered without any other incident than the overtaking and passing of a very down-the-road-looking man in a phaeton and three, who took one glance at Miss Taverner as she went by, and whipped up his horses in the vain attempt to catch up with her. A golden beauty driving a curricle-and-four down the Brighton road was, after all, no everyday occurrence.

But the phaeton was soon left behind, and Miss Taverner reached Pease Pottage, confident that she must have gained considerably on her brother. Beside the Black Swan inn a toll-gate, on the right, gave entrance to the road to Horsham, and on the left the superb beeches and hazel undergrowth of Tilgate Forest must at any other time have tempted Miss Taverner to draw rein. But her ambition was centred on overtaking Peregrine; she passed the woods with no more than a glance, and an exclamation of delight, and had the satisfaction, half a mile on, of seeing her brother's curricle a few hundred yards ahead of her.

She had been easing her leaders, but she let them do their full share now. Peregrine glanced once over his shoulder, and whipped up his team. The two curricles raced down a straight stretch of road, the second slowly gaining on the first. A sharp bend came into sight; Peregrine took it at a gallop, lost control, and ran his near-side wheels into the bank. Judith saw Hinkson jump down and run to the horses' heads, caught a glimpse of the sort of turmoil that not infrequently enlivened Peregrine's journeys, and drove past him with a triumphant twirl of her whip over her head.

It would take Peregrine some minutes to set matters to rights, she knew, and once past him she steadied to a more respectable pace, and came presently into Hand Cross at a strict trot.

Hand Cross was not remarkable for its size or beauty, but its chief inn, the Red Lion, a gabled building with tall chimney-stacks and a line of white posts linked by chains, enjoyed a good deal of custom. A number of post-horses were stabled there, and it was whispered in knowledgeable circles that the casks of excellent brandy in its cellars were used to be delivered under cover of night, and had rendered no duty at any port.

As Miss Taverner drove up the street towards the inn, she saw only one vehicle drawn up under the shade of the two big trees that stood outside. It was a curricle with a tiger sitting up behind. Something in the tilt of his hat was familiar; in another minute a clearer view of the whole was obtained, and Miss Taverner recognised not only the tiger, but also the team of blood-chestnuts that were harnessed to the curricle.

She came up alongside, heard Henry cry in his shrill voice: 'Lordy, guv'nor, if it ain't that there Miss Taverner!' and saw her guardian standing in the doorway of the inn with a glass in his hand. She met his startled, incredulous gaze for a moment as she went by, bowed slightly, and proceeded on her way at an increased speed.

Judson twisted round in his seat to look behind. Miss Taverner, despising herself, was yet unable to refrain from asking what his lordship was doing.

'I think, miss, he means to come after you,' replied Judson ominously. 'If I may say so, miss, his lordship doesn't look best pleased.'

Miss Taverner gave a short laugh, and set her horses at a dangerous gallop down the hill. 'I don't mean to let him come up with me. He has to pay his reckoning before he can start. If I can reach Cuckfield and be away with a fresh team before he catches me —'

'But Miss Judith, you can't race those chestnuts!' cried the groom, aghast.

'We will see. We don't know when they were put-to after all.'

'For God's sake, miss, don't take them down the hill at the gallop! You'll have us overturned!'

She said coolly: 'I am driving this curricle, Judson. Confine your attention to the view, if you please. I do not know when I have seen finer bursts of country than on this road.'

The vale which was opening out before them as they raced down the hill was indeed beautiful, with its copses, and winding roads, and glimpses of warm-tiled roofs amongst the trees, but Judson, clinging to his seat, hoped fervently that his mistress would not permit it to distract her attention. He cast an alarmed look at her profile, and was relieved to see that her gaze was fixed on the road.

At the foot of the hill the road cut through Staplefield Common, and ran on to Cuckfield through three miles of undulating country. The team was responding gallantly, but when they were pulled up at the toll-gate at Whiteman's Green their flanks were heaving and foam-flecked. Every moment wasted at the gate seemed an age to Miss Taverner, glancing continually over her shoulder. The ticket was handed up just as she caught the sound of hooves thundering behind her. The gate was pushed slowly open; she started her team with a jerk, urged them into a canter, and was away again by the time Judson reported the Earl to have reached the gate.

The way was now hollow, running between banks covered with a thick tangle of hazels. There were bends in it that ever and again hid the pursuing curricle from view, but the sound of the chestnuts' hooves seemed to Miss Taverner to be coming inexorably closer. She held grimly to the crown of the road, determined with a queer mixture of obstinacy and unreasoning panic to prevent Worth from passing her.

She feather-edged a corner, almost scraping the wheels of a post-chaise coming in the opposite direction, heard Judson gasp beside her, and gave a reckless little laugh. 'How near is he?' she demanded.

'Close behind you, miss. For the Lord's sake steady them at the next bend! It's sharper than you know.'

One of the leaders stumbled, but she held him up, and pressed on. The bend came into sight; she checked slightly, and hugged the left side of the road, secure in the conviction that the Earl would not dare shoot his horses past on the corner. A sharp, compelling blast on a horn sounded immediately behind her; a chestnut head crept up alongside, and in another instant the Earl had flashed by, his team at a full gallop.

She gazed after him in a kind of horrified wonder, believing for a moment that the chestnuts were bolting. But their headlong pace was checked gradually; they dropped into a canter; continued so for a little way; and then clattered into Cuckfield at a smart trot.

Her own team was blown; she could only follow in the Earl's wake through the narrow street to the centre of the town.

He reached the King's Head considerably in advance of her and by the time she had pulled up before it he was standing on the ground awaiting her, and a couple of ostlers, shrilly instructed by Henry, were leading off his horses.

'Blow up for the change, Judson!' said Miss Taverner sharply.

The groom, however, was looking at Worth, and did not obey her. The Earl laid his hand on the curricle, and said curtly: 'You will be pleased to alight, Miss Taverner.'

She glanced down into his face, and experienced a sensation of shock. She had seen the Earl supercilious, she had seen him scornful, but never had she encountered in him a look so blazingly angry. The breath caught in her throat, but she said with tolerable composure: 'By no means, Lord Worth. You were averse, I believe, from my driving to Brighton in Peregrine's curricle. You must know that I have submitted to your decree, and have engaged to race him there in my own curricle instead.'

'Miss Taverner, must I request you again to get down?'

'I shall not get down, sir. Time is precious. I wait only for the change.'

His eyes met hers; he said with a menace she could not mistake in his voice: 'Your race is run. I have a good deal to say to you. If you choose it shall be said here in the open street, but I think you will prefer to hear it alone!'

A flush of mortification at being thus addressed before the groom and the waiting ostlers, spread over her cheeks. She could not doubt that the Earl would be as good as his word, and with one furious look shot at him from under her brows, she gave the reins to Judson, and allowed the Earl to assist her to alight. His fingers grasped her wrist ungently, and released it the instant her feet were upon the ground. He said: 'Go into the inn!' and turned to give instructions to the ostlers.

There was nothing for it but to obey him. Holding her head proudly erect, Miss Taverner went into the King's Head, followed by the landlord, who had been standing just outside, and who ushered her at once into one of his private parlours and desired to know what refreshment he might bring her.

She declined every offer of tea, coffee, or lemonade, and stripping off her gloves stood by the table in the centre of the room, jerking them between her hands. In the space of a few minutes the door opened to admit the Earl. He came in with a firm stride, and said without preamble: 'You will finish your journey by post-chaise, Miss Taverner. I have hired one for you, and it should be ready in a few minutes.'

Her eyes flashed; she exclaimed: 'How dare you? How dare you? I shall finish as I began! This interference in the way I choose to travel passes all bounds!'

'Miss Taverner,' said the Earl, 'I shall not remind you that you are my ward, for it is a fact you must be well aware of, but I shall give you a warning that may not come amiss. While I hold the reins you will run as I choose, and by God! ma'am, if you try to take the bit between your teeth it will be very much the worse for you!'

This way of putting the matter was scarcely calculated to mollify Miss Taverner, nor did the consciousness of being in the wrong act on her temper as it should. She was white with anger, her lips tightly compressed. She heard the Earl in quick-breathing silence, and when he had done, said in a low, trembling voice: 'I admit no right in you to order my movements. My fortune is in your hands, and I have been content to have it so, but at the outset I told you that your authority extended no further than to the management of my affairs. Upon every occasion you have intervened where you had neither cause nor right. I have hitherto submitted, because I do not choose to be for ever at loggerheads with one to whom, to my misfortune, I am in some sort tied. But this goes beyond what my patience can suffer. You are not to be the judge of the propriety of my actions! If it pleases me to drive a curricle to Brighton it is no business of yours!'

'Do you think I will permit *my* ward to make herself the talk of the town? Do you think it suits my pride to have my ward drive down to Brighton wind-blown, dishevelled, a butt for every kind of coarse wit, an object of disgust to any person of taste and refinement? Take a look at yourself, my good girl!'

He seized her by the shoulders as he spoke, and twisted her round to face the mirror that hung over the mantelpiece. She saw to her annoyance that her hair, escaping from under the close hat she wore, was whipped into a tangle, and her habit powdered with dust. It made her more angry than ever. She wrenched herself free, and cried: 'Yes, an object of disgust for you and any other dandy, I daresay! Do you think I care for your good opinion? It is a matter of the supremest indifference to me! From the moment when I first set eyes on you I have disliked you – yes, and mistrusted you too! I do not know what your motive has been in trying to overcome my dislike, but you have not succeeded!'

'Evidently not,' he said, a grim smile curling the corners of his mouth. 'I can readily believe that, but I shall be obliged to you if you will tell me what I have done to earn your mistrust.'

Having no very clear idea, but, woman-like, having merely used the most wounding phrases she could think of, she ignored this home-question, and said: 'Do not imagine that I am not well aware of the reason for this unmannerly outburst in you! You are less concerned with the appearance I may present than with having had your own commands set aside! *You* must always be the master; you cannot bear to have your will gainsaid.'

'Very true; I cannot,' he replied. 'I might say the same of you, Miss Taverner. A strong desire of having your own way has led you into a scrape which might, were I not here to enforce your obedience to my commands, have damaged your reputation more seriously than you know. These hoyden-tricks may do very well in the wilds of Yorkshire; I am happy to say that I know nothing of the manners obtaining there; but they will not serve here. You have been grossly at fault. Your own principles should tell you so; it should not be necessary for me to inform you of it. As for your obliging description of my character, I shall take leave to tell you that this guardianship, which was foisted on to my shoulders, and which has been from the outset a source of trouble and annoyance to me, comprises more than the mere management of your fortune. You had the goodness once, Miss Taverner, to inform me that you were glad you were not my daughter. So am I glad, but however little I may relish the post I stand to you in the place of a father, and if you do not obey me I shall be strongly tempted to use you as I have very little doubt your father would if he could see you at this moment.'

'I have only one thing to be thankful for!' cried Judith. 'It is that in a very short time now it will be out of your power to threaten me or to interfere in my concerns! You may be certain of this at least, Lord Worth: once your guardianship of me ends I shall not willingly see you again!'

'Thank you! You have now given full rein to your temper, and can have no more to say,' he replied, and turned, and held open the door. 'Your chaise should be ready by this time, ma'am.'

She moved towards the door, but before she could reach it, Peregrine had come hastily into the room, looking hot, and rather more dusty and dishevelled than she was herself.

'What the devil's amiss?' demanded Peregrine. 'I thought you had been half-way to Brighton by now! I have had the wretchedest luck, I can tell you!'

'Lord Worth,' said Judith, controlling her voice with an effort, 'has seen proper to declare our race at an end. It does not suit his dignity to have his ward drive herself into Brighton.'

'Much we care for that!' said Peregrine. 'Damme, Worth, this is a wager! You can't stop my sister now!'

'I will say what I have to say to you later,' replied Worth, unpleasantly. 'Miss Taverner, I am waiting to hand you into your chaise!'

'You may continue your journey,' she said. 'When my brother is with me I need no protection but his.'

'As we have seen,' he remarked sardonically. 'Well, I warned you, Miss Taverner, that I should compel your obedience.'

He came forward, but Peregrine stepped quickly between them with his fists up, and said sharply: 'And I will warn you, sir, to leave my sister alone!'

'I am afraid that noble gesture is wasted on me,' said Worth. 'Console yourself with the reflection that if I did hit you, you would be more than sorry to have provoked me to it.'

Miss Taverner pushed by her brother. 'Do not make a scene, Perry, I beg of you! I am ready to go with you, Lord Worth.'

He bowed; she went past him out of the room, and a couple of minutes later she was being handed up into the waiting chaise. The door was shut on her; she heard her guardian give an order to the post-boys, and sank back into a corner of the chaise as the horses moved forward.

She found that she was trembling, her thoughts in confusion, and a lump in her throat. All her pleasure in going to Brighton was at an end; she knew herself to be the wretchedest creature alive. There could be no defending her conduct; she had realised at Horley how indecorous it was, and had now the mortification of having earned Worth's condemnation. He thought of her with disgust; he had not scrupled to humiliate her, nor to address her in terms of the most galling contempt. It was small wonder that she should have lost her temper with him: he had been unpardonable. The better understanding which had seemed to be growing up between them was quite at an end. She did not care; unless he begged her pardon she could not bring herself to meet him again without feelings of the strongest revulsion, and she was pretty sure that he never would beg her pardon. Her credit with him was utterly destroyed; he was odious, insolent, overbearing, and she herself little better than vulgar Lady Lade.

These agitating reflections produced their natural result. Tears poured silently down Miss Taverner's cheeks, and picturesque villages, turnpikes, and views passed unnoticed. When she was at last set down at the house on the Marine Parade, not even the sight of the sea had the power to elevate her spirits. She hurried into the house with her veil pulled down, and almost ran up the stairs to indulge her misery in the seclusion of her own bedchamber.

Seventeen

$\mathcal{I}$T WAS MANY DAYS BEFORE MISS TAVERNER COULD BE
restored to the enjoyment of composure, and long before
the evils of her journey ceased to be felt. She struggled to support
her spirits, but they were quite worn down, and although she
might assume an air of calm cheerfulness, her reflections were all
mortifying, and her heart very heavy.

Peregrine's arrival in Brighton, half an hour later than her
own, brought her no comfort. What had passed between him
and Worth she did not ask, nor he divulge. He came to her
sulky, half-defiant, half-shamefaced, ready to abuse Worth, but
reluctant to discuss the cause of their disagreement. It was evident that Worth had not spared him. Judith's spirits sank still
lower. She felt herself to have bred dissension between the two
men, and no acknowledgment now (which would indeed have
been hard to make) of having deserved Worth's censure would
avail to soften Peregrine's indignation. No good could come of
talking over the affair; it must be left to time to remedy the
harm that had been done. Nor could she expect Peregrine to
see it all as she did. He was conscious of having done wrong,
perhaps secretly sorry for it, but it was after all no great matter:
he could forget everything but Worth's part in it in a very short
while, and sally forth with tolerable light-heartedness to take a
look at Brighton.

When Mrs Scattergood was set down at the house it was some hours later, and Judith was able to meet her with the appearance at least of composure. But it was a hard case to be obliged to listen to her reproaches, and to give her some account of what had passed at Cuckfield. But even Mrs Scattergood could not talk for ever, and by the time they sat down to dinner she was ready to forget it all, and turn her thoughts to what Brighton offered in the way of entertainment.

The house on the Marine Parade was neat, and sufficiently commodious to satisfy its tenants. They could have wished that the drawing-rooms had been more handsome, but were obliged to admit that the furnishings of the whole, though not rich, were above what was generally to be found in houses let out for hire at the seaside. The want of elegance was soon remedied by the arrangement of all the pretty trifles and hangings which Mrs Scattergood had had the forethought to bring from Brook Street in one of her many trunks. The first evening passed quietly in making themselves at home; both ladies went early to bed, the elder to place slices of raw veal on her face to prevent wrinkles, and the younger to lie awake half the night in fruitless reflection.

This wretchedness could not long endure. In the morning the sight of the sun sparkling on the sea produced an alleviation; and the air, which was fresh and salt-tanged, invigorated the spirits. Some feeling of lowness must still remain, but misery could not persist. It was in anticipation of a day of interest and pleasure that Judith joined her brother and Mrs Scattergood in the breakfast-parlour.

From the circumstance of her eyes having been full of tears when her chaise had driven into Brighton the day before, Judith had been hardly conscious of her surroundings, and had not even looked up to see the Pavilion, which was placed to catch the traveller's gaze immediately upon entering the town.

That must therefore be the first object of their morning's walk, and soon after breakfast the two ladies set out together, accompanied as far as the Steyne by Peregrine, who was bound for Ragget's club.

Five minutes' walk along the sea-front brought them to the southern end of the Steyne, and a view, though not the best, of the Pavilion was at once obtained. They bent their steps inland, and began to walk up the glazed red-brick pavement of the Steyne, past the neat gardens laid out in geometrical designs, past Donaldson's Circulating Library, until Pavilion Parade was reached, and they stood immediately before the gleaming and costly edifice itself.

The Pavilion, which had been built for the Prince Regent by Mr Henry Holland, occupied a frontage of four hundred and eighty feet, and stood in ten acres of ground. It had been designed in accordance with a vague idea conceived by the Prince upon being sent a present of some Chinese wallpaper, and startling and original was the result. At first glance the sight-seeing visitor might well imagine himself to have strayed into some land of make-believe, so gorgeous and unconventional was the palace. The Greek, the Moorish, and the Russian styles predominated. It was fronted by an Ionic colonnade and entablature; a succession of green-roofed domes and minarets rose above a running battlement that surmounted the upper line of the whole building; and two cones, equal in height to the central and largest dome, crowned each wing. The pinnacles and the minarets, which were placed at every angle of the structure, were made of Bath stone, the rest of the palace of stuccoed brick. In front of each of the wings was an open arcade composed of arches, separated by octagonal columns, and ornamented by trellis-work. The entrance was upon the western side, but the principal front, which Mrs Scattergood and Miss Taverner were gazing at, was to the east, and opened on to a lawn, which was separated from the parade by a low wall, and a dwarf enclosure. A captious critic had once remarked, on first seeing the palace, that it was as though St Paul's had littered, and brought forth a brood of cupolas, but no such profane thought crossed Miss Taverner's mind. If the Pavilion had not been conceived with quite that simplicity of taste which was proper, it was not for her to cavil; she was not to be setting up her judgment in opposition to Mr Holland's.

'Is it not a noble edifice?' said Mrs Scattergood, who could never see it without being struck afresh by its magnificence. 'The stables alone cost seventy thousand pounds to build, you know. I am sure you can never have seen a palace to equal it! Carlton House is nothing to it! *That* is unpretentious to the point of meanness; *this* must instantly catch the eye, and hold the visitor spellbound with admiration!'

'Very true; it is something quite out of the common, indeed.'

'And the interior! – But you will see! We shall be invited to one of the musical parties, of course. Every apartment of the most noble dimensions, and the whole fitted up with a degree of elegance beyond what is imaginable!'

They walked on to obtain a view of the stables, which were placed at the northern end of the grounds. A short distance brought them to the New Road, and turning down this they soon found themselves in North Street, a steep, crowded highway, which was always in a bustle of traffic. Several of the principal coach-offices were situated in it, and the two ladies paused for a few minutes to watch the departure of one of the stages to London. A number of shops displaying attractive wares made their progress slow, but they presently reached Promenade Grove, on the south-western side of the Pavilion, and sat down to rest for a while under the scanty shade of the poplars that fringed it.

Here were displayed a neatness and a propriety of taste which must have delighted a more critical observer than Miss

Taverner. She exclaimed, and was enchanted, and after a short interval of repose declared her intention of exploring the numerous bowers and zigzag alleys in which the grove was laid out. Mrs Scattergood was very willing, and half an hour was spent in wandering about and admiring the beauty of the flowers, which grew in profusion in a number of formal beds. The grove was not crowded, for the fashionable hour for promenading was later in the day, when an orchestra dispensed music from a wooden box in the centre, but during the course of their stroll the two ladies met several persons with whom they were acquainted, and learned from one of these that although the Prince Regent was not yet in residence at the Pavilion, he was expected to arrive at the end of the week. Colonel McMahon, his secretary, was already in Brighton.

A glance at her watch informed Mrs Scattergood that the morning was already considerably advanced, and as they had come out with the intention of visiting one of the libraries, and taking out a subscription, both ladies now left the grove, and, passing the Castle inn, made their way across the Steyne to Donaldson's library.

Accustomed as she was by this time to the superiority of the London libraries, Miss Taverner was yet amazed at the spaciousness and elegance of Donaldson's. The collection of books was large; the morning papers and the most valuable of the periodical publications were arranged on tables for the use of subscribers; and the rooms, which were many, were fitted up with a taste that was seldom met with. Card parties and music were to be had there any evening during the season, and throughout the day a constant stream of fashionables coming, some to exchange a book, others to meet their acquaintances or to show off new gowns, produced a continuous scene of animation.

Mrs Scattergood and her charge reached home again a little time after midday, to find that Peregrine had returned before them, and was seated in the bow-window of the drawing-room on the first floor, busily engaged in focusing a telescope on to the bathing-machines lined up along the beach below. It had not taken him long to discover that one of the more popular amusements obtaining amongst the Corinthians at Brighton was to train a telescope on to these machines (which, unlike those at Scarborough or Ramsgate, had no awnings) in the hope of catching a glimpse of Beauty about to enter the sea, and he had lost no time in purchasing a telescope for his own use.

Mrs Scattergood exclaimed at him, and abused him roundly for being an odious, vulgar boy, but as the summer was not yet far enough advanced to tempt ladies to indulge in sea-bathing, he was able to refute all her accusations, and offer her the telescope, so that she might see with her own eyes that the only object of interest on the shore was a stout gentleman in a scarlet suit, cautiously dipping one foot into the water. She indignantly declined taking a peep through the telescope, and removing it from his grasp, shut it up, and inexorably drove him down to the dining parlour, where a cold luncheon was set out upon the table.

The question to occupy their thoughts during lunch was what was to be done with the rest of the day. It was Wednesday, and no ball offered. These took place at the Castle inn and the Old Ship alternately. Wednesdays and Fridays were devoted to card-assemblies, and although Mrs Scattergood would have been very happy to have spent the evening playing Commerce or Casino, she knew that her charge was not fond of cards. Happily, Peregrine had provided for their entertainment in a burst of brotherly affection, and had not only engaged a box at the theatre, but was willing to take Judith driving all the afternoon.

She was very glad to exchange a card-assembly for the theatre, but the mere mention of driving with him was sufficient to put her out of countenance and bring a blush to her cheeks. She declined it, excusing herself on the score of being tired from her morning's ramble about the town. He did not press it, but went off shortly after luncheon to seek other amusement. Mrs Scattergood retired to her bedchamber, and Judith sat down in the drawing-room to occupy herself with her netting-box, and to look out of the window at the lively scene presenting itself on the parade.

She was not left long in silence. A caller was presently announced, and she got up in a little confusion to welcome Captain Audley.

It was hard to meet his eyes, but from his first question it was made apparent that Worth had not told him of the previous day's escapade. He asked her if she had enjoyed a tolerably comfortable journey; he had too much delicacy of feeling, she was sure, to have put such a question had he been aware of the facts. She returned a rather constrained answer, and made haste to introduce some other topic for conversation. It was not difficult; as he sat down beside her on the window-seat he desired to know how she liked Brighton, and on that subject she could be animated enough, free from all agitating reflections.

'Oh, I am quite delighted with it!' she said. 'To be sure, it is not so large, but it is a thousand times better than Scarborough. And I was used to think that nothing could be! But Brighton passes anything I have ever seen. I wish I might stay here for ever.'

'You would soon wish yourself back in London when the autumn came,' he replied, smiling. 'It is very well on a bright summer's day, but you will find after a while that there is a sameness that makes it all seem insipid.'

'I cannot believe it. Do you find it so?'

'I? No, indeed; did you not tell me I had the happiest disposition? But every young lady is soon bored by Brighton, I assure you. It is not at all the thing to continue being pleased with it.'

'I daresay those same young ladies would declare themselves bored in London as easily. For my part, even though the balls and the assemblies palled I could gaze for ever on such a prospect as this.'

'I venture to think that the first sober-looking morning will make you change your mind. Or do you refer not to the sea, after all, but to Golden Ball instead? That, I agree, is a prospect one cannot soon tire of.'

She leaned forward to look down into the road, and following the direction of the Captain's eyes, looked with amused appreciation at a chocolate-coloured barouche, drawn by white horses, which was being driven slowly down the parade by a tall, thin gentleman, who had so exaggerated an air of fashion that he must in any company be remarkable.

'You forget,' she replied, 'Mr Hughes Ball is a sight I have enjoyed in London these six or seven months. He lives in Brook Street, you know, and once did me the honour of calling on me. Who is that queer old gentleman with powdered hair, and a rose in his button-hole? How odd he looks, to be sure!'

'What, do you not know Old Blue Hanger?' demanded the Captain. 'My dear Miss Taverner, that is Lord Coleraine. You may know him by his green coat, and his powder. You must have met his brother in town.'

'Oh, Colonel Hanger! Yes, I have met him, of course.'

'And disliked him very thoroughly,' said the Captain, with a twinkle. 'He is not such a bad fellow, but to tell you the truth, the Regent's intimates are never excessively well-liked by the rest of the world. Here is one of them tittuping up the parade now. You must go far before you will find McMahon's equal. There, the little man in the blue and buff uniform, bowing and scraping before Lady Downshire.'

She remarked: 'So that is the Regent's secretary! He is very ugly.'

'Very ugly, and up to no good.'

Colonel McMahon, having parted from Lady Downshire, was coming slowly along the parade. As though aware of the two pairs of eyes observing his progress, he glanced up as he passed the house, and seeing Miss Taverner, stared very hard at her with an expression of critical approval. She drew back at once, reddening, but the Captain merely said: 'Do not be surprised at his quizzing you, Miss Taverner. He has very queer manners.'

Soon after he proposed escorting her for a stroll, to see Rossi's statue of the Regent, which was placed in front of Royal Crescent; and upon her agreeing readily to the expedition, it was not long before they had left the house, and were walking up the parade, enjoying on the one side the majestic grandeur of the sea, and on the other the rows of elegant habitations, adorned with columns, pilasters, and entablatures of the Corinthian order, which had been erected during the past dozen years. There was nothing to offend wherever the eye might chance to light: all was in the neatest style, and a series of well-kept squares and crescents saved the parade from too uniform an appearance, and relieved the eye with their welcome patches of verdure.

Mrs Scattergood met them upon their return to the house, and having exclaimed at seeing her young cousin (whom she had not expected to be in Brighton for some days), extended a cordial invitation to him to accompany them to the play that evening. He accepted with evident pleasure, and after sitting with the ladies for a little while, took his leave of them with a promise of meeting them again later at the theatre.

The theatre, which Mrs Scattergood and Miss Taverner had passed during the course of their morning's walk, was situated in the New Road, and though not large, was a handsome building, fitted up with every attention to comfort. The pit and gallery were roomy, and two tiers of lofty boxes, ornamented with gold-fringed draperies, provided ample accommodation for the more genteel part of the audience. The Regent's box, on the left of the stage, which was separated from the others by a richly gilt iron lattice-work, was empty, but nearly all the others were occupied. Miss Taverner's time, before the curtain went up, was fully engaged in bowing to those of her acquaintance who were present; Mrs Scattergood's in closely observing every cap and turban in the house, and preferring her own to them all.

During the first interval several gentlemen visited their box, among them Colonel McMahon, who came in on the heels of Mr Lewis, and begged leave to recall himself to Mrs Scattergood's memory. She was obliged to introduce him to Miss Taverner, to whom he at once attached himself, remaining by her side throughout the interval, and alternately diverting and disgusting her with the obsequiousness and affectation of his manners. He professed himself to be all amazement at not having met her before, and upon hearing that she had not yet had the honour of being presented to the Prince Regent, assured her that she might depend on receiving a card of invitation to the Pavilion in the very near future.

'I venture to think,' he said impressively, 'that you will be pleased alike by the interior of the Pavilion, and by its Royal owner. Such manners are not often met with. You will find His Highness condescending to the highest degree. No one was ever more affable! You will like him excessively, and I am emboldened to say that I can engage for him being particularly pleased with *you*.'

She could hardly keep her countenance as she thanked him, and was glad that the interval was nearly over. It was time for him to return to his place; he made her a low bow, and went away rubbing his hands together.

During the second interval a circumstance occurred to destroy all Miss Taverner's pleasure. She became aware of being closely scrutinised, and glancing towards the opposite boxes found that the Earl of Barrymore was fixedly regarding her through his quizzing-glass.

She recognised him at once, and knew from the slight smile on his lips that he had recognised her. He nudged his companion, pointed her out, and very palpably asked a question. Miss Taverner could guess its import, and with a heightened colour turned away.

She took care not to glance in that direction again, but Peregrine, chancing to look round the house, exclaimed suddenly: 'Who is that fellow who keeps staring into our box? I have a very good mind to step round and ask him what he means by it!'

'I do not think I should notice his impertinence, if I were you,' replied the Captain. 'It is only Cripplegate, and the Barrymores, you know, cannot be held accountable for their odd manners. If you had known Hellgate, the late Earl, you would think nothing of this man.'

Peregrine was frowning across the house. 'Yes, but he seems actually to be trying to catch our attention. Ju, you do not know him, do you?'

She looked fleetingly towards the opposite door. The Earl kissed his hand to her, and Captain Audley turned to her with a surprised question in his eyes. 'My dear Miss Taverner, are you acquainted with Barrymore?'

She said in a good deal of confusion: 'No, no! I have never spoken to him in my life.'

'Well, I think perhaps I will go round and inform him of it,' said the Captain, rising from his chair.

She laid her hand on his sleeve, and said with strong agitation: 'It is of no consequence! I am persuaded he mistakes me for another. See, he has found his error for himself, and is no longer looking this way! Pray sit down again, Captain Audley!'

Civility obliged him to comply, though he looked to be far from satisfied. But the third act commenced almost immediately, and as the Earl went away before the farce no further annoyance was suffered that evening.

But the effects of his having recognised in Miss Taverner the curricle-driver at Horley were soon felt. Knowledge of her identity did not prevent him from describing the circumstances under which he had first met her, and by the time she entered the Assembly-rooms at the Old Ship with Mrs Scattergood on the following evening her name was being bandied about pretty freely, and two ladies who had hitherto treated her with marked amiability bowed with such cold civility that she felt almost ready to sink.

The rooms were full, and a large part of the gathering was composed of officers, with whom, from the circumstance of a Cavalry barracks being situated a little way out of the town on the Lewes road, Brighton always teemed. The Master of Cere-monies presented several of the younger ones to Miss Taverner, but she stood up for the first two dances with Captain Audley.

It might have been her fancy, but she thought that she could detect a shade of reserve in his manner, a grave look in his usu-ally merry eyes. After a little while she said as lightly as she could: 'I daresay you have heard by this time of my shocking conduct, Captain Audley. Are you disgusted? Do you think you should stand up with such a sad character as myself?'

'You refer to your drive from town, I collect. *I* should not have described it in such terms.'

'But you do not approve of it. I can see that you think ill of me for having done it.'

He smiled. 'My countenance must be singularly deceptive, then. I think ill of you! No, indeed, I do not!'

'Your brother is very angry with me.'

He returned no answer, and after a moment or two she said with a little laugh: 'It was not so very bad, after all.'

'Certainly not. What *you* do could never be bad. Let us say rather that it was not very wise.'

She was conscious of a constriction in her throat; she overcame it, and replied: 'I am sure I do not care. Such an excessive regard for public opinion is what I have no patience with. Your brother is not here to-night, I think.'

'He was engaged to dine with some friends, but I daresay he will be here presently.'

They went down the dance at this moment, and when they stood opposite to each other again another topic for conversation came up, and continued to occupy them for the rest of the time they were together.

As she walked back beside the Captain to where they had left Mrs Scattergood, Miss Taverner saw that Worth had entered the room, and was standing talking earnestly to her chaperon. From the glance Mrs Scattergood cast in her direction she felt sure that she was the subject under discussion, and it was consequently in a very stiff manner that she greeted her guardian.

His bow was formal, his countenance unsmiling; and for the few minutes that he remained beside them he talked the merest commonplace. Tuesday's events were not referred to, but that they held a prominent place in his thoughts Miss Taverner could not doubt. All the mortifications of her last meeting with him were vividly recalled to her memory by the sight of him, and no softening in his manner, no kinder light in his eyes came to alleviate her discomfort. Upon her civility being claimed towards an officer who approached to lead her out for the next dance, the Earl walked away to the other end of the room, and presently took his place in another set opposite a young lady in a diaphanous gown of yellow sarcenet. He left the ballroom before tea, and without once having asked his ward to stand up with him. She saw him go, and was wretched indeed. As for his taste, she thought very poorly of it, for she could not perceive the least degree of beauty in the lady in yellow sarcenet – nothing, in fact, to have made it worth the Earl's while to have attended the ball.

The evening provided her with a fair sample of what she guessed she would be obliged to endure until her escapade was forgotten. Several dowagers eyed her with a good deal of severity, and her particular friends seemed to have agreed amongst themselves to behave towards her as though nothing had happened, which they did so carefully that her spirits sank lower than ever. The gentlemen saw the affair as a famous joke; they were ready enough to talk of it, and to applaud her daring; and the boldest amongst them quizzed her with a kind of familiar gallantry which galled her pride beyond bearing. To make matters worse Mrs Scattergood bemoaned the results of her imprudence all the way home, and prophesied that the evils of such conduct would be felt for many a long day.

At the end of the week the Regent arrived in Brighton, accompanied by his brother the Duke of Cumberland; and somewhat to Miss Taverner's surprise a card was received by Mrs Scattergood inviting them both to an evening party at the Pavilion on the following Tuesday. The royal brothers were seen in church on Sunday: the elder stout, with a sallow sort of handsomeness, and an air of great fashion; the younger lean, extremely tall, and with his black-avised countenance disfigured by a scar from a wound received in Tournai.

Miss Taverner could not forbear looking at him with a good deal of interest, for the scandals attaching to his name were many, and he was generally credited with nearly every form of vice, including murder. Only a couple of years before his valet had committed suicide, and there were still any number of persons who did not scruple to hint that the unfortunate man had not met his end in the way that was officially given out. The Duke of Clarence, who, like every one of his brothers but Cumberland himself, was an invincible and an indiscreet talker, had referred to that particular scandal upon one occasion, and while assuring Miss Taverner that there was no truth in it, had added: 'Ernest is not a bad sort, only if he knows where you have a tender spot on your foot he likes to tread on it.' Looking at the Duke of Cumberland's face, Miss Taverner could well believe this to be true.

Before the party at the Pavilion took place Judith had the comfort of knowing that her cousin was in Brighton. He and her uncle arrived at the Castle inn on Monday at four o'clock, having come down from the White Horse Cellar, in Piccadilly, in a little under six hours, travelling post; and called at Marine Parade after dinner. Peregrine had driven out to Worthing earlier in the day, and was not yet back, but both the ladies were at home, and while Mrs Scattergood was engaged with the Admiral, Judith was able to take her cousin apart, and pour into his ears an account of her disgrace and its cause.

He listened to her with an expression of concern, and twice pressed her hand with a look of such sympathetic understanding that she was hard put to it not to burst into tears of self-pity. The relief of being able to unburden her heart was great; and the knowledge that there was one at least who did not condemn her induced her to show a more marked degree of preference for her cousin than she was aware of doing.

'You see how bad I have been,' she said with a trembling smile. 'But I should never have done it if Lord Worth had not laid it down so positively that I was not to go with Perry.'

'The impropriety of *your* behaviour is nothing when compared with the total want of delicacy *he* has shown!' he replied warmly. 'You were at fault; your action was ill-judged, but I can readily perceive how you were provoked into doing it. Lord Worth will be content with nothing less than a complete ascendancy over your mind! I have watched with alarm his growing influence over you; it is evident that he thought you would meekly obey his arbitrary commands. Do not be unhappy! He has been betrayed into showing himself to you in his true

colours, and *that* must be of benefit. He is autocratic; the mild-
ness of manner which he has lately assumed towards you is as
false as his pretended regard for you. He cares nothing for you,
my dear cousin; no man who could address you in the humili-
ating terms you have described to me!'

She was considerably taken aback by the vehemence of this
speech, nor did its import produce any of that comfort which was
presumably its object. The evils of her situation seemed to
become greater; she said in a desponding tone: 'He has never given
me any reason for suspecting him of having a regard for me.'

He looked at her intently. 'To me it has seemed otherwise. I
have sometimes been afraid that you were even inclined to
return his partiality.'

'Certainly not!' she said emphatically. 'Such a notion is
absurd! I care nothing for his good opinion, and look forward
to the day when I shall be freed from his guardianship.'

He said with meaning: 'And I, too, look forward to that
day, Judith.'

Upon the following evening Mrs Scattergood and Miss
Taverner drove in a closed carriage to the Pavilion, and were
set down at the domed porch punctually at nine o'clock, and
ushered through an octagonal vestibule, which was lit by a
Chinese lantern suspended from the centre of the tented roof,
into the entrance hall, a square apartment with a ceiling
painted to represent an azure sky with fleecy clouds. Here
they were able to leave their shawls, and to peep anxiously at
their reflections in the mirror over the marble mantelpiece.
Mrs Scattergood gave their names to one of the flunkeys who
stood on either side of the door at the back of the hall; the
man announced them, and they passed through the door into
the Chinese Gallery.

A numerous company was gathered here, and the Prince
Regent was standing in the central division of the gallery in a

position to welcome his guests as they came in. His resplendent figure instantly caught the eye, for he had a great inclination towards finery, and his girth, which was considerable, did not prevent him from wearing the most gorgeous waistcoats and coloured coats. His doctors had forbidden him on pain of death to remedy the defects of his figure with tight-lacing, and since he was always very anxious over the state of his own health, he obeyed them. But in spite of his corpulence, and the lines of dissipation that marred his countenance, there were still some traces to be found of the Prince Florizel who had captivated the world thirty-odd years before.

As Mrs Scattergood, rising from a deep curtsy, begged leave to present Miss Taverner, he smiled, and shook hands with a good-humoured condescension which had often endeared many people to him whom he afterwards contrived without the least difficulty to alienate. With that easy courtesy he knew so well how to assume he insisted that he remembered Mrs Scattergood well, was happy to see her again (and in such looks), and very glad to make the acquaintance of her young friend. It was difficult to realise that so affable a prince had done what he could to assist in oversetting his father's precarious reason, had discarded two wives, and heartlessly abandoned any friend of whom he had happened to tire. Miss Taverner knew him to be selfish, capricious, given over to every form of excess, but she could not remember it when he turned to her and said with his attractive smile and air of kindness: 'You must know, Miss Taverner, that from *one* member of my family I have heard so much in your praise that I have been anxious indeed to meet you!'

She hardly knew where to look, but chancing to meet his eyes, which were twinkling archly, she was emboldened to return his smile, and to murmur that he was very kind.

'Is this your first visit to Brighton?' he inquired. 'Do you make a long stay? It is a town I have come to regard as so peculiarly my own that it will not be out of place for me to bid you welcome to it.'

'Thank you, sir. It is my first visit. If I could indulge my inclination I believe I should stay here for ever.'

'That is famous!' he said jovially. 'That is how I feel, I can tell you, Miss Taverner. It is many years since I first came to Brighton – we called it Brighthelmstone in those days, you know – but you see what a hold it took on my fancy! I was constrained to build myself a little summer palace here, and I give you my word that whenever I can I come down to live in it.'

'And I am sure it is no wonder, sir!' said Mrs Scattergood, to whom this speech was partially addressed. 'I have frequently been describing to Miss Taverner the beauty and elegance of the Pavilion. Nothing could ever equal it!'

He smiled, and seemed pleased, though he deprecated her praise with a protesting movement of his hand. 'I believe it to be a little out of the common,' he acknowledged. 'I do not wish to say that it is by any means perfect, but it suits *me*, and has been admired by those whose taste and judgment I depend upon. Miss Taverner will be interested, I daresay, in some of the examples of Chinese art she will find here. The light immediately above us, for instance, ma'am,' he continued, pointing upwards to a horizontal skylight of stained glass set in the middle of the ceiling, 'represents Lin-Shin, the god of thunder, surrounded, as you see, by drums, and flying.'

Miss Taverner looked, and admired; he invited her cordially to inspect whatever she had in mind to, and seemed as though he would have volunteered to guide her round the gallery himself, had he not been obliged to turn away from her to receive another guest who had just been announced.

Mrs Scattergood and Miss Taverner withdrew to where an acquaintance of the former was standing, and while the two elder ladies stood chatting together Miss Taverner had leisure to look about her and to be astonished.

Her view of the exterior of the Pavilion had led her to expect the interior to be of more than ordinary splendour, but she had not been prepared for what met her gaze. The gallery in which she stood was of immense length, and partially separated into five unequal divisions by a trellis-work of what looked to be bamboo, but which, upon closer inspection, turned out to be painted iron. The central division was surrounded by a Chinese canopy of similar trellis-work, hung with bells. Above, a coved ceiling projected through the upper floor, and had set in it the light towards which the Regent had directed her notice. A chimney-piece in brass and iron, worked in further imitation of bamboo, was placed directly facing the middle entrance, and on either side of it two niches, lined with yellow marble, contained cabinets. There seemed, as far as Miss Taverner could see, to be corresponding niches in the other divisions, as well as two recesses with a porcelain pagoda in each. Stained glass lanterns hung from the angles of the ceiling, and in addition to these a soft light was thrown by branches concealed in the glass tulips and lotus-flowers which adorned the three mantelpieces in the gallery. The extreme compartments were occupied by two staircases, also made in imitation of bamboo, and two doors, which, being fronted with looking-glass, made the perspective of the gallery seem interminable. The walls were battened and covered with canvas painted with peach-blossom as a ground-colour, on which rocks, trees, shrubs, birds, and flowers were pencilled in pale blue. All the couches and chairs were of ivory figured with black, and the daylight was admitted only through the lights in the several coved roofs, and through the stained-glass window above one of the staircases. The corresponding window over the other staircase was merely imitative.

While she was looking about her, and wondering at what she saw, a footman had come up with a tray of refreshments; she took a cup of coffee from it, and turned to find Mr Brummell at her elbow, dressed in the plainest of black coats and knee-breeches, and looking singularly out of place in the midst of such splendid surroundings. 'Spellbound, Miss Taverner?' he inquired.

'Mr Brummell! I did not know you were in Brighton! Yes, indeed: it is all very – very beautiful – quite extraordinary!' She saw the faint, incredulous smile he used to check applause, and gave a relieved sigh. 'You do not like it either!' she said.

'I thought you had decided it was all very beautiful?'

'Well, I expect it is. It must be, of course, for everyone is in raptures over it.'

'Have you heard me express myself rapturously over it?'

'No, but –'

'Then there is no reason for you to be sure of its beauty.'

She smiled. 'Pray do not snub me, Mr Brummell! If you are to do that I shall be left without any support in this horrid censorious world. You must know that I am a little in disgrace.'

'I have heard rumours. If you think my advice of value I have some for you.'

'Yes?' she said eagerly.

He flicked open his snuff-box in his inimitable way and took a pinch. 'Drive your phaeton,' he said. 'You are really very stupid not to have thought of it for yourself.'

'Drive my phaeton?' she repeated.

'Of course. Upon every occasion, and where you would be least expected to do so. Did I not tell you once, Miss Taverner, never to admit a fault?'

She said slowly: 'I see. You are right; that is what I should have done at once. I am in your debt.'

People were beginning to move down the gallery towards the looking-glass doors at the north end. These had been flung open into the Music Room, where a concert was to be given. The Regent called to Mr Brummell, desiring his opinion on a piece of Sèvres he had been showing to one of his guests; Miss Taverner rejoined her chaperon, and taking her place in the procession soon found herself in a huge room which cast anything she had yet seen into the shade.

At first sight it was all a blaze of red and gold, but after her first gasp of astonishment she was able to take a clearer view of the whole, and to see that she was standing, not in some fantastic dream-palace, but in a square apartment with rectangular recesses at each end, fitted up in a style of Oriental splendour. The square part was surmounted by a cornice ornamented with shield-work, and supported by reticulated columns, shimmering with gold-leaf. Above this was an octagon gallery formed by a series of elliptical arches, and pierced by windows of the same shape. A convex cove rose over this, topped by leaf ornaments in gold and chocolate; and above this was the central dome, lined with a scale-work of glittering green and gold. In the middle of it a vast foliated decoration was placed, from whose calyx depended an enormous lustre of cut-glass in the shape of a pagoda. To this was attached by chains a lamp made to resemble a huge water-lily, coloured crimson and gold and white. Four gilded dragons clung to the under-side of the lamp, and below them hung a smaller glass water-lily.

The recesses at the north and south ends of the room were canopied by convex curves of imitation bamboo, bound by ribands, and contained the four doorways of the apartment, each one of which was set under a canopy of crimson and gold, embellished with bells and dragons. These canopies were held up by gilt columns, entwined by yet more dragons. The walls were hung with twelve views of the neighbourhood of Pekin, executed in bright yellow on a crimson background, and set in frames enwreathed by dragons. Still more dragons writhed above the window draperies, which were of blue and crimson satin and yellow silk. The floor was covered by a gigantic Axminster carpet where golden suns, stars, serpents, and dragons ran riot on a pale blue ground; and the sofas and chairs were upholstered in yellow and dove-coloured satin.

A fire burned in the fireplace of statuary marble on the western wall, and above it, on the mantel-shelf, a large clock presented an appearance of the most striking incongruity, for although its base was entwined by an inevitable dragon, upon the top were grouped, rather surprisingly, Venus and Cupid, with the Peacock of Love, and Mars climbing up to them.

Miss Taverner was quite overpowered, and could only blink at what she saw. The heat of the room was oppressive; all the ladies were fanning themselves. Miss Taverner began to feel a little faint; dragons and lights started to dance oddly before her eyes, and had she not at that moment found a chair to sink into she believed she must have lost possession of her senses.

She recovered in a few minutes, and was able to enjoy the concert. The Regent, who had been taught to play the violoncello in his youth by Crossbill, and was very musical, beat time with one foot; the Duke of Cumberland stared all the prettiest women out of countenance; Mr Brummell gazed before him with an air of weary patience; and Sir John Lade, who looked for all the world like a stage-coachman strayed by mistake into the Pavilion, went to sleep in the corner of a sofa, and snored gently till it was time to go home.

Eighteen

Upon the following morning Miss Taverner despatched her groom post-haste to London to fetch down her phaeton, and no sooner had it arrived, and her horses been rested, than she startled Brighton by driving it to Donaldson's at the fashionable hour to change her book. No one observing her air of calm assurance could have guessed what an effort it cost her to appear thus unconcerned. She met Captain Audley on the Steyne, and took him up beside her, and drove him to the Chalybeate Spring at Hove and back again. At the ball at the Castle inn that evening one or two people ventured to comment on it. She raised her brows and said coolly: 'My phaeton? Yes, it has just arrived from town. Some trifling fault made it necessary for me to send it to the coachmaker's, which is why you have seen me walking lately. You must know that I am used to drive myself wherever I go.' She passed on with a smile and a bow.

'Excellent, Miss Taverner!' murmured Mr Brummell. 'You are so apt a pupil that if I were only *ten* years younger I believe I should propose for your hand.'

She laughed. 'I cannot suppose it possible. Did you ever propose to any lady, sir?'

'Yes, once,' replied Mr Brummell in a voice of gentle melancholy. 'But it came to nothing. I discovered that she actually ate cabbage, so what could I do but cut the connection?'

If Miss Taverner's phaeton did not succeed in putting an end to all criticism of her drive from town it did silence a good many tongues. Her habit of driving herself all over Brighton was soon looked on as an idiosyncrasy allowable in a lady with a fortune of eighty thousand pounds. But although the dowagers, with one or two exceptions, might agree to look indulgently on her oddities there was one person who gave no sign of having forgiven her. Lord Worth continued to hold aloof, and when they met conducted himself towards her with a cold civility that showed her how fresh in his mind were the events at Cuckfield. Having frequently assured herself and him that nothing could exceed her dislike of him, there was no other course open to her than to treat him with similar coldness, and to flirt with Captain Audley. The Captain was all readiness to oblige her, and by the time they had twice danced half the evening together, and twice been seen driving along the parade in the perch-phaeton it began to be pretty freely circulated that the Captain was to be the lucky man.

Even Mrs Scattergood began to take a serious view of the affair, and having watched in silence for a week at last ventured to broach the subject one evening after dinner. 'Judith, my love,' she said, very busy with the yards of fringe she was making, 'did I tell you that I met Lady Downshire in East Street this morning? You must know that I walked back to Westfield Lodge with her.'

'No, you did not tell me,' replied Miss Taverner, laying down her book. 'Was there any reason why you should?'

'Oh, none in the world! But I must own I was rather taken aback by her asking me when your engagement to Charles Audley was to be made known. I did not know what to say.'

Judith laughed. 'Dear ma'am, I hope you told her that you did not know?'

Mrs Scattergood shot her a quick look. 'To be sure, I told her that I had no apprehension of any such engagement taking place. But the case is, you see, that people are beginning to wonder at the preference you show for Charles. You must not be offended with me for speaking plain.'

'Offended! How should I be?'

Mrs Scattergood began to look a little alarmed. 'But Judith, is it possible that you can be contemplating marriage with Charles?'

Miss Taverner smiled saucily, and said: 'I am persuaded you can no longer see to make your fringe, ma'am. Let me ring for some working-candles to be brought you!'

'Pray do not be so teasing!' besought her chaperon. 'I have nothing in the world to say against Charles. Indeed, I have the highest value for him; but a younger son, my dear, and without the least prospect of enlargement! for it is not to be supposed that Worth will stay single to oblige him, you know. I could tell you of any number of young ladies who have set their caps at him. He will certainly be thinking of getting married one day soon.'

'I shall be happy to wish him joy whenever that may be!' said Miss Taverner sharply. She picked up her book, read a few lines, lowered it again, and inquired hopefully: 'Was it he who told you to discover whether I mean to marry Captain Audley or not?'

'Worth? No, my dear, upon my word it was not. He has not spoken to me of it at all.'

Miss Taverner resumed her book with an expression so forbidding that Mrs Scattergood judged it wisest to say no more.

She was at a loss to know what to think. A natural shrewdness had induced her to suppose from the outset that Judith stood in very little danger of falling in love with the Captain. A hint that people were beginning to couple their names should have been enough, if she did not mean to marry him, to make her behave with more circumspection; but it had no effect on her at all. She continued to flirt with the Captain, and her brother, in high good-humour, remarked to Mr Taverner that he believed the pair would make a match of it yet.

'Audley and your sister!' said his cousin, turning a little pale. 'Surely it is not possible!'

'Not possible! Why not?' asked Peregrine. 'He is a capital fellow, I can tell you; not at all like Worth. I thought the instant I clapped eyes on him that he would do very well for Judith. It's my belief that they have some sort of an understanding. I taxed Ju with it, but she only coloured up and laughed, and would not give me an answer.'

Peregrine's own affairs soon took a turn for the better. He had lately fallen into the habit of driving over to Worthing twice a week, and spending the night with the Fairfords; and he was able to inform Judith on his return from one of these expeditions that Sir Geoffrey, being dissatisfied with the uncertainty of his daughter's engagement, was coming to Brighton to seek an interview with Lord Worth.

'We shall see how *that* may answer,' said Peregrine in a tone of strong satisfaction. 'However little Worth may attend to my entreaties, he cannot fail to pay heed to a man of Sir Geoffrey's age and consequence. I fancy the wedding-day will be soon fixed.'

'I do not depend upon it, though I am sure I wish it may,' Judith replied. 'I shall own myself surprised if Sir Geoffrey finds his lordship any more persuadable than we have done.'

Peregrine, however, continued sanguine, and in a very few days events proved him to have been justified. They were sitting down to dinner in Marine Parade one evening when the butler brought in Sir Geoffrey's card. Peregrine ran out to welcome him and learn his news, while Mrs Scattergood cast an anxious eye over the dish of buttered lobster, and sent down a message to the cook to serve up the raised giblet-pie as well as the fricando of veal. She was still wondering whether the cheese-cakes would go round and lamenting that a particularly good open tart syllabub should have been all ate up at luncheon when Peregrine brought their visitor into the dining-parlour. Peregrine's countenance conveyed the intelligence of good news to his sister immediately; his eyes sparkled, and as Judith rose to shake hands with Sir Geoffrey, he burst out with: 'You were wrong, Ju! It is all in a way to be done! I knew how it would be! I am to be married at the end of June. Now wish me joy!'

She turned her eyes towards him with a look of amazement in them. She had not thought it to be possible. 'Indeed, indeed, I do wish you joy! But how is this? Lord Worth agrees?'

'Ay, to be sure he does. Why should he not? But Sir Geoffrey will tell it all to us later. For my part I am satisfied with the mere fact.'

She was obliged to control her impatience to know how it had all come about, what arguments had been used to prevail with Worth, and to beg Sir Geoffrey to be seated. The impropriety of discussing his interview with Worth before the servants was generally felt, and it was not until they were all gathered in the drawing-room later that their curiosity could be satisfied.

It was not in Sir Geoffrey's power to remain long with them; he had made no provision for spending the night in Brighton, and wished to be back in Worthing before it grew dark. There was very little to tell them, after all; he had guessed that Lord Worth's refusal to consent to the marriage taking place arose from scruples natural in a man standing in his position. It had been so; his lordship had felt all the evils of a marriage entered into too young, but upon Sir Geoffrey's representation to him of the proved durability of Peregrine's affections (for six months, at the age of nineteen, was certainly a period) he had been induced to relent.

'There was no difficulty, then?' Judith inquired, fixing her eyes on his face. 'Yet when I spoke of it to him he answered me in such a way that I believed nothing could win him over! This is wonderful indeed! There is no accounting for it.'

'There was a little difficulty,' acknowledged Sir Geoffrey. 'His lordship felt a good deal of reluctance, which I was able, however, to overcome. I am not acquainted with him, do not think I have exchanged two words with him before to-day, so that I cannot conjecture what may have been in his mind. He is a reserved man; I do not pretend to read his thoughts. I own that it seemed to me that something more than a doubt of the young people being of an age to contemplate matrimony weighed with him.'

'What made you think so?' Miss Taverner asked quickly. 'He can have had no other reason!'

Sir Geoffrey set the tips of his fingers together. 'Well, well, I might be mistaken. His manners, which are inclined to be abrupt, may easily have misled me. But upon my making known to him the object of my call his first words were of refusal. That he had no objection to my daughter's character or her situation in life he at once made clear to me, however.'

'Objection!' cried Peregrine, with strong indignation. 'What objection could he have, sir?'

'None, I trust,' replied Sir Geoffrey placidly. 'But his countenance led me to suppose that my application was very unwelcome. He said positively that you were too young. I ventured to remind him that a six-months' engagement was his own suggestion, whereupon he exclaimed with a degree of annoyance that surprised me that he had been guilty of a piece of the most unconscionable folly in consenting to any engagement at all.'

'Well, and so I thought at the time,' remarked Mrs Scattergood. 'It seemed to me highly nonsensical, as I daresay it did to you, sir. For I quite depended on it being no more than a passing fancy with them both, you know.'

'But why? Why?' demanded Judith, striking the palms of her hands together. 'A doubt of Peregrine's not being old enough could not weigh so heavily with him. I am at a loss to understand him! What did he say then? How did you prevail?'

'I must hope,' said Sir Geoffrey, with a smile, 'that the reasonableness of my arguments induced his lordship to relent, but I am more than a little persuaded of his not having heard above half of them. His own reflections seemed to absorb him.'

'Ah, I daresay!' nodded Mrs Scattergood. 'His father was just the same. You might talk to him by the hour together, as I am sure I have done often, and find at the end that he had been thinking of something quite different.'

'As to that, ma'am, I cannot accuse his lordship of letting his mind wander from the *subject* of my visit. All I meant to say was that his own thoughts operated on his judgment more than my arguments. He took several turns about the room, and upon Captain Audley coming in at that moment briefly informed him of the reason of my being there.'

'Captain Audley! Ah, *there* you found an ally!'

'Yes, Miss Taverner, it was as you say. Audley immediately advised his brother to consent. With the greatest good nature he declared himself to be in the fullest sympathy with Peregrine's impatience. He said there could be no object in delay. Lord Worth looked at him as though he would have spoken, but said nothing. Captain Audley, after the shortest of pauses, remarked: "As well now as later." Lord Worth continued looking at him for a moment, without, however, giving me the impression of attending very closely to him, and suddenly replied: "Very well. Let it be as you wish."'

'So much for prejudice!' said Peregrine. 'But I knew how it would be when he came face to face with you, sir. And now you see what a disagreeable fellow we have for a guardian! Ay, you do not like me to say it, Maria, but you know it is so.'

'I confess I had been thinking his lordship very much what you had described to me,' said Sir Geoffrey, 'but I am bound to say that from the moment of his giving his consent nothing could have exceeded his amiability. These fashionable men have their whims and oddities, you know. I found him perfectly ready to discuss the details with me; we talked over the settlements, and what income it would be proper for Peregrine to enjoy until he comes of age, and found ourselves in the most complete agreement. He pressed me with the utmost civility to dine with him – an invitation I should have been happy to have accepted had I not felt it incumbent on me to lose no time in coming to set *your* mind at rest, my dear Perry.'

'Well, and I am sure it has all ended very much to Worth's credit,' said Mrs Scattergood. 'You and I, my dear sir, can easily understand his scruples, however little these impatient young people may.'

Shortly after this Sir Geoffrey got up to take his leave of them, and until the tea-table was brought in the others were fully occupied in talking over what had passed. A knock on the front door put them in the expectation of receiving another visitor, but in a few minutes the butler came in with a note for Peregrine which had been brought round by hand from the Steyne. It was from Worth, requesting Peregrine to call at his house on the following morning for the purpose of discussing the marriage settlements. Judith listened to it being read aloud, and turned away to pick up one of the volumes of *Self-Control* from the sofa-table. But not even Laura's passage down the Amazon had the power to hold her interest. It was evident that Worth had no desire to meet her; he would otherwise have appointed a meeting with Peregrine in Marine Parade.

The interview next morning served to put Peregrine in a mood of the greatest good humour. Worth became once more a very tolerable sort of fellow, and if his harshness at Cuckfield was not quite forgotten it was in a fair way to being forgiven.

The first person to share the news was Mr Bernard Taverner, whom Peregrine met in East Street, outside the post office. Peregrine had been feeling a good deal of coldness towards his cousin ever since the affair of his frustrated duel, but his present happiness made him at one with the whole world, and induced him to extend a cordial invitation to Mr Taverner to drink tea with them in Marine Parade that evening. The invitation was accepted, and shortly after nine o'clock Mr Taverner's knock sounded on the door, and he was ushered into the drawing-room, to entertain the ladies with an account of the races, which he had been attending that afternoon, to wish Peregrine joy, and to make himself generally so agreeable that Mrs Scattergood, feeling all the undoubted attraction of air and manner, could almost find it in her to be sorry that his situation in life made him so ineligible a suitor. He had never been a favourite with her, but she did him the justice to acknowledge that he bore the news of his cousin's approaching nuptials well – very much better, she guessed, than the Admiral would when next they had the doubtful pleasure of seeing him.

Peregrine's marriage naturally formed the topic of a great part of their conversation. He was in spirits, and when he had talked over all his own plans, found it easy to quiz his sister, to exclaim at her ill-luck in being obliged to see him married before herself, and to throw out a good many dark hints that she would not be long in following him to the altar. 'I do not mention any names,' he said roguishly. 'I am all discretion, you know! But it is safe to say that it will not be a certain gentleman who was bred to the *sea*, nor a tall, thin *commoner* with his calves gone to grass, nor that cursed rum touch who took you and Maria to the British Gallery, nor –'

'How can you talk so, Perry?' interrupted his sister, turning her head away.

'Oh, I would not betray you for the world!' he replied incorrigibly. 'If you have a preference for a *red* coat that is nothing out of the way! With females a red coat is everything, and if there is *one* officer amongst your acquaintance who is more dashing and gallant than the rest, I am sure no one can have the least notion who *he* may be!'

She was put quite out of countenance by this speech, and did not know how to meet her cousin's grave look. Mrs Scattergood began to scold, for such talk did not suit her sense of propriety, but her efforts to check Peregrine only provoked him to be more teasing than ever. It was left to Mr Taverner to give the conversation a more proper direction, which he did by saying suddenly: 'By the by, Perry, all this talk of being married puts me in mind of something I had to say to you. You will be enlarging your household, I daresay. Have you room for another groom? I am turning away a very good sort of man, and should be happy to find him an eligible situation. He leaves me for no fault, but I am putting down my carriage, you know, and unlike you wish to reduce my household.'

'Putting down your carriage!' exclaimed Peregrine, his thoughts instantly diverted. 'How comes this about? Do not tell me *your* pockets are to let!'

'It is not as bad as that,' replied Mr Taverner, with a slight smile. 'But I like to be beforehand with the world when I can, and I believe it will be prudent for me to retrench a little. My father keeps his carriage, of course, so I beg you will not be fancying me forced to walk. But if you have a place for my lad in your stables I should be glad to recommend him to you.'

'Oh, certainly, there must always be something for a second groom to do,' said Peregrine good-naturedly. 'Let him come and see me. I will engage for Hinkson's being obliged to you at least!'

'I can readily believe that *he* may well be tired of the road to Worthing,' said Mr Taverner slyly.

If Peregrine could have had his way Hinkson would have seen even more of that road, but happily for him Sir Geoffrey Fairford's fondness for his son-in-law was not quite enough to make him view with complacence that young gentleman's presence in his house every day of the week. He had laid it down as a rule that Peregrine might only visit Harriet on Mondays and Thursdays, but since Lady Fairford's solicitude would not allow her to permit Peregrine to drive back to Brighton after dark these visits always lasted until the following day, and the lovers were not so very much to be pitied after all.

Mr Taverner thought it was rather Judith who should be pitied, and said as much to her one evening at the Assembly at the Castle inn. 'Perry neglects you sadly,' he remarked. 'He thinks of nothing but being at Worthing.'

'I assure you I don't regard it. It is very natural that he should.'

'You will be lonely when he is married.'

'A little, perhaps. I don't think of it, however.'

He took her empty glass of lemonade from her, and set it down. 'He should count himself fortunate to possess such a sister.' He picked up her shawl, and placed it carefully round her shoulders. 'There is something I must say to you, Judith. In your own house Mrs Scattergood is always beside you; I can never get you alone. Will you walk out with me into the garden? It is a very mild night; I do not think you can take a chill.'

Her heart sank; she replied in a little confusion: 'I had rather – that is, there can be no occasion for that degree of privacy, cousin, surely.'

'Do not refuse me!' he said. 'Do you not owe me this much at least, that I should be allowed five minutes alone with you?'

'I owe you a great deal,' she said. 'You have been all that is kind, but I beg you to believe that no purpose can be served by – by what you suggest.'

They were standing in one of the rooms adjoining the ballroom, and since another set was forming there no one but themselves now remained in the smaller apartment. Mr Taverner glanced round, and then clasping Judith's hand, held it fast between both of his, and said: 'Then let me speak now, for I can no longer be silent! Judith – dearest, sweetest cousin! – is there to be no hope for me? You do not look at me! you turn your head away! God knows I have little enough to offer you: nothing indeed but a heart that has been wholly your own from the first moment of setting eyes on you! Your circumstances and mine – alas, so widely apart! – have held me silent, but it will not do! I cannot continue so, be the event what it may! I have been forced to see others soliciting what I have not dared to ask. But it has grown to be more than a man may bear! Judith, I entreat you, look at me!'

She did contrive to raise her eyes to his face, but it was with considerable agitation that she answered: 'I beg of you to say no more! Dear cousin, for your *friendship* I am and shall always be grateful, but if I have (unwittingly, believe me) led you to suppose that tenderer sentiments –' Her voice became totally suspended; she made a gesture, imploring him to say no more.

'How could I – how could any man – know you and not love you? I cannot offer you a title, I cannot offer you wealth –'

She recovered her voice enough to say: '*That* would not weigh with me if my affections had been touched! I give you pain: forgive me! But it can never be. Let us not speak of it again!'

'Once before I asked you if there were another man. You told me "No", and I believe it was true then. But now! *Now* could you return that answer?'

A deep flush suffused her cheeks. 'You have no right to ask me such a question,' she said.

'No,' he replied, 'I have no right, but this I must and will say, Judith! – No man, I care not who he may be, can feel for you what I do! While Worth continues to be your guardian I know well that you will never be permitted to marry me, but in a very little while now you will be free, and no considerations of that –'

'My refusal has nothing to do with Worth's wishes!' she said quickly. 'I should desire always to be your friend; I esteem and value you as a cousin, but I cannot love you! Do not tease me further, I beg of you! Come, may we not remain good friends?'

He controlled himself with a strong effort, and after looking steadily into her face for a moment or two, raised her hand to his lips, and passionately kissed it.

A very dry voice said immediately behind them: 'You will forgive me for intruding upon you, Miss Taverner, I trust.'

Miss Taverner snatched her hand away and turned. 'Lord Worth! You – you startled me!'

'Evidently,' he said. 'I am charged with the office of finding you. Your carriage is spoken for, and Mrs Scattergood grows anxious.'

'Thank you. I will come at once,' she murmured. 'Good night, cousin!'

'Will you not let me take you back to Mrs Scattergood?' he asked quietly.

She shook her head. She was still sadly out of countenance, and it was quite meekly that she laid her hand on the Earl's proffered arm, and allowed him to lead her away. Once out of earshot she managed to say, though in a very small voice: 'I daresay it may have looked very particular to you, but you are quite mistaken.'

'In what?' said the Earl coldly.

'In what you are thinking!'

'If you are able to read my thoughts at this moment you must be very clever.'

'You are the most disagreeable man I have ever met!' said Miss Taverner, a break in her voice.

'You have told me as much before, Miss Taverner, and my memory, I assure you, is peculiarly retentive. Console yourself with the reflection that in a short time now you will be able to forget my very existence.'

She said unsteadily: 'I do not suppose that I look forward to that day more eagerly than you.'

'I have never made any secret of the fact that my guardianship of you has been irksome in the extreme. But do not anticipate too much, Miss Taverner. You are still my ward. These affecting passages with your cousin would be better postponed.'

'If you imagine I have – I have an understanding with Mr Bernard Taverner you are wrong!' she said. 'I am not going to marry him!'

He looked down at her, and it seemed for a moment as though he was about to say something. Then Mrs Scattergood came up to them, and the opportunity was lost. He escorted both ladies out to their carriage, and it was only at parting that Miss Taverner could trust her voice sufficiently to say: 'I have been wanting to thank you, Lord Worth, for giving your consent to Peregrine's marriage.'

'You have nothing to thank me for,' he replied rather curtly, and bowed, and stood back to let the carriage move forward.

Nineteen

$\mathcal{W}$HY SHE HAD BEEN SO ANXIOUS TO INFORM HER GUARDIAN that she did not mean to marry Mr Bernard Taverner was a question that occupied Miss Taverner's mind for an appreciable time. If an answer to the riddle did occur to her she at least would not admit it to be the correct one, and as no alternative answer presented itself to her she was forced to conclude that the agitation of the moment had made her speak at random.

Mrs Scattergood, observing her spirits to be low, supposed that she must be looking forward with a good deal of melancholy to her brother's marriage, and did what she could to cheer her up by promising to stay with her for as long as her companionship was required, and by prophesying many pleasant visits to the young couple at Beverley. But the truth was that the prospect of being separated from Peregrine was not oppressing Miss Taverner's spirits as much as the thought of her own approaching freedom. She did not know what was to become of her. Lord Worth was provoking, tyrannical, and very often odious, but he managed her fortune for her to admiration, and disposed of importunate suitors in a way that she could not hope to equal. She might quarrel with him, and resent his interference in her schemes, but while he stood behind her she had a feeling of security which she had scarcely been aware of until now when she was so near to having his protection withdrawn.

And when he was not being disagreeable and over-bearing he had been kind to her. He had given her a recipe for snuff, and allowed her to drive his greys, and invited her to stay in his house. Until that unfortunate encounter at Cuckfield she had been liking him very well. Naturally she could never like him after his intolerable behaviour on that fatal day, but in spite of that the thought that in a short while she would be able to forget his very existence had so lowering an effect upon her that she was hard put to it to keep the tears from her eyes. And if, as an alternative to this course, he intended her to marry his brother he would find that he had made a mistake. She foresaw that she was doomed to a lonely spinsterhood.

Meanwhile she continued to take her part in all the gaieties that Brighton had to offer, squandered a good deal of money, and drove over with Peregrine to spend a couple of days in Worthing. That experience was one which she was not tempted to repeat, for while she could value Sir Geoffrey's worth as she ought, and be grateful to Lady Fairford for her motherly kindness, the spectacle of two happy lovers was not one that was likely to elevate her spirits. After the one visit she was resolute in refusing all other invitations, and when urged by Peregrine to accompany him said playfully that now that he had at last engaged a groom who knew one end of a horse from the other it was no longer a source of anxiety to see him drive off without her.

Peregrine protested loudly against this aspersion being cast on his driving, but admitted under pressure that Tyler was a better groom than Hinkson. Hinkson had never found favour with Miss Taverner. She thought (in the idiom employed by Mr Fitzjohn) that he was cow-handed, and she disliked his square, pugnacious face even more than his rough manners. Mr Bernard Taverner's man was very much more to her taste. He knew his work, could handle a team, and was not only respectful, but did

not regale his young master's ears with grim tales of the Ring –
a fault in Hinkson which Miss Taverner had always strongly
deprecated. She had not the least hesitation in attributing to
Hinkson such of Peregrine's vulgar expressions as *a bunch of fives,
drawing his cork, wisty castors,* and *milling a canister,* and hoped that
the excellence of his new groom would gradually wean him
from his predilection for Hinkson.

Hinkson, as might have been expected, showed signs of
resenting Tyler's presence, and was always ready with some
excuse to prevent his being taken over to Worthing in his stead.
Judith learned from her own groom that a good deal of dissension was rife in the stables, Hinkson being a rough customer,
very ready with his fists, and suspicious of his fellows. Judith
mentioned the matter to her brother, representing to him the
advisability of turning the man away, but he only laughed, and
said that she was prejudiced against him. She admitted it to be
true. She neither liked nor trusted Hinkson, and thought that
his face, with its broken nose and rugged lines, was almost vil-
lainous. But not even when Tyler brought the tilbury round
one Thursday in Hinkson's stead because Hinkson had been
imbibing Blue Ruin rather too freely in a neighbouring tavern
could Peregrine be induced to say that he would dismiss the
man. All he did say was: 'Oh well, it's the first time he's been
bosky, after all! Stark Naked puts us all under the table once in
a while, you know, Ju.'

'I wish you would not use that horrid cant. A moment ago
you said he had been drinking Blue Ruin.'

'It's the same thing,' grinned Peregrine. 'You can call it a
Flash of Lightning, if you like, or Old Tom. It means gin, my
dear.' He laughed at her face of disgust, gave her a careless
embrace, and with a glance at the clock exclaimed that it was
after three already, and he must be off. Her only satisfaction
was in seeing him drive away with a competent groom up

beside him instead of one who would have been more at home in a prize ring.

The road to Worthing ran through the village of Hove, past the ruins of Aldrington, and along the low cliffs to New Shoreham and Lancing, and thus on by Sompting and Broadwater. Peregrine drove past the end of the Steyne and up on to the East Cliff at a sedate pace, and just beyond the Old Ship was about to let his horses show their paces along the less crowded West Cliff when a light phaeton suddenly swept round the corner of West Street, and its driver, catching sight of him, pulled up his horses and signalled to him to stop.

Peregrine obediently drew rein alongside the phaeton, and hoped that his guardian did not mean to detain him long. 'How do you do? I am just on my way to Worthing.'

'Then I have caught you in time,' replied the Earl. 'I want your signature to one or two documents.'

Peregrine pulled a face. 'Now?' he asked.

'Yes, certainly now. There is also another matter of business which I must discuss with you, but I hardly think the street is a suitable place for that.'

'But could I not call on you to-morrow?' said Peregrine.

'My good boy, is your engagement in Worthing so pressing that you cannot spare me half an hour? To-morrow might suit you better, but it would be highly inconvenient to me. I am going to the races.'

'Oh well!' sighed Peregrine. 'I suppose I must come then, if you make such a point of it.'

The Earl felt his horses' mouths with a movement of his long fingers on the reins. 'I have often had it in mind to ask you, Peregrine, why your father omitted to send you up to Oxford,' he remarked. 'It would have done you so much good.'

Peregrine reddened, turned his horses, and followed rather sulkily in the wake of the phaeton.

The house which Worth rented on the Steyne stood on the corner of St James's Street, and had the advantage of a yard and stables to the rear. Worth led the way into the cobbled alley that ran behind the house, drove his phaeton into the yard, and got down. Henry scrambled from his perch and took charge of the horses, just as Peregrine's tilbury entered the yard.

'You had better tell your man to take the horses into the stable,' said the Earl, stripping off his gloves.

'I thought he might as well walk them up and down,' objected Peregrine. 'I shall not be as long as *that*, surely?'

'Just as you please,' shrugged the Earl. 'They are not my horses.'

'Oh, very well, do as his lordship says, Tyler,' said Peregrine, climbing down from his seat. 'I shall want them again in half an hour, mind!'

This was said in a firm tone that was meant to indicate to the Earl that half an hour was the limit Peregrine had fixed to the interview, but as Worth was already strolling away towards some iron steps leading up to a back door into the house it was doubtful whether he had heard the speech. Peregrine went up the stairs behind him wishing that he were ten years older, and able to assume a manner ten times more assured than the Earl's own.

The door opened into a passage that ran from the hall to the back of the house. It was not locked, and the Earl led Peregrine through it to his book-room, a square apartment with windows on to St James's Street. The room was furnished in a somewhat sombre style, and the net blinds that hung across the window while preventing the curious from looking in also obscured a good deal of light.

The Earl tossed his gloves on to the table and turned to see Peregrine glancing about him rather disparagingly. He smiled, and said: 'Yes, you are really better off on the Marine Parade, are you not?'

Peregrine looked quickly across at him. 'Then this *was* the house my sister wanted!'

'Why, of course! Had you not guessed as much?'

'Well, I did not think a great deal about it,' confessed Peregrine. 'It was Judith who was so set on –' He stopped, and laughed ruefully. 'To tell you the truth, I don't know which of the two she *did* want!' he said.

'She very naturally wanted the one I told her she was not to have,' replied the Earl, moving over to a console-table where a decanter of wine and two glasses had been placed. 'Fortunately I was able to read her intention just in time to retrieve my own mistake in ever mentioning this house.'

'Ay, and devilish cross you made her,' said Peregrine.

'There is nothing very new in that,' said the Earl in his driest voice.

'Oh, she had not been disliking you for a long time then, you know,' said Peregrine, inspecting a round table snuff-box with a loose lid that stood on the Earl's desk. 'In fact, quite the reverse.'

The Earl was standing with his back to the room, but he glanced over his shoulder, holding the decanter poised for a moment over one of the glasses. 'Indeed! What may that mean?'

'Lord, nothing in particular!' said Peregrine. 'What should it mean?'

'I wish I knew,' said the Earl, and returned to his task of filling the glasses.

Peregrine looked at him rather sharply, and after fidgeting with the lid of the snuff-box for a moment blurted out: 'May I ask you a question, sir?'

'Certainly,' said the Earl, replacing the stopper in the decanter. 'What is it?'

'I daresay you won't like it, and of course I may be wrong,' said Peregrine, 'but I am Judith's brother, and I did think at one time, when my cousin hinted at it, that you might be – well, what I wish to ask you is – is, in short –'

'I know exactly what you wish to ask me,' said the Earl, handing him one of the glasses.

'Oh!' Peregrine accepted the glass, and looked at him doubtfully.

'I can appreciate your anxiety,' continued the Earl, a trifle maliciously. 'The thought of being saddled with me as a brother-in-law must be extremely unnerving.'

'I did not mean that!' said Peregrine hastily. 'Moreover, I don't believe there is the least fear – I mean, chance – of it coming to pass.'

'Possibly not,' said the Earl. 'But "fear" was probably the right word. Would you like to continue this conversation, or shall we turn to your own affairs?'

'I thought you would not like it,' said Peregrine, not without a certain satisfaction. 'Ay, let us by all means settle the business. I am ready.'

'Well, sit down,' said the Earl, opening one of the drawers in his desk. 'This is the deed of settlement I want you to sign.' He took out an official-looking document and gave it to Peregrine.

Peregrine reached out his hand for a pen, but was checked by the Earl's raised brows.

'I am flattered by this blind trust in my integrity,' Worth said, 'but I beg you won't sign papers without first reading them.'

'Of course I should not do so in the ordinary way! But you are my guardian, ain't you? Oh Lord, what stuff it is! There's no making head or tail of it!' With which pessimistic utterance Peregrine fortified himself with a gulp of wine, and leaned back in his chair to peruse the document. 'I knew what it would be! Aforesaid and hereinafter until there is no sense to be made of it!' He raised his glass to his lips again and sipped. Then he lowered it and looked at the Earl. 'What *is* this?' he asked.

The Earl had seated himself at his desk, and was glancing over another of the documents that awaited Peregrine's signature.

'That, my dear Peregrine, is what Brummell would describe as the hot, intoxicating liquor so much drunk by the lower orders. In a word, it is port.'

'Well, I thought it was, but it seems to me to taste very odd.'

'I am sorry that you should think so,' replied the Earl politely. 'You have the distinction of being alone in that opinion.'

'Oh, I did not mean to say that it was not good port!' said Peregrine, blushing furiously. 'I am not a judge. I've no doubt of it being capital stuff!' He took another sip, and returned to the task of mastering the deed of settlement. The Earl sat with his elbow on the desk, and his chin resting on his hand, watching him.

The words began to move queerly under Peregrine's eyes. He blinked, and was conscious all at once of a strong feeling of lassitude. Something in his head was making a buzzing sound; his ears felt thick, as though wool had been stuffed in them. He looked up, pressing a hand to his forehead. 'I beg pardon – don't feel quite the thing. A sudden dizziness – can't understand it.' He lifted his half-empty wine-glass to his lips, but paused before he drank, staring at Worth with a look of frightened suspicion in his eyes.

The Earl was sitting quite still, impassively regarding him. One of the cut-steel buttons on his coat attracted and held Peregrine's cloudy gaze until he forced himself to look away from it. His brain felt a little stupid; he found himself speculating on the snowy folds of Worth's cravat. He himself had tried so often to achieve a Water-fall, and always failed. 'I can't tie mine like that,' he said. 'Water-fall.'

'You will one day,' answered the Earl.

'My head feels so queer,' Peregrine muttered.

'The room is a trifle hot. I will open the window in a minute. Go on reading.'

Peregrine dragged his eyes away from that fascinating cravat and tried to focus them on the Earl's face. He made an effort to collect his wandering wits. The paper he was holding slipped from his fingers to the ground. 'No!' he said. 'It's not the room!' He staggered to his feet and stood swaying. 'Why do you look at me like that? The wine! What have you put in the wine? By God, you sh-shall answer me!'

He stared at his glass in a kind of bemused horror, and in that instant Worth was on his feet, and in one swift movement had got behind him, and seized him, gripping the boy's right hand from over his shoulder in a cruel hold that clenched Peregrine's fingers tightly round the wine-glass. His left arm was round Peregrine, forcing the boy back against his shoulder.

Peregrine struggled like a madman, but the dreadful lassitude was stealing over him. He panted: 'No, no, I won't! I won't! You devil, let me go! What have you done to me? What –' His own hand, with that other grasping it, tilted the rest of the wine down his throat. He seemed to have no power to resist; he choked, spluttered, and saw the room begin to spin round like a kaleidoscope. 'The wine!' he said thickly. 'The wine!'

He heard Worth's voice say as from a long way off: 'I am sorry, Peregrine, but there was no alternative. There is nothing to be afraid of.'

He tried to speak, but could not; he was dimly aware of being lifted bodily from the ground; he saw Worth's face above him, and then he slid into unconsciousness.

The Earl laid him down on the couch against one wall and loosened the folds of his cravat. He stood frowning down at him for a minute, his fingers lightly clasping one slack wrist, his eyes watchfully intent on Peregrine's face. Then he moved away to where the empty wine-glass lay on the carpet, picked it up, and put it on the table, and went out of the room, locking the door behind him.

There was no one in the hall. The Earl let himself out through the back door on to the iron steps, and went down them into the yard. The tiger met him, and grinned impishly. The Earl looked him over. 'Well, Henry?'

'Shapley's not back yet from wherever it was you sent him off to, guv'nor, and you know werry well you let the under-groom go off for the day.'

'I had not forgotten it. Did you do what I told you?'

'O' course I did what you told me!' answered Henry, aggrieved. 'Don't I always? *I* knew he wouldn't say no to anything out of a bottle. "Flesh-and-blood this is," I says to him, but Lord love yer, guv'nor, he wouldn't have known different if I'd said it was daffy! He tosses it off, and smacks his lips, and I'm blessed if he didn't sit down right there under my werry nose, and drop off to sleep! *I* never seen anything like it in all my puff!'

'The sooner you forget that you saw it at all, the better,' commented the Earl. 'Where is Hinkson?'

'Oh, him!' Henry sniffed disparagingly and jerked a thumb over his shoulder. 'Putting the horses to, he is, which is about all he's good for, and not so werry good at that either, if you was to ask me.'

'Don't be jealous, Henry. You have done your part very well, but you cannot do everything,' said the Earl, and walked across the yard to the stables just as Hinkson led out Peregrine's two horses. 'Get those horses put to, Ned. Any trouble?'

'No, my lord, not at my end of the business – not yet, that is. But Tyler's been getting smoky about me. I gammoned him I was boozy, and he thought he'd left me safe under the table. But I'm scared of this, my lord; properly scared I am. Broad daylight!'

'There you are, what did I tell you, guv'nor?' demanded Henry scornfully. 'Him a prize-fighter! You'd have done better to let me handle the whole job. You'll have that chicken-hearted shifter handing Jem Tyler over to a beak if you ain't careful.'

Hinkson turned on him wrathfully, but upon the tiger saying at once: 'Yes, you pop in a hit at me, and see what you get from

my guv'nor!' a slow grin spread over his unprepossessing countenance, and with an apologetic look at the Earl he went on
harnessing the horses to the tilbury. Henry cast a professional
eye over the buckles, and watched with considerable interest his
master and Hinkson hoist the inanimate form of Jem Tyler into
the tilbury, and cover it with a rug.

Hinkson gathered up the reins and said gruffly: 'I won't fail
you, my lord.'

'No, because if you did you'd lose a fatter purse than you've
ever fought for, or ever will!' retorted Henry.

'And when all's clear,' said Hinkson, settling himself on the
box-seat, and addressing the tiger, 'I shall come back into this
yard and wring your skinny neck, my lad!' With which he
jerked the reins, and drove out of the yard into the alley.

The Earl watched him go, and turned to look down at his
tiger. 'You know me, don't you, Henry? One word of this on
your tongue and it is I who will wring your neck, long before
Hinkson has the chance of doing it. Off with you now!'

'*And* I'd let you, guv'nor, which is more than what I would
that lump o' lard!' replied Henry, unabashed.

An hour later Captain Audley went softly into the book-room
and shut the door behind him. The Earl was writing at his desk,
but he looked up and smiled faintly. Captain Audley glanced
across at Peregrine's still form. 'Julian, are you quite sure − ?'

'Perfectly.'

Captain Audley walked to the couch and bent over it. 'It
seems a damned shame,' he said, and straightened himself. 'What
have you done with the groom?'

'The groom,' said Worth, picking up a wafer and sealing his
letter, 'has been taken to a spot somewhere near Lancing, and
shipped aboard a certain highly suspicious vessel bound for the
West Indies. Whether he ever reaches his destination is
extremely problematical, I imagine.'

'Good God, Worth, you can't do that!'

'I have done it – or, rather, Hinkson has done it for me,' replied the Earl calmly.

'But Julian, the risk! What if Hinkson turns on you?'

'He won't.'

'You're mad!' Captain Audley exclaimed. 'What should stop him?'

'You must think I choose my tools badly,' commented the Earl.

The Captain glanced towards Peregrine again. 'I think you're a damned cold-blooded devil,' he said.

'Possibly,' said Worth. 'Nevertheless, I am sorry for the boy. But the date of his marriage being fixed was his death-warrant. He must be put out of the way, and really I think I have chosen quite as kind a way of doing it as I could.'

'Yes, I know, and I see it had to be, but – well, I don't like it, Julian, and there you have it! How I'm to face Judith Taverner with this on my conscience –'

'You can comfort yourself with the reflection that it is not on your conscience at all, but on mine,' interrupted the Earl.

'She is going to the Pavilion to-night,' said Captain Audley inconsequently.

'Yes, and so am I,' replied the Earl. 'Do you go too, or do you propose to sit and mourn over Peregrine's plight?'

'Oh, be quiet, Julian! I suppose I must go, but I tell you frankly I feel little better than a murderer!'

'In that case you would be wise to order dinner to be put forward,' recommended the Earl. 'You will feel better when you have eaten and drunk.'

'How are you going to get him out of the house?' asked the Captain, looking towards the couch again.

'Very simply. Evans will come in by the back way and I shall give the boy over to him. He will do the rest.'

'Well, I hope to God it does not all fail!' said Captain Audley devoutly.

But no hitch occurred in the Earl's plans. At eleven o'clock a plain coach drove unobtrusively into the alley, and a couple of sturdy-looking men got out, and softly entered the yard through the unlocked gate. No one was stirring above the stables, and the men made no sound as they went up the iron steps to the back door. It was opened to them by the Earl, who had changed his cloth coat and pale yellow pantaloons for knee-breeches, and a satin coat. He pointed silently to the book-room. Five minutes later he had seen Peregrine's limp body, wrapped round in a frieze cloak, put into the coach, and had returned to the house, and locked the back door. Then he examined the set of his cravat in the mirror that hung in the hall, picked up his hat and gloves and walked out of the house, across the Steyne to the Pavilion.

Twenty

MISS TAVERNER'S FIRST VISIT TO THE PAVILION HAD SOON been followed by others, for the Regent, while at Brighton, liked to hold informal parties in his summer-palace, and was always very easy of access, and affable to the humblest of his guests. It was not to be supposed that he should feel as much interest in Peregrine as in his sister, but even Peregrine had been invited to dine at the Pavilion once, and had gone there in a state of considerable awe, and returned home dazzled by the magnificence of the state apartments, and slightly fuddled by the Regent's famous Diabolino brandy. He had tried to describe the Banqueting-room to his sister, but he had retained so confused an impression of it that he could only say that he had sat at an immensely long table, under a thirty-foot lustre, all glass pearls, and rubies, and tassels of brilliants, which hung from a dome painted like an eastern sky, with the foliage of a giant plantain tree spreading over it. He had thought no chains had been strong enough to hold such a lustre; he had not been able to take his eyes from it. For the rest he dimly remembered golden pillars, and silver chequer-work, huge Chinese paintings on a groundwork of inlaid pearl, mirrors flashing back the lights of the lustres, crimson draperies and chairs, and piers between the windows covered with fluted silks of pale blue. He had counted five rosewood sideboards, and four doors of rich japan-work. He had never been in such a room in his life. As for the entertainment he had had, nothing was ever like it! Such a very handsome dinner, with he dared not say how many wines to drink, and no less than a dozen sorts of snuff placed on the table as soon as the covers were removed!

The Regent did not invite ladies to his dinner-parties, because there was no hostess to receive them, but they flocked to his concerts, and his receptions. Mrs Scattergood, remembering pleasant evenings spent at the Pavilion when Mrs Fitzherbert received guests there, shook her head, and said: 'Ah, poor soul! People may say what they please, but I shall always hold that she was his true wife. And so, I hear, does the Princess of Wales, though it is an odd thing for *her* to say, to be sure!'

'Yet you would have had me accept Clarence's offer,' remarked Miss Taverner.

'No, indeed, I would not. *That* was nothing but a notion that just entered my head. These morganatic marriages are not at all the thing, though for my part I could never find it in me to blame Mrs Fitzherbert for marrying the Prince. He was so extremely handsome! He is a little stout now, but I shall always think of him as I first saw him, in a pink satin coat sewn with pearls, and a complexion any female would have given her eyes to possess!'

'His complexion is very sallow now,' observed Miss Taverner. 'I am afraid he has a sickly constitution.'

But although Mrs Scattergood would allow that the Regent did not enjoy the best of health, she could not be brought to see that time and self-indulgence had coarsened his features. He was the fairy-prince of her girlhood, and she would listen to nothing said in his disparagement. Miss Taverner was sorry for it, since the frequent visits to the Pavilion were not entirely to her taste. The Regent was fifty years old, but he had an eye to a pretty woman, and although there was nothing in his manner to alarm her, Miss Taverner could not be at her ease with

him. Mrs Scattergood, whose native shrewdness was overset by
the distinguishing notice the Regent bestowed on her, spoke of
his attitude to her charge as fatherly, and said that Judith should
consider herself honoured by his kindness. She wondered that
Judith should not care to go to the Pavilion, and reminded her
that Royal invitations were tantamount to commands. So Miss
Taverner allowed herself to be taken there two or three times a
week, until the glories of the Gallery, and the Music Room, and
the Saloon became so well known to her that they no longer
seemed at all out of the common. She had the treat of hearing
Viotti play the violin there, and Wiepart the harp; she had been
present at a very select and convivial party, when the Regent,
after listening to several glees, was prevailed upon to sing *By the
gaily flowing glass*, for the edification of the company; she had
been shown such objects of vertu as the tortoiseshell table in the
Green Drawing-room, and the pagodas in the Saloon; and she
had had the doubtful honour of receiving the advances of the
Duke of Cumberland. She could not feel that the Pavilion held
any further surprises for her, and when she set out with Mrs
Scattergood for Thursday's party there, quite shocked that good
lady by announcing that she had rather have been going to the
ball at the Old Ship.

Upon their arrival at the Pavilion it was discovered that this
was not to be one of the Regent's musical gatherings, but a conversable evening spent in the Gallery and the over-heated
Saloon. This was a big, round apartment, the centre of the suite
on the eastern front of the building, surmounted by the inevitable cupola, and enlarged by two semi-circular recesses. Ruby
and gold were the predominant colours, and several magnificent
lustres, reflected in long pier-glasses, gave to the room an efful-
gence that was as remarkable as it was dazzling.

Miss Taverner looked about her to see whether any of her
acquaintance were present, and had the satisfaction of observing

Captain Audley in conversation with Lord Petersham, whom she had not known to be in Brighton. Captain Audley caught sight of her, and at once brought his companion over to her side. 'Come now, Petersham, I insist on your showing it to Miss Taverner!' he said gaily, as Judith shook hands with his lordship. 'I know she will be delighted with it. My dear Miss Taverner, this lucky fellow has got a new snuff-box, which is the prettiest I have seen these ten years!'

'Oh, Lord Petersham has all the prettiest snuff-boxes in his possession!' smiled Miss Taverner. 'I have one to match each gown, but he has one for every day in the year. Do, pray, show me this new one, sir! Ah yes, it is charming indeed. Sèvres, I think?'

'Yes,' acknowledged Petersham, in his gentle way. 'It is a nice box for summer, but it would not do for winter wear, you know.'

'No,' said Miss Taverner seriously. 'I believe you are right.'

'These niceties are beyond me,' complained the Captain. 'I suppose I may as well go bury myself now you are got on to the subject of snuff together. You will be talking till midnight.'

'Oh no!' said his lordship. 'To talk on any subject till midnight would be a great bore. But you put me in mind of something very important. Where is Worth? Has he put his name down for some of the Martinique snuff Fribourg and Treyer are importing?'

'He has not told me, but you may ask him yourself. He will be here later in the evening. Do not on any account look to the right, Miss Taverner! Monk Lewis is eagerly awaiting his opportunity to approach you, and once he succeeds in engaging your attention you will not be rid of him under half an hour. I never knew a man to talk so much!'

Mr Lewis, however, the author of that celebrated novel *Ambrosio, or the Monk*, was not one to be easily baulked of his prey. He soon button-holed Miss Taverner, and proceeded to fulfil Captain Audley's prediction until she was rescued from him by Sir John Lade, who came up to inquire whether she had a fancy to sell her bays. She had no such fancy, nor did she care for Sir John, who smelled of the stables, and used the language of his own grooms, but she was grateful to him for interrupting the flow of Mr Lewis's conversation, and treated his repeated offers to buy her horses with more patience than could have been expected of her.

The temperature at which the Regent kept his rooms was always hard to bear, and by half-past eleven Miss Taverner had developed a headache, and was thinking longingly of her bed. But card tables had been set out in the Green Drawing-room, which adjoined the Saloon on the south side, and Mrs Scattergood was happily engaged in a rubber of Casino there, and would be certain to remain for another hour. Miss Taverner wondered why her guardian did not come, and decided privately that the party was more than ordinarily insipid. She was just about to sit down on a ruby silk ottoman as far as possible from the fire when her name was spoken, and she looked up to see the Regent at her elbow.

'At last I am able to snatch two words with you!' said the Regent jovially. 'I do not know how it is, but I have not had the chance to come near you all night. Now that will not do, you know! And I have something very pretty to show you, too: something which, I flatter myself, will take your fancy.'

She smiled, and returned a civil answer. A faint aroma of Maraschino hung about him, and although he was not by any means the worse for drink, she could not help suspecting that he had taken just enough to make him a little reckless.

'Yes, yes, you shall see it!' he promised. 'And you shall take it away with you, too, if you care to please *me*. But it is not here; we must slip into the Yellow Drawing-room to find it. Come, let me offer you my arm! I do not believe you have seen that room, have you? It is quite my favourite.'

'No, sir, I do not recall – But perhaps Mrs Scattergood –'

'Oh, stuff and nonsense!' said the Regent. 'Mrs Scattergood is very well occupied, I assure you, and will not miss you. And if she did, you know, you have only to tell her you were with me, and she can have not the slightest objection.'

Miss Taverner tried to think of an excuse, and could hit upon none. She did not know what to say, for how could a mere Miss Taverner, from Yorkshire, presume to rebuff a Prince-Regent who was old enough to be her father? She ought not to go with him, and yet how was she to refuse? It would be to insult him, and that was unthinkable. She let him tuck her hand in his arm, and tried to think that the squeeze he gave it was not intentional. He led her to one of the folding-doors at the north end of the saloon, and ushered her into the Yellow Drawing-room.

'There!' he said. 'Is not this a great deal better than to be trying to talk in the midst of a crowd of other people? This is my private drawing-room, not vast, you see, but exactly the sort of apartment where one can be cosy and informal.'

Miss Taverner could not help reflecting that 'cosy' was not the adjective she would have used to describe the Yellow Drawing-room. Hot it certainly was, and extremely airless, but a room more than fifty feet long and over thirty feet wide, with a ceiling supported by white and gold pillars, enwreathed by serpents, and spreading into umbrella capitals hung with bells, hardly seemed to her an apartment designed for informal use. Nor could she feel that five doors panelled with plate-glass enhanced the comfort of the room. The draperies over the windows were of striped satin; there were any number of inlaid Buhl tables, bearing pieces of Asiatic porcelain; and the walls, which were white with gilt borderings, were embellished by Chinese pictures, lanterns, and flying dragons. The chairs and sofas were upholstered in blue and yellow satin, and the cabinet-maker who had constructed them had had the tasteful and original idea of placing a Chinese figure with a bell in either hand on the back of every one.

'Well, how does it strike you? Do you like it?' demanded the Regent.

'Extremely elegant! It is something quite out of the common, sir,' murmured Miss Taverner, wishing that he had not shut the door into the Saloon.

'Yes, *that* I flatter myself it certainly is,' he said with a good deal of satisfaction. 'But I will tell you something, my dear: your pretty curls are precisely the colour of my gilding! Now, is not that odd? You must allow me to tell you that you make a charming picture.' He laughed at her evident confusion, and pinched her cheek. 'No, no, there is no need to colour up! You do not need *me* to tell you what a little beauty you are, when you can see yourself in the mirror whichever way you turn.'

He was standing very close to her, one hand fondling her wrist, and his eyes fixed on her face in a greedy way that made her feel hotter than ever, and more than a little frightened. She pretended to be interested in the Vulliamy timepiece that stood on the mantelshelf, and moved towards the fireplace, saying: 'You have so many beautiful things in the Pavilion, sir, one is continually in a state of admiration.'

'Yes, yes, I daresay, but the most beautiful thing in it only came to it an hour ago,' he replied, following her.

Regent or no, she must try to check this amorous mood. She said as lightly as she could: 'You were going to show me something, sir. What can it be, I wonder? May I see it before we return to the Saloon?'

'Oh, no hurry for that!' he replied. 'But you shall certainly see it, for it is your own, you know. There!' He picked up a Petitot snuff-box from one of the tables, and closed her fingers on it. 'That is an odd gift for a lady, is it not? But I fancy you like snuff-boxes better than trinkets.'

'I do not know what to say, sir,' faltered Miss Taverner. 'You are very good. I – I thank you, and assure you I shall treasure it, and – and always feel myself to have been honoured indeed.'

'Come, come, come!' said the Regent, smiling broadly. 'That is not how I like to be thanked! Supposing we were to forget all this ceremony, eh?'

He was standing so close to her now that she could feel the warmth of his body. He was going to kiss her; his hand was stealing up her bare arm; his breath was on her averted cheek. His grossness, the very scent with which he lavishly sprinkled his clothes, revolted her. Her impulse was to thrust him away, and to run back into the Saloon, but she felt curiously weak, and the heat of the room was making her head spin.

His arm encircled her waist; he said caressingly: 'Why, here is a shy little miss! But you must not be shy with me, must you?'

Miss Taverner had the oddest sensation of being hot and cold at once. She said in an uncertain voice: 'Forgive me, sir, but the room is so close – I am afraid – I must – sit down for a moment!' She made a feeble attempt to disengage herself from his hold, and then, for the first time in her life, quietly fainted away.

She regained consciousness a minute or two later, and was aware first of feeling very sick, and then of being in strange, glittering surroundings. A peevish voice was saying loudly: 'Nonsense! no such thing! She was overpowered by the heat! Most unfortunate! quite extraordinary! I never heard of such a thing. Fainting in the Pavilion! Really, it is a damned awkward situation! I would not have had it happen for the world.'

Miss Taverner recognised the voice, felt a cool hand on her brow, and shuddered uncontrollably. She gave a fluttering sob, and opened her eyes, and found herself looking straight up into her guardian's face. She stared for a moment. 'Oh, it's you!' she murmured thankfully.

'Yes, it's I,' Worth said in his level voice. 'You will be better in a minute. Don't try to get up.'

She groped for his hand. 'Please stay. Please don't go away and leave me here.'

His hand closed reassuringly on hers. There was a curious expression on his face, as though he was surprised at something. 'There is nothing to alarm you,' he said. 'I am not going away, but I want to procure you a glass of wine.'

'I don't know how I came to faint,' she said childishly. 'I have never done so before. But I did not know what to do, and –'

'You fainted from the heat,' he interposed. There was a note of finality in his voice; he did not seem to want her to say any more. He disengaged his hand and rose. 'I am going to get you something to drink.'

Miss Taverner watched him walk away, and tried to marshal her wits into order. It dawned on her that she was lying at full length on a sofa in the Regent's Yellow Drawing-room, and that the Regent himself was present, looking sulky, and very much aggrieved. She managed to sit up, and to put her feet to the ground, though her head swam unpleasantly. She now remembered with tolerable clarity the events which had preceded her swoon. How Worth came to be there she had no notion; nor could she imagine what had possessed her to cling to his hand like a frightened schoolgirl. She said, trying to speak with composure: 'I must beg your pardon, sir, for being so troublesome. I have disgraced myself indeed.'

The Regent's brow cleared a little. 'Oh, not at all! not at all! I daresay the room was a trifle warm. But you are better now; you will not object to my shutting the window again?'

She looked round, and saw that the striped curtains had been pulled back, and one of the long windows flung open. 'Certainly, sir. I am quite recovered, I assure you.'

The Regent hurried over to the window, and shut it. 'The night air is very treacherous,' he said severely. 'And I am particularly susceptible to chills. It was shockingly careless of Worth – however, I say nothing, and we must *trust* that no harm will come of it.'

She assented, leaning her aching head on her hand. The Regent regarded her with considerable anxiety, and wished that Worth would make haste to come back. Miss Taverner was looking very sickly, and it would be extremely awkward if she were to swoon again. There had never been anything so unlucky, to be sure. How could he guess that the girl was such a prudish little fool? McMahon – to whom he would have something to say presently – had grossly misled him. And as for that damned fellow Worth not concerning himself with his ward, that was another of McMahon's unforgivable blunders. Worth had stalked in without ceremony, without so much as common courtesy, and not only had he not believed a word his Prince had said, but he had had the insolence to show it. It was really a great deal too bad of the girl to place him in such an uncomfortable situation. For he had done nothing, nothing at all! But to be found clasping a swooning female in his arms, to be forced to explain it all in a great hurry to the girl's guardian, wounded his dignity, always his most vulnerable spot. He had been made to appear ridiculous: he would find it hard to forgive Miss Taverner. However, she did seem to be behaving more sensibly now; he had had a horrid fright upon her first coming-to, that she was going to pour out some nonsensical, untruthful version of the affair to Worth.

He peered at her anxiously. She still looked very pale. If he had not been bound to consider his own health he would have felt tempted to open the window again. 'A glass of wine will make you feel very much more the thing,' he said hopefully.

'Yes, sir. It is nothing, and I am ashamed to have put you to so much trouble. I beg you will not neglect your other guests for my sake. Your absence will be remarked. If Mrs Scattergood could be sent for –'

'Certainly, if you wish it – immediately!' he said. 'Though she is playing cards, you know, and I daresay it would cause a little talk, which you would not like.'

'Oh no! You are very right, sir,' she answered submissively. 'Lord Worth will know what is best to be done.'

The Earl came back into the room at that moment, with a glass in his hand. 'I see you are better, Miss Taverner. May I suggest, sir, that it would be advisable for you to return to the Saloon? You need not scruple to leave Miss Taverner in my charge.'

The Regent was perfectly ready to follow this piece of advice, even though he might resent the manner in which it was given. He begged Miss Taverner not to think of leaving the drawing-room until she felt herself to be quite recovered; assured her that he did not at all regard the trouble she had made; and went out by the door into the Chinese Gallery, which Worth was holding open for him.

The Earl shut the door, and came back to Miss Taverner's side. He obliged her to drink some of the wine he had brought. The relief she had felt on first seeing him had by now given place to mortification at being found in so compromising a situation. She said with difficulty: 'I did not know you were in the Pavilion. You must wonder at finding me in this room, I daresay, but –'

'Miss Taverner, how came you to do such a thing?' he interrupted. 'I entered the Saloon to be met by the intelligence, conveyed to me by Brummell, that you had slipped away with the Regent. I came immediately to put an end to so improper a tête-à-tête, and I found you fainting in the Regent's arms. You will tell me at once, if you please, what this means! What has happened in this room?'

'Oh, nothing, nothing, upon my honour!' she said wretchedly. 'It was the heat, only the heat!'

'Why are you here?' he demanded. 'What purpose can you have had in going apart with the Regent? Careless of your reputation I know you to be, but I had not thought it possible that you could behave with such imprudence!'

She was stung into replying: 'How could I help going with him when he pressed me to as he did? What was I to say? Mrs Scattergood was in the card-room; you were not present. How could I know what I should do or say when no less a person than the Prince-Regent requested my company? These reproaches might have been spared! You cannot know the circumstances. Say no more! You may think me what you please: I am sure I do not care!'

'No,' said the Earl with strong feeling, 'I am well aware of that at least! But while I have authority over you I must and will censure such conduct.'

She managed to get up, though her knees still shook. 'It does not signify talking. You are determined to despise me.'

There was a moment's silence. '*I* determined to despise you?' said the Earl in an altered tone. 'What nonsense is this?'

'I have not forgotten what you said to me *that* day – at Cuckfield.'

'Do you imagine I have forgotten that day?' said the Earl sternly. 'Your opinion of me, which you so freely expressed, is not likely to be soon wiped from my memory, I assure you.'

She found to her dismay that tears were rolling down her cheeks. She averted her face, and said in a broken whisper: 'My carriage – Mrs Scattergood – I must go home!'

'A message shall be conveyed to Mrs Scattergood when she leaves the card-room,' he said. 'I will take you home as soon as you are sufficiently recovered.' He paused, and added: 'You must not cry, Clorinda. That is a worse reproach to me than any I have bestowed on you.'

'I am not crying,' replied Miss Taverner, groping in her reticule for her handkerchief. 'It is just that I have a headache.'

'I see,' said the Earl.

Miss Taverner dried her eyes, and said huskily: 'I am sorry you should have the troublesome office of taking me home. I am quite ready. But if only Mrs Scattergood could be fetched –'

'To summon Mrs Scattergood from the card-table would give rise to the sort of public curiosity I am endeavouring to avoid,' he replied. 'Come! Your mistrust of me surely cannot be so great that you will not allow me to convey you a few hundred yards in your own carriage.'

She raised her head at that. 'If I did indeed say that on that hateful day I beg your pardon,' she added. 'You have never given me – would never give me, I am persuaded – the least cause for mistrusting you.' She saw the frown in his eyes, and wondered at it. 'You are still angry. You don't believe me when I say that I am sorry.'

He put out his hand quickly. 'My dear child! Of course I believe you. If I looked angry you must blame circumstance, which has forced me to –' He broke off, and smiled at her. 'Shall we put the memory of that day at Cuckfield out of mind?'

'If you please,' whispered Miss Taverner. 'I am aware – have been aware almost from the start – that I ought not to have driven myself from London as I did.'

'Miss Taverner,' he said, 'I am seriously alarmed. Are you sure that you are yourself?'

She smiled, but shook her head. 'I am not sufficiently myself to quarrel with you to-night, provoke me how you may.'

'Poor Clorinda! I won't provoke you any more, I promise,' he said, and drawing her hand through his arm, led her to the door into the Chinese Gallery and so out to her carriage.

Twenty-One

$\mathcal{M}$R BRUMMELL, WHO HAD ELECTED TO STROLL ACROSS FROM his lodgings on the Steyne to the Earl of Worth's house on the morning after the party at the Pavilion, set the red Pekin sweetmeat-box of carved lacquer down on the table with tender care, and sighed. 'Yes,' he said. 'I am inclined to hazard the opinion that it is quite genuine. Ch'ien Lung. Pray remove it from my sight.'

The Earl restored the box to its place in the cabinet. 'I found it in Lewes, of all unlikely places. Charles will not allow it to be worth a guinea.'

'Charles's opinions on old lac leave me supremely indifferent,' said Brummell. He crossed one leg, beautifully sheathed in a pale biscuit-coloured pantaloon, over the other, and leaned his head against the back of the chair to look lazily up at Worth. 'Well, I have seen the Great Man,' he said. 'You are quite out of favour, you know.'

The Earl gave a short laugh. 'Yes, until he wants my judgment on a horse or a brand of snuff. Did you come to tell me that?'

'Not at all. I came to tell you that he has taken a chill for which he apparently holds you responsible.'

'I can only say that I hope it may prove fatal,' replied the Earl.

'He seems to think that probable,' said Brummell. 'I left him on the point of being cupped. I am not unreasonable; if he likes to make being cupped a hobby it is quite his own affair; but he had the deplorable bad taste to tell me how much blood he had had taken from him these thirty years. It will come to this, you know, that I shall be obliged to drop him. I begin to think that I made a great mistake to bring him into fashion at all.'

'He doesn't do you much credit, certainly,' remarked the Earl with the glimmer of a smile.

'On the contrary, he does me considerable credit,' said Brummell. 'You must have forgotten what he was like before I took him up. He was used to flaunt abroad in green velvet and spangles. Which reminds me, you will like to know that I punished him for you after you had left last night. He actually asked my opinion of that coat he was wearing.' He inhaled a pinch of snuff, and delicately dusted his fingers. 'I thought he was going to burst into tears,' he said reflectively.

At this moment the door was quickly flung open, and Captain Audley came into the room. He looked straight across at his brother, and said without preamble: 'Are you at liberty, Julian? Miss Taverner is here, and wishes to see you – on a matter of grave importance.'

The Earl turned, and their eyes met for an instant. 'Miss Taverner wishes to see me?' repeated the Earl, a slight inflection of surprise in his voice.

'Urgently,' said Captain Audley.

'Then pray bring her in,' said the Earl calmly. He walked to the door. 'My dear Miss Taverner, will you not come in? I do not know what Charles is about to leave you standing in the hall.'

Judith came swiftly towards him. She was dressed in her driving-habit, and she looked unusually pale. 'Lord Worth, something has happened to Perry!' she said. 'I have come at once to you.'

He drew her into the saloon, and shut the door behind her. 'Indeed! I am extremely sorry to hear it. What is it? Has he overturned his curricle?'

Her eyes alighted on Brummell, who had risen at her entrance and was regarding her with an expression of civil concern. 'I beg your pardon. I thought you were alone. You must forgive me for breaking in on you so abruptly, but I hardly know what I am about. I have just learned that Perry did not go to Worthing yesterday!'

The Earl raised his brows. 'From whom have you learned this? Are you quite sure?'

'Oh yes, there can be no mistake. I have spoken with Lady Fairford. She and Miss Fairford have come over to Brighton to make some purchases. I was driving up East Street when I saw them. I stopped, and before I could speak Lady Fairford had asked me whether Peregrine was indisposed that he had not kept his engagement with them yesterday.' She paused, and lifted her hand to her cheek. 'Perhaps you will think I am needlessly alarmed – there may be a dozen simple explanations! I tell myself so, but – I cannot believe it! Lord Worth, Perry left me yesterday afternoon, and he is not back!'

One of Mr Brummell's mobile brows went up. He glanced from Worth to Charles Audley, but said nothing.

The Earl drew a chair forward. 'Yes, I think there might be several explanations,' he said. 'Will you not be seated? Charles, pour out a glass of wine for Miss Taverner.'

She made a gesture of refusal. 'Thank you, thank you, I do not want anything. What explanation can there be? All I can think is that some accident has befallen him, but even that will not do, for how is it possible that I should not have heard of it by now? He was not alone; his groom was with him. Lord Worth, what has happened to Perry?'

'I am afraid I can scarcely answer that question,' replied the Earl. 'But since he was accompanied by his groom, it seems safe to assume that he has not met with an accident. The more probable explanation is that he has gone off to see a cock-fight, or something of that sort, and did not wish you to know of it.'

'Oh,' she said eagerly, 'do you think that might be so? It is quite true that he would not wish me to know. But the Fairfords – oh no, he would not have made so positive an engagement – he was to accompany them to an Assembly – if he had not meant to keep it!'

'Well, let us suppose that he did mean to keep it,' said the Earl. 'From my knowledge of him I should not imagine that if, at the last moment, some acquaintance desired him to go off to see a mill, or some cocking, he would find him very hard to persuade.'

'No, perhaps not,' she conceded doubtfully. 'But would he not have returned by now?'

'Apparently not,' said the Earl.

The matter-of-fact way he spoke had its effect on her. She tried to smile, and said with a faint blush: 'You make my fears sound ridiculous. Of course something of the kind must have occurred. Ten to one I shall find him at home when I get there. Only – Lord Worth, do you indeed think that? You do not see any need for anxiety?'

'Not yet, at all events,' he replied. 'If you have no news of him by dinner-time, send me word, and I will come round to discuss what is best to be done. Meanwhile, I will certainly make inquiries on the Worthing road. I think, if I were you, I would not mention the matter to anyone. If Peregrine were to return and find the whole town talking of his escapade, he might not be best pleased.'

'You are very right. I shall say nothing. Of course, there must be some very simple reason for his disappearing.' She got up. 'I must not stay. Mrs Scattergood will be wondering what has become of me.'

Captain Audley, who had retired to the window, stepped forward. 'You will allow me to accompany you?' he said.

She smiled. 'Yes, indeed, I should be glad. I daresay we shall find Perry in Marine Parade after all. Mr Brummell, I wish you had not been here, for I am aware how I must have sunk in your estimation! You told me once never to betray emotion, and here I am, on the high road to hysterics! No, no, do not come out with me, Lord Worth! Captain Audley has me in charge.'

The Earl, however, accompanied her to her phaeton, handed her up into it, and saw her drive off. When he returned to the saloon he found Mr Brummell standing where he had left him, sipping a glass of Madeira. Mr Brummell said in his pensive way: 'It occurs to me, Julian, that though *I* might not be so well informed, the news of a mill to be fought in the district must have reached *your* ears.'

'You would think so,' replied the Earl shortly.

Mr Brummell looked at him over the rim of his wine-glass. 'Well, do you know, I do think so,' he said. 'The cocking was a better notion, and if *you* are satisfied with it, it would be absurd for *me* to cavil.'

'I am not in the least satisfied with it,' said the Earl. 'But something had to be said. If you have any suggestion to offer I shall be glad to hear it. What is in your mind, George?'

'Who,' asked Mr Brummell, 'is the heir to Peregrine's fortune?'

'To a great extent, his sister.'

Mr Brummell shook his head. 'I cannot feel that Miss Taverner would be guilty of the impropriety of murdering her brother.'

The Earl poured himself out a glass of wine, and tasted it before he answered. 'Murder, George, is a very strong word,' he said. 'There was also a groom, and a tilbury, and a pair of horses.'

'True,' agreed Brummell. 'Yet I am of the opinion that a resourceful person might – at a pinch – find the means of disposing of a groom, a tilbury, and even a pair of horses.'

'It is a possibility that has already occurred to me. It is not, however, one that I intend to present to Miss Taverner.'

Mr Brummell set down his glass, and opened his snuff-box again. 'How many years have I known you, Julian?' he inquired.

'Precisely eighteen,' replied the Earl, with disastrous promptness.

'Nonsense!' said Brummell, considerably startled. 'It was not as long ago as that, surely, that I joined the regiment?'

'You were gazetted to the 10th Hussars in June of '94, and you left us in '98 – upon the regiment's being moved to Manchester,' said the Earl inexorably.

'I remember *that*,' admitted Brummell. 'But how very shocking! I must be thirty-four or five!'

'Thirty-four,' said the Earl.

'My dear Julian, I beg you won't mention it to anyone!' said Brummell earnestly.

'I won't. What was it you wanted to say?'

'Oh, merely that during the years I have known you I have always thought you a man of considerable resource,' said Brummell.

'I am obliged to you,' said the Earl. 'You have only to add that the most determined suitor to Miss Taverner's hand is one Charles Audley, and we shall understand one another tolerably well.'

'But I have known you for eighteen years,' objected Brummell. 'And it does seem to me that I have seen another determined suitor – a very civil gentleman who is, I think, a cousin.'

'Admiral Taverner's son,' said the Earl briefly.

Brummell nodded. 'Yes, I met the Admiral in Brook Street once. He is a fellow, now, who would send his plate up twice for soup. I am perfectly willing to suspect any son of his.'

'Yes,' said the Earl, 'I rather fancy that if nothing is heard of Peregrine, suspicion will point to Mr Bernard Taverner. That would be unfortunate for Mr Bernard Taverner.'

'I collect,' remarked Brummell, 'that the gentleman in question is no friend of yours.'

'So little my friend,' replied the Earl, 'that I shall own myself surprised if he does not presently set it about that it was I who caused Peregrine, and his groom, his tilbury, and his horses to disappear.'

'Which is absurd,' said Brummell.

'Which,' agreed the Earl, 'is naturally absurd, my dear George.'

In Marine Parade Miss Taverner spent an uncomfortable day, running to the window at the least sound of carriage wheels stopping outside the house, and trying to think of some good reason for Peregrine's prolonged absence. While Mrs Scattergood did her best to reassure her, it was evident that she too felt a considerable degree of alarm, and when, at six o'clock, there was still no sign of Peregrine, it was she, and not Miss Taverner, who sent a footman round to the Steyne with an urgent note for the Earl of Worth.

He came at once, and was ushered into the drawing-room, where both ladies were awaiting him. Miss Taverner was looking pale, and greeted him with a rather wan smile. 'He has not come back,' she said, trying to speak calmly.

'No, so I am informed,' he replied. 'And you, I perceive, have been fancying him dead this hour and more.'

His coolness, though it might argue a lack of sensibility, had always the power to allay any extraordinary irritation of nerves in her. She had been thinking Peregrine dead, but she at once felt such fears to be nonsensical. But Mrs Scattergood exclaimed, with a strong shudder: 'How can you say such things? If that is what you think —'

'No, it is what Miss Taverner thinks,' he answered. 'Am I right, my ward?'

'Lord Worth, what am I to think? He has disappeared. I know no more than that.'

'You would do well not to imagine more,' he said. 'Your brother is an extremely careless young man, but because he has chosen to slip off on some adventure without letting anyone know of it, is no reason to be in despair.'

'It will not do,' she said. '*You* know how much reason I have to fear the worst. All day long I have been recalling that duel, the attempt to shoot him on Finchley Common — even his illness in your house! Have you forgotten these things?'

'No,' he replied, 'I have not forgotten them. I am leaving for London to-night. I can get no news of him on the Worthing road. You must try to trust me, Miss Taverner. Meanwhile, I wish that you will remain in Brighton, and continue as much as possible your ordinary pursuits. Until we have more precise information it would be undesirable to start any public hue and cry. The fewer people who know of Peregrine's disappearance the better.'

'I have told no one but my cousin,' she said. 'You can have no objection to that.'

'None at all,' he said with a grim little smile. 'I should even be interested to hear how he received the news.'

'With a concern that did him more honour that your sneer does you, Lord Worth!' she retorted fierily.

'I can believe it. Have you ever asked yourself, Miss Taverner, who would be the person most interested in Peregrine's death?'

'Don't, don't use that dreadful word!' besought Mrs Scattergood. 'Not but what I think you are right. I never did like the man!'

Miss Taverner got up swiftly, and stood leaning one hand on the table, her eyes fixed on the Earl's face. 'You forget, I think, that you are speaking of one who is nearly related to me: of one, moreover, who has earned my trust in a way that must for ever preclude my lending ear to such suspicions. Had my cousin wished to kill Peregrine he would not have stopped his duel with Farnaby last year.'

'I had certainly forgotten that,' agreed the Earl.

'Perhaps you might, but I never shall. Mr Bernard Taverner had nothing to do with Perry's disappearance. He dined with friends, and was with them until past midnight.'

'And was it not Mr Bernard Taverner who recently introduced a servant of his own into your household – a servant who, by the oddest coincidence, is also missing at this moment?' inquired the Earl.

Mrs Scattergood gave a sharp scream. 'Mercy on me, so he did! Oh dear, what will become of us? I shall not sleep a wink to-night!'

'Lord Worth, you shall not make these insinuations!' Miss Taverner said. 'If Peregrine was overpowered, so too must Tyler have been.'

'Miss Taverner, you have said that you fear Peregrine may have met with foul play. If your cousin is to be above suspicion, whom do you mean to choose for your villain? Since he has only one arm, Charles, I fear, is ineligible. There remains myself.'

Her eyes sank. 'You are wrong. There is another,' she said, in a low voice. 'I have – always held him in mind, even though every feeling must be outraged by such a thought! But my father did not trust him. I cannot get that out of my head.'

'Are you referring to your uncle?' asked the Earl. She nodded. 'I see. Your cousin, meanwhile, to remain blameless. It does not seem to me very likely, but time will show. I shall hope to be able to send you more certain tidings in a day or two. Until then, I can only advise you to wait with as much patience as you can.'

'What do you mean to do in London?' asked Mrs Scattergood. 'Do you think Perry can have gone there?'

'I have no idea,' answered the Earl. 'I am hoping that the Bow Street Runners will be able to help me to find out.' He held out his hand, and Miss Taverner put hers into it. 'Goodbye,' he said curtly. 'Keep a stout heart, Clorinda.' He bowed, and in another minute was gone.

'What was that he called you?' asked Mrs Scattergood, momentarily diverted.

'Nothing,' replied Miss Taverner, flushing. 'A stupid jest, that is all.'

She saw her cousin on the following morning, when he called to inquire whether any news had been heard of Peregrine. She informed him of Worth's having gone to London, and requested him not to mention Peregrine's absence to anyone. He said quickly: 'I should certainly not speak of your affairs without leave, but why do you particularly wish me to be silent? Is this Lord Worth's doing?'

'He thinks it best not to spread it abroad. I daresay he may be right. I must be guided by him.'

He took a turn about the room, and presently said with a little reserve: 'I am aware that it is not for me to criticise. But what reason can he have for wishing to keep Perry's disappearance secret? You tell me he has gone to Bow Street: that would be well done indeed – if he may be believed. *You* are to do nothing, to set no inquiries on foot: it is all to be left to him. Does he know that I am in this secret?'

'Yes,' she said. 'Certainly he knows.'

He looked at her intently. 'Ah, I understand! I am suspect.'

'Not by me,' she answered.

'No,' he said with a slight smile, 'but by him. If anything has happened to Perry – which God forbid! – Worth will do his utmost to lay it at my door. The very fact of my having recommended Tyler to Perry, though I did it to avert this very event, gives him a weapon.'

'You did it to avert – you placed him with Perry to guard him?'

'Yes, to guard him. I have been uneasy these many weeks. Judith, who put the man Hinkson in Perry's service?'

'Hinkson! Why, no one! Perry stood in need of a groom; Hinkson applied for the post. I know nothing more than that, cousin.'

'Nor I, but I have long believed him to be in Worth's pay.'

'What reason have you for saying such a thing? I cannot credit it!'

'The man was never a groom in his life. There is part of my reason for you. For the rest, can you tell me why Perry's groom should be seen going into Worth's house? I have seen that.'

She was startled, but a moment's reflection caused her to reply with a good deal of calm sense: 'When I have had occasion to send a message to Lord Worth, Hinkson has very often been charged with it. I cannot allow his having been seen by you to be a reason for supposing him in Worth's pay.'

'Where was Hinkson yesterday when Perry set out for Worthing?'

'He was in some tavern – I cannot tell you which. He was drunk.'

'Or he wished it to be thought that he was drunk. One more question, and I have done. Where was Lord Worth that night?'

'At the Pavilion,' she answered at once. 'I was – I was taken faint there, and he brought me home.'

'He was there throughout the evening?'

'No,' she said slowly, 'he came late.'

He faced her, frowning. 'Judith, I have no proof, nor do I wish to make accusations which may well be unfounded, but I tell you frankly I have a profound conviction that Worth knows more of this affair than he has disclosed.'

She got up with a hasty movement. 'Oh, I cannot bear it!' she cried. 'Is it not enough that I should be almost distraught with anxiety for Perry? Must I also be tortured by such suspicions as these? I would not listen to Worth when he warned me against you, and I will not listen to you! Please leave me! I am in no case to talk to you, or anyone.'

'Forgive me!' he said. 'I should not have troubled you with my suspicions. Forget what I have said. I will do everything that lies in my power to aid you in this search. To see you in such distress –' He broke off, and caught her hand in his, holding it very tightly. 'If I could have spared you this anxiety! It is a damnable business!' He spoke with real feeling; both air and countenance showed him to be strongly moved. He pressed her hand to his lips for an instant, and with a last, eloquent look went quickly out of the room.

He left her wretched indeed. She knew not what to believe, nor whom to trust, and as the morning wore on, and no news of Peregrine came, her spirits grew more and more oppressed, until she found herself even looking on Mrs Scattergood with doubt. Mrs Scattergood did what she could to induce her to walk out with her and take the air, but Judith felt herself quite unequal to it, and begged with so much earnestness to be left in solitude, that the good lady judged it wisest to humour her, and set off alone to try and find some new publication upon the shelves of the circulating library sufficiently enthralling to distract even the most overwrought mind.

She had not been gone above ten minutes when Sir Geoffrey Fairford's card was brought up to Miss Taverner's room, where she was laid down to rest. Her feelings, on reading it, were all of thankfulness, for on Sir Geoffrey's integrity at least she could place absolute dependence. She got up, and with trembling fingers tidied her hair, and adjusted her dress. Within five minutes she was in the drawing-room, clasping both Sir Geoffrey's hands with a look of relief so heartfelt, that the circumstance of their being but barely acquainted was forgotten, and Sir Geoffrey, drawing her to the sofa, obliged her to sit down, and commanded her, as though she had been his own daughter, to put him in possession of all the facts.

He was on his way to London, to seek out Lord Worth, but he would not go without first visiting Judith, and learning from her whether any tidings of Peregrine had been received. She was grateful indeed. If he were to make it his business to join in the search for Peregrine she might be assured of everything possible being done. She told him what she knew as collectedly as she could, and had the comfort of knowing that, although he considered the case to be extraordinary, he did not feel it to be desperate. His judgment was calm, his opinions so much those of a man of sense and experience, that he had to be attended to. He was able to soothe the more violent of her fears, and when he presently went away, he left her tolerably composed, and even hopeful of a happy issue.

A visit from Captain Audley helped still further to restore her to some degree of tranquillity. He came in shortly after Mrs Scattergood's return, and bore Miss Taverner off for a drive. She at first declined it, but allowed herself in the end to be persuaded.

'Miss Taverner,' he said, 'you are for moping indoors, and indulging your fancy in every flight of the most horrid imagination! Confess, you have been picturing dungeons, oubliettes, ambushes – in a word, all the terrors that lurk between the pages of the best romances! But it will not do: we live in the nineteenth century, and instead of receiving demands for a fabulous ransom, you are a great deal more likely to find that Perry has posted off to buy some horse which he has been informed is so perfect in all its paces that it would be a shocking thing to miss the chance of striking a bargain. Ten to one, the explanation will be something very like that, and when you scold him for giving you such a fright he will be mightily indignant, talk of the letter he sent you through the post, and discover it in the pocket of his driving-cloak.'

'Ah, if I could only think so!' she sighed.

'You will find that it is so, I assure you. Meanwhile, I have a strict charge laid on me not to allow you to fret. You are to regard me, if you please, as Worth's proxy, and in that character I command you, Miss Taverner, to put on your driving-habit, and come with me. Look out of the window, and tell me if you can be ungrateful enough to refuse!'

She did look out, and smiled faintly to see Worth's team of greys being led up and down by a groom. 'At any other time I should be tempted,' she said. 'But to-day –'

'Miss Taverner, do you dare to oppose my brother in this fashion?' he demanded. 'I cannot credit it!'

Mrs Scattergood added her persuasions to his. Miss Taverner submitted, and was soon sitting on the box-seat of the curricle, the reins in her capable hands. Captain Audley, exerting himself to divert her, was by turns audacious, droll, witty, sensible, but none of his sallies drew so animated a look, nor so unforced a smile from her as his offer, when the curricle drew up on Marine Parade again, to escort her to London if no news of Peregrine was heard within the week.

'I don't doubt we *shall* have news,' he said, 'but if we do not by Thursday next, I will engage to go with you and Maria to town, and to conduct you to Bow Street myself.'

'Oh, if you would!' she said. 'To be staying here, unable to do anything to the purpose, ignorant of the steps Lord Worth is taking – it is not to be borne!'

'You have my promise,' he said. 'But until then try to do as Worth bade you. Be patient, do not set tongues wagging, and do not imagine the worst!' He handed her down from the curricle, saw her into the house, and nodded to the groom to get up on the box-seat. His gaiety had fallen from him when the door was closed behind Miss Taverner. As he was driven back to the Steyne he was frowning, in a way that induced the groom to suppose that his arm must be causing him a good deal of pain.

He dined alone, but went out afterwards to stroll down the Steyne. Nine o'clock was the fashionable hour of promenade there, and he had not gone far before he had met half a dozen people he knew. Several inquiries were made concerning Worth's whereabouts, but the news of Peregrine's disappearance did not seem to have got about, and Worth's having gone up to London on a matter of business was not much wondered at. Captain Audley had just repeated this explanation of his brother's absence for the fifth time, when he saw Mr Bernard Taverner walking towards him, evidently with the intention of accosting him. He made his bow to the two ladies who were regretting Worth's departure, and moved on to meet Mr Taverner.

'I am glad to have this chance of speaking with you,' Bernard Taverner said. 'I do not like to be for ever calling in Marine Parade for tidings. Has anything been heard of my cousin?'

'I do not know what my brother may have heard,' replied the Captain. '*I* have heard nothing.'

Mr Taverner fell into step beside him, and said with an air of grave reflection: 'Your brother hopes to get news of him in London, I collect. Is there any reason to suppose that Peregrine should have gone there?'

'Oh, I am afraid I am not enough in Worth's confidence to be able to answer you. You may depend upon it, however, that *he* had sufficient reason for going to London. My brother, Mr Taverner, is by no means a fool.'

Mr Taverner inclined his head. 'You are not aware what plans Lord Worth has made for discovering what has become of my cousin?'

'No, he left in haste, and told me very little. I am sorry for it: *you*, I am persuaded, must be anxious to know.'

'Yes,' said Mr Taverner quietly. 'I am indeed anxious to know that proper measures have been taken.'

'You may be sure of it,' replied the Captain. 'But we should not be discussing it in such a public place as this, you know. I was on my way to the Castle. Do you care to accompany me?'

Mr Taverner assented, and walked with him in silence to the inn. They went into the tap-room. The Captain called for a bottle of wine, and led the way to one of the tables against the wall. 'I can really tell you nothing that you do not already know,' he said. 'It is a most unaccountable business, but if there has been foul play I will back Worth to bring it home to the proper quarter.'

'Lord Worth suspects there has been foul play, then?'

'Well, what can one think?' said Captain Audley. 'Does it not bear all the appearance of it?'

'Yes,' replied Mr Taverner. 'I think it does, Captain Audley.'

'Do not breathe as much to Miss Taverner, however. She is already suffering great anxiety, you know.'

'It is not to be wondered at. *Her* situation is wretched indeed!'

The Captain glanced at him under drooping eyelids. 'You must not think that she is forgotten because Worth has left Brighton,' he said. 'I have the intention of escorting her to London on Thursday if nothing should be heard of Peregrine in the meantime.'

'Escorting her to London! For what purpose? What good can she do there?' exclaimed Mr Taverner.

'As to that, none, I suppose, but you will find that she wishes to go. It is very understandable, after all.'

'Understandable, yes, but I am surprised at Lord Worth's allowing it.'

The Captain smiled and picked up the wine bottle. 'Are you?' he said. 'Perhaps my brother has a reason for that as well.'

He began to pour out the wine, but his left hand was still unused to doing the work of his right, and some of the liquid was spilled, and splashed on to his immaculate breeches. He said with a good deal of annoyance: 'Can you perform the simplest office with your left hand? I cannot, as you see. Damnation!' He set the bottle down, and snatching his handkerchief from his pocket, dabbed angrily at the stain on his knee. But in pulling out his handkerchief he caught up something else as well, which fluttered to the floor between his chair and Taverner's. He looked down, and made a swift movement to retrieve it.

Mr Taverner was before him, however. His fingers closed on the paper just as Captain Audley reached for it. He looked at it for one moment, and then raised his eyes to the Captain's face. 'Am I to wish you joy, Captain Audley?' he asked in a measured voice. 'I had no idea that you were contemplating matrimony, but since you carry a special licence in your pocket, I must suppose the happy day to be imminent.'

The Captain took the paper from him rather quickly, and stuffed it back into his pocket. 'Oh Lord, no!' he said easily. 'It is not for me, my dear fellow. A friend of mine is about to be married, and charged me with procuring the licence, that is all!'

'I see,' said Mr Taverner politely.

Twenty-Two

*S*UNDAY DRAGGED PAST WITHOUT BRINGING ANY NEWS OF
Peregrine to his sister. She went to church with Mrs
Scattergood in the morning, and on coming out after the service
was hailed by her uncle, who came hobbling towards her, leaning
upon his stick. She had not seen him since some days before
Peregrine's disappearance, and so strong was her mistrust of him
that she found it hard to greet him with the distinction their relationship demanded. He did not look to be in health; his usually
red cheeks had a sallow tinge, but he ascribed it all to his gout,
which had kept him indoors for the past week. This, he told his
niece, was his first day out. She experienced a strong feeling of suspicion upon his so pointedly telling her this, but forced herself,
from a wish not to be backward in any attention that was due to
him, to inquire whether he had tried the Warm Bath. He had done
so, but without receiving much benefit from it. It was evident that
he did not wish to make his own health the subject of his conversation; he begged his niece to give him her arm to his carriage,
and was no sooner walking slowly away with her than he looked
anxiously round into her face, and said in a low tone: 'You know,
I should have been with you two days ago, my dear, had I not been
aground with this curst foot of mine. It is a dreadful business! I do
not know what to say to you. I would not have had such a thing
happen for the world! Ay, poor girl, I see how you feel it!'

His hand squeezed hers; meeting his eyes she saw so troubled an expression in them that she could almost have acquitted him. She thanked him, and said: 'I do not let myself despair, sir. I believe Lord Worth will find Peregrine.'

'Ay, and so I hope he may do,' he answered. 'It is a dreadful business, a dreadful business!'

'My cousin is not with you today, sir?' she observed, not wishing to discuss Peregrine's fate with him.

'Eh?' he said, recalling himself with a start. 'Oh no! Did you not know Bernard has gone off to do what he can for you? Ay, so it is. He set off last night; could not be kicking his heels in Brighton with his cousins under the hatches, as we say. Ah, my dear, if you knew the depth of my boy's regard for you – but I do not mean to tease you, I am sure, and this is no time to be talking of bridals.'

They had reached the carriage by this time, and he climbed into it, groaning a little. Miss Taverner was resolute in declining his offer to convey her to her door, but she could not believe his sympathy to be quite hypocritical, and took leave of him with more kindness than she would have thought it possible to feel for him.

Monday brought her a letter from Sir Geoffrey Fairford. He wrote from Reddish's hotel, in St James's Street. He had seen Worth, and although he was not able to give her any news of Peregrine, he was confident that a very few days must put them in possession of all the facts. He wrote in haste, and meant to carry his letter to the Post Office, that there might be no delay in its despatch. He could only counsel her not to lose hope, and assure her that her guardian was doing all that lay in his power to bring about a happy issue.

With this brief note she had to be satisfied. Her dependence was now on Captain Audley's promise to escort her to London. Every day spent in wretched suspense at Brighton was harder to bear than the last. Mrs Scattergood's attempts to keep up her spirits, alternating as they did with fits of the gloomiest foreboding, could only make matters worse. She so obviously gave Peregrine up for lost, that Judith could not feel her company to be any support; and since at the end of three days she was unable to sleep without the assistance of drops of laudanum, and spent the greater part of her time on a couch, with a bottle of smelling salts in one hand, and a damp handkerchief in the other, the only advantage of her presence was that she gave Judith something to do in looking after her.

No tidings came from Worth. Judith believed him to be in London, but even Captain Audley could give her no certain intelligence on this point.

On Wednesday morning, more from an inability to be still than from any real expectation of finding a letter from her guardian, Miss Taverner put on a street dress, and a hat, and went out to call at the Post Office. But the night-mail had brought no letter for her, and it was with a heavy heart that she walked back to Marine Parade. She was within sight of her house when she suddenly heard her name called, and turned quickly round to see her cousin jumping down from a light travelling carriage which had drawn up behind her.

She hurried to meet him, her countenance expressing all the eagerness she felt on beholding him. 'Cousin! Oh, have you discovered something? Tell me, tell me!'

He grasped the hands which she held out to him, and said in a repressed voice: 'I was on my way to your house. But this is better still. I believe – I trust – that I have discovered something.'

His face, which was very pale, led her to suppose that his news must be bad. Her own cheeks grew white; she just found strength to utter: 'What is it? Oh, do not keep me in suspense! I can bear anything but that!'

'I think I have found him,' he said with an effort.

Her eyes dilated. 'Found him! O God, not dead?'

'No, no!' he replied quickly. 'But in what case I dare not say!'

'Where?' she demanded. 'Why do you not take me to him at once? Why do we stand here wasting time? Where is he?'

'I will take you to him,' he said. 'It is some little distance, but I have brought a carriage for you. Will you come with me?'

'Good God, of course I will come!' she cried. 'Let me but run home to leave a message for Mrs Scattergood, and we may start immediately!'

His clasp on her hand tightened. 'Judith, most solemnly I beg of you not to do that! A message to Mrs Scattergood will ruin all. You do not know the whole.'

'What are you trying to tell me?' she said. 'How could a message to Mrs Scattergood ruin all?'

'Cousin, every suspicion has been confirmed. You are not meant to find Peregrine. The place where I shall take you is hidden away in the depths of the country. I believe him to be held there – you may guess by whom.'

She had the sensation of having received a blow that robbed her of all power of speech. She made a queer little gesture, as though to ward something off, and without a word turned, and hurried towards the carriage.

He assisted her to get into it, and took his place beside her. The steps were folded up, and in a moment the horses were turned about, and driven at a trot up the Steyne towards the London road.

Though the day was sunny, and very warm, Judith was shivering. She managed to articulate one word. 'Worth?'

'Yes,' he answered. 'It was he who kidnapped Perry; how I know not.'

'Oh no!' she whispered. 'Oh no, oh no!'

He said in a constrained voice: 'Does it mean so much to you that it should be he?'

She managed to control herself enough to say: 'What proof have you? Why should he do so? This is not credible!'

'Do you think Perry's fortune is not enough to tempt him?'

'He is not heir –' She broke off, and pressed her hands together in her lap. 'Oh, it would be too vile! I will not believe it!'

'You are the heir,' he said. 'But do not flatter yourself you were ever destined to be Worth's bride, cousin. Had I not discovered by the veriest chance the plot that was being hatched you would have been forced, by some devilish trick or other, into marrying Charles Audley.'

'Impossible!' she said. 'No, that I cannot believe! Captain Audley has no thought of marrying me.'

'Yet Captain Audley was to take you to London tomorrow, and Captain Audley carries a special licence in his pocket.'

'What!' she exclaimed.

'I have seen it,' he said.

She was utterly dumbfounded, and could only stare at him. After a moment he continued: 'I imagine that you were to be safety tied up to him in the few days that remain before you come of age. Have you considered that by Friday you will be free from Worth's guardianship?'

'What can that signify?' she said. 'Oh, it will not do, cousin! Captain Audley is a man of honour, incapable of such baseness!'

'Money can drive a man to measures more desperate than you have any notion of,' he said, a hard note in his voice. 'Worth has made attempt after attempt on Perry's life. You know it to be true!'

'No,' she said faintly. 'I do not know it to be true. I cannot think – my head feels empty! I must wait until I have seen Perry. How far do we have to travel?'

'You would not know the place. It is some miles west of Henfield. I was led to it by a series of circumstances – but I will not weary you with all the miserable details.'

She did not speak; her senses were almost overpowered; she could only lean back in her corner, trying to conjure up every recollection that should prove or disprove his accusations. He looked at her compassionately, but seemed to understand her need of silence. Once he said, as though impelled: 'If I could have spared you! But I could not!'

She tried to answer him, but her voice failed. She turned her head away to stare blindly out of the window.

The carriage was bowling along at a brisk pace, only checking at the turnpikes. For many miles Judith was scarcely aware of the distance they were covering, but when they left the pike-road and branched off on to a rough lane she roused herself, and looking at her cousin in a blank way, said: 'Have we to go much farther? We must have come a long way. Should we not change horses?'

'It will not be necessary,' he replied. 'This pair can accomplish the journey, for the carriage is a light one. We have only another ten miles to go. An hour should see us safely arrived.'

'If I find Perry – alive, all the rest can – *must* – be borne!' she said. 'Forgive me for being so silent a companion! I cannot talk of it.'

He pressed her hand. 'I understand. When we arrive will be time enough for all that must be said.'

'Is – is Lord Worth at this place?' she asked.

'No, he is in London. You need not fear having to meet him.'

'But why has he – why is Perry kept in this place you are taking me to? If all you have said is true, how comes he to be alive? Surely –'

'You will know presently,' he said.

She said no more. The carriage was jolting along a twisting lane between high, tangled hedgerows; a scent of hay was wafted in on the warm air; occasionally she caught a glimpse of a vista of rolling fields, with a blue background of hills in the distance.

As they plunged deeper into the country, and she felt herself to be within reach of Peregrine, the numbness that had been clogging her brain gave way to an impatience to arrive. She turned to her cousin and demanded: 'Are we never to reach this place? Why did you not have the horses changed half-way?'

'We are nearly there now,' he answered.

In another five minutes the weary horses had turned in through a gateway, and were going at a jog-trot up the rough cart-track that led between rank fields to a fair-sized cottage, nestling in a hollow of the ground. It was surrounded by a fenced garden, and a huddle of outhouses. A few hens were to be seen, and a pig was rootling amongst some cabbages at the back of the cottage. Judith, leaning forward to see more plainly, turned with an expression of surprise on her face. 'But this is nothing but a villager's cottage!' she exclaimed. 'Is Perry kept *here*?'

He opened the door and sprang out, letting down the steps for her. She could scarcely wait, but almost jumped down on to the ground, and pushing open the low gate, walked quickly up the path to the cottage.

The door was opened before she had time to knock on it by an old woman with wispy grey hair, and the rather vacant look in her eyes which belongs to the very deaf. She dropped a curtsy to Judith, and in the same breath begged her to step in, and to excuse her not hearing very plain.

Judith swung round to face her cousin, her brows drawing close over the bridge of her nose. 'Peregrine?' she said sharply.

He laid a hand that shook on her arm. 'Go in, cousin, I cannot explain it to you on the doorstep.'

She saw his coachman leading the horses round to one of the barns at the back of the house. Her eyes darkened with suspicion. 'Where is Peregrine?'

'For God's sake, Judith, let us go in! I will tell you everything, but not before this woman!'

She looked down at the deaf woman, who was still holding the door, and nodding and smiling at her, and then stepped over the threshold into a narrow passage with some stairs at the end of it. Bernard Taverner threw open a door and disclosed a low-pitched but roomy apartment with windows at each end, which was evidently the parlour. Judith went in without hesitation, and waited for him to close the door again. 'Peregrine is not here?' she said.

He shook his head. 'No. I could think of no other way to bring you. Do not judge me too harshly! To deceive you with such seeming heartlessness has been the most painful thing of all! But you would never have come with me. You would have gone to town with Audley, and been tricked into marrying him. You must – you *shall* forgive me!'

'Where is Peregrine?' she interrupted.

'I believe him to be dead. I do not know. Do you think if I did I would not have led you to him? Worth made away with him –'

'Worth!' she said. 'No, not Worth! I am asking *you*! What have you done to Perry? Answer me!'

'Judith, I swear to you I know no more than you do what has become of him! I had no hand in that. What do I care for Peregrine, or his fortune? Have I proved myself so false that you can believe *that* of me? It is you I want, have wanted from the day I first saw you! I never meant it to be like this, but what could I do, what other course was open to me? Nothing I could have said would have prevented you from going to London with Audley, and once you were in his and Worth's hands, what hope had I of saving you from that iniquitous marriage? Again and again I have warned you not to trust Worth, but you have not heeded me! Then came Peregrine's disappearance, and once more you would not listen to me. Even so, I should have shrunk from taking this step had I not

seen the marriage-licence in Audley's possession. But I knew
then that if I was to save you from being the victim of Worth's
fiendish schemes I must act drastically – treacherously, if you
will! – but yet because I love you!'

She sank down on a chair beside the table, and buried her
face in her hands. 'What does that matter?' she asked. 'I do not
know whether you are speaking the truth or not; I do not care.
Perry is all that signifies.' Her hands fell; she stretched them out
to him. 'Cousin, whatever you have done I can forgive, if you
will only tell me Perry is not dead!'

He went down on his knees by her chair, grasping her hands.
'I cannot tell you. I do not know. It was not I who made away
with him. Perhaps he is not dead; if you will marry me we will –'

'Marry you!' she cried. 'I shall never marry you!'

He rose and walked away from her to the window. With his
back to her he said: 'You must marry me.'

She stared at him. 'Are you mad?'

He shook his head. 'Not mad. Desperate.'

She said nothing. She was looking about her as though she
had just realised the significance of this cottage, lost in the
Weald. After a moment he said in a quieter tone: 'I must try to
make you understand.'

'I do understand,' she said. The fingers of her right hand
clenched and unclenched. 'I understand why I was not to leave
a message for Mrs Scattergood, why you would not change
horses on the road. The woman who lives in this place – is she
in your pay?'

'Yes,' he replied curtly.

'I hope you pay her handsomely,' she said.

'Judith, you hate me for this, but you have nothing to fear
from me, I promise you!'

'You are mistaken; I do not fear you.'

'You have no need. I want you to be my wife –'

'Would you want me to be your wife if I were not possessed of a fortune?' she said scathingly.

'Yes! Oh, I shan't deny I need your fortune, but my love for you is real! Too real to allow of my doing anything *now* that could set you more against me! I am aware how much I have injured my own cause by this step I have taken. It is for me to show you in what respect I hold you. I shall not presume even to touch you without your leave, even though I must keep you here until I have your promise to marry me!'

'You will not get it, I assure you.'

'Ah, you do not understand. You have not considered! That I should be obliged to point out to you – But it must be done! Judith, do you know that a fortnight – a week – spent in my company, hidden away from your friends, must make it impossible for you to refuse? Your reputation would be so damaged that even Worth himself must counsel you to marry me! In plain words, cousin –'

A voice from the other end of the room interposed coolly: 'You need not speak any more plain words, Mr Taverner. You have said quite enough to compromise yourself.'

Judith gave a cry and turned. The Earl of Worth was seated astride the window-sill at the back of the room. He was wearing riding-dress, and he carried his gloves and his whip in his hand. As Judith started up from her chair he swung his other leg over the sill and stepped quickly into the room, tossing his gloves and whip on to the table.

'You!' The word burst from Bernard Taverner's pale lips. He had spun round at the sound of the Earl's voice, and stood swaying on the balls of his feet, glaring across the room, for one moment before he sprang.

Miss Taverner uttered a shriek of terror, but before it had died on her lips it was all over. At one moment the Earl seemed in danger of being murdered by her cousin, at the next Bernard Taverner had gone down before a crashing blow to the jaw, and was lying on the floor with an overturned chair beside him, and the Earl standing over him with his fists clenched, and a look on his face that made Miss Taverner run forward and clasp her hands about his arm. 'Oh no!' she gasped. 'You must not! Lord Worth, I beg of you –'

He looked down at her, and the expression that had frightened her died out of his eyes. 'I beg your pardon, Clorinda,' he said. 'I was rather forgetting your presence. You may get up, Mr Taverner. We will finish this when Miss Taverner is not by.'

Bernard Taverner had struggled on to one elbow. He dragged himself to his feet, and stood leaning heavily against the wall, trying to regain full possession of his senses. The Earl picked up the fallen chair and handed Miss Taverner to it. 'I owe you an apology,' he said. 'You have had an uncomfortable sort of a morning, and I am afraid that was my doing.'

She said: 'Peregrine – he said it was you who kidnapped Peregrine!'

'That,' said the Earl, 'is probably the only correct information he has given you.'

She turned very white. 'Correct!'

'Perfectly correct,' he said, his gaze resting mockingly on Taverner's face.

'I don't understand! Oh, you could not have done so!'

'Thank you, Clorinda,' he said, with a faint smile. 'But the fact remains that I did.'

She glanced towards her cousin, and saw that he was staring at Worth with a mixture of horror and incredulity in his eyes. She got up. 'Oh, what are you saying? Where is Perry? For God's sake, tell me, one of you!'

'By this time,' said the Earl, 'Peregrine is probably in Marine Parade. Don't look so surprised, Mr Taverner: you cannot seriously have imagined that I should permit you to ship my ward off to the West Indies.'

'In Marine Parade!' Judith repeated. 'The West Indies! Bernard! Oh no, no!'

Bernard Taverner passed a hand across his eyes. 'It's a lie! I did not have Peregrine put away!'

'No,' agreed the Earl. 'You did your best, but you reckoned without me. However, you may console yourself with the reflection that your careful arrangements were not wasted. The master of that highly suspicious vessel off Lancing was quite sat-isfied to receive Tyler in Peregrine's stead. In fact, I am inclined to doubt whether he even appreciated that an exchange had been made. I was quite sure, you see, that you would not expect to see Tyler back again in Brighton. That would have been too dangerous, I feel. So it was really very safe for me to dispose of him precisely as he meant to dispose of Peregrine.'

'Lord Worth, you may attempt to foist this monstrous story on to me if you please,' Mr Taverner said. 'You will find it hard to prove.'

'I might have found it hard to prove had you not so oblig-ingly abducted Miss Taverner today,' said the Earl. 'That error of judgment, my dear sir, has made it so easy for me to prove the rest that I am confident you will not put me to the trouble of offering my proof to a Grand Jury.'

Miss Taverner sank back into her chair. 'All those other attempts – *you* made? But the duel! Ah no, that at least cannot have been your doing!'

'I am sorry to disillusion you, Miss Taverner,' said the Earl implacably, 'but that duel was Mr Bernard Taverner's first attempt to dispose of Peregrine. The news of it was brought to me by my tiger, who, by a fortunate coincidence, was in the gallery of the Cock-Pit Royal when the quarrel between Peregrine and Farnaby took place. By the way, Miss Taverner, while I have grave doubts of that surgeon's ability to recognise your cousin, I have a reasonable dependence on his recognising *me*.'

She exclaimed: 'It was you who stopped the duel? Oh, fool that I was! But you did not tell me! Why did you let me think it was my cousin who had done it?'

'I had several reasons, Miss Taverner, all of them good ones.'

Bernard Taverner lifted a hand to his cravat and mechanically straightened it. He moved across to the empty fireplace and stood by it, leaning his arm on the mantelpiece. An ugly bruise was beginning to disfigure his face; he looked to be very much shaken, but he said with all his customary calmness of manner: 'Pray continue! You are blessed with a lively imagination, but I fancy that any jury would require more precise information than this before convicting me of so wild a crime. You accuse me of contriving that duel, but I should be interested to hear what proof you would offer to your Grand Jury.'

'If I could have brought proof to bear you would not be at large to-day, Mr Taverner.'

Judith was looking at the Earl in wonderment. 'When did you suspect that the duel was brought about by my cousin?' she asked.

'Almost immediately. You may perhaps remember bringing me word once of Peregrine's being got into a bad set of company. You mentioned Farnaby's name, and it crossed my mind that I had seen Farnaby in your cousin's company once or twice. At the time my only suspicion was that there might conceivably be a plot on hand to bleed Peregrine of his fortune at cards. I dealt with that by frightening Peregrine with a threat to send him back to Yorkshire if I found he had contracted debts of honour above what his allowance would cover. I thought also that a discreet inquiry into the state of Mr Taverner's finances might not be inopportune. I admit, however, that I was so far from suspecting the truth that I committed the imprudence of sanctioning Peregrine's betrothal to Miss Harriet Fairford. In doing that I undoubtedly placed him in jeopardy of his life. While Peregrine remained single there was no pressing need to be rid of him. I imagine that before he arranged for the boy's death your cousin would have made sure of you, had his hand not been forced. The betrothal made it necessary for him to act quickly. Mr Farnaby was hired to shoot Peregrine in a duel, and might well have succeeded had he chosen a less public spot for the forcing on of that quarrel. Upon learning from my tiger what was intended I set him to discover the surgeon Fitzjohn meant to employ. The rest was simplicity itself.'

Judith pressed her hands to her cheeks. 'It is too terrible! too shocking! Ever since that day Peregrine has been in danger!'

'Hardly that,' replied the Earl. 'I have had him carefully watched ever since then. I believe Ned Hinkson has never been a favourite with you, Miss Taverner, but you will admit that his prompt action on Finchley Common last year compensated for his lack of skill on the box. He is by profession a pugilist, and although I have reason to believe that my tiger – a somewhat severe critic – doubts his ability to shine in the Ring, I myself feel that, given a patron, he may do very well indeed.'

'Hinkson!' Miss Taverner exclaimed. 'Oh, I have been blind indeed!'

'I am aware that an attempt was once made to hold my cousin up on Finchley Common,' Bernard Taverner said contemptuously. 'Is that also to be put to my account?'

'I am quite sure that it might be put to your account,' replied the Earl, 'but I scarcely think a jury would be interested. But they might be interested in a certain jar of snuff at present in my possession, and still more interested in the effects of that snuff upon the human system.'

Bernard Taverner's hand closed convulsively on the edge of the mantelpiece. 'I fear I am far from understanding you now, my lord,' he said.

'Are you?' said the Earl. 'Have you never wondered why that snuff did not seem to affect Peregrine? I concede you a certain amount of forethought in thinking of a means of poisoning your cousin through a medium on which I am known to be an expert; but you might have considered, I should have thought, that while I might certainly be suspected of having put up the snuff, if its being poisoned were ever discovered, there was also a strong probability that I should be the very person to make that discovery. The circumstance of the mixture being heavily scented was enough to make me suspicious. I found the opportunity, while he was staying in my house, to abstract Peregrine's snuff-box. It was a little difficult to determine the exact proportions of the three sorts used in making the original mixture, but I believe I succeeded fairly well. At all events, Peregrine detected no difference.'

'His illness in your house!' Miss Taverner cried. 'That cough! Good God, is this possible?'

'Oh yes,' said the Earl in his matter-of-fact way. 'Scented snuffs have long been a means of poisoning people. You may remember, Miss Taverner, that I found an excuse to send Hinkson up to Brook Street while you were at Worth?'

'Yes,' she said. 'You wanted the lease of the house.'

'Not at all. I wanted the rest of Peregrine's snuff. He had told me where the jar was kept, and Hinkson was easily able to find an opportunity to go up to his dressing-room and exchange the jar for another, similar one, that I had given him. Later, when I was in town again, I visited the principal snuff-shops in the whole of London – a wearing task, but one which repaid me. That particular mixture is not a common one; during the month of December only three four-pound jars of it were sold in town. One was bought at Fribourg and Treyer's by Lord Edward Bentinck; one was sold by Wishart to the Duke of Sussex; and the third was sold by Pontet, in Pall Mall, to a gentleman who paid for it on the spot, and took it away with him, leaving no name. The description of that gentleman with which the shopman was obliging enough to furnish me was exact enough not only to satisfy me, but also to embolden me to suppose that he would have no difficulty in recognising his customer again at need. Do you think a jury would be interested in that, Mr Taverner?'

Bernard Taverner was still clenching the edge of the mantelpiece. A rather ghastly smile parted his lips. 'Interested – but not convinced, Lord Worth.'

'Very well,' said the Earl. 'We must pass on then to your next and last attempt. I will do you the justice to say that I don't think it was one you would have made had not the fixed date of Peregrine's marriage made it imperative for you to get rid of him at once. You were hard-pressed, Mr Taverner, and a little too desperate to consider whether I might not be taking a hand in the affair. From the moment of Peregrine's wedding-day being made known you have not made one movement out of your lodgings that has not been at once reported to me. You suspected Hinkson, but Hinkson was not the person who shadowed you. You have had on your heels a far more noted figure, one who must be as well known as I am myself. You have even thrown him a shilling for holding your horse. Don't you know my tiger when you see him, Mr Taverner?'

Bernard Taverner's eyes were fixed on the Earl's face. He swallowed once, but said nothing.

The Earl took a pinch of snuff. 'On the whole,' he said reflectively, 'I believe Henry enjoyed the task. It was a little beneath his dignity, but he is extremely attached to me, Mr Taverner – a far more reliable tool, I assure you, than any of your not very efficient hirelings – and he obeyed me implicitly in not letting you out of his sight. You would be surprised at his resourcefulness. When you drove your gig over to New Shoreham to strike a bargain with that seafaring friend of yours you took Henry with you, curled up in the boot. His description of that mode of travel is profane but very graphic. I am anticipating, however. Your first action was to introduce a creature of your own into Peregrine's household – a somewhat foolhardy proceeding, if I may say so. It would have been wiser to have risked coming into the fore-ground at that juncture, my dear sir. You should have disposed of Peregrine yourself. Well, you made arrangements to have Peregrine transported out to sea. Was he then to be dropped overboard? It would be interesting to know what precise fate lay in store for him. I can only trust that it may have befallen Tyler, whose task was undoubtedly to have overpowered Peregrine at a convenient moment during his drive to Worthing, and to have handed him over to the captain of that vessel. To make doubly sure, Tyler tried to drink Hinkson under the table before setting out. But Hinkson has a harder head than you would believe pos-sible, and instead of remaining under the table, he came to me. I waylaid Peregrine on the West Cliff, and requested him to come back with me to my house on a matter of business. Once I had him under my roof I gave him drugged wine to drink, while Henry performed the same office for Tyler. Hinkson then drove Tyler to the rendezvous you had appointed, Mr Taverner, and delivered him up to your engaging friends. It was he who wrote you the message which you thought came from Tyler, telling you that he had done his part, and would meet you in London. Peregrine was carried out of my house that evening and taken aboard my yacht, which was lying in New Shoreham harbour.'

'Oh, how could you?' Judith broke in. 'What he must have suffered!'

He smiled. 'Charles felt very much as you appear to do, Miss Taverner. Fortunately I am not so tender-hearted. Peregrine has suffered nothing worse than a severe headache, and a week's cruise in excellent weather. He has not been imagining himself in any danger, for I gave my captain a letter of explanation to be delivered to him when he came to his senses.'

'You might have told me!' Judith said.

'I might, had I not had an ardent desire to try your cousin into betraying himself,' replied the Earl coolly. 'It was with that object that I left Brighton. Charles did the rest. He led Mr Bernard Taverner to believe – did he not, my dear sir? – that he and I had concocted a scheme to lure you to town, and there to force you into marriage with one or other of us. He dropped a special licence under Mr Taverner's nose and left the rest to his own ingenuity. You took fright, sir, precisely as you were meant to, and this is the outcome. The game is up!'

'But – but you?' demanded Miss Taverner, in a bewildered voice. 'Where were you, Lord Worth? How could you know that my cousin meant to bring me here?'

'I did not know. But when Henry was able to report to Charles that your cousin had left Brighton on Saturday night, Charles sent the tidings to me express, and I returned to Brighton on Sunday night, where I have been ever since, waiting for your cousin to move. Henry followed you to the Post Office this morning, witnessed your meeting with Mr Taverner, and ran to tell me of it. I could have overtaken you at any moment during your drive here had I wanted to.'

'Oh, it was not fair!' exclaimed Miss Taverner indignantly. 'You should have told me! I am very grateful to you for all the rest, but this –' She got up from her chair, rather flushed, and glanced towards her cousin. He was still standing before the fireplace, his face rigid, and almost bloodless. She shuddered. 'I trusted you!' she said. 'All the time you were trying to murder Perry I believed you to be our friend. My uncle I did suspect, but you never!'

He said in a constricted voice: 'Whatever I may have done, my father had no hand in. I admit nothing. Arrest me, if you choose. Lord Worth has yet to prove his accusations.'

Her mouth trembled. 'I cannot answer you. Your kindness, your professions of regard for me – all false! Oh, it is horrible!'

'My regard for you at least was not false!' he said hoarsely. 'That was so real, grew to be so – But it does not signify talking!'

'If you stood in such desperate need of money,' she said haltingly, 'could you not have told us? We should have been so happy to have assisted you out of your difficulties!'

He winced at that, but the Earl said in his most damping tone: 'Possibly, but it is conceivable that I might have had something to say to that, my ward. Nor do I imagine that with a fortune of twelve thousand pounds a year to tempt him Mr Taverner would have been satisfied with becoming your pensioner. May I suggest that you leave this matter in my hands now, Miss Taverner? You have nothing further to fear from your cousin, and you cannot profitably continue this discussion. You will find that the chaise that is to convey you back to Brighton has arrived by now. I want you to go out to it, and to leave me to wind up this affair in my own way.'

She looked up at him doubtfully. 'You are not going to come with me?' she asked.

'I must ask you to excuse me, Miss Taverner. I have still something to do here.'

She let him lead her to the door, but as he opened it, and would have bowed her out, she laid her hand on his arm, and said under her breath: 'I don't want him to be arrested!'

'You may safely leave everything to me, Miss Taverner. There will be no scandal.'

She cast a glance at her cousin, and looked up again at the Earl. 'Very well. I – I will go. But I – I don't want you to be hurt, Lord Worth!'

He smiled rather grimly. 'You need not be alarmed, my child. I shan't be.'

'But –'

'Go, Miss Taverner,' he said quietly.

Miss Taverner, recognising the note of finality in his voice, obeyed him.

She found that a chaise-and-four, with the Earl's crest on the panels, was waiting for her outside the cottage. She got into it, and sank back against the cushions. It moved forward, and closing her eyes, Miss Taverner gave herself up to reflection. The events of the past hours, the shock of finding her cousin to be a villain, could not soon be recovered from. The drive to Brighton, which had seemed so interminable earlier in the day, was now too short to allow her sufficient time to compose her thoughts. These were in confusion; it would be many hours before she could be calm again, many hours before her mind would be capable of receiving other and happier impressions.

The chaise bore her smoothly to Brighton, and she found Peregrine awaiting her in Marine Parade. She threw herself into his arms, her overcharged spirits finding relief in a burst of tears. 'Oh, Perry, Perry, how *brown* you look!' she sobbed.

'Well, there is nothing to cry about in that, is there?' asked Peregrine, considerably surprised.

'No, oh no!' wept Miss Taverner, laying her cheek against his shoulder. 'It is only that I am so thankful!'

Twenty-Three

*I*F MISS TAVERNER EXPECTED TO FIND HER BROTHER indignant at the treatment he had undergone she was soon informed of her mistake. He had had a capital time.

'Nothing could be like it!' he told her over and over again. 'I must have a yacht of my own. If Worth won't consent to it it will be the greatest shame imaginable! I am persuaded Harriet would like it above all things. I wish Worth had come here to-night, I cannot conceive why he should not. Evans – he is Worth's captain, you know: a first-rate fellow! – Evans says I have a great aptitude. Never in the least sick – and we ran into a pretty ground-swell on Tuesday, I can tell you! But it made no odds to me, never felt better in my life!'

'But Perry, when you awoke from that drug, were you not sadly alarmed?'

'No, why should I be? I had a devilish headache, but that soon went off, and then Evans gave me Worth's letter.'

'What must your feelings have been when you read it! He told you the whole?'

'Oh yes, I was excessively shocked! But ever since he had the impudence to interfere over that duel I have not at all liked my cousin, you know.'

'But Perry, he did not interfere! It was he who –'

'Ay, so it was; I was forgetting. But it's all one: I have been thinking him a shabby fellow these several months.'

'We have not valued Lord Worth's protection as we should,' said Judith, colouring faintly. 'If we had trusted him more, been upon kinder terms, perhaps he need not have put you away, or —'

'Lord, there's nothing in that!' Peregrine declared. 'I am precious glad he did, because I had never been to sea before in my life. I would not have missed it for the world! To own the truth, I did not above half like coming ashore again, except, of course, for seeing you and Harriet. However, I am quite determined to set up a yacht of my own, only it will cost a good deal, I daresay, and ten to one Worth won't hear of it.'

'I wish,' said Miss Taverner, with some asperity, 'that you would give your thoughts a more proper direction! Towards Lord Worth we must be all obligation. Without his protection I am very much disposed to think that you and I should have made but wretched work of everything.'

'It is very true, upon my honour! I assure you I am quite in charity with him. But then, you know, I never disliked him as much as you did, though he has often been amazingly disagreeable.'

Miss Taverner's flush deepened. 'Yes, at first I did dislike him. The circumstances of our —'

'Lord, I shall never forget the day we called in Cavendish Square, and found that it was he who was our guardian! You were as mad as fire!'

'It is a recollection that *should* be forgotten,' replied Miss Taverner. 'Lord Worth's *manners* are — are not always conciliating, but of the propriety of his *motives* we can never stand in doubt. We owe him a debt of gratitude, Perry.'

'I am very sensible of it. To be sure, we were completely taken in by my cousin. And to drug me, and put me aboard his yacht — Lord, I thought he was going to murder me when he forced that stuff down my throat! — was the neatest piece of work! I had no notion I should like being upon the sea so much! Evans was in a great pucker lest I should be angry at it, but, "Lord," I said, "you need not think I shall try to swim to shore! This is beyond anything great!"'

Miss Taverner sighed, and gave up the struggle. Peregrine continued to talk of his experiences at sea until it was time to go to bed. Miss Taverner could only be glad that since he had formed the intention of driving to Worthing upon the following day any further descriptions of ground-swells, squalls, wearing, luffing, squaring the yards, or reefing the sails must fall to Miss Fairford's lot instead of hers. It was a melancholy reflection that although she would have been ready to swear, a day before, that she could not have borne to have let him out of her sight again, if he should be restored to her, three hours of his company were enough to make her look forward with complaisance to his leaving her directly after breakfast next morning. Even when he was not recounting his adventures his conversation had a nautical flavour. He talked of crowding all sail to Worthing, of bringing to, and hauling his wind, and of making out a friend at cable's length. An empty wine-bottle became a marine officer, landsmen on board a ship were live lumber, and a passer-by in the street was described as being as round as a nine-pounder. A number of sea-shanties being sung loudly and inaccurately all over the house finally alienated even Mrs Scattergood's sympathy, and by eleven o'clock on Thursday nothing could have exceeded both ladies' anxious solicitude to set him on his way to Worthing.

Miss Taverner then sat down to await her guardian. He did not come. Only Captain Audley called in Marine Parade that morning, and when Miss Taverner asked, as carelessly as she could, whether his lordship was in Brighton, the Captain merely said: 'Julian? Oh yes, he is here, but I fancy you won't see him to-day. York arrived in Brighton yesterday, you know.'

Miss Taverner, who was inclined to rate her claims quite as high as the Duke of York's said: 'Indeed!' in a cold voice, and turned the subject.

There was no appearance of Worth at the ball that night, but upon Miss Taverner's return to Marine Parade she found a note from him lying on the table in the hall. She broke the seal at once, and eagerly spread open the single sheet.

> *Old Steyne, June 25th, 1812.*
>
> *Dear Miss Taverner. – I shall do myself the honour of waiting on you to-morrow morning at noon, if this should be convenient to you, for the purpose of resigning into your charge the documents relating to your affairs with which I have been entrusted during the period of my guardianship. Yours, etc.,*
>
> *Worth.*

Miss Taverner read this missive with a sinking heart, and slowly folded it up again. Mrs Scattergood, observing her downcast look, hoped that she had not had bad news. 'Oh dear me, no!' said Miss Taverner.

Breakfast, upon the following morning, was enlivened by the appearance of Peregrine, who had driven back from Worthing so early on purpose to wish his sister many happy returns of her birthday. He thought himself a very good brother to have remembered the event, and would have bought her a present if Harriet had put him in mind of the date sooner. However, they would go out together after breakfast, and she should choose her own present, which would be a much better thing, after all. He admired the quilted parasol of shaded silk which Mrs Scattergood had given Judith, and said there was no need to inquire who had sent the huge bouquet of red roses which graced the table. 'They come from Audley, I'll be bound.'

'Yes,' agreed Miss Taverner, with a marked lack of enthusiasm. 'I have had a letter from my uncle also. You may read it, if you choose. It is painful: one cannot but pity him. He seems to have known only part of what my cousin intended.'

'Oh well, don't let us be thinking of him now!' said Peregrine. 'We are very well rid of the pair of them. Only fancy, though! Worth told Sir Geoffrey the whole, when he saw him in town this week. Sir Geoffrey thinks Worth a very tolerable sort of a fellow.' He poured himself out a cup of coffee. 'Now, what would you like to do to-day? You have only to give it a name; I am quite at your disposal. Shall we drive over to Lewes? I believe there is a castle, or some such thing, to be seen there.'

'Thank you, Perry,' she said, touched by this handsome offer. 'But Lord Worth is coming to see me this morning. I was thinking that you should stay at home with me. You will want to thank him for all that he has done.'

'Oh, certainly!' said Peregrine. 'I shall be very glad to meet him, to be sure. I want to talk to him about my yacht, you know.'

Shortly before noon Peregrine, who was seated in the window of the drawing-room, quizzing the passers-by, announced that Worth was approaching. 'My dear Ju,' he said in tones of awe, 'only look at the coat he is wearing! I wonder whether Weston made it? Do but look at the set of it across the shoulder!'

Miss Taverner declined leaning out of the window to stare at his lordship, and begged her brother to draw in his head. Instead of doing anything of the kind Peregrine waved to attract Worth's attention, and, upon the Earl looking up, was instantly struck by the exquisite arrangement of his cravat. He turned, and said impressively: 'I do not care if he does give me one of his set-downs; I must know how he ties his cravat!'

The Earl had knocked on the door by this time, and in a few moments his step was heard on the stairs. Peregrine went out to meet him. 'Come up, sir! We are both here!' he said. 'How do you do? You are the most complete hand indeed, you know! My head, when I awoke! My mouth too! There was never anything like it!'

'Was it very bad?' inquired the Earl, leisurely mounting the last three stairs.

'Oh, beyond anything! But I don't mean to complain; I have had a famous time of it! But come into the drawing-room! My sister is there, and I have something very particular to say to you. Ju, here is Lord Worth.'

Miss Taverner, who, for reasons best known to herself, had suddenly become absorbed in her embroidery, laid aside the frame and got up. She shook hands with the Earl, but before she could speak Peregrine was off again.

'I wish you would tell me, sir, what you call that way of tying your cravat! It is devilish natty!'

'I don't call it anything,' replied Worth. 'It is a fashion of my own. You are none the worse for your adventure, Miss Taverner?'

'Oh, a fashion of your own! That means, I daresay, that it will be all the crack in a week. Is it very difficult to do?'

'Yes, very,' said the Earl. 'Is that the particular thing you wanted to say to me? I am highly flattered.'

'Oh no, that was not it! You must know that I took a great fancy for the sea – never was upon a yacht before in my life, and had no notion what it could be like. Such a degree of comfort in so small a space! And then, sailing the vessel, you know! Evans thinks I have a natural aptitude for it. It was a pity I had to come ashore so soon, for there is a great deal about a ship I have not learned yet.'

The Earl's attention seemed to be fixed on Miss Taverner, but he turned his head at that, and said in some amusement: 'Is there indeed? Well, I am happy to know that you are not going to challenge me to a duel (as you once did) for putting you on board my yacht.'

'Challenge you to a duel! Good God, no! Of course, I don't say that I should have gone aboard willingly if you had asked me to, because *then* I knew nothing of being at sea, but that is all changed now, and I am excessively grateful to you.'

'Lord Worth,' interposed Miss Taverner, 'Perry and I feel we owe you an apology for not treating you with that degree of confidence, which –'

'No, I don't,' objected Peregrine. 'I never mistrusted him, Ju. It was you who did that. All I ever said of him was – But that don't signify!'

'All you ever said of me was that I was the most unamiable person of your acquaintance,' said the Earl. He flicked open his snuff-box and offered it to Peregrine.

Peregrine looked as though he could hardly believe his eyes, and blurted out: 'You have never done *that* before, sir!'

'I am in an unusually mellow mood to-day,' explained the Earl.

Peregrine took a pinch, and his sister, seizing the opportunity for speech afforded by him being slightly overcome by the honour of being invited to help himself out of the Earl's box, said: 'Lord Worth knows, I hope, that it is many months since I was foolish enough to mistrust him.'

'Lord Worth is much obliged to you, Miss Taverner,' said the Earl.

She raised her eyes rather shyly to his, and saw that he was still looking amused. She said with an admonitory glance at Peregrine: 'Had we been more in the habit of attending to you perhaps none of the measures you have had to take for Peregrine's safety would have been necessary. I think we do owe you an apology; and we are very grateful to you for your care, are we not, Perry?'

'Yes, of course,' replied Peregrine, brushing some grains of snuff from his sleeve. 'Extremely so, and *I* more than my sister, sir, because if you had not put me away as you did, I might never have taken it into my head to go for a cruise my whole life long. And that does not bear thinking of, for sailing a yacht, you know, has even curricle-racing beat to a standstill. *I* like it better, at all events.'

'I hope you do it better,' commented the Earl.

'Well, I believe I shall,' said Peregrine eagerly. 'And that is what I wanted to ask you. Nothing will ever satisfy me until I may have a yacht of my own! Pray do not say no! I daresay that is what you mean to do, but only consider! If it does mean that I must have a larger allowance, you cannot object to that, surely! And Harriet would like it excessively! I told her how enchanted she would be, and she agreed to it at once. But you must give me an answer soon, if you please, because the case is that Evans knows of just such a vessel as would suit me – two-masted, fore-and-aft rigged: the neatest little craft imaginable, he says! She is lying in Southampton Water. I forget who owns her, but she is to be sold privately, and Evans says I could not do better than to snap her up before it becomes generally know. And Evans has a cousin who would be the very man to put in command of her. He says –'

'Peregrine,' interrupted the Earl, 'do you know where to find Evans?'

'Why, he will be on board the *Seamew*, I suppose.'

'No,' said the Earl. 'At the present moment he is somewhere in the town. Possibly at the Crown and Anchor, or, failing that, the Greyhound. I am sure you will be able to find him if you search Brighton carefully. And when you do find him, give him a message from me that I shall be obliged to him if he will kidnap you again, and take you for a long, long cruise.'

'Oh,' said Peregrine, with a grin, 'he would not have to kidnap me, I can tell you! But can I have a yacht?'

'You can have a dozen yachts,' replied the Earl, 'if only you will go away!'

'I was sure you would agree!' declared Peregrine radiantly. 'I could not conceive of any reason why you should not! And do you think Evans's cousin –'

'Yes,' said the Earl. 'I am persuaded Evans's cousin will be the very man for you. You had better go and talk it over with Evans before he leaves Brighton.'

Peregrine was a good deal struck by this suggestion. 'Upon my word, that is a capital notion! I believe I will do it at once, if you don't mind my leaving you?'

'I can bear it,' said the Earl. 'Let me advise you not to lose any time in setting out.'

'Well, I think I had best be off at once,' said Peregrine. 'And when I have talked it over with Evans I will come and tell you all about it.'

'Thank you very much,' said the Earl gravely. 'I shall be on the watch for you, I assure you.'

Miss Taverner turned away to hide a smile, and after a final promise to call at the Earl's house later in the day Peregrine took himself off.

The Earl looked at Miss Taverner, his brows lifting a little. 'I perceive that it is you and not Peregrine who must bear me a grudge for that kidnapping,' he said. 'Really, I had no idea it would produce such unnerving results. I am exceedingly sorry.'

She laughed. 'I think it is Harriet who is to be pitied.'

'I must remember to make her my apologies. May I felicitate you, Miss Taverner, on having attained your majority?'

'Thank you,' murmured Miss Taverner. 'Perhaps it is I who should felicitate you on being rid of a charge which I believe has been very irksome.'

'Yes,' remarked the Earl thoughtfully. 'I do not think you missed many opportunities to flout my authority.'

She bit her lip. 'If you had used me with more courtesy, more – more consideration, I should not have done so. *You* missed no opportunity to vex me!'

'But I should not have done so had not *you* made the temptation irresistible,' he pointed out.

'I believe,' said Miss Taverner coldly, 'that you have some papers you wish to hand over to me.'

'I have,' he replied. 'But on second thoughts I have decided – with your permission, of course – to send them instead to your lawyer.'

'I am sure I do not know who is to look after my affairs for me,' said Miss Taverner.

'That will be a task for your husband,' he answered.

'I have not got a husband,' said Miss Taverner pettishly.

'Very true, but that can soon be remedied. Now that you are free from *my* shackles your suitors will flock to the house.'

'You are extremely good, but I have no wish to marry any of them. I confess I did not like it at the time, but lately I have been glad that you refused your consent to them all. Which puts me in mind, Lord Worth, of what I wish to say to you.' She drew a deep breath, and embarked on the speech she had prepared. 'I have not always appeared to be sensible of the care you have bestowed on me, but I know now that it has been unceasing. I am deeply grateful for your kindness during the past –'

'My what?' demanded the Earl.

She said stiffly: 'Your *many* kindnesses.'

'But I thought I was the most odious, provoking, detestable creature alive?'

She regarded him with a smouldering eye. 'Yes, you are!' she said. 'Civility compelled me to try at least to thank you for the services you have rendered me, but if you will have none of it, I assure you I do not care! You put me in the horridest situation when you encouraged my cousin to make off with me; you had not the common courtesy to call to see how I did yesterday; you wrote me instead the most odious letter (and I daresay if he had not been away you would have told Mr Blackader to do it to save you the trouble!); and now you come to visit me in one of your disagreeable moods, and try to make me lose my temper!

Well, I shall not do it, but I shall take leave to tell you, my lord, that however glad you may be to be rid of your ward you cannot be as glad as I am to be rid of my guardian!'

His eyes were alight with laughter. 'I am very sorry to have put you in a horrid situation,' he said. 'I did not come to see you yesterday because you were still my ward then; I had no idea of writing you an odious letter (and Mr Blackader is *not* away); and I am not in one of my disagreeable moods. But I *am* very glad to be rid of my ward.'

'I know *that*,' said Miss Taverner crossly.

'I imagine you might, but do you know why, Clorinda?'

'I wish you will not call me by that name!'

He took her hands in his. She made a half-hearted attempt to pull them away, and averted her face. 'I shall call you just what I choose,' said the Earl, smiling. 'Are the recollections that name conjures up still so painful?'

'You used me abominably!' said Miss Taverner in a very small voice.

'It is very true,' said the Earl. 'I did use you abominably, and I have been waiting ever since to do it again. Now, Miss Taverner, you are not my ward, and I *am* going to do it again!'

Every feeling of propriety should have prompted Miss Taverner to resist. She did indeed blush rosily, but although her hands moved in the Earl's it was only to return the clasp of his fingers. For a moment he held her so, looking down into her face; then he let go her hands and swept her into his arms.

Mrs Scattergood, quietly coming into the room just then, stood transfixed on the threshold, gazing in blank amazement at the spectacle of her charge locked in the Earl of Worth's embrace. He was standing with his back to the door, and Mrs Scattergood, recovering from her astonishment just in time, whisked herself out of the room again before her presence had even been suspected.

'Now do you know why I am glad to be rid of my ward?' demanded the Earl.

'Oh,' said Miss Taverner foolishly, 'I was afraid you meant me to marry your brother!'

'Were you indeed? And was all the determined flirting I have been watching between you merely to show me how willing you were to oblige me? Nonsensical child! I have been in love with you almost from the first moment of setting eyes on you.'

'Oh, this is dreadful!' said Miss Taverner, shaken by remorse. 'I disliked you amazingly for weeks!'

The Earl kissed her again. 'You are wholly adorable,' he said.

'No, I am not,' replied Miss Taverner, as soon as she was able. 'I am as disagreeable as you are. You would like to beat me. You said you would once, and I believe you meant it!'

'If I only said it once I am astonished at my own forbearance. I have wanted to beat you at least a dozen times, and came very near doing it once – at Cuckfield. But I still think you adorable. Give me your hand.'

She held it out, and he slipped a ring on the third finger. 'You see, I *had* got a birthday present for you, Clorinda.'

Miss Taverner raised the hand shyly to touch the Earl's cheek. He caught it, and pressed it to his lips. She blushed, and said: 'I thought – after Cuckfield – I had no power to attach you any more. You made me so unhappy! There was no continued observance, none of that distinguishing notice which had become, insensibly, so necessary to my comfort!'

'That *I* should have given you one moment's pain!' he said. 'But your words to me at Cuckfield, the tone in which you uttered them, convinced me that nothing could avail to banish that disgust of me which our first meeting had given you.'

She smiled saucily up at him. 'You must be so well aware of how little delicacy of principle I have that I need have no scruple in telling you that it is many weeks since I have recalled that first meeting without feeling a strong desire of having your shocking conduct repeated. But after Cuckfield all seemed at an end! I had offended beyond forgiveness. And then the mortification of being found by you in the Yellow Drawing-room that miserable evening! Shall I ever forget my dismay at what you must have been thinking!'

'That evening?' he said, holding her closer. 'Shall *I* ever forget the look that came into your eyes when you opened them, and saw me; or the way your hand clung to mine! Till then I had thought my case to be hopeless. But you begged me not to leave you! Had Prinney not been standing at my elbow I must have thrown every consideration of honour to the winds, and spoken *then*! But his being there compelled me to remain silent, and by the time he was gone all the impropriety of speaking to you while I was still your guardian had been recollected. I had come, moreover, straight from delivering Peregrine into my captain's hands! I shall not allow the evils of your situation to have been comparable to mine!'

'There *was* a constraint,' she agreed. 'I was sensible of it even when you forgave me for my conduct at Cuckfield. It was not until you knocked my cousin down that I dared to entertain the notion that your affection had re-animated towards me. But your expression then! No mere indignation at my cousin's villainy, I was persuaded, could have brought that look into your face! I thought you were going to kill him!'

'I had momentarily forgotten your presence. You must forgive me for having given way to impulse.'

'Oh,' said Miss Taverner archly, 'there can be no need for apology when you consider how much I am in the habit of staying in towns where a *prize-fight* is to take place! To own the truth, I had not the least objection to seeing you knock my cousin down. I would have liked to have done it myself. And until then, you know, I had never suspected that you *could* knock a man down.'

'Never suspected that I could knock a man down?' repeated the Earl, a good deal surprised.

'No, how should I? I was used to think you were just a dandy. But Captain Audley once said you had the most punishing left imaginable, and although I did not know what he meant at the time, it occurred to me when you hit my cousin that frightful blow that perhaps that was it. For you did use your left hand, did you not?'

'Yes,' said the Earl gravely. 'I expect I did.'

'You were so quick too!' said Miss Taverner admiringly. 'I quite thought my cousin would have borne you backwards through the window, for he rushed on you with such fury! But I daresay you have been in the habit of boxing a little.'

'Yes,' said the Earl again. His lips quivered. 'I think I may be said to have been in the habit of boxing a little.'

'You are laughing at me!' said Miss Taverner suspiciously.

'My darling,' said the Earl, 'I used to spar with the great Jem himself!'

'Oh?' said Miss Taverner. 'And was he a good boxer?'

'He was the greatest of them all,' replied the Earl.

'Oh no!' said Miss Taverner, glad to be able to display her knowledge. 'Belcher was the greatest of them all. I have often heard my father say so.'

'There is nothing for it,' said the Earl, 'I shall have to kiss you again, Clorinda. Jem Belcher was the man I meant.'

'Good God!' cried Miss Taverner, struck by a sudden thought. 'I had no notion – Oh, I do hope you did not kill my cousin!'

'Not quite,' said the Earl.

'And I was afraid you might be hurt! You must have thought me ridiculous!'

'I thought you enchanting,' said the Earl.

Ten minutes later Peregrine came running up the stairs, and entered the drawing-room in his usual tempestuous fashion.

'Oh, sir, can you come and speak with Evans?' he asked, address-ing himself to his guardian. 'He thinks I should make a bid for that yacht at once if I want her.'

'I have not the least desire to speak to Evans,' replied the Earl.

'But Evans says she is a splendid vessel! He says she sails a point nearer to the wind than your *Seamew*!'

'Even that fails to awaken any desire in me to speak to him. I have some shocking news to break to you: I have just become engaged to your sister.'

'But it won't take you above a quarter of – What's that you say? Engaged to my sister? Oh, Lord, I was afraid that would happen!'

'Peregrine!' said Judith.

'Well, I was,' he insisted. 'Harriet said she was sure you were in love with him all the time. I hoped it would be Charles, but she said there was no question of that. I'm sure I wish you very happy. I should not be interrupting you, I suppose, but this is devilish urgent, and it won't take above a quarter of an hour, you know. Worth, I wish you will come with me to hear what Evans says for yourself!'

'Peregrine,' said the Earl in a gently persuasive voice, 'take Evans, take my whole crew, and the *Seamew* as well, if you like, and go to Southampton, and see this vessel for yourself. Only do not talk any more to me about it!'

'Do you mean I can buy her?' asked Peregrine eagerly.

'You can buy a fleet of yachts for all I care,' said his lordship.

'I'll be off at once!' said Peregrine, and hurried out of the room.

'My dear!' said Miss Taverner, rather perturbed. 'You should not have told him to go to Southampton! He is quite capable of setting out in a chaise immediately!'

'I hope very much that he may. If I had had the presence of mind I would have told him to take Henry with him. I am per-suaded they would find themselves a good deal in sympathy. Henry will be even less pleased at the news of our engagement than Peregrine – and almost as hard to silence.'

'Indeed, when I think of Henry's views on my sex I am astonished at your daring to propose to me at all,' said Miss Taverner. 'I hope you are not offended by the circumstance of Perry not liking it extremely. He will when he knows you better, I promise.'

The Earl smiled. 'No, I am not offended,' he said. 'I was prepared for worse. I am consoling myself with the reflection that your brother's way of receiving the news cannot be more unflattering to *me* than my tiger's opinion of it will be to *you*, my darling!'

Also Available

Georgette Heyer trade paperbacks available from Sourcebooks

An Infamous Army
Black Sheep
Charity Girl
The Conqueror
Cotillion
False Colours
Faro's Daughter
Friday's Child
Lady of Quality
My Lord John
Royal Escape
Simon the Coldheart
The Spanish Bride
The Reluctant Widow

About the Author

*A*UTHOR OF OVER FIFTY BOOKS, GEORGETTE HEYER IS ONE of the best-known and best-loved of all historical novelists, making the Regency period her own. Her first novel, *The Black Moth*, published in 1921, was written at the age of fifteen to amuse her convalescent brother; her last was *My Lord John*. Although most famous for her historical novels, she also wrote twelve detective stories. Georgette Heyer died in 1974 at the age of seventy-one.